THE PROMISE OF YALTA

THE PROMISE OF YALTA

Bernard Melunsky

Book Guild Publishing
Sussex, England

First published in Great Britain in 2009 by
The Book Guild Ltd
Pavilion View
19 New Road
Brighton, BN1 1UF

Copyright © Bernard Melunsky 2009
Jacket design, map and author's photograph by Tobias Melunsky

The right of Bernard Melunsky to be identified as the author of this work has been asserted by him in accordance with the Copyright, Designs and Patents Act 1988.

All rights reserved. No part of this publication may be reproduced, transmitted, or stored in a retrieval system, in any form or by any means, without permission in writing from the publisher, nor be otherwise circulated in any form of binding or cover other than that in which it is published and without a similar condition being imposed on the subsequent purchaser.

While some of the characters in this book were real people, this is a work of fiction. Any resemblance between the novel's imaginary characters and any real person is purely coincidental.

Typesetting in Baskerville by
Keyboard Services, Luton, Bedfordshire

Printed and bound in Great Britain by
Athenaeum Press Ltd, Gateshead

A catalogue record for this book is available from
The British Library

ISBN 978 1 84624 359 2

For Barbara

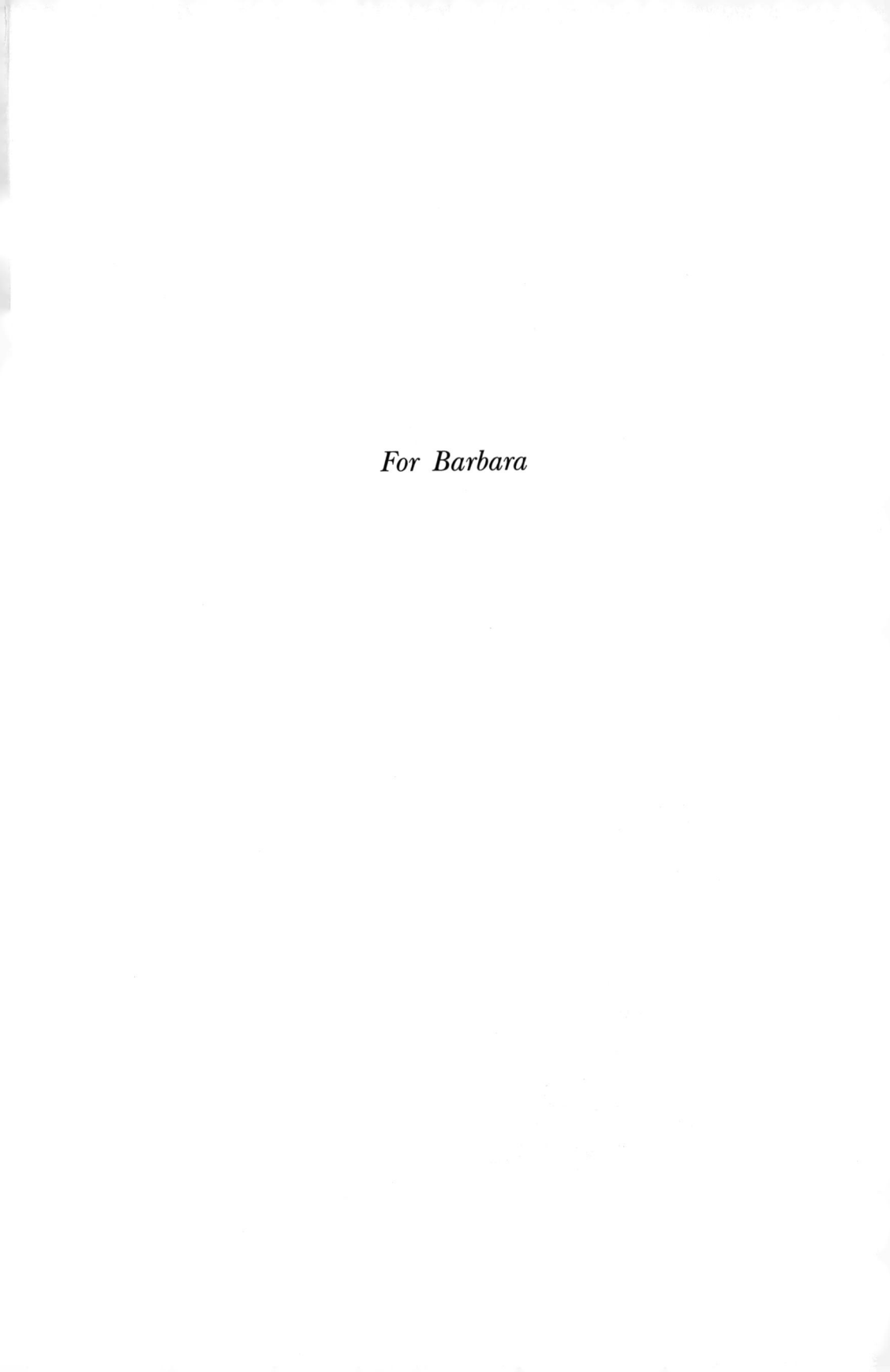

Residences of the Allied Leaders at the Yalta Conference - February 4 - 11, 1945
Livadia Palace - Franklin D. Roosevelt
Yusupov Palace - Joseph V. Stalin
Vorontsov Palace - Winston S. Churchill

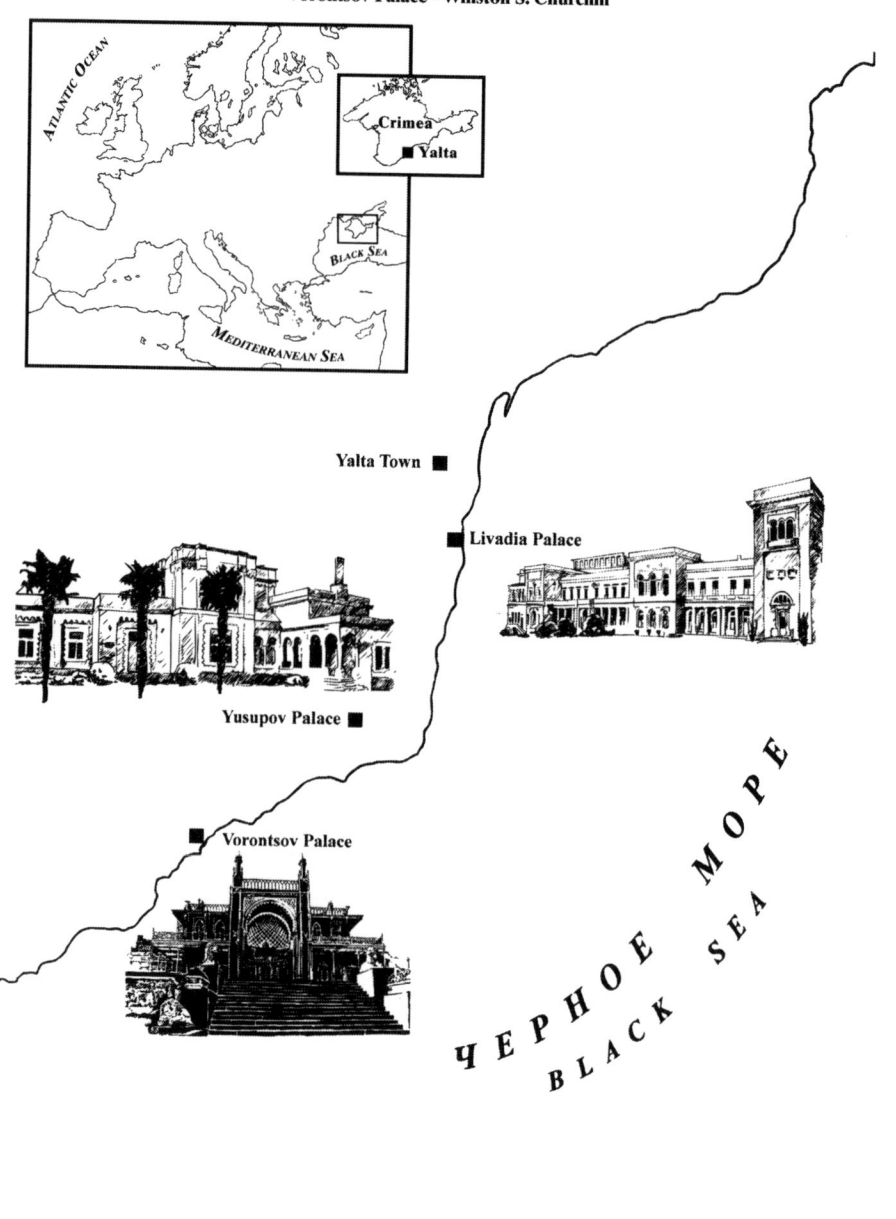

1

Crimea, February 3, 1945

Our flight took us across the battered countries of Europe and over contested, cruel seas. The war was far from finished, the peace an unwritten page.

As we droned to our destination, the Prime Minister slept like a baby, escaping, in dreams of imperial colours, the difficulties of how to finish off the enemy and how to impose his global strategy on sceptical allies. Seated behind him, I dozed fitfully, wrapped in my personal preoccupations, dreading the worst news but clinging to a few well-worn hopes.

Finally, we came down through a layer of grey mist and bumped onto the runway at Saki aerodrome, 80 miles from Yalta, just after noon. Winston awoke with a splutter of discontent. Deep snow lay piled around the bleak landing field. The strip itself was wet and glistening. I could see the cracks on the tarmac as our Skymaster, a gift from the Yanks, taxied along, propellers howling. The flags of the three Allied nations blustered about in the crisp breeze. As the plane lumbered towards the reception party, I peered through the window. The only distant person I could recognise, by the sun glinting weakly on his little spectacles, was Molotov, dismally dour, wearing a black coat and a fur hat, like a bureaucrat at a minor dignitary's funeral.

From the scowl on Winston's face as he got ready to leave the aircraft, he clearly felt his prejudices about the conference venue were justified. In military greatcoat, he moved slowly to the doorway, muttering to himself. Behind him, Sarah looked round, caught my eye and gave a smile of complicity. We both knew we would have our hands full at Yalta coping with the old lion's moods and demands.

He walked slowly, gingerly down the steps from the plane into the chill air of the western Crimea. As he did so, his frown was replaced by a benevolent smile, suitable for the elder statesman role he had decided to play at this conference. It was probably the only one left to him now that the war had bled us dry of power and influence.

He was the oldest and most experienced of the Big Three. He'd been in the British cabinet at a time when the Empire was still strong, when Stalin was no more than an anti-Tsarist plotter on the run and Roosevelt a novice naval official. Now *they* were the senior partners.

Ah, but surely there was still scope for shaping events, he had told us on the flight. He could cajole Franklin back into line, and do business with Stalin despite all the omens. It was a question of give and take, simple as that.

Winston, these days, was plagued by the problems of mollifying his partners and keeping their ambitions in check. It had been so straightforward in 1940 when he had no option but to concentrate all his concerns on the desperate cause of survival. Rally the nation, and the Empire, cock a snoot at Hitler, keep going at all costs until the Americans came to our rescue!

At the airport, Red Army troops in smart dress uniform, white gloves, shiny leather boots, gleaming buttons lined the route from the plane to the reception party. Winston nodded appreciatively. Nothing pleased him more than the colourfully romantic side of soldiering.

Molotov greeted him with a wintry smile and Winston beamed back cherubically at the pasty-faced Commissar of Foreign Affairs and his minion Vyshinsky, whom I remembered for his role as the vindictive prosecutor in Stalin's show trials of the late 1930s. Behind them smiled bushy-browed Gromyko, wearing a gangster-style hat, possibly bought in the United States where he was ambassador. He was darkly handsome despite a fleshy nose. But a dashing, stiff-creased matinée idol Anthony Eden, he was not! Anthony, our Foreign Secretary, was adored by the women of Britain – not a bad asset for a prime minister in waiting.

To my surprise Podbirski was in the Soviet party too. How high had he risen, and at whose expense? Our eyes locked briefly and I raised my eyebrows. He gave me just the hint of a smile. Was it possible that he might have news for me?

A Russian interpreter began intoning a welcome on behalf of Stalin, who had not deigned to be present. Winston continued to smile beatifically, while the rest of us stood behind him on the tarmac. I turned sideways to look into the sardonic gaze of Alan Brooke, Chief of the Imperial General Staff, our senior military planner, who made no effort to hide his disdain at this pretence of unity.

An army band struck up 'God Save the King' and then our party, led by Winston, head thrust forward, cigar in his mouth, strode towards Roosevelt's plane. The aircraft, nickamed 'The Sacred Cow' and specially designed inside for the disabled President, had landed 20 minutes or so before us. FDR was carried from it, looking grey and washed out. He was bundled efficiently into a jeep by secret service men, as though he were some indigent old family retainer. His dark navy cape, which so often gave him an arrogant flamboyancy, today seemed to hang about his shoulders like an old woman's shawl. A cigarette drooped from his mouth. It gave him the look of Bogart on a bad, bad morning after. I remembered from newsreels the jaunty angle of his cigarette holder in times past. Not today. As the band played 'The Star-Spangled Banner', he held a shabby trilby to his heart and gaped bleakly into space, while Winston, in his military peaked cap, saluted with jaw-jutting solemnity and Molotov looked stolidly ahead. Then Roosevelt, ferried in the jeep, and Winston, marching alongside, inspected an army guard, which snapped fiercely to attention, fixed bayonets pointing to the sky.

I stood beside Sarah who stared at the President and whispered: 'That poor man looks like death – and there's still the drive across the mountains. Why do they have to do that to him?'

'Perhaps they want to show him something.'

'Perhaps they want to shake the last bit of life out of his bones,' she snorted.

Roosevelt's physical condition had shocked us all when he'd come to Malta a few days earlier for pre-conference talks with Winston. Now he looked even worse than before. His neck was too scrawny for his collar – the sight of this, both sad and comical, made me think, uncomfortably, of thin-throated Chamberlain waving empty promises of peace in the air.

Like many of us, Sarah had a respectful love of the President despite his current vague and off-handed manner towards Winston. That was politics, forced on him by others, she believed.

I asked her what Winston had been saying as he left the aircraft.

'He was singing. Very softly, under his breath. "Keep the Home Fires Burning".'

I groaned.

'That was the last war,' I whispered.

'But still appropriate. He says they couldn't have chosen a more ghastly spot for this meeting if they'd looked all over the world.'

'It seemed the best compromise, if Stalin couldn't leave Russia.'

'*Wouldn't*, you mean!'

'I thought you quite liked him,' I teased, knowing how she'd enjoyed the moment when the Soviet dictator had solemnly risen from his seat and drunk a toast to her at the Tehran Conference just over a year before.

'Oh, Uncle Joe can be awfully nice in a ruffian sort of way. Quite funny too. Not exactly Noel Coward – but he tries hard.'

Dear Sarah, I thought. How she had tried too. It wasn't easy being a child of Winston Churchill. Her way of coping, before the war, had been by rebellion. But she'd come through her family and marital tribulations, and today looked as glamorous as a film star under the leaden skies of the airfield, her steely blue air force coat and WRAF cap enhancing the sparkle of her dark red hair.

'Anyway, why not Moscow, if he couldn't tear himself away?' she asked. 'I'd love to have seen the Bolshoi. This place is far from everything. So bleak and so cold.'

I reminded her that Yalta, to the south-east on the Black Sea coast, would be much milder, and added: 'Perhaps the Politburo have the health of their visitors in mind.'

'How big-hearted of you, Jimmy. I hadn't realised you were so tolerant of the Bear people. Do you have a Ninotchka pining for you in the Kremlin?'

I pretended not to hear. Fighter planes patrolled overhead, the band still played, the wind whistled.

Three large tents had been set up at the end of the runway, and after the ceremonies we headed towards them for refreshments. Sarah, along with her father and other bigwigs, went into one of them. I was directed to another where we lesser species were offered sparkling wine, vodka, caviar, smoked sturgeon, suckling pig and the rest – fare that was to become nauseatingly familiar in the days ahead.

Podbirski was observing me from across the tent. He caught my eye, and I gave a discreet nod back. A few minutes later, he came up to me, grinning widely. He'd gone almost completely bald, which made him look even more pig-like than before. His face was flushed and he'd put on a lot of weight. Obviously, he was having a good war.

'Jimmy, am so glad to see.'

'Me too, Anatoly.'

'So, we both are surviving,' he observed. 'Is good.'

I fixed my gaze on the medals adorning his uniform.

'Some of us are doing better than others.'

'Ah, is just, how you say, ornaments? Yes?'

'Still, better than nothing.'

'But you, even better, Jimmy. You advise to Mr Churchill.'

'No I pass on his advice to others,' I said. 'Just a humble secretary.'

'I, also, am humble,' he smiled.

'Can you tell me anything?' I asked.

'Is better not talk here.'

'But later?'

He nodded slightly in reply. I saw beads of perspiration on his forehead. It was warm inside the tent. I knew I shouldn't try to push him, but couldn't help asking: 'When, Anatoly? Can I expect some news of her? What should I do?'

He considered this.

'Maybe pray. You sometimes pray, Jimmy?'

'I've been known to.'

'Your God is on our side, too, now that we great allies?'

'I've never thought about that. When I pray, it's more superstition than belief.'

'You not believe in God?' he said, looking, or pretending to look, shocked. 'Is bad thing for Christian, Jimmy.'

'Don't tell me you've found religion, Anatoly?'

He glanced around quickly. The tent was almost empty now, with just a few Soviet officials and soldiers guzzling the last of the food and drink. It was time to move on to Yalta. No one was showing the slightest interest in us.

'Is no such thing in my country,' he said in a low voice, though quite jovially. 'But different with you in England.'

'So I'm told. I've heard there are still believers scattered here and there.'

'You joke again. Mr Churchill, he believes in God?'

'Oh, yes. Winston is always giving advice to the Almighty.'

He let himself laugh aloud, almost as if he'd forgotten where we were.

'Jimmy, always you make funny jokes. Is good.'

Then he shook my hand.

'We talk again at Yalta, my friend.'

He walked to a trestle table, poured himself a glass of Champagne and drank it at one gulp.

Outside the marquee, the clouds were thickening ominously. A fleet of black limousines was lined up to load us in for the long haul over the mountains.

The journey was mostly on potholed, winding roads. The first stretch from Saki to Simferopol was over rolling snow-covered country. We saw only a few trees still standing, skeletal survivors of the holocaust of war. Just about every house on the route had been destroyed. The few peasants we caught a glimpse of wore sullen faces. The bloated bodies of cattle and horses lay beside burned-out tanks with swastikas still visible on the charred sides and overturned, gutted railway carriages.

For large parts of the route, the road was lined by unsmiling, stocky Red Army troops, men and women, snapping to attention and saluting with a swift thrust of their rifles in front of them as the cars passed by. I had a vision of expressionless Soviet automatons stretching all the way back across Europe.

On the way we stopped for more refreshments and to relieve ourselves. It was bitterly cold along this mountain road and the grey sky was spitting sleet. I stood peeing next to a Russian foreign ministry interpreter whom I'd known slightly in Moscow just before the war.

I asked him about the Soviet advance into Germany, and he told me it was hard going but they'd get through, come what may.

'So, you may see Berlin soon,' he said. 'You have been there before, I believe.'

'Yes.'
'When were you there?'
'The first time was 1931.'
'Ah, 1931. That year I was at the university in Leningrad. A very happy time. You went to Germany for studies?'

'Sort of,' was all I said, for I wanted to get back to the relative warmth of the car without going into any explanation. But he persisted. Maybe that was his real job.

'In those days it was very exciting, I believe,' he said. 'Many girls, many parties.'

'Exciting in a lot of ways,' I said grudgingly.

'Ah, you went there to fight the fascists?'

I smiled politely and walked away.

I wondered what they had taught him in Leningrad about what was going on in Germany, and who was battling whom.

2

Berlin

Germany had always loomed large in my life. I grew up within earshot of the Great War. From our village on the south coast of England you could hear the thunder of the shells in France. I'd been told my father was over there, fighting the Germans. What I didn't know was why he was fighting or what sort of enemies he was up against. What, exactly, *were* Germans? My mother made no effort to explain these things to me, though my grandfather spoke of the Germans with loathing.

I was seven when my mother told me my father had been killed. 'Fallen' was the word she used. 'Your father has fallen.' I wondered why she was wearing such a sombre face simply because he had tumbled down steps or tripped over a stone. However, the meaning was soon made clear. He was gone and he wasn't ever coming back.

I can't say that I felt any great sadness or despair. I had barely known him. On the few visits from the fighting in France, he was kind to me, in my memory, but never overtly tender.

Apart from the memories, all I had of him was a photograph of a serious man in uniform and some toy soldiers he'd brought me as a present on his last visit. All he had ever done, in my memory, was visit. I never thought of him as a part of home, which consisted of my mother and myself.

The toy soldiers – made of lead and painted in khaki or grey uniforms – mattered more to me than a vague father, although it sometimes made my child's eyes smart to remember how he had taught me to play with them.

One day, soon after my father's death, Douglas Winterton visited us. He and my father had been close friends, in England and in France. He told me about my father's sense of humour, sense of duty and hopes for me. His main hope was that I should grow up to be someone who behaved decently to his fellow man.

'Like Christ?' I asked.

'Certainly,' Douglas smiled. 'But you don't have to be a good Christian to be a good man.'

'Douglas!' admonished my mother.

'Can a German be a good man?' I asked. 'Grandpa says they're all monsters.'

'Go and play in the garden, James,' said my mother.

My mother, Elizabeth, was a beautiful and desirable woman. I knew that because I'd overheard two army officers discussing her at our house after my father's funeral service.

'The widow's a damn good-looking wench,' one of them said.

'A beauty, and she'll be snapped up soon – if there's anyone left to snap her up,' said the other.

When I reported this conversation to my mother, she allowed herself a rare smile.

'Who will snap you up?' I asked fearfully. 'Not a dragon.'

'No, James. No one is going to snap me up. He was making a joke.'

I had a pretty normal sort of childhood for a middle-class English boy, progressing from home to prep school, to public school. But often I found myself wondering what sort of man my father really was. Douglas painted a heroic picture, but my mother generally managed to change the subject if asked about him. His own parents seemed too pained by his loss to talk about him to me.

At school, having a father killed in battle was a badge of honour, but so many others shared this distinction that it seemed almost abnormal for a child to have both parents living.

The father of my friend Gerald Cross was a general. He shook his son's hand on one Parents Day as though Gerald was a soldier rather than a 12-year-old.

To me, he said: 'Good man. Keep it up, keep it up.'

Afterwards, I confided to Gerald that I wished my father had been a general too.

'Why?' asked Gerald, mystified.

'Don't know,' I muttered.

'What *was* your father, Bexley?'

'A captain.'

'That's jolly good. Generals are complete asses.'

'Why?'

'Just you believe me,' said Gerald darkly.

Even as a boy in his early teens, Gerald was starkly handsome with straight jet-black hair and classical features. His eyes flashed with humour, anger, insolence and passion. He always dressed neatly and crisply, whether in cricket flannels or blazer and tie. By contrast, I had straw-coloured unkempt hair on a very ordinary face, which my mother once scathingly said 'reveals your father's peasant bloodline', and never took much care about my clothes.

Gerald and I were the only two in our form to study German, rather than French, as an optional second language. It united us against a mainstream of boys who couldn't understand why anyone should want to speak 'the Boche lingo'.

Once, confronted by a menacing gang out to beat us up for our linguistic aberration, Gerald confounded them by saying with complete sang-froid: 'We're only learning it so we can interrogate them in the next war.'

The group dispersed in some confusion, and I was given an early lesson in the art of necessary duplicity.

'D'you think there *will* be a next war?' I asked Gerald.

'I hope not. I don't want to end up like my father, going on and on and on about how he won every battle he fought.'

'You mean you wouldn't fight?'

'Not bloody likely. I've become a pacifist.'

'I think *I'd* join the army,' I said.

'Well, you've probably got more reason than me, Bexley.'

By the time I'd reached my late teens, I wanted to look further afield for clues about my father and his death. I'd visited some of the battlefields of France on a school trip but found the melancholic atmosphere too uncomfortable. There was only gloom, grief and hopelessness there. My father had died fighting against Germany, so perhaps being among Germans might tell me something about him. What I wanted was not some cold name on a forbidding monument but the doubts, hatreds, courage, fears of the real person.

That was why, after taking the Cambridge exam and opting to read history at my father's college, Trinity, I broached the idea of delaying my entrance for a year so I could travel to Germany. My mother opposed this and she controlled the trust fund that could finance my travels. However, Douglas, by now an economics don at Trinity, reacted with enthusiasm to my plan.

He said Germany's future was hanging in the balance, and what happened there could affect all Europe. Going there would open my eyes.

My mother protested that Germany had become a dreadful, perilous place, with rabble fighting on the streets, loose morals and hatred of Britain for winning the war.

'We need our young people to be aware of the world and its problems, not to behave like rabbits,' Douglas said.

'Rabbits?' she said.

'Not an enlightened species,' he said. 'Over-indulgent and far too timid for the life they live. Also, easily blinded by sudden flashes of light.'

'I thought you liked rabbits,' she said.

'In a stew,' he replied. 'Sometimes.'

'I once cooked Douglas and your father a rabbit stew,' my mother explained to me. 'A long time ago. It was a disaster.'

'But delicious, none the less,' said Douglas.

He winked at me.

My mother told me later that she was often scared by Douglas's ideas but didn't mind his fleeting visits because they reminded her of happy pre-war days.

'We were young,' she sighed. 'People knew what they were and what was expected of them. But, as Douglas says, we can't always live in the past.'

So, despite her scorn for post-war Germany, she agreed that I should visit Berlin before going up to Cambridge, on condition that I spend my time there usefully, preferably in learning to speak the language like a native.

'That might help in the diplomatic service,' she said. 'Or in business.'

Berlin, when I arrived in 1931, was an exciting, dangerous, vivid, depressing and profoundly apocalyptic world on the verge of self-destructive eruption.

The big question then was which rough beast would emerge triumphant from the flames? Would it wear the Nazi brown shirt or carry the Communist red flag?

My eyes began to open to the dark chasms of life.

Frau Siegendorff, my landlady, was a grey-haired widow, a lot older than my mother, stouter and much less careful about her appearance.

When I told her that my father had died on the Western Front in 1918, she exclaimed: 'Ach, your poor mother! And, for what? I wish that my Hans had stayed here and made money rather than going off to die for the Fatherland. For what? Here there is only hardship.'

She spoke to me in German, as I'd asked her to do.

'I like to have foreigners in my house,' she said. 'We Germans are too full of contempt for others. We envy too much. That was why the fool of a Kaiser started the war. You are too young to remember, Herr Bexley. And in the end, what has it brought us? Poverty and bitterness.'

We were sitting at her solid oak dinner table along with several other lodgers, giving their earnest attention to the mutton, dumplings and boiled carrots in front of them.

'And yet somehow we are still alive,' remarked Dr Bergsen, one of the lodgers, with a mischievous smile. 'At least in this house we dine well.'

'Yes, for now, for today, I can still afford to buy meat – don't ask about the cost, though! But others must go to the soup kitchens for warm food. And that is how God punishes us for choosing war.'

The house, which had seen better days, was in Wilmersdorf, close to Berlin's affluent, decadent West End but a million miles away from its lurid modernity. Frau Siegendorff had been left an annuity whose value had all but vanished in the crippling inflation of the twenties.

A framed photograph on the dining-room mantelpiece showed her husband with strong, clear eyes, briskly brushed hair and a hint of cynical humour on his face. Another was of her son Gregor, a blond young man looking with cool disdain at the camera. She said vaguely that he was in Hamburg, 'learning a career'.

I ventured that the main cause of Germany's misery was the punitive Versailles Treaty imposed by the victorious Allies.

'No, no, we cannot always blame others,' cried Frau Siegendorff. 'It's the German people who are voting for Hitler, not you

English or the French. It's our people who want that Austrian nobody to be their leader.'

Adolf Hitler's Nazi party had made spectacular gains in recent elections, pledging to restore Germany's grandeur and destroy its enemies. He railed in blood-dripping, Dark Ages phraseology against Jews and Communists, generally lumping them together.

'My dear, respected Frau Siegendorff, do not despair,' said Dr Bergsen, a courteous, scholarly lawyer in his late forties. 'He is a politician like the others. Perhaps a little more vulgar than the others. If he ever should come into the Reichstag he will calm down.'

'I am surprised that you, Herr Doktor Bergsen, should think well of that scoundrel!' she exclaimed.

'I do not think kindly or well of him, my dear lady, but why should we Germans despair because such a man plays upon the prejudices of the ignorant. It is true the Brownshirts did better than we expected in these elections, but not in the big cities, not in our Berlin, where the people have more culture.'

The other lodgers chose to say nothing. Berlin was a risky place to talk politics openly unless you had good reasons for nailing your colours to the mast. Most people preferred to keep their thoughts to themselves, or to confide only in trusted friends.

Some of the Berliners I'd met were attracted by Hitler, but deplored the street brawling crudity of his followers. Others, while appalled by the man, believed Nazism was a passing phase.

Dr Bergsen, Jewish and cultivated, was one of the latter. If he had any great concern about the future, he never showed it.

He spoke to me in English when we were alone. He had a great and romantic love of England, although he'd never visited the country. He was bachelor, a small, round-faced man with receding hair and wire-rimmed spectacles.

'Ah, Cambridge,' he said, reflectively, when I told him I was headed there. 'I wanted to study in Cambridge, but then came the war, and afterwards, impossible. Where could one get the money to go there?'

We'd been sitting and reading in the parlour – he, an evening newspaper published by the liberal Ullstein Press; I, *The Magic Mountain*.

'Did you want to study law at Cambridge, Herr Dr Bergsen?'

I used his full title, in the German manner, out of respect. He was a formal man – a middle-class German of his time – who always wore a suit and a tie.

'*Ja*, but also to drink from the English literature. Hardy, Dickens, H.G. Wells. We have good writers too. Thomas Mann (here he pointed to the book I was reading) is a good writer also. But Trollope, Dickens, Bernard Shaw; such humour. Only in England could they have *blühen* – how do you say, flower?'

'Yes, flourished.'

'Ah, flourished. I must remember, flourished. Only in a country where there is such a tolerance.'

'But in Germany, Herr Dr Bergsen, there is so much exciting art today!'

I'd been staggered by the power and bite of the paintings and theatre in Berlin. Razor wit and raw satire sprang out of the pavements. Grosz and Dix in garish colours depicted the uncaring rich. Brecht splashed his plays with sharp street humour and invective.

'Because they believe they must provocative – *mein Gott*, why can I not express?' Dr Bergsen raised his hands in exasperation.

'You always make yourself clear,' I said. 'Your English is good.'

'It could have been, it could have been, when I was young, yes? But now, what use is English to me? Better I should learn Hebrew. That is what the Zionists tell me. Even the Yiddish of the Ostjuden is not good enough for them.'

He despised the Jews who had flooded in from eastern Europe in recent years, seeing their alien dress, ways and language as a blot on German culture.

Feeling emboldened by his small confidences, I asked: 'What do you really think will happen in Germany, Herr Dr Bergsen?'

'Since the war, we have had already one revolution and governments of the left, and the centre and the centre right, and maybe there will finally be one of the extreme Brown right or the extreme Red left. Who knows? Then the *karussell* will begin again. *Karussell* is the right word?'

'Carousel, merry-go-round, yes. And you don't feel threatened?'

'Always in Germany there was anti-Semitism. It is in the blood, like some weakness of the body, although perhaps it gets worse now because of so many of these people from the east. The

German Jews have learned to live with dislike against them for hundreds of years. So why should I be threatened? I am a German citizen of the Hebrew faith. Some Jewish have taken even the Christian faith. Still, they are not completely accepted. If the Nazis win to power, for a short time, every *Volkisch* – nationalistic, you would say – German will spit on me, yes? But afterwards I will still be here. They will always need patriots to fight if there is a war.'

He pointed to a small veteran's badge on his jacket lapel.

'Yes, I am proud I fought even though it was against Englishmen. Against your father, Herr Bexley, I am sad to say. Your father, did he hate the Germans?'

'I don't know. If he hated anyone, it was probably the Allied generals.'

'Ach, all the generals are always stupid. The military mind is not, how you say, subtle? Our generals say the army was stabbed in the back, and that is why we lost the war. But it was the military class who betrayed us. They wanted the war.'

'How does the army regard Hitler?' I asked.

'They will use him if they can. They will make him in power if he can give them aeroplanes and weapons and make them again to be strong. But he will not be used so easily. He is not a fool, that little corporal.'

He said this with some admiration.

'Hitler – *ja*, he is a strong character. And what a speaker! I went once to the Sportpalast, with a colleague of mine who is a member of the NSDAP, the Nazi Party – but a nice fellow, not a Jew hater – and there I heard Hitler speak. He makes you to listen to every word. It was, how you say, *hynotisch*.'

'Hypnotic,' I said.

'For cetain, he talks like a monster, but he is also a politician. When he shouts some crazy ideas, some of them, it is to get votes. Trust me, Herr Bexley, he is a politician and politicians change their spots – *ja*? – when they come in government.'

I shook my head. The Brownshirts were marching around Berlin shouting 'Perish Judah', attacking Jews and Jewish businesses, and an intelligent Jew could talk like this!

He smiled at my gesture and said soothingly: 'All will be well, Herr Bexley.'

3

Yalta, February 3–4, 1945

It was night, after a bone-juddering journey, when we reached the wooded hills surrounding Yalta and the bizarrely magnificent mansion housing the main British delegation. Our base was the Vorontsov Palace, named after an Anglophile aristocrat who'd built it a century earlier. In the dark, we walked up a vast stone staircase to the main entrance and could make out the Moorish shape of the arched central portal. The lit-up interior, with its spaciousness, restored grandeur, chandeliers, blazing log fires and the rest, made the horrors of the Crimean countryside seem hundreds of years away.

'Crikey,' joked Sarah. 'Just like home.'

We laughed. No one in our company lived in such style. The Churchills themselves owned a relatively modest country house in the weald of Kent.

'Of course, Papa was born with a silver spoon in his mouth,' Sarah added.

'Indeed, I was,' said her father. 'Unfortunately, it was sold along with the other cutlery.'

He seemed in a jovial mood as he glanced about him, though Sarah whispered to me he had grumbled mightily during the journey from Saki, apologising for bringing her to 'this hole'.

Until a few months before, the Vorontsov had been the headquarters of Von Manstein, Hitler's favourite general. The Germans pulled out in a hurry, leaving an utter shambles inside, though the buildings were not destroyed.

The Russians had done marvels. Everything from crockery to chambermaids to food had been imported from Moscow for our comfort. I recognised a couple of waiters who'd been at the Metropole Hotel in Moscow in 1939, but they gave no sign that they remembered me. After nibbling at dinner, I went upstairs to the bedroom I was sharing with several other flunkies and quickly fell asleep. We were all fatigued.

Even Winston retired early.

I woke at seven o'clock, just as the sun was rising. It was Sunday, but I knew there would be no church bells in this country. I scratched at some insect bites. There was a queue for the only upstairs bathroom. I managed to find an outdoor tap for a cold-water wash.

I doubted if the primitive toilet facilities were part of a deliberate policy. The Russians took pride in being good hosts, but Soviet policy was not aimed at improving creature comforts or personal hygiene for the masses; there'd been a severe shortage throughout the country of baths – and even more so, for obscure reasons of proletarian priorities, bath plugs – since the revolution.

After washing, I went into the gardens. The buildings took my breath away. They were an architectural pastiche of Scottish baronial and Arabian Nights extravaganza. The entrance was reached by a stone staircase between sculpted life-size white lions, one dozing contendedly, another just awakening and a third alert and suspicious. Behind the building, rose the shiny snow-covered granite cliffs of the coastal mountain range, brushed by a few puffy clouds in the brightening blue sky.

The grounds sloped gently down to the glinting Black Sea. I walked in friendly sun-dappled light through cypresses and pines, imagining myself in pre-war Amalfi. The illusion of 1930s luxury was confirmed by breakfast: fish, meat and fruit that were undreamed of in wartime Europe, and freshly baked bread. I took what I thought was a glass of orange juice and found it was mixed with Champagne.

Some of the delegation, housed a short distance away from the palace, arrived moaning about their lot. 'Black Hole of Calcutta,' one of them said. 'Seven chaps to one bloody room!'

I bumped into Sarah. She was much amused at the sanitary arrangements afflicting almost everyone but Winston and her.

'I saw a couple of generals and admirals wandering around in their dressing-gowns with tin cans for washing,' she said. 'They were not at their best. Very disgruntled. I shouldn't be surprised if we launched an attack against Moscow today.'

'And you?' I asked. 'Were you queuing in your dressing-gown as well?'

'Oh, no,' she said with a little look of horror. 'I'm using Papa's bathroom downstairs.'

'How nice for you,' I said. 'As it happens, I'm one of the tin can brigade. Reminds me of my prep school. And some of the chaps lodging down the road are pretty upset, crowded quarters, bedding on the floor, lice.'

Sarah tried, but failed, to conceal a grin.

'Sorry, darling,' she giggled. 'But you all have to remember there's a war on.'

'Really, Sarah, you're impossible sometimes,' I remonstrated, though not without smiling myself. 'And I wouldn't joke about the conditions in front of some of those chaps. You'll recognise them from the blotches on their faces where the bed bugs attacked them. They're not amused.'

'Listen, ducky,' she said seriously. 'There are people fighting and dying for their country all over the world. And what have some of those little squirts ever done in this war except carry someone else's briefcase?'

'Spoken like a true Churchill,' I said.

She smiled an acknowledgement and we went to Winston's bedroom.

He was sitting up, pinkly, in bed, reading papers from a despatch box in the sunny room. He looked up and smiled.

'My good friend Marshal Stalin has done us proud, has he not? I hope you both have slept peacefully, as indeed we all should have done. "Be not afeard; the isle is full of noises, sounds and sweet airs that give delight and hurt not."'

'Darling Papa,' Sarah said. 'Your delivery is perfect. Everyone knows I inherited my small thespian talent from you. But is Yalta going to be as idyllic as that?'

'Does Caliban mock? The coming days will tell, Sarah. I have no illusions as to the designs and rapaciousness of our hosts. But for now let us enjoy the sweet airs. Last night, before retiring, I had an opportunity to look at some of the paintings downstairs in the dining-room. Two of them are copies of family portraits of the Herberts at Wilton. A thoughtful touch, is it not?'

'I'm pleased you're feeling comfortable and content, Papa,' said Sarah with a loving smile.

'Everything thus far appears as it should be. Do you not agree, Mr Bexley?'

'Yes, Prime Minister.'

'Some of the delegation down the road are in rather cramped accommodation in what are called sanatoria, I gather,' said Sarah.

'Ah, well,' sighed Winston. 'They will have to bear it with as much fortitude as they can muster. We must all make further sacrifices – as I informed the House quite recently. Much depends on this conference. Weighty matters will be decided. We few gathered here hold in our hands the future of the world. Is that not worth some days of cramped accommodation? I myself well remember the confines of my captivity in the Transvaal. But I did not shrink from the hardship.'

'You escaped, Papa.'

'So I did,' Winston chuckled. 'And you are to be commended, Sarah, as my aide-de-camp, for drawing my attention to the conditions of these, um, stoical and brave members of our party. I do not feel it is something I should raise with Marshal Stalin – certainly not before he has agreed to a representative government in Poland – but pray tell them that I fully appreciate their commitment to the cause.'

He was enjoying himself.

'Yes, Papa, I'm sure Mr Bexley will convey your appreciation to his friends in the sanatoria, who will take great comfort from your concern,' Sarah said with a straight face.

'And you, Sarah? You have no cause for complaint?'

'I did just mention to one of the waiters last night that there seemed to be no lemon peel in the cocktails. The poor wretch went very pale indeed. But I noticed this morning that they were planting a fully grown lemon tree in the Orangery. And it was loaded with fruit.'

'An excellent omen,' Winston said. 'Civilisation depends for its continuance on that balance of service and courtesy between, um, masters and, um, servants...'

At which, he broke off to shout for his long-suffering valet.

'Sawyers, Sawyers! Where are my damn slippers? Have you run my bath yet?'

We could hear Sawyers scampering about his business.

'And are we prepared sufficiently, Mr Bexley?' Winston turned to me.

For a second, I thought he was asking me about his bath. Then I grasped his meaning.

'The Foreign Secretary thinks...' I began.

'I know what Anthony thinks,' he growled. 'He never ceases to nag me about it. He fears chaos because of a certain lack of consultation in the past few days between the Americans and us. Certainly, the President did appear to be somewhat distracted at Malta, but that was perhaps natural after his long voyage. He has never succumbed to the anti-British feelings of some of his compatriots. Do you believe my old friend is going to let me down, Mr Bexley?'

I did not feel it would be politic for me to say I thought that Roosevelt had been unwilling at Malta to engage in serious discussion for reasons of policy rather than fatigue. My duty as a private secretary was to convey information not conjecture.

'No, Prime Minister,' I said, searching for words. 'Not deliberately, but the Russians might try to capitalise on the situation if the President is indeed distracted. I gather Mr Roosevelt has not yet read the briefs prepared for him.'

'The President knows the issues a great deal better than does his State Department,' Winston rapped out. 'I have no fears on that score. What else?'

'The Foreign Secretary is increasingly pessimistic about the Polish situation.'

'Yes, Anthony has not been backward in conveying his concerns. He is apprehensive. And so am I, so am I. We went to war on a sacred pledge to Poland, and we must strive to see it restored to its independence with all its freedoms intact. You and Mr Eden need have no fears on that score. We will get guarantees of it, even though the Red Army is now the master of that house.'

Winston then suddenly switched tone and tactics and looked at me with a curious, nasty schoolboy glint in his eye.

'The joint chiefs will be meeting this morning,' he said. 'They'll keep me in the dark about their scheming. Do you have a reliable source of information?'

I said I had. I didn't mention that the source was my old school friend Gerald Cross.

'Then find out what the devil they're up to behind my back,' he growled as he returned to his papers, waving Sarah and me away.

Then he shouted: 'Hurry it up, damn it, Sawyers!'

After we'd left the room, Sarah said to me: 'If we win the war, the nation will owe Sawyers a huge debt.'

The first morning of the conference was like the slow start to a symphony. There were hints of what was to come, but no theme was yet fully developed.

Before noon, the British military chiefs of staff held a short meeting. Afterwards, I sought out Gerald and asked him what had happened. At school and Cambridge he'd been a pacifist, but had joined up on the outbreak of war and been wounded in Normandy. He was now a staff officer – Captain Cross.

'Spying for your master, eh?' he smiled.

'Can you give me the broad picture, Gerald?' I urged.

'I suppose you've got to have something to give the old man.'

He outlined briefly some of the issues discussed. They included differences between the Americans and us over the best way to attack Germany from the west, while the Russians closed in from the east.

'And Greece?' I asked, knowing this was dear to Winston's heart: he feared the military chiefs were bent on thwarting his desire to keep British troops on the liberated mainland to help prevent it falling to the Communists in a civil war.

'The P.M. already knows he's got his way on that, for now. *Entre nous*, old chap, has he gone a bit gaga of late? He does get bees in his bonnet!'

'Ah, Gerald, your chaps haven't enough grey matter to realise that waging this war is a complex business. It's not just winning that matters. We have to see how things are going to pan out afterwards.'

'That may be so, but the first thing is to do the winning bit,' Gerald retorted. 'You should've stayed in khaki, James.'

'Most of the time, I wish I had.'

After lunch, I got my first close-up look at Stalin. I'd watched him from afar in Red Square on May Day 1939, reviewing troops and workers, and seen him portrayed as the heroic, dark-haired figure of destiny in a million touched-up photographs and idealised posters. This was uncomfortably different. I was within a few feet of him as he and his entourage, surrounded by bodyguards, swept into the Vorontsov Palace for a chat with Winston. He wore a double-breasted grey coat and black leather boots. About his figure and features, there was nothing heroic. He was short and squat and he moved with a purposeful, ungainly shuffle. His face was pock-marked, his eyes a nasty yellowish-brown, his breath (from the whiff I got as he moved past me) stinking of foul tobacco. He was the sort of man you'd give a wide berth to if encountered on a dark street. But despite his unsavoury physical appearance, he carried with him an aura of immense controlled power. Here was someone who meant business and knew he had the wherewithal to conduct it successfully. A Mafia boss of bosses, yes – but without the need to combat the law; for he *was* the law.

He was staying a short distance away at the former palace of Prince Yusupov, one of the conspirators who killed Rasputin. This was an interesting choice given Stalin's fear of assassination, though the residence with its clear view of the sea and of the approaches to the hills provided him with excellent security from external attack.

His first meeting with Winston was what diplomats call a courtesy call, though it's doubtful that Stalin cared about such a concept. He had certain objectives, and nothing much else mattered, no matter that he might have a reluctant respect for and possibly envy of Winston's qualities – the Prime Minister's ability, for example, to evoke feelings of warm regard, even love, from his own countrymen. Stalin also seemed to have an element of genuine affection for Roosevelt (especially now that the President looked as though he was at death's door, and who knew how difficult it might be to put one over his probable successor, that inexperienced – and therefore unpredictable – Mr Truman?) But J.V. Stalin, one knew, didn't really trust these wartime allies in the long run. They were against the way he ran Russia and always had been, and always would be, despite the present marriage of convenience.

The most significant thing at this meeting was a reaffirmation of the basic war aim – that Germany had to be finished off as quickly as possible. No dithering, as in the past. No lack of resolve, allowing Hitler to stage surprise attacks. End it all, and soon, in a two-pronged attack! Exactly how we could all work together to do this, how we could make the Germans pay for their acts, and how we might live together afterwards were matters for discussion at the conference.

Stalin was highly optimistic about the Red Army's progress through Poland into Germany.

'Pockets of Germans are being mopped up,' he said, showing rotting teeth in what was less a smile than a grimace of triumph.

'Ah, yes, good,' said Winston, though he would dearly have loved Anglo-American forces to win the race to Berlin. Montgomery could do it. However, this was not the American ambition.

'We, too, will very shortly launch a new offensive, in the west,' he added, trying to sound more positive than he felt. 'In three or four weeks time.'

'Good,' said Stalin.

He knew about the dissension among his allies, and was pleased to hear from Winston's own lips that they were taking their time, and hence that Berlin was not the prize they sought.

Winston grunted, then a small gleam of innocent happiness came into his eyes. He would show off his pride and joy to this crafty fellow, as venomous as an adder and far more slippery, but none the less a valued ally – for the moment. He led the way to his map room, which provided a bird's-eye view of war zones and military strengths, and the two veteran battlers, who both fancied themselves as knowing more about warfare than their generals, exchanged views on tactics.

Then Stalin left, no doubt relieved that he had done his duty as the conference host towards his eldest guest, and happy to know that Soviet soldiers would raise the Red Flag over Hitler's Reichstag and show the world who took the lead in blasting the Nazis off the face of the earth.

4

Berlin

Frau Siegendorff introduced her as 'Fraulein Jung from London'.
 The young woman corrected her with just the trace of a smile: 'Young, actually, and I'm a Freudian.'
 Dr Bergsen smiled enormously and said: 'Also, me.' Then he laughed heartily at some private joke.
 Her name was Dorothy Young, and she wore a faded floral dress, which served only to enhance the rest of her. She lit up Frau Siegendorff's dining-room. Her ginger hair was done in a severe style, fiercely combed away from the forehead and in a bun at the back. She had a wide mouth and large eyes that stretched to give her a slightly oriental look. She wore bright red lipstick. Her nose was Cleopatra-like long, her figure enticingly fulsome.
 She didn't say much, but she was like a bright tropical flower in the sombre dining-room where reproductions of old devotional paintings hung on the dark walls and heavy furnishings cluttered the space.
 After dinner, she and I sat together on a large leather sofa and talked. She was only a few years older than me but seemed decades ahead in sophistication and experience of life.
 'Why have I landed up in Berlin?' she replied to my question. 'Curiosity of a kind, I suppose. I want to, well, to look around and see what's what.'
 I waited for her to expand on her reasons. All she did, though, was to light a cigarette and inhale deeply.
 I told her I was bound for Cambridge, and described the envy felt by Dr Bergsen. She laughed when I talked about his love of England and its culture.
 'He's Jewish, I suppose?' she said.
 'Does that matter?'
 'Oh, come off it. Just to wonder if someone is Jewish doesn't make one a Nazi.'

'In this country, it more or less does.'

In truth, anti-Semitism in Germany was not the exclusive property of Nazis. Complaints that the Jews were 'not really Germans' were commonplace in Berlin. I had come across anti-Jewish statements in England too – sometimes from my mother and her friends – though rarely expressed as crassly or openly as in Germany.

'You oughtn't to jump to conclusions,' Dorothy said. 'You barely know me, and you've already got me pigeon-holed – English woman, *ergo* dim and prejudiced.'

She smiled as she said this. She was not as conventionally pretty as some of the girls I'd known, but when she smiled fully she was beautiful.

'I never meant that. But you'll come to see that in Germany comments from foreigners about "Jewishness" amount to political statements.'

'In that case I'm lucky to have met you so soon, Herr Bexley. Thank you for instructing me.'

'You're being juvenile,' I retorted.

'And you've been bloody presumptuous!'

We glared at each other in anger for a moment, then she said: 'Look, let's not argue over this. I'd hate to come across you in London or somewhere knowing you were thinking "Oh, God, here's that bigoted bitch I met in Berlin." I'm not remotely anti-Semitic. So, can we forget all this?'

'Yes, let's.'

'In any case, I'm Jewish myself, for what it's worth.'

'Then I'm sorry for bringing it up,' I said, embarrassed.

'Why? It's a superstition I was born into. Hardly my fault, and hardly something to feel ashamed about. Certainly not in this country.'

'No, but why come here when you're bound to get insulted?'

'Because I'm bloody-minded, and I certainly wasn't going to let any fascist gangsters stop me from going where I please.'

'What did your parents think?'

'My parents?' She raised her eyebrows. 'Why on earth should they matter? They've always thought I was a bit mad, I suppose, but they didn't raise any objections. They know where I stand. Mind you, they'd approve of the food that Frau S dishes up. Stodgy and Central European. How I hated it as a child. My grandmother cooked a bit like that, but with more imagination. At least she flavoured the dumplings. She came to England as a young girl, from Latvia.'

'To study?'

'No, silly!' Dorothy laughed. 'To work as a servant, but she always preached education. I suppose she'd have loved the thought of me going to university if she were still alive.'

'And might you go to university?'

'Possibly.'

'Cambridge?' I asked.

'Anywhere but there! Elitist and they won't even give women degrees, for God's sake! Mind you, a lot of interesting things are going on there. Politically.'

'Despite which, you wouldn't be seen dead there?'

'I was baiting you, darling. You bait easily. Now don't go all moody on me. Go on, call me an emancipated bitch. Get it out of your system.'

I found myself laughing.

'What?' she asked, bemused.

'You remind me of a chap in my house at school,' I said. 'Biggins. He couldn't resist being sarcastic and nasty, especially to the younger kids, accusing them of wetting their beds because they missed home, that sort of thing. Baiting them.'

'Oh God,' said Dorothy. 'And I'm like that?'

'A bit. Only Biggins had pimples, and he was fat. And smelly.'

'Thanks! Was your school awful?'

'I don't think it scarred me. I actually enjoyed some aspects.'

'Oh dear, don't tell me you're one of those rugger buggers,' she said.

'I was never much good at rugby, and I'm not one of the others, either.'

'What a relief!' she said, adding quickly: 'But don't get the wrong idea ducky. I'm liberated, not promiscuous.'

I changed the subject and asked her about the 'interesting' political developments at Cambridge.

'Oh, you know, new thinking about society,' she said airily.

'Marxism, you mean? The answer to all ills.'

'Things can't stay the way they are,' she snapped. 'Do you know what it's like to be without work and without hope? Have you ever come across real hardship, seen the world as it really is?'

'Probably not.'

'Then curb your schoolboy sarcasm.'

We said a frosty good-night to each other.

After that we had some friendlier chats, keeping well away from ideological tracks. I showed her some of the seamier sides of Berlin nightlife. She was amused by, but not attracted to, the scabrous froth of the West End cabarets and clubs.

'You won't get too attached to this sort of nonsense, will you, *liebling*?' she said, pecking me lightly on the cheek after one such excursion.

'I'm on a learning curve,' I said.

'As long as you curve leftwards.'

A few days later, she told me she was leaving Frau Siegendorff's house and going to stay with friends.

'I'll sleep on the floor until I get a job and can afford a place of my own.'

'Keep in touch.'

'Oh, we'll bump into each other again,' she said vaguely.

Dr Bergsen asked me about her one evening after she'd left.

'The lovely Fraulein Young, you meet her sometimes, yes?'

'No. Passing ships in the night.'

'Passing, yes, but you both go in the same direction. To English universities. And she liked you, I could tell.'

'I can assure you, Herr Doktor Bergsen, nothing could be further from the truth. If anything, she thinks I'm just a kid likely to fall into wicked ways.'

'Ach, I don't believe. You are young foreigners in my beautiful city. She also must be lonely.'

I doubted she was. It was hard to see how anyone – let alone a woman of her beauty – could be lonely in Berlin, which offered diversions to even the most friendless of strangers. You couldn't help being affected by the strange, stimulating mixture of gaiety and foreboding in the streets. Despite the political storm clouds and vicious brawling between Nazi gangs and their opponents, many people, especially the young, still pursued daily happiness, as though without a care in the world. They gossiped in coffee shops, laughed at the constant, chirpy, sharp Berlin witticisms, made love, argued about trivial things. And yet, whatever they said or did, however they acted, almost everyone – even those who like Dr Bergsen put a heavy gloss of optimism on the future – seemed to know, deep down, that something awful was coming. They accepted its inevitability with gallows humour or manic abandon, often masking a deep inner depression.

Everyone, that is, except the young left-wing radicals I met, mainly in beer cellars in dingy working-class areas, where you had to be careful not to stumble on to groups of brown-shirted SA thugs who loved nothing better than beating the sense and sometimes the life out of anyone who might be against them. The young leftists I was getting to know believed that Nazism could be confronted and beaten. They were mostly Social Democrats – Sozis. Together with the Communists they would have been a formidable force, but members of the two groups hated and distrusted each other far too much to unite. The Communists thought that democratic socialism threatened the Soviet Union even more than did fascism. To them, Nazism was merely the last gasp of capitalism, the final dying convulsion before the Great Dawn of Proletarian Dictatorship. There was a humourless fervour about the Communists, whereas the Sozis managed to combine sincerity of purpose with the sceptical, slangy humour of Berlin.

For a foreigner like myself, Berlin seemed the most fascinating, if frightening city in the world. I was making friends, improving my German and doing voluntary work for a charity trying to alleviate malnutrition among children in the capital.

One night at a raucous party in the room of a young Social Democrat friend, Klaus Friedrich, who lived in one of the ugly, crowded tenement blocks that disfigured the narrow streets of the workers' district of Neukölln, I spotted a face I knew. She wore her hair long now, had no make-up and was dressed as shabbily as any poverty stricken proletarian housewife.

'*Liebling*,' she cried when she saw me.

My heart pounded. It was Dorothy. We embraced in a comradely fashion and I kissed her on both cheeks.

'I never expected to meet you in this company,' she said.

'I'm not surprised to see you, though.'

'Oh, that's funny, because it's only by chance that I'm here. Dieter knows some of these people.'

She waved vaguely around, though whether to point out Dieter or to indicate 'these people' was unclear.

'You've changed your hairstyle,' I said.

'You noticed! And how is Frau S, and that sad Dr Bergsen?'

I gave her what little gossip I had and we discussed, with the sort of guardedness that was commonplace in left-wing Berlin, what we'd been doing in the past few months.

She had a part-time teaching job that left her plenty of spare time to 'see things'. She was not more explicit and I didn't push.

I told her about my friendship with Klaus and other socialists, and also about my work among the half-starved street children of Berlin.

'Typical do-gooding!' she said scornfully.

'You'd rather they went hungry?' I asked caustically.

'If it furthers the revolution, yes.'

'God, Dorothy. I suppose you'd just walk right by a starving kid and do nothing?'

'Of course, I wouldn't if I had money or food to give. But I wouldn't be a Lady Bountiful. All *you* people are doing, really, is papering over the cracks.'

'If you want to call it that,' I said angrily.

She smiled at me, and said affectionately: 'Don't take it to heart, *liebling*. Actually, it's quite nice to have a down-to-earth spat with you.'

My anger faded.

'We should do it more often,' I said.

We clinked together our glasses of beer.

'Look, love,' she said suddenly. 'I'll give you a telephone number in case you have a sudden burning desire to see me. Ask for Dieter's friend Dorothy and I'll reach you at the Siegendorff ménage. All right?'

She fished a pencil and scrap of paper out of her cheap handbag and wrote a number.

'Contact me before you go back to Blighty,' she said.

Then, with a smile, she disappeared into the crowd of smoke and noisy young things. I asked my friend Klaus who Dieter was.

'*Mensch!*' he exclaimed. 'I don't know who brought that commie arsehole along. He's that blond-haired one over there. For sure, I didn't invite such a dumb head. He's the sort who if Stalin farts he puts it in a bottle and sniffs it for kicks.'

Klaus himself hated following any line. He was sandy-haired

and freckled, a pocket Hercules who wore his beliefs lightly and had a visceral dislike of fanatics at either end of the political spectrum. He scrapped with Nazis because he despised them and enjoyed punching them, not because anyone told him to do it. He got his kicks from danger, large or small. He'd suggest escapades, some of which I joined in, like climbing illicitly into the zoo at night and painting anti-Nazi slogans on the walls. One said: 'On no account should visitors feed a Goebbels to the animals; it's poisonous.'

A few weeks after the party in Neukölln, I telephoned the number Dorothy had given me and explained to a neutral male voice that I wanted to leave a message for her. He grunted that he'd pass it on. I asked him to tell her I'd meet her at Schwannecke's at lunchtime the next day if she could make it.

'Schwannecke's?' he said, astonished.

Somewhat to my surprise, she arrived, on time, in an ankle-length check dress with a midriff belt and buckle that showed off her body very well and managed to turn several heads. She'd put on lipstick and eye shadow and looked like a well-heeled Berlin woman about town.

Schwannecke's was a bar and restaurant near the fashionable Kurfürstendamm, a haunt of the intelligentsia. Its interior was narrow, and the hum of conversation incessant and insistent. I'd chosen it out of mischievousness.

'This is rather jolly, isn't it?' she said with schoolgirl enthusiasm.

'The bourgeoisie behaving like human beings?'

She laughed and touched my hand.

'You're trying to goad me, *liebling*. These are bohemian bourgeoisie, so they don't quite count as the enemy.'

'You look quite at home,' I taunted her.

'Stop it, Jimmy, I want to enjoy this place. The comrades can be frightfully boring sometimes – oops, for God's sake don't tell Stalin I said that.'

'So, you've joined the Party ranks?'

'Shh,' she whispered. 'I'm still not a member, but please don't go saying those things in public. This isn't Soho, you know.'

'You look gorgeous, anyway. A ravishing revolutionary.'

'I borrowed the outfit and the make-up. Tomorrow, we'll make the revolution. Today, I wanted to make an impression on Schwannecke's. I think I may have succeeded.'

I agreed that she had. Her mixture of intelligence, radicalism and voluptuous beauty intoxicated me. We ordered wine and sandwiches and giggled our way through the next hour or so. She was totally unlike anyone I'd ever met. I was entranced by the fact that she'd obviously come to Germany to fight the Nazis, and yet retained such an allure of femininity. In that short time in Schwannecke's we established a kind of intimacy; two young English people, serious-minded but capable of frivolity in the midst of Germanic intellectual intensity.

In between laughing and drinking, we talked about the differences in our upbringings: me in my comfortable environments at home and school; she escaping from the confines of a poor Jewish family in the East End of London. Her family had scraped to send her and her sisters to good schools, which gave her the poise and confidence to get work in a film studio as secretary to a production manager.

'That's where I learned to speak posh. I should have been an actress.'

'What stopped you?'

'Someone told me I was good at imitation but poor at interpretation.'

She told me of the rage she'd felt at the inequalities of wealth in Britain, at the hypocrisy of the upper classes and politicians. She was still a schoolgirl when she turned towards the far Left and Marxism.

'Eventually, I knew I had to come to Germany. This is where the revolution's going to spread next.'

'Which is one reason why Hitler's so popular,' I said.

'Don't worry, darling, he'll get his head cracked in due course.'

'Why not now?'

'When the time is ripe.'

I couldn't see the logic of allowing the Nazis to get stronger and stronger before stopping them in their tracks – all Dorothy would say was 'the crisis in capitalism will lead to a general collapse' – but I almost wanted to believe that she was right. I was drawn to her idealistic belief in a fair deal for all, workers as well as bosses. Who could not want that? Wasn't it gloriously heroic for a spirited, attractive, young woman to fight for it?

I felt she knew about life, while all I knew about was the trappings of privilege. And, of course, there was something irresistible about her, a look, a feeling, a scent. I had been in love before, but they were juvenile emotions, compared to this. It was her fervour as well as her body that I coveted.

When we swayed out into the street, the dark of the afternoon was already closing in.

'I'd better get back to Dieter's place,' she said vaguely. 'There's a meeting, pamphlets to distribute...'

'Come and say hello to the folks at Frau S's,' I suggested.

'No, better not,' she mumbled.

I was clutching her hand.

'Why do you want me to?' she asked.

'I like your company,' I said lightly. 'Then I'll escort you to Dieter's place.'

No one was visible at Frau Siegendorff's house, so we went up to my room. All I could offer Dorothy was a bottle of beer. I had no idea what might happen. I just wanted to be with her.

Once the door was closed, she slumped on to the bed, kicked off her shoes and curled up, drifting quickly into sleep. I sat in the armchair and tried to read *The Magic Mountain* before dozing off myself.

She woke me with a gentle nudge.

'Have to go, *liebling*,' she said softly.

I opened my eyes.

'Are you sure? We could have a meal somewhere.'

'In Cambridge, darling, if ever I get there.'

'And in Berlin?'

'Oh, we're bound to bump into each other again. Everyone does. But don't phone that number again. They're a bit jittery these days.'

Then she kissed me lightly on the cheek and left.

I forced myself to accept that there would be no romance between us. She was here on serious business. I had better forget her, no matter how difficult.

I met another girl.

Frau Siegendorff said the daughter of some acquaintances would be happy to give me some lessons in German conversation without charge.

Magda was about the same age as me, very pretty, with long blonde hair, which she sometimes wore in tresses, and big blue eyes. She was pleasant, cheerful and full of laughter. The family, like so many, had fallen on hard times, but still managed to live in relative comfort. She was a good antidote to my unrequited feelings for Dorothy. She showed me with pride the great imperial classical buildings and took me for excursions to Wannsee, with its lake, parks and villas, and other beauty spots. One evening, we kissed passionately and clung to each other.

The next day, I went to the house, eager to see her, excited at the idea of her physical presence. Her elder sister answered the doorbell and suggested I wait in the drawing-room. I walked into the room where her father was reading a Nazi newspaper. He saw my look of surprise and laughed it off by saying: 'So, we have to read some of the rubbish too, to know what's going on in our troubled country.'

Just then, his wife came in, and said: 'We are not National Socialists here, Herr Bexley.'

'I never thought...' I began.

Magda's father poked at the newspaper with his pipe.

'But some of the things that Hitler says make good sense. Of course, I would never vote for that rabble, but, you know, the others have failed us for so long.'

I muttered that it was for the Germans to decide their future.

The father jumped on this.

'Ah, but it is Great Britain and her friends, especially France, which marches in and occupies our territory with such arrogance, that have made so many people here vote for the National Socialists. We have lost our territory, we are not even allowed to have a proper army or navy. Is that just?'

I shook my head. I couldn't argue against the fact that the Versailles Treaty was iniquitous.

'Well, and Herr Hitler says he will correct this injustice and many other injustices,' he said. 'Some people are asking, Should he not be given the chance?'

'At least, Hitler has an honest face,' said his wife.

He said: 'And, naturally, I do not agree with all the rubbish about the Jewish conspiracies, and so forth, but the Jews in Germany have very great influence, too much.'

Magda entered. Her face flushed when she saw *Der Angriff* – Goebbels' newspaper – in her father's hand.

Outside, in the warmth of a summer's day, she said: 'I wish they wouldn't read such things. My father isn't a violent person.

It's all just talk. It's politics. I know nothing about those things, Jimmy. It will all blow over, these bad times. Also, as my father says, Hitler only wants to make right all the wrongs we have suffered.'

'And the threats against the Jews?' I asked.

'Oh, the Jews,' she said, dismissively. 'Of course, that is wrong. But they bring it on themselves too. They should become more like us, perhaps, and not be so greedy. But, Jimmy, I don't want to talk about all these things.'

'Okay,' I said.

'There are some good Jews too,' she said. 'My mother will go only to see a Jewish doctor. They are the best. But the others...'

We walked in silence.

'You probably know about them better than I do,' she said. 'Probably in England it's different.'

I knew very little about Jews in England. I'd known a few Jewish boys at school. They seemed nice enough chaps, even if sensitive, aloof, nervous of rejection. And I knew Dorothy.

'Oh, Jimmy, let's not spoil this beautiful day by thinking about all the bad things in life,' Magda said. 'We will go to the zoo and see all the animals.'

But the day had been ruined for me. Magda and her family were unimaginative, but basically law abiding – not that different from so many people I'd come across in England – and yet they were being drawn into something that reeked of an evil I'd never encountered before.

At the zoo, Magda put her arm through mine. I did not push her away, but I felt uneasy and apart from her. For me, the zoo was a place of brilliantly forbidden nights where one daubed caustic anti-Nazi witticisms on the walls and laughed at them in the company of brave friends. It was not this daytime menagerie where iron bars enclosed the animals, much as the lies of the Nazis were beginning to trap the ordinary people of Germany in cages of the mind.

At the end of the day Magda kissed me sweetly, oblivious to my feelings of depression and distaste.

I wrote her a note, saying how I'd enjoyed our time together, but that I would soon be returning to England. A few days later I received a short letter from her: 'Dear Jimmy – I hope you will enjoy the rest of your stay. I wish you every happiness in the future.'

I was relieved that this little interlude had ended, and that I could breathe a little more freely. Magda, despite her physical charms, soon disappeared from my mind.

One morning, Dr Bergsen said he would like to show me the classical antiquities at the new Pergamon museum.

'My work is a little less these days,' he explained. 'So I have the time to be a little your guide to our culture.'

It was a lovely morning as we strolled along a quiet residential street towards the tram stop, inhaling the wonderfully light, energising air of Berlin. People were walking busily to work, or pushing prams or carrying bags of shopping.

I'd told him about my conversation with Magda and her parents, and said I still couldn't understand how it had come to this – that normal, ordinary, possibly quite decent people could turn into supporters of racist extremism.

'You want to know why ordinary people say these things? Because you stole our colonies, our industries, our money. You British wanted we should be ashamed to be German, but actually you make us proud of it, you make those people full of hatred because of their humiliation.'

I said gloomily: 'So, you blame *us* for Hitler?'

'You know, my dear friend, how much I love of England and its culture. But who else to blame? These people believe he is their saviour from what has been done to them. They have seen here nearly a Bolshevik revolution, and for long time all they had to eat was turnips. Naturally, they will follow a man who tells them he will end all this suffering and make Germany great again.'

Just then we began to hear some shouting and singing, and a truck heaved into view, carrying a horde of Brownshirts, some with swastika flags, some hanging on to the outside of the vehicle. They were singing a song about beating the daylights out of the Red Flag. As they passed us, a couple of them jeered. They'd driven on for a few seconds before the truck stopped and several of them got off and swaggered towards us. They were quite young, almost schoolboys, although the lout in command was older, leathery, a veteran of some kind of fighting. It was he who, ignoring me, jabbed his finger in Dr Bergsen's face and said with a menacing grin: 'Soon, soon. Soon we'll deal with you, Jew scum.'

None of the people in the street stopped or even looked at us. It was as though, for them, the scene was not taking place.

'Leave him alone,' I said in English, and then in German.

'It's okay, Jimmy. Is nothing,' said Dr Bergsen.

The leader looked at me and grinned. I could see that several of his front teeth were missing.

'This is not your country, Englishman. You can have this Jew if you want. Take him back to England.'

His comrades laughed loudly.

Dr Bergsen pointed to his lapel badge and said: 'I am a veteran of the war. I fought for Germany.'

The man looked hard into his face.

'The only badge that counts with me is your foul Jewish face. The only badge you deserve is one that says "I am a piece of Jewish shit".'

His comrades roared with laughter, though one or two, it seemed to me, were disconcerted at the insults being heaped on an old soldier. Their leader, though, was not finished yet.

'Soon,' he repeated to Dr Bergsen, this time without a smile. 'Soon.'

He pushed him hard in the chest and sent him falling to the ground.

Then, with a slight head movement, he signalled to the others that they should move on. I helped Dr Bergsen to his feet. The Brownshirts climbed back on to the truck which drove off. They were gone from sight, but we could still hear the anti-Semitic slogans.

I asked Dr Bergsen if he was all right. He seemed pale and shaken.

'Thank you, my dear Herr Bexley. I am not hurt. Ach, they are only ignorant criminals. They drink, they shout, sometimes they attack. But it will all pass. Perhaps one day Hitler will realise what is going on and deal with them.'

I felt like grabbing him by the lapel, which held his veteran's badge, to shake him into some kind of realisation of what was happening in Germany.

He tried to regain his cheerfulness during our excursion to the museum.

'Look at all this beauty,' he said, pointing out the flowing forms of some Greek sculpture. 'It always will survive, *nicht wahr?*'

I said it would, but deep down I was unsure what, if anything, might survive this age. I felt a great anger, not least with myself for lacking the courage to punch the leader of that Brownshirt truckload. I wanted to wipe that smirk off his face, to destroy his ignorant certainty.

I wanted someone to do it *now*, and to every Nazi in Germany.

5

Yalta, February 4, 1945

The room has dark wood panelling on the walls and ceiling. It is exactly the sort of place for an intimate, confidential talk between friends. Not too large, but with enough space for a solid desk, a settee, occasional tables and chairs. On a mild, sunny afternoon like today, you can look through the window across the gardens to the calm, twinkling sea. The two men sit together on a sofa with crimson upholstery, darker than blood. The Georgian Wolf is calling on the New York Patrician.

Stalin's sneer-set face cracks into a friendly smile as Roosevelt pumps his hand enthusiastically in greeting. The Marshal, having removed his coat, wears a uniform with modest decorations. The President is in shirtsleeves and sports a multicoloured striped tie, conveying optimism. Because FDR has not risen to his feet to greet his visitor, you may deduce that he is incapable of standing, but no wheelchair is in evidence, no crutches. This is a man who still strives to conceal from the world, and perhaps from himself, that he is anything but the able-bodied athletic world-in-his-hands fellow of his twenties. Even today, as the old, familiar, confident Roosevelt grin lights up the room, there is a raffish air about his appearance. Then you notice the pallor in his face.

The two men embark on a conversation, which each hopes will cement their relationship. With lovers it is the eyes that speak, with statesmen it is the meaning behind the words, true or false, that matters most. The two do not speak each other's language but interpreters render the utterances as best they can. Apart from the leaders and their interpreters, the only other person present is Molotov, who does not speak but sits and observes expressionlessly.

'I am happy to see you again,' Stalin tells Roosevelt.

He means this. He likes the President because that poor,

crippled man has got the heart of a lion. Men of such courage, who can fight from the front and overcome their pain, are worth liking, even if they are adversaries. It doesn't enter Stalin's mind that if Roosevelt were a Soviet rather than American citizen he would have to be crushed like a beetle and a confession of wrongdoing extracted from him with methods perfected by the Inquisition and the Gestapo, as well as the pre- and post-Revolutionary secret police of the Russian empire. It doesn't enter his mind that he can be fond of Roosevelt because the President is not a rival in the sense that Trotsky, Bukharin and the rest were rivals for power. If his mind were to run along these lines, he would brush off the thought by concluding that there was nothing personal involved in getting rid of those scum and the thousands like them because what they challenged was not him alone, but the whole structure of the true Soviet system. Ask Molotov, ask Jewish Kaganovich, or fat-hipped Malenkov, or peasant-faced Khrushchev, or slimy little Beria. All would agree that even though Trotsky was a smart-arsed bourgeois intellectual and Bukharin was a self-righteous, right-wing prig, they would never have been liquidated merely for their characteristics. It was what they stood for that condemned them, not their perverted personalities.

Joseph Vissarionovich Stalin looks closely into Roosevelt's eyes and sees that the fire that was there at Tehran has begun to die out. Soon it will be gone. Molotov has already advised his chief of this, and has said: 'This is to our advantage.' Stalin has some respect for Molotov, a useful man in his way, but knows he lacks the imagination of a statesman. What good would it do to ride like a Cossack over an ally like Roosevelt? For the sake of appearances, as much as of high policy, care must be taken not to over-exploit the American's frailty.

This has nothing to do with sentimentality – a trait that Stalin learned to suppress even before his days in the conspiratorial revolutionary underground at the turn of the century – though he has not forgotten that it was this man, soon after he became President in 1933, who decided the United States should give diplomatic recognition to the Soviet Union.

'You are comfortable here, Mr President?' he asks. 'You and your delegation are comfortable?'

Roosevelt is in residence at the Livadia Palace, a graceful

white building, stately but not grandiose, its porticoes and pillars in perfect proportion to its size. This is where the main political sessions of the conference will take place.

'Very,' says Roosevelt. 'It's a beautiful place. Magnificent setting. I understand it was once the summer palace of the Tsar?'

'And later, after the People's Revolution, a sanatorium for workers.'

'Then it's exactly right for this conference since we all need some peace and quiet to recover from our recent troubles,' the President observes.

The interpreter feels it necessary to point out to the Marshal that Roosevelt's remark is intended as a self-deprecatory joke, referring to the shock German Ardennes offensive – frantically repulsed by the western Allies only a few weeks ago – or to the obstructionist attitudes of Prime Minister Churchill, rather than as any criticism of the Soviet Union's conduct of the war.

'I know that, of course,' says Stalin gruffly in Russian to the interpreter. 'Confine yourself to translating his remarks, Pavlov.'

To Roosevelt, he says, gesturing around with his hand: 'Yes, we have tried to make sure it is a restful place once more. You know, the Nazi swine ransacked everything here. What they did not destroy, they took away with them, no doubt for Goering's art collection.'

'They are a bunch of bastards,' says Roosevelt angrily.

He despises the idea of looting of cultural treasures. When you destroy art, you destroy civilisation. He thinks of the burning of books in Germany and the denigration of what the Nazi ignoramuses call 'degenerate art'. He puts to the back of his mind the knowledge that the man sitting opposite him has turned churches into barns and has ruled that the only worthwhile art is that which illuminates the benefits of the Soviet system.

'I want you to know, sir,' Roosevelt says emphatically, 'that I am today more bloodthirsty than I was a year ago.'

He has been fired up by the sights of devastation on the journey from Saki to Yalta, and he wants to let Stalin know the United States is going to be totally ruthless towards the Germans, without any of Winston's outdated scruples about treating one's defeated foe with decency and magnanimity unless they are war criminals – though he is not going to go along with Treasury Secretary Morgenthau's idea of transforming Germany into an agricultural and pastoral country.

He has committed men to war himself, young men to the slaughter on steamy Pacific islands and on the hellish beaches of Normandy, and he hasn't always slept easily. But what the Germans did in the Crimea was a deliberate act of criminality, not a necessary struggle in defence of one's country and its liberties. He is convinced the Red Army was right to be as brutal as necessary in forcing its enemies from the peninsula.

Stalin nods. This is the point he has been making and will continue to make: war is not about looking at maps and moving paper armies. War is about beating the invading enemy back with ferocity and then punishing him for the invasion. That is war. Diplomacy is making sure he will not do the same thing again without the risk of war.

'We are all more bloodthirsty now,' he says. 'But I must tell you that what has happened in Crimea is nothing compared to what these savages have done in Ukraine. Here, they did not have the time to destroy everything in a planned way. In Ukraine, they destroyed with method and calculation.'

'Savages,' agrees Roosevelt.

His memory is not what it was, but he remembers that Stalin did his own destructive work in Ukraine some years before, causing famine and the deaths of millions – yes, millions – because he wanted to rush the Soviet Union into modernisation. He puts this out of his mind quickly.

'You have heard, Mr President, that a few days ago the People's Army liberated a terrible concentration camp in Poland?' Stalin asks.

Roosevelt nods. He cannot find anything adequate to say about the horrors of Auschwitz. He is far from ignorant about how Nazi extermination policies have been put into practice. For years, he has been reading intercepted transcripts between German officials dealing with the killing of Jews and their transportation to camps built for nothing less than mass murder.

Stalin says laconically: 'Many people – millions – were murdered there.'

'We'll make the bastards pay, Marshal,' says Roosevelt.

Discussing the military situation, Stalin is much more pessimistic than he had shown himself to be in his meeting with Churchill.

'When will the Red Army get to Berlin?' Roosevelt asks. 'You know, Marshal, I've got a lot riding on that. I've been taking bets that you guys will get to Berlin before General MacArthur takes Manila. Am I going to win my bets?'

'Communists do not bet on the future,' says Stalin with a straight face. 'We make it happen. But I am sure you are going to lose your bets, Mr President. I would like to help if I could, but we have difficult fighting ahead, very difficult, before we reach Berlin.'

He searches his pockets, then turns to stony-faced Molotov.

'As usual, Molotov, I have no money. Can you make sure we can give some kopeks to the President when he loses his bets?'

Molotov nods seriously. They make a great double act, Roosevelt thinks. He chuckles. This Joe Stalin is as shrewd a guy as you will get. He brings out the best in me. Winston used to do that too.

'You know, I'm going to hold you to that, Marshal,' FDR says in that elegant New England Brahmin voice, which the Russians sense rather than comprehend. 'We'll have it written into the protocols of the conference: Marshal Stalin pledges to reimburse President Roosevelt for lost bets on overestimating the speed of the Red Army's advance.'

Brief flicker of a smile from Stalin. He stubs out a cigarette, gives a short smoker's cough and says: 'Perhaps to help you even more, Mr President, so you can have a small chance of winning your gamble, I will order Zhukov to concentrate everything on getting to Berlin as quick as he can. But it is not so easy as some people think to fight our way to Berlin. It is not like we are taking a train trip from Paris to Rome, or to Amsterdam.'

This is a jibe at what Stalin considers the relatively easy ride the Allied troops have been getting on the western front, despite the so-called Battle of the Bulge in the Ardennes Forest, which caught the Americans and British with their pants down and ended complacency about a swift end to the German war.

Roosevelt doesn't rise to the bait. He wants this conversation to run smoothly and along certain lines. He is trying to draw Stalin into the cosy FDR fellowship – and how many people have been able to resist the charm and wit of this president? – so he alters the focus of the discussion, although not so radically as to alert his sparring partner.

'When you do get to Berlin,' he asks, 'will you find Hitler is still there? Or do you think he will run away from there?'

He wants to have Stalin's insights into the thinking of a fellow dictator, especially in the face of inevitable defeat.

He knows Churchill would have stayed in London and died fighting if Hitler had invaded Britain. And if the Japs had ever managed to get as far as the United States mainland, and had sent rapid patrols to Washington or Hyde Park, he believes that he himself, wheelchair-bound but pistol in hand, would have done the same rather than flee to some underground redoubt.

But dictators are different. They deal in destiny. They believe their personal survival is tied up with the triumph of the states they rule.

Stalin shrugs as he ponders this question. He too has wondered about Hitler. Undoubtedly a man of genius, admirable in the way he disposes of his domestic opponents, but misguided. If he'd been even half reasonable, the two of them, Stalin and Hitler, could have worked things out sensibly. A division of spoils. Mastery of all Europe. Living space for the Germans, security for the Russians. Molotov had met the man and thought him unstable, with too many bees in his bonnet. But then what can you expect of a teetotal, non-smoking vegetarian who is scared of women and of Jews? A sensible man knows how treat women (with the kindness of a strong and punitive hand) and how to handle the oily, untrustworthy, greedy Jews. There are other ways of doing this than trying to kill off a whole race. Stop them from practising their superstitions, yes. Deport them wholesale to somewhere far away, certainly. But murder the whole grasping race, without even the pretence of trials? Ridiculous. Only a madman would think he could get away with that.

'I believe he will try to escape if there is a chance of carrying on the war,' Stalin says eventually.

Then, unexpectedly, he adds: 'But perhaps there is another way for him. Perhaps Mr Churchill will offer him a separate peace.'

'Winston?' Roosevelt laughs in amazement. 'Never in a thousand years.'

Stalin is smiling sardonically. He genuinely does suspect that Britain, and perhaps even America, will agree to a truce with the Germans in the west, allowing the enemy to move all its legions to the eastern front against the Soviet homeland.

The President – all his old divide-and-rule instincts sharpening his mind – seizes the moment. This is the time to show Stalin exactly where he stands.

So, having made a loyal statement in regard to his old friend Churchill – dear old Winston who used to revitalise him so much with his verbal wizardry and wit but who these days, to be frank, often bores him (which is the worst of sins in the world of Franklin Delano Roosevelt) – he indulges in some fairly pointed jibes at the expense of the Prime Minister and his antiquated ideas. He knows these will appeal to Stalin, the unsentimental revolutionary hard man, the realist. Winston's had his glorious day – and we will, naturally, never forget how he alone, in a world of defeatists, cowards, isolationists, opportunists, stood up against the all-conquering Nazi onslaught. But now, now there are two Great Powers only left in the world. To make this point, the President sets the scene by recalling an episode at Tehran, more than a year ago when Stalin, in a gruffly genial way, had suggested the best way to punish the German army would be to round up and shoot 50,000 officers. To be honest, not even Roosevelt was quite sure whether Stalin was being serious or not. But Winston had no doubts. He'd turned purple and spluttered that Britain would never stand for such barbarity. FDR had by this stage noted the twinkle in Stalin's eye and suggested, jocularly, a compromise of 49,000 executions. Churchill had eventually stomped out of the dinner in disgust, to be brought back only by the coaxings and explanations of a beaming, conciliatory Stalin.

Now, at Yalta, Roosevelt says with a smile: 'I sincerely hope, my dear Marshal, that this time you will again propose a toast to the execution of 50,000 German officers.'

As wisecracks go, while this is not, Roosevelt knows, in the Jack Benny class, he calculates it will go down well with Stalin. The Marshal merely nods enigmatically, but Roosevelt is pretty sure he has forged another bond between them.

In fact, what Stalin is thinking is as follows. This dying President will go to any lengths to ingratiate himself with me. Is this because of his illness, or because this is what the Americans want? Well, we will see. He and I equally loathe the British.

The Americans can never forget that they had to fight the British for their independence. So, in a way, did we. Churchill once asked me to forgive him for trying to strangle the Soviet Union at its birth. I told him, with my tongue in my cheek, 'All that is in the past, and the past belongs to God.' Well, maybe that was not entirely in jest. I studied in a seminary, after all, and God is just another word for history.

Roosevelt, meanwhile, thinks he is doing a pretty good job at stoking up Stalin's suspicions of the British and must continue with this line.

'I will tell you something indiscreet,' he says with his charming, dazzling grin still present in that haggard face. 'It is something I would not wish to say in front of Mr Churchill.'

Stalin perks up at this, half smiles at Roosevelt, inviting the indiscretion to issue forth. Could it be something scandalous? he wonders. Could this sexless pudding of a man Churchill be fucking the wife of one of his cabinet members?

'It is this,' says the President. 'The Prime Minister wants to build up France into a strong European power capable of holding the line on the border with Germany until the British army can recover to full strength.'

He is hinting at the obvious: that Churchill fears post-war Europe being dominated by one power, namely the Soviet Union.

Stalin sinks back into his chair, a little disappointed. Is that all? And so what if the perfidious British are going to use their traditional cross-Channel enemy for their own purposes? They have always acted in such a duplicitous way.

Still, he takes the point behind Roosevelt's gossip: the Americans are not going to join the British in a common united negotiating position at Yalta. This is gratifying, though not conclusive. He knows full well that in diplomacy as in politics, as in human relations, you are a fool if you trust anyone. Especially someone who tries to ingratiate himself or herself (and, by God, he knows all about the wily ways of women, from wives and mistresses to his beloved, wayward little daughter Svetlana) with you. Only the stupid, timid rabbit will trust the fox bearing gifts.

And suddenly his suspicion is vindicated. This fox, this President whom he admires as much as he pities, displays his cunning once more. All this talk is only feigned camaraderie. Here is the real point of it all. Roosevelt has dangled the carrot of a Great Alliance, but there is a quid pro quo.

'To get back to the military situation. You know, Marshal Stalin, we hope we can all finish off this Hitler sonofabitch as fast as possible, so we can throw everything we've got at the Japanese.'

Stalin smiles inwardly. This is the sort of talk he understands, and what he has come to expect from his negotiating partner at his best. So, the man is nearly on his deathbed, but his mind still functions well.

'Yes, of course,' says Stalin. 'That, too, must be undertaken.'

Roosevelt looks at him steadily. The unasked question is: When will Stalin be able to help out in Asia? He'd agreed at Tehran that he would join in the war against Japan, but Roosevelt is seeking confirmation of the pledge and details about precisely when, how and in return for what it will be consummated. FDR knows the Japanese are fanatical defenders and the Pacific War is likely to run on into 1946 or beyond, even if the Soviet Union comes in heavily. The US will have to invade the homeland eventually at an astronomic cost in the lives of American boys.

If Stalin makes good his promise it could save maybe a million US lives. How can one even imagine what a million body bags lying all together on the ground would look like? But he cannot rush things. This oriental bargaining partner of his gives nothing for nothing. So he conveys the unasked question in his steady gaze.

'Of course,' Stalin says slowly, 'the Japanese will have to be defeated, but first, first we must smash Hitler, we must smash German aggression for ever.'

And here he smashes his fist on to the arm of the settee. It is a gesture of resolve that is not lost on Roosevelt. This man, FDR thinks, is as ruthless as ever. We *will* have him on our side against the Japs. But don't rush him. I have to handle this right. With a guy like Joseph Stalin, it's all about making deals.

Having smashed his fist, Stalin smiles amiably. Molotov coughs discreetly. Stalin says: 'Now, it is time for the plenary session, I think.'

Roosevelt checks his watch and says: 'Yes, it's three minutes to five.'

'I have enjoyed meeting you once more like this, Mr President.'

'That's a mutual enjoyment, Marshal,' Roosevelt beams.

Neither man has mentioned the question of atomic weapons. They are both aware that the scientists at Los Alamos in the New Mexico desert are working with the military towards building a bomb of this type. But neither man seriously believes that such a device – even if it works – will affect the outcome of World War Two. Both these leaders deal in the art of the possible, not in science fiction.

6

Berlin

I was disturbed by the reactions of both Dr Bergsen and myself to the incident in which he'd been insulted and assaulted by Nazi Brownshirts. How was it possible that he, the target of such hatred, could bring himself to believe that this monster of racist fascism would simply disappear one fine day? And why had I done nothing to protect him? I'd protested, but that was about all. I should have fought in his defence, even if I would certainly have been knocked silly. Why hadn't I? It wasn't that I feared a bloody nose – I'd received and given worse at school. Nor was I a pacifist like Gerald. If it ever came to war, I told myself, I'd fight to the death even if I did end up like my father – a forgotten hero of a forgotten cause. The idea that *he* might have died pointlessly made me even more despondent. Perhaps, I thought in a moment of deep depression, my grandfather hadn't been so far off the beam in seeing Germany and Germans as intrinsically evil – and then I recalled the decent people I knew in Germany who would never be dragged into supporting Hitler.

Dr Bergsen never volunteered much about his family or relations. I gathered that his mother was dead and his father was living somewhere in Germany, but I didn't know whether he had brothers or sisters or cousins or uncles or aunts. So it was a complete surprise when he invited me to dinner with his nephew.

'I think you will like Leo,' he said. 'Also, he speaks English good.'

Leo Roth – the son of Dr Bergsen's only sister – was a few years older than me. He had a full head of curly dark hair, a high forehead and a long, slightly ridged nose, on which sat a pair of horn-rimmed spectacles; he looked like a scholar. From the moment I arrived at the restaurant, I could see that Dr Bergsen was extremely proud of him.

'Leo is going to become a *berühmter* – how do you say? – scientist,' Dr Bergsen said.

'Famous,' I said.

'Yes, famous around the world.'

'No, Uncle Samuel, I am not going to be another Einstein,' Leo said, quite earnestly.

'Einstein, ha!' said Dr Bergsen dismissively. 'You will be better than him. That fellow, he thinks so much of himself. On everything, he is an expert. Germany, he does not like; war, he does not like. So who is there who likes war? But still we have to fight for our country.'

'He is a great genius, though, Uncle,' said Leo, with a tolerant, affectionate smile. 'He has made the greatest discoveries since Newton.'

'Newton, *ja*. *There* was a man. But what he discovered was solid. The Law of Gravity, no? You can see it all the time you open your eyes. Look!'

He dropped his teaspoon to the floor.

'See!' he said triumphantly. 'But this Einstein, what does he prove? That nothing is real? So I believe. That nothing is solid like it looks?'

He held out his hand to me.

'Touch this, Herr Bexley. Is not this solid?'

He waved the same hand around the room, which was full of very solid citizens chomping away at their substantial meals.

'It is merely an illusion, Uncle Samuel,' laughed Leo. 'Everything consists largely of empty space.'

'Like your head, Leopold, like your head,' said Dr Bergsen in good humour.

I was touched by the real affection between these two. If anything in this world of ours was sturdy and permanent, it seemed to me that it was this bond between them.

When we'd finished our meal, Dr Bergsen took out his gold pocket watch and announced regretfully that he needed to return to his office to see a client. Business was slow these days, because of the economic depression and because of all the uncertainty, he said, so he could not neglect a valuable client.

'A rich lady. She is of the Jewish faith and is already frightened by this National Socialist business. To America, she wants to run. While she makes a visit there to see how much she likes, she wants my firm to look after her – I do not have the English word – *angelegenheiten*.'

'Her affairs,' said Leo. 'She must trust you, Uncle.'

'Trust? Of course, she trusts. And perhaps there is more than trust.'

He smiled, like a child who hopes to shock his parents.

'Then perhaps you should go with her to America,' said Leo teasingly.

'No, no,' he said quickly, frowning. 'I should not have said. She is rich, I am poor. She is old, I am not so old. She is in many ways foolish, I am a little more clever. But I must go to talk to her; I must tell her there is no need to run away from Germany. All is solid here.'

He stood to go, and Leo and I also rose.

'Sit, my dear young people,' said Dr Bergsen. 'Sit and talk for a little longer between yourselves.'

After he'd left, Leo and I, in a roundabout fashion, both expressed our fears that Dr Bergsen was far too optimistic about the future. I didn't tell Leo about the incident with the storm troopers. I didn't want to upset him. He was intelligent enough to know that that sort of thing was going on all the time, and that things would get worse, not better.

Dr Bergsen had told him I was going up to Cambridge. Leo said he was a bit envious because of interesting developments there.

'A friend of mine said something similar, but she meant political things,' I remarked.

'I don't really care about that sort of excitement,' Leo said. 'I was talking only about science.'

He was doing research in theoretical physics at Göttingen University. He was more interested in talking about his field than about German politics. It was all a bit above my head. He told me he was studying the structure of atom nuclei.

'Your great Professor Rutherford at the Cavendish Laboratory – and it was he, incidentally, not Einstein, who discovered that the atom consists mainly of emptiness – has postulated the existence of particles known as neutrons. It would explain so much about the universe, about everything, if this could be proved. Why, for instance, the nucleus simply doesn't blow up.'

'Would it matter if it did?' I asked.

Leo laughed. 'Of course. If that happened, even the illusion of our existence would not survive.'

'It sounds fascinating, but if the Nazis come to power will they let such research continue? Don't they consider that sort of thing to be "Jewish science"?'

'Who can say, for sure what they will do?' he shrugged. 'Perhaps they will be persuaded by some of the "pure" German scientists who are also working on studies that may prove to be very significant.'

'Significant?'

'I could explain, perhaps,' he smiled. 'But where should I start? You are familiar with quantum mechanics?'

I clapped my hand to my head.

'No, Leo, please forget that I asked.'

'Then I will spare both of us further anguish. It is no more than the basic physics of the atom, but perhaps this does not interest you.'

'I have a very small brain.'

'Not so small, I'm sure. I hope that the brains of our leading Nazis prove much, much smaller. There is a very sinister possibility about the enormous energy that would be available if we learned how to split the atom. A part of me hopes that Hitler and his friends find the whole idea of "Jewish" science so repulsive that they will not go down the road of atomic physics.'

'If that happens, you'll be out of a job here, won't you?' I asked.

'Probably, but if they were to see the potential of atom research, I for one – and I believe others too – would not be prepared to work for them.'

'Why not try for a research grant at Cambridge?'

'Because we are still talking about probabilities. I hope that I am more realistic about the future than my dear uncle, but who can say for certain what the future holds for this country?'

'But, Leo, you know as well as I do that the Nazis could be in power one day, and soon. If that happens...'

'I think it is probably more a question of *when* than if,' he said somberly. 'One hopes it will be later rather than sooner.'

'Since you're pretty sure what's going to happen, why not get out now?' I asked.

'I'm sure, but not certain,' he smiled. 'At the heart of German atomic physics is the principle of uncertainty.'

'You ought at least to make some kind of preparation,' I urged.
'Like Uncle Samuel's rich lady friend?'
'Leo, be serious!'
'All right, my friend. Look, I couldn't run away even if I wanted to. I couldn't go and leave behind my mother, my sisters, my grandfather. My uncle.'
'Make them leave too!'
'It's not as easy as you seem to think. This is my home.'
'It's not as if...' I said, in exasperation, but stopped myself from completing the sentence.

Leo, however, knew what was in my mind.

'You were going to say that it is not as if I'm taking some kind of political or moral stand to try to prevent this catastrophe. The answer to that may sound strange to you, but I'm a scientist, Jimmy, not a politician. I want to look for answers, not create them. These people – the idealists, the opportunists, the whole gang of politicians from every side – they think they can change the world. I am not so arrogant, I hope.'

'But, Leo, this is more than mere politics, isn't it? This is about the fate of Germany. For God's sake, what will happen if – or when – the Nazis take power?'

'They will turn Germany, and perhaps more than just Germany, into a cultural and humanistic wasteland. It will be a tragedy, but politics isn't my field. Some of my colleagues are committed to one ideology or the other. I don't believe that such an attitude makes them better scientists.'

'But when it happens?' I persisted.

'Then we will have to see,' he said sadly.

I was left with the sickening feeling that Leo was being as ostrich-like as his uncle, despite all his rationalisations. Did he really believe it was possible to stand aside from all the dirty politics of our age, or was he, like me, wary of making a commitment to something as nebulous as an idea? It must be the latter, I thought. His research work was aimed at proving the truths of theories, or being unable to prove them. In politics, all one could do (if one was unable to embrace a creed with blind faith) was to hold on to some kind of hope. The only proof would be in the sweet or bitter taste of the outcome.

* * *

One night, I returned late to my lodgings at Frau Siegendorff's house and wandered into her living-room, where a light was on.

Sitting in an armchair, one foot over the armrest, was a fair-haired young man in a casual tweed jacket and grey trousers. He smiled amiably at me, and said, in good English: 'I am Gregor, the prodigal son of the household. You must be the Englishman, out of whose arse my mother thinks the sun shines.'

'Everyone here is very friendly to me,' I said cautiously.

'Naturally. They always think every foreigner is more cultured and more wealthy and, ergo, better than themselves.'

He went to a cupboard and brought out a bottle of red wine, offering me a glass and pouring it.

'*Zum wohl*,' I said.

'Bottoms up,' Gregor replied, laughing. 'An appropriate greeting in Berlin, yes?'

I asked how his studies were going.

'Is that what she told you?' he laughed. 'That I am student? Not really, my friend. I work at this and that, you understand, when the need arises. Luckily the old girl gives me an allowance.'

'Times are hard,' I said neutrally.

'Oh, yes, they are hard,' he agreed.

I reckoned that he must be only a few years older than me.

'What would you like to do, Gregor?'

'Do? You mean what sort of respectable job would I like to have? I don't have those sorts of aims. I will serve my country.'

'In the army? Like your father?'

'Eventually, it will perhaps come to that, but before then there is much work to do. I will let you in on something – that's correct way of saying, yes? My mother doesn't know this, but she probably guesses it: I am a National Socialist.'

'Good Lord!' I couldn't help saying.

Gregor laughed.

'You are shocked, my friend,' he said gleefully. 'I am pleased it shocks you that a young German boy should embrace the future of his country. You foreigners are all alike. You see things so simplified – simplistically, I should say.'

'How did this happen?' I asked.

Again he laughed.

'You think it is like a case of influenza, yes? You think that if I go to bed and rest then it will go away. You think that it is only the unemployed and the criminals who flock to the Party. You are wrong, my friend.'

He poured me another glass of the excellent wine.

'It's okay, yes?' he asked politely, and I nodded.

'I'm sorry that I have joked with you,' he went on. 'What you want to know is how a young man from a background like this (he swept his arm around the respectable, conformist, slightly claustrophobic middle-class room, heavy with dark furniture and traditional Christianity) comes to join a revolutionary party like the NSDAP?'

'Yes.'

'Because you do not perhaps – not yet – have the experience of how old fools can bring your country to its knees and let it lie in its own shit. My father, a good man and a good soldier, died so that Germany could have the land and the wealth it deserved – not so that it must be the beggar of the world. And not that it must have beggars on the streets. Your father, I think, also died for love of his country.'

'I don't know why he died.'

'To preserve your Empire,' he said. 'It was something to fight for. In Germany, even before the war, a lot was rotten. The way we were taught to respect religion and authority above all. But this was the authority of age and education, not the leadership of a prophet. And then we lose the war – and not because our soldiers were beaten, but because the politicians wanted it. And the result? Poverty, misery, national shame – and the same old people saying the same old things.'

His face was getting flushed, whether from the wine or revolutionary fervour I could not tell.

'So what should we – the youth – do?' he asked. 'I do not think we can just sit back and do nothing. Do you think that, Englishman?'

'Would your father, do you think, approve of a party that wants to destroy democracy?'

'Democracy – that is a rich man's weapon to make life more safe for the rich. Naturally, he would approve. He was a patriot who died for this country. He never knew about democracy and he would not think much of this democracy. What is democracy but talk, talk, talk and do nothing except make yourself richer? Adolf Hitler does not want to destroy, he wants to build a new order. It is the Bolsheviks who want to destroy.'

I said no to another glass of wine. I felt uncomfortable drinking with the enemy. Gregor poured himself another glass, the last bit of wine from the bottle.

'What would *your* father think?' he asked. 'The decent English soldier. What would he think about the way my country is in chaos?'

'I think that the last thing he would want is another war, in which perhaps you and I might die,' I said.

'There will not be another war,' Gregor said forcefully. 'Not unless your country forces us into it because you do not want Germany to be strong.'

I stood up and said good-night. He raised a hand to delay me.

'I know you want to ask about the Jews, no?' he drawled. 'I do not believe that every Jew is bad. It's true they have damaged us and they are everywhere running things and they are behind the Communists. But some of the chosen people are quite decent. I do not believe that we should harm them physically, though we must get free of their grip. Look, don't tell my mother, but I myself have had a Jewish girlfriend. She was excellent to make love with.'

He laughed at the memory, and then turned serious again.

'It's true there have been isolated attacks on Jewish businesses and people. Some killings, even. But most of those who do such things are not real National Socialists; they are criminals and Communist provocateurs. Don't worry, my friend. Sleep easily. When Adolf Hitler becomes leader of Germany he will not tolerate such excesses. Believe me. The Jews will lose their power, but not their lives.'

I shook my head and went to bed.

The next day, he'd gone off again.

I told Frau S that I'd met her son briefly.

'*Ja*,' she sighed. 'He is a good boy.'

But she looked as though she wanted to weep.

I had by now decided to go back to England. I enjoyed Berlin and was tempted to stay, and perhaps do something to oppose Nazism, but I felt this would be little more than a gesture to ease my conscience. The time was not ripe for foreigners to intervene in the affairs of Germany, I thought, and cursed my inability to suspend logical thought. Why could I not just *act?*

I went to Neukölln to say goodbye to Klaus. We drank beer in a noisy tavern frequented by Sozis, where the mood was unusually optimistic and even more boisterous than I'd known it before. Klaus told me why.

'Together with the trade unions, we have made a common front to fight the Brownshirts, and maybe the Communists will join us. In Neukölln, and some other places, they are a little bit more friendly to us than Moscow would like them to be.'

After a few hours of drinking, as we walked towards a tram stop, an excited voice hailed me from across the street. It was Dorothy. With her was Dieter, the Communist – young, blond-haired, muscular, with cold and hard eyes.

We chatted briefly, then Dieter and Dorothy looked at each other, and he invited us for a nightcap.

Klaus agreed, joking: 'Is it okay to have a Sozi in your room, comrade?'

'Why not?' said Dieter without a trace of humour or irony.

We went to a tenement building, from whose windows I could make out hammer and sickle flags waving. Dieter's room was up several flights of stairs. It was evident that Dorothy was living there too. A petticoat and her floral dress hung on a line strung across part of the room, and I could see lipstick and a woman's hairbrush on top of a cupboard. The room itself, apart from this intrusion of femininity, was like a shrine to Communism. The walls were hung with red flags, pictures of Lenin, Stalin and the German Communist Party chief Thalmann. One striking poster showed a steadfast worker in overalls holding a garish crimson flag emblazoned with Cyrillic writing.

'What does that say?' I asked.

'The USSR is the crack brigade of the world proletariat,' said Dorothy with pride.

'You know Russian?' I asked.

'I'm learning,' she smiled. 'Teaching English and learning Russian.'

In this setting, accompanied by much schnapps, we discussed the way the future was to pan out. Klaus and Dieter were soon discussing strategic possibilities for joint action against Brownshirt gangs.

'Why is this happening?' I asked Dorothy.

'It's a local thing. It doesn't mean much, but a few fascist heads may get broken.'

'Which is a good thing, surely?'

'As long as it doesn't turn into something more concrete,' she said in a low voice. 'We can never work with the Social Democrats in the long run.'

'We?'

She nodded: 'The Party. I took the plunge – it's terribly liberating. You must have guessed. You won't tell a soul in England, will you?'

'You aren't ashamed of it?' I teased.

'*Liebling*, we're still pals, aren't we? These are difficult times all over. I'll explain everything some day.'

'It's your business, but, Jesus, Dorothy, if this alliance in Neukölln works, then why not all over Germany? Can't you see the dangers of Hitler?'

'Of course,' she said, somewhat smugly. 'We aren't blind to that, but objectively the SPD is a tool of the fascists.'

Her eyes were burning with a zeal I hadn't seen in her before.

'How can social democracy be a "tool" when they risk their necks fighting Nazis?'

'Oh, Jimmy, you're being formalistic. They offer no solution to the real problems, they hate the Soviet Union, they split the true proletariat. They siphon off support from the only force that can change the world for the better, the Party.'

'Formalistic?' I asked.

'You see things as they appear to be, not as they really are in Marxist terms. It's a simple concept: the Social Democrats may *say* they are against Nazism, but their actions help the Nazis in the long run.'

'Well I think that's exactly what *your* actions do. If you don't fight Hitler, you bloody well help him.'

'In your short-sighted eyes,' she sighed. 'That's formalism. In our eyes, we are the only long-term enemy of the Nazis.'

'This is *Alice Through the Looking Glass*,' I exclaimed in frustration. 'I just can't see how, when you're fighting what could be a losing battle, you can afford to reject the help of anyone, let alone another leftist party. That's not policy, it's lunacy.'

She looked at me sympathetically, as though I was the greatest simpleton she'd ever come across.

'It's essential for the German Communist Party to represent the majority of the working class and it is, therefore, the prime task of German Communists to smash the Social Democratic Party. Those are Stalin's words.'

She said this as though it were a biblical injunction, which I supposed it was for her, and then gave me a smug smile as if to say: There, I've proved my point conclusively.

'But Dieter appears to be conspiring to break Comrade Stalin's official line,' I observed, feeling I was up against a brick wall.

'In some cases it may be possible to make short-term accommodations. There are comrades who believe this has become necessary.'

Dieter and Klaus were laughing together in a comradely way. It was the first time in the evening that Dieter had shown any emotion, though his laughter sounded hollow to me.

'They seem to be hitting it off pretty well,' I said. 'Hope Moscow doesn't get wind of this.'

'Oh, Jimmy,' she said wearily. 'This is a battle for the future. It's complex.'

I told her about the Nazi attack on Dr Bergsen and said that it had made me think about staying on and joining the Social Democrat fighters.

'Don't!' she said. 'You'd only get hurt, or locked up. You're not really committed, *liebling*. You'd be better off letting people know what's really going on.'

'You don't think I should stay in Berlin?'

I felt a curious mixture of relief and disappointment.

'Not for political reasons. It isn't your battle.'

'Are you saying that only the Marxists have the right to fight?'

'It's not a football tournament, Jimmy,' she said fiercely. 'It's not only who wins; it's also what comes after. You'd get your head broken for nothing. I'm committed to something. You're just in a romantic phase. Have you asked yourself why you're so keen on getting beaten to death in Berlin?'

'Not simply to impress you,' I grinned.

She made a comical grimace.

'I would hope not, *liebling*,' she said.

'Anyway, I'm touched at your concern for my safety.'

'I'm concerned that you don't risk your neck before you know why you're doing it.'

'Are comrades allowed that sort of sentimental emotion?'

'Oh, belt up, you idiot!' she laughed. 'Go back and get an education.'

'As it happens, I *have* decided to go back. Perhaps we can take this up again some day in England.'

'Some day,' she said. 'If I ever return.'

'What do you mean?'

'I don't know yet. It's not in my hands. Please don't get curious about me.'

'I'll try not to.'

7

Yalta, February 4, 1945

The drive to the Livadia Palace at disconcerting speed around a winding mountain road gave vistas of the sparkling Black Sea bay lapping the coast of greater Yalta and beyond. It was easy to see why the Russian upper crust – Tsarist and Bolshevik – had taken this place as their winter retreat.

From the guarded gateway of the palace, our cars drove up a long lane shaded by a rich variety of coastal trees, cypress, cedar, yew and bay. Glimpses of well-armed Russian troops in the grounds were no doubt intended as much to remind us that we were under surveillance as that we were safe from outside attack.

We came to a halt on a circular gravel path and walked between tall Corinthian columns into a spacious hall, from where one could look out across the bay to Yalta town and the blue-green mountains surrounding it. Beyond the entrance hall was the rectangular conference room, which had once been the imperial ballroom, a chandeliered setting for dancing and romance. It had immense arched windows all along its sides, from almost floor to ceiling level, a fine Grecian sculpture of a pensive woman and a huge marble fireplace, with logs blazing away. I doubted whether the fire was necessary on this mild afternoon, but the Russians presumably wanted to make FDR as warm as possible. Close to the fireplace was a large oval table, covered with a plain white cloth. Around it were placed solid straight-backed chairs for the delegates.

I sat behind Winston and marvelled at the spectacle – the leaders of the largest military alliance the world had ever known sitting down, shoulder to shoulder, to argue over the great issues of the day and plan the future.

Knights of the Round Table? No, I decided, not enough nobility of spirit; more like a gathering of tribal elders to haggle about the boundaries, jurisdiction and administration of the settlements under their control.

Stalin, all benevolence, asked Roosevelt to preside. FDR looked around as though bemused by the honour, but quickly pulled himself together and said the topic of this session should be the military situation in Europe.

Everyone here knew Germany was on its last legs; but it still had to be battered to the ground, flattened by bombers, invaded and conquered by hardened soldiers. Hitler would not surrender. His legacy mattered more to him than the sufferings of his civilians and soldiers. But would some high-ranking Nazi figure be prepared to defy him and lay down Germany's arms? It was assumed that this would not happen until the very end. First, Berlin would have to be captured and all of the Reich occupied.

Roosevelt poured great buckets of flattery on the Russians.

'I must tell you that when the news came that the Red Army had advanced twenty-five kilometres into Germany, I doubt whether even the Soviet people were more thrilled than the folk of the United States and the people of Great Britain.'

In front of me, Winston nodded agreement. Inwardly, he was probably wincing. The Soviet offensive was too fast, too threatening.

Stalin beamed his pleasure, but couldn't resist having a dig at his allies.

'We launched our winter offensive because it was our moral duty to our allies. We were not bound to do so and we received no request to do so.'

In other words, he implied, Soviet troops attacked through Poland to help relieve the British and American armies who had been caught on the hop by the desperate, last-gasp Nazi thrust in the Ardennes. There was also the scarcely veiled rebuke that the Russian willingness to attack was in total contrast to our dithering a few years before over opening a second front in France to take the heat off Russia.

Winston chose to ignore the undercurrent of one-upmanship. He gave the impression of being delighted that the ructions were a thing of the past.

'There was absolutely no need to bargain with you, my dear Marshal,' he said warmly. 'We knew you could be depended upon to do the right thing.'

Turning to Anthony Eden, he muttered: 'He has blood on

his hands but he delivers what he promises. We have no reason not to trust him on that score.'

Eden, smiling, shook his head but this might have been at the impropriety of Winston's remark rather than in disagreement.

Stalin's interpreter for the meeting – Ivan Maisky, a little man with a clipped beard who'd been ambassador in London in the thirties and early forties, and a darling of British left-wing intellectuals – said something to his chief. Had he picked up Winston's stage whisper? If he had, and had passed it on, it did not appear to upset Stalin in the slightest. He would have taken it as a supreme compliment.

'You know how many fascists have been killed?' Stalin said with a wolfish grin. 'Three hundred thousand dead and one hundred thousand captured. Our artillery shattered the bastards; the prisoners we took were too dazed to know even where they were.'

At this, Roosevelt's ashen face cracked into a smile.

Putting morality to one side, one had to be impressed with Stalin in action. What was on view was no wild, bulging-eyed Hitler-like tyrant. He was the wise, unflappable chairman of the board. Mostly, he sat impassively but alertly in his seat and listened, occasionally asking a question, making a point. His subordinates – the bureaucrats and the military planners – were completely under his thumb. The British and American leaders, in contrast, had to contend with a democratic amount of consultation, even disagreement. Sometimes when Winston went into one of his verbal flows, Eden twitched with impatience. And when Roosevelt seemed to be losing the thread of the discussion, his long-time confidant Harry Hopkins passed him a note to set him back on track. But there was never any question of Stalin being challenged by his underlings. At times he made a big thing of consulting Molotov or someone else, but this was purely for effect. He, and he alone, was in charge, and everyone in his delegation knew it and feared him because of it.

'That man is a mystery to me,' said Winston as we drove away after the talks. 'A mystery.'

I recalled his earlier confident view that he could do business with Stalin the pragmatic dictator, but decided to say nothing. If the Prime Minister wanted your view, he asked for it.

'So many times I've been certain that I knew every crevice of his mind, and so many times have I been deceived. What makes him tick, eh, Bexley?'

'As an observer, Prime Minister, I'd say he's learned in a very hard school that to remain in power in the Kremlin you can't ever show your hand. You have to be devious.'

'Devious?' Winston snarled. 'Is that all you can offer? We're all devious. President Roosevelt, Stalin, yes even myself. We have to be devious. The heavy burden of statecraft in times of peril demands that we be devious. I expected more from you than a platitude.'

I stayed silent. It was better to accept the lashing and wait for the storm to abate, as it often did amid the torrent of words.

'Even that blackguard Hitler is not so stupid that he cannot be devious; but the difference is that only a naif would be taken in by him. Neville, poor man, was taken in by him because Neville was himself completely lacking in the necessary degree of deviousness to enable him to detect it in others. Yes, Bexley, you have to be a snake to spot a snake. I learned that as a subaltern in India.'

His anger was going, as swiftly as it had come. I settled back in my seat, hoping he would drone on about his adventures in the Raj. He didn't.

'But that man Stalin is so rare a species of snake that a mere cobra like myself, a mere performing reptile, cannot penetrate his layers. The very first time I met him I was struck by his depths. That was at Moscow in 1942. Do you remember my astonishment, nay bewilderment, when it descended upon me that this was no ordinary personage?'

'No, Prime Minister,' I said. 'I was not there.'

'You did not accompany me?'

'I was in North Africa, Prime Minister.'

'So you were, so you were. With the gallant Eighth Army, whose leadership had taxed me grievously.'

I kept silent, but I could see that Winston read my feelings from my face.

I braced myself for a tirade of abuse. Instead, he peered at me and allowed himself the merest glimmer of a smile.

'I admire loyalty. You believe I should have left your commander *in situ*. It is a point of view. The Army of the Nile had indeed fought with resolution and great courage – despite the humiliation of Tobruk – but the men were low in morale, were they not? They needed the vigour of a new guiding hand. And that was the reason I felt it necessary to replace General Wavell.'

'It was General Auchinleck you replaced, Prime Minister.'

'Yes, yes. What of it? I am talking now of Auchinleck. He is a fine soldier, but I had to prod, prod, prod for offensive action against Rommel. I needed a victory very badly at the time.'

I knew his reasons. For years, he had withstood the batterings of bad tidings and grim prognostications. Winston wanted immediate results, whatever the odds, against the German Afrika Korps. Auchinleck, a great and loyal military man, wanted victory, too. But he preferred to wait until his forces were ready to strike.

'Never mind, never mind,' Winston said. 'Memory plays tricks on old men. I can recall as clear as a bell events of my childhood, of my parents, India, the Sudan, South Africa, and yet the things that happened only last year sometimes get muddled. Well, well, it matters little. When I come to write the chronicle of this war, I shall have the assistance of keen-memoried young men like you, shall I not?'

'I would be honoured, Prime Minister.'

'And that is why I am conveying to you my lack of comprehension of that man from the Kremlin. In Moscow, when I had to break the news to him that there would be no second front in 1942, no invasion of occupied Europe to take the pressure off the Red Army, he was full of understanding one day, boorish, even insulting, the next. It would pain me to relay to you some of his worst barbs. He had the temerity to accuse our soldiers of cowardice. I was in no mood to tolerate this. I determined to leave Russia forthwith but was persuaded that I should give it another go. Accordingly, I put aside my personal feelings for the sake of our wartime alliance.

'We met again, and the man was all charm; a different person entirely, genial, flattering. I wish I could say I had worked him out, Bexley. He remains a damned enigma. Can one ever rely upon the word of such a one?'

Our car had arrived at the entrance to the Vorontsov, and I was spared a reply.

'How I wish I could once again be an ordinary soldier in the field,' Winston muttered.

I knew, of course, that he had never been an ordinary soldier, and never an ordinary man. His ancestry and his character had propelled him beyond the ranks. He did not have the layers of intrigue that had formed and now enveloped Stalin. With Winston, you got, and always had got, exactly what you saw. That was his strength and his weakness.

The formal dinner that night was in the Tsar's old panelled billiard room at the Livadia. Possibly because of his waning powers, Roosevelt didn't do his usual pre-party trick of mixing the cocktails himself. Neither Winston nor Stalin minded this at all. Winston preferred his drink uncluttered and straightforward; Stalin made a show at banquets of tossing back vodka after vodka, but it was never clear how much of what he drank was alcohol and how much pure water. He preferred to get other people drunk.

To begin with, the talk was inconsequential: the Black Sea coast and its benevolent climate, its hunting, its lavish villas. My thoughts turned to the doomed Tsar Nicholas and his courtiers whiling away the time with chat and gossip, knocking balls round a table, unaware or uncaring of the coming revolutionary storm.

Then Stalin got to his feet, and the room fell silent. He gazed around at all the faces, focusing on each. I sensed the dread that his Politburo and other gatherings of subordinates must feel when he rose to pronounce or to denounce.

This time, though, he seemed almost jovial after initial penetrating stares. The yellow eyes glinted, but without apparent malice. He wanted to propose a toast to Winston.

'I will never forget how you supported Russia at the time of our greatest need when Hitler attacked us in 1941,' he said.

Winston inclined his head, beaming his thanks.

'Of course,' Stalin said, stained teeth spreading into a snide smile beneath the moustache. 'Of course, why did you do this? I understand perfectly why you did this. You did this because you wished to achieve only one thing at this time: defeating that despicable fascist bastard, Hitler.'

That is how it came out in the translation by the interpreter Pavlov but those with even a smattering of Russian knew that the adjectives describing the Führer were considerably more coarse and colourful.

After we had all poured some fiery vodka down our throats, Winston hauled himself out of his chair, looked serious, tugged at his lapels as though about to address the Lord Mayor's luncheon, and said he too would like to propose a toast.

There was a respectful silence during which his stern gaze slowly lightened and a twinkle came into his eyes.

'I should like us all to drink to the proletarian masses of the world,' he said. 'Let us hope that they will, sooner rather than later, lose their chains.'

This raised a sardonic little smile from Stalin.

Winston was in his element, rambling down all sorts of avenues.

'While I am constantly, um, beaten up as a reactionary, permit me to boast that I alone among the heads of government here can be thrown out at any time by the voters of my country.'

He paused, perhaps waiting for acclaim.

Stalin looked stolidly ahead, unimpressed.

Roosevelt seemed unconcerned. His tight-lipped staff, though, had expressions of disapproval; their boss wouldn't have to face the voters for another four years, and it was plain silly of this die-hard imperialist to try to score points off the head of the world's greatest democracy, or to take an undiplomatic swipe at their Soviet ally, despot though he might be.

Stalin broke the uncomfortable silence: 'It seems that the Prime Minister is scared of these elections?'

Winston's face went slightly crimson. He knew he'd overdone it, but being Winston, he was not about to climb down.

'Not only do I not fear an election,' he said, lips coming together in clenched defiance, 'I am proud of the historic right of the British people to change their government (here he fixed his gaze directly on Stalin) at any time they see fit!'

FDR now stared ahead open-mouthed, either because he was gasping for consciousness and ideas, or because he was amazed at Winston's recklessness.

The evening began to unravel.

First, Stalin and Roosevelt agreed with each other that the

peace should be written and preserved by the Big Powers – and, by definition, bugger the small powers!

'We three are the great powers,' said Stalin. 'Who else does anyone think should share this table with us?'

He laughed scornfully and indicated the table, groaning with food – fried chicken Southern style and Russian sparkling wine among other goodies from capitalist and Communist stores. Food for kings, not third-rate autocrats!

Winston disagreed. He quoted: 'The eagle should permit the small birds to sing, and care not wherefore they sing.'

Then Stalin got into a huff when Roosevelt told him that his allies called him Uncle Joe. Stalin must have known this, but chose to take umbrage.

'Extremely insecure fellow,' Eden muttered to me.

'How long do I have to remain here?' Stalin asked angrily.

'Half an hour,' called Winston genially, when this was translated.

It seemed to have degenerated into a saloon – or playground – spat.

But, of course, Stalin was only pretending to be upset. It was a useful little ploy to make them think that vanity might be a weak point with him. Let them analyse the incident to see how they might exploit such a 'weakness' for their own ends; he had his sights on bigger goals.

He allowed himself to be persuaded to stay.

As the dinner rumbled on, I left the room, to relieve myself and clear my head. It had been a long evening, and still the bombast and chatter went on as if the map of the world could be redesigned over alcohol and tobacco.

Outside the dining area, I encountered Ed Brewster. He was regarded as a coming man in the State Department and I'd thought he might come to Yalta, so it wasn't that much of a surprise. When he saw me, his face burst into its familiar, wide all-American grin. I'd known him first at Cambridge where he'd arrived with Iowa cornstalks in his hair, but full of ideas.

He grasped my hand as firmly as ever and said: 'Good to see you again, Jim.'

He was a tall man, a little broader in the midriff than the loping undergraduate I'd first known, but still handsome, a full head of dark, wavy hair, tinged, I noted, with a few streaks of grey, his eyes generous and twinkling.

Meeting him again made me tetchy though. He said he envied me for having seen action, and I reminded him that he'd once written to me of the futility of England fighting alone against Germany.

'We were getting that kind of intelligence,' he said with a twinge of embarrassment. 'Diplomats, spies – they were sure you guys couldn't hang on for long. Besides, there were people, high up, who wanted to believe you'd sue for peace soon so *we* wouldn't have to get involved.'

'Lucky they were wrong, wasn't it?'

'I was misled,' he shrugged. 'But I was never a defeatist. Once we got into it, I was desperate to join up, only they wouldn't let me. Too valuable, or some such bullshit. So, I genuinely do envy and admire you, Jim.'

'I managed to avoid getting killed. Nothing to write home about.'

'And now you're in Winston's inner circle.'

'I fetch and carry for him.'

'Same old Jim Bexley. You always were too goddam modest for your own good. What you're doing for the old boy is vital for the war effort.'

I sought irony in his voice or face, but found none.

'In the same way as his valet is,' I said.

'You'll probably end up with a knighthood.'

'You never give up, do you?' I smiled.

I couldn't help liking him, despite everything. He'd charmed his way through life.

We wandered outside, so we could talk more frankly. No one followed us. He asked for my views on the conference. I mentioned our fears about Roosevelt's health.

'He *is* one pretty sick guy,' Ed grimaced. 'No one knows what it is or exactly how serious, but it's sure as hell not good. What *we're* scared of is that he's going to let Stalin ride over him. Winston may still be our best hope to stop this. Is he as pig-headed as ever?'

He was, I said. But it was difficult when the Yanks undermined him.

'I don't make policy,' Ed said. 'There are some guys who reckon you people don't see the reality of the times. Interfering in European politics like it was the bad old days. Take Greece

– hey, personally I totally approve of you stuffing the Reds, but to some people it reeks a bit of colonial meddling. Myself, I'm an Anglophile at heart.'

'Bit of an unfashionable position in Washington, I gather.'

'I don't spread it about much,' he smiled.

'Does anyone there think we have a future?' I asked, choosing to bypass Greece, about which I felt equivocal. Did we have the right to intervene there any more than Stalin could dictate the way Poland was ruled?

'That's the way it goes, buddy. Good days, bad days. One day it'll be our turn – or the Ruskies,' he said.

We stood in thoughtful silence for half a minute.

'Look, the way Roosevelt is cosying up to Stalin stinks,' he said. 'It's immoral, suicidal, against our best interests. In the long run, it's going to have to be us versus them. Cooperation ain't in their vocabulary. If we make policy on the basis that they believe in real cooperation with us, then, brother, the whole world's going to be in the soup again. We don't need their help to lick the Japs.'

Having got this off his chest, he shifted to personal things, talking about life in Washington and his marriage.

'It's all about give and take. I don't care for the social whirl, she thrives on it.'

'Really?'

'Loves it. She hosts soirées. Anyone who's anyone is welcome, except the Reds and Nazis of course. Sometimes it seems we got half of Congress in our place. Republicans and Democrats. She says she needs the contacts for her causes. Negro rights, women's rights, things like that. She reckons Roosevelt has sold his soul to Stalin.'

'And so do you?'

'I was brought up on the New Deal, but FDR's not the man he was.'

'None of us are.'

'I know what you're getting at. I'm an old married man these days.'

'Wow!'

'Spare me the sarcasm,' he laughed. 'I'm sort of respectable, and she turns a blind eye if I lapse, if you know what I mean? No secrets. She doesn't resent it if I have a little fun.'

'You've always had your little fun,' I pointed out.

'When I got married, I thought it was over. Still, a man's a man.'

We stood, smoking, in silence.

Then he said in a low voice: 'You know, they're watching me all the time, listening.'

'Who?'

'My guys, yours, theirs.'

'They watch everyone, Ed. Why you in particular?'

'My past, my present, my future – everything smells funny to them. Listen: a word of advice. This whole place is bugged. The bedrooms, the dining-rooms, the johns. Everything. They've got bugs in the trees and in their buttonholes, and probably up their butts. Don't say anything you don't want them to hear.'

'One doesn't have to assume that every casual word is pored over.'

'One sure as hell does, buddy. So, listen, Jim – this is from an old pal, and I don't care who's listening – is Winston going to stay tough? Someone needs to be resolute. We have to be sure we don't throw away things to them. We'll keep our promises. They won't. Roosevelt doesn't understand that. Does Churchill?'

His face was pressed close to mine, and he didn't give me time to answer.

'You've got to tell Winston. Tell him to dig his heels in, to stonewall ... what's that cricketing term?'

'Block?'

'Yeah, with a straight bat, though I could never figure out why it has to be straight.'

'Cricket's a game of morality.'

'Unlike Big Power diplomacy.'

'I take your point about Winston, but I can't predict. Still, you know his style. Resolute. If you're concerned, take it up with our Foreign Office people.'

'I can't. I can talk to you because they know we're old friends. It doesn't raise suspicions. But, Jim, no shit, a lot of us are darn concerned.'

I presumed he was talking about some of the State Department crew who had long disliked FDR's way of conducting diplomacy without informing them.

We walked back inside and I saw Podbirski, among a group

of delegates standing outside the dining-room. He seemed to be looking out for someone. He caught my eye and made a small head movement to show I should follow him through a small door into the Italian garden.

Ed may have noticed the contact, but gave no sign that he had.

'See you later, pal,' he said.

I strolled, as nonchalantly as I could, in the direction Podbirski had indicated. As I did so, I felt almost as though I were no longer my own person, that I was being tugged in some way between Podbirski's probable machinations and Ed's obsessions. I shouldn't have gone outside again. I needed to get back to the dinner – Winston wanted me there so I could write a report for the Cabinet – but I was getting desperate for information.

8

Yalta, February 4–5, 1945

In the shadows of an alcove between two pillars in the Italian garden, the glowing red tip of a cigarette revealed the presence of Podbirski.

It was a warm night, and though it was too dark to see the lush, coastal foliage, the air was full of the scents and insect sounds of the sheltered sub-tropical garden, an internal courtyard of the palace enclosed by a rectangular gallery supported by Doric pillars.

'Is okay here,' he said. 'Everyone drink too much to worry about us.'

'Have you got a message, Anatoly?'

'I see you talk to that fellow,' he said. 'American. Brewster. You trust?'

'I've known him for years,' I said.

'We learn here in Russia, all the time: don't trust even old friends. Sometimes they more dangerous than new friends.'

'Anatoly, did you drag me out here to give me advice on friendship?'

'Is difficult, Jimmy. I try to tell you something. Sometimes can trust friend if he trades with you. How you say, barters?'

'Trades what? I think you've come to the wrong market, chum.'

'Not secrets!' he said impatiently. 'You think I try to recruit Mr Churchill's private secretary as spy? We trade favours. I do you favour. Later on, you do me one, maybe.'

I was not innocent of the ways of Soviet agents provocateurs and their ilk, but I was surprised at his clumsy approach.

'I could never agree to that, Anatoly. I never would. You know that.'

'I just want to tell you. For record, as you say.'

'And for the record, *Nyet*, Anatoly.'

He stubbed his cigarette against a pillar till he was sure it was out. Then he carefully brushed the ash stain from the pillar and put the burnt-out cigarette end in his pocket.

'Of course, of course. This is not market place. All I want is to give some information. For free. Nothing in exchange.'

'Oh, yes?'

'Our friend. Soon perhaps you meet her. Then you know you can trust me.'

'You're sure of that?' I asked. 'She's coming here?'

'Maybe. Maybe not yet. But you will meet, I hope. And, Jimmy, this is not official business, you understand. This is freelance. Good-night, my friend.'

'Anatoly...' I began, but he'd disappeared into the shadows.

Back in the dining-room, the banquet was beginning to break up.

Roosevelt and Stalin had already left. Churchill, Eden and Stettinius, the American Sectretary of State, were still conversing. As they moved towards the door, Winston, puffing out clouds of cigar smoke, suddenly said: 'On the whole, on reflection, I think that while the rights of small nations should be protected, they should not have a voice in the great matters of international import. They cannot be permitted to throw a spanner in the works if they object to something we agree upon.'

Anthony turned red in the face. The long years of having to do the bidding of prime ministers unskilled, to his mind, in diplomatic matters and ignorant of the true motives of their adversaries, was taking its toll. Always, I felt about Eden, there was a volcano beneath that suave exterior waiting to erupt in undiplomatic fury. Now it did.

'That is a nonsensical formulation,' he burst out.

'What? What? Nonsensical, you say?' Winston spluttered.

'The idea that they can't be allowed to throw a spanner in the works, as you put it, is ridiculous. If you accept this idea, this Russian idea, the small powers will have no reason to sign on to the United Nations.'

'I am thinking of the realities of the international situation,' Winston puffed out his chest.

'Really, Winston, you cannot say one thing one minute, and something completely different the next. It makes my job impossible. If you accept the Russian position on voting, we can say goodbye to ever holding a United Nations conference.'

'Your job?' said Winston, bristling ominously. 'You forget, sir, that you hold your high office at my discretion.'

'I've resigned before and I'll do it again if I have to,' Anthony said in a strained voice.

I could see the veins standing out on his temple, the famous flashing smile transformed into thin-lipped violent antipathy to the man – the only man – who stood in his way to the ultimate prize of British politics.

Winston glowered.

Anthony continued, slowly bringing himself under control: 'Isn't protecting the weaker countries the reason we went to war against Hitler? I must advise you, Prime Minister, that I am prepared to go before the House of Commons and put the issue to the vote.'

He had made a huge effort to douse his overt anger and spoke with icy calm, all the more forceful for being deliberate and controlled.

Winston made no response, but walked away briskly.

Though it had begun as no more than a spat over policy, it was an uncomfortable revelation of the subterranean animosity between an old man heading towards the end of his power and a Young Turk itching to take over.

Only a spat, perhaps, but one that would make FDR purr with pleasure when Stettinius passed on the gossip. The President was much better at juggling his subordinates, keeping them off balance, than Winston in his blunt way ever could be, and would never have allowed an argument like this to develop in public. It would confirm his view that Winston was a spent force among his own circle, as well as on the international stage.

Next morning at breakfast a waiter brought me a tray with coffee in a silver pot and a cup and saucer. I looked up from a Cabinet memo I was reading, smiled and nodded my thanks. He failed to return my smile. I noticed a small envelope under the saucer. I lifted it and slipped it, unseen I hoped, into my jacket pocket. My mind was racing, but I managed to finish reading the government document before walking casually into the garden and strolling to a pond where no guards seemed to be loitering. I opened the letter and read it almost at a glance. The envelope was addressed to Mr James Bexley, British Delegation. I recognised the handwriting immediately.

The note said: 'I will try to see you.'

Nothing else.

I walked slowly back to the dining-room, took a cup from the table and approached the waiter with a request for more coffee. He looked terrified. I smiled, handed him the cup and said, out of the corner of my mouth: 'The person who gave you letter. Where is she?' He said nothing and I could tell he was much too scared to divulge anything, so I dropped the subject.

Throughout the morning, I kept thinking of the note. Did it mean she was in Yalta already, or that she was trying to get here? I wondered how she'd managed to get the message to me. Had she been helped by a friend, possibly Podbirski? Had she perhaps been forced to write the note?

Sarah came into the Private Secretary's office and was concerned to find me looking anxious. I told her I had a slight headache, nothing more.

'All the vodka and wine last night, I expect,' she smiled. 'Papa was quite put out because Uncle Joe wouldn't drink the King's health – what a silly thing to refuse – but said that otherwise it went very well except that he and Anthony had a little tiff afterwards. Were you there?'

'I was.'

'Well, what happened, Jimmy?' she asked impatiently.

I gave her a brief report on what had been said.

'Why did Anthony get so steamed up?'

'He believes, and I go along with him, for what it's worth, that Stalin's views on small countries are about as humane as Himmler's on the Jews.'

'I'm sure Papa does too,' Sarah said. 'But sometimes he needs to provoke those closest to him, and you know he regards Anthony almost as a son. Anyway, Papa was quite contrite this morning, like a little boy who's been naughty, so I'm sure they'll kiss and be friends again.'

'Good,' I said.

'What is the matter, Jimmy?' she asked solicitously. 'Homesick? Affair of the heart?'

'Well...' I hesitated, feeling it would be unfair to tell the Prime Minister's daughter something that she could not be expected to keep from him.

'You don't have to say, if you don't want to,' she said.

'There *is* a girl,' I admitted, adding quickly: 'Not here, of course.'

'A Russian?'

Her eyes were wide.

'I'd better not say any more, Sarah.'

'I know. She's a ballerina.'

I shook my head, smiling.

'Good. Not your type. She's on the stage, though? She's done Chekhov?'

'No,' I said. 'Not even warm.'

'Not a member of the acting profession?' Sarah asked with mock horror.

'Actually, Sarah, she's a duchess.'

Sarah laughed, remembering a time when she had poured her heart out to me, a sympathetic journalist, because of the pressures she was under from Winston and Clementine for wanting to marry a music hall violinist and comedian, Vic Oliver, and I had asked: 'Would it have made any difference if Vic was a Shakespearean actor?'

She'd replied: 'Not even if it was Henry Irving himself. They'd like me to marry a duke, at the very least. They want me to be a bloody duchess, and I just want to be me.'

Now, at the Vorontsov, she said: 'Then I can't see what the problem could be.'

'Even if this room weren't full of microphones, I don't think it would be fair to tell you. Fair to you, that is.'

'Right,' she said abruptly, and I knew she felt a little hurt.

'It's just ... an old episode,' I said weakly.

'They're often the most difficult.'

A bit later, Winston sent for me. Though it was past noon, he was still in bed, looking spruce in a bright red dressing-gown emblazoned with fearsome yellow dragons breathing fire.

'I want you to be present at a meeting,' he said. 'The Foreign Secretary is coming to see me in a few minutes. I need a witness. I trust he is not going to be unpleasant, but if he is, then I need you to chronicle everything in detail. I will correct the proofs, of course.'

This last was said with a twinkle in his eye, to show me that he wasn't really fearful of the conversation.

Anthony came in, immaculately tailored and groomed. He smiled as his eye took in Winston's gaudy dressing-gown. He frowned when he saw me.

'I thought we might have a talk in private,' he said.

'And that is exactly what we are to have,' Winston beamed. 'Pray take no notice of Mr Bexley. He is engaged on other matters, but I need him close by.'

Anthony seemed about to take issue with my presence, but then thought better of it.

'Very well,' he said briskly. 'I wanted to see you, Winston, because we will need today to make clear that the French have to be engaged in the occupation of Germany.'

There was to be no argument. Anthony was offering a peace token. Winston seized it, though he might have preferred a decent war of words.

'Yes, yes, of course. I am in concert with you, Anthony. I always defer to your judgement on these matters. We will insist upon it.'

'Thank you, Winston. We need to be strong on this. You know how the President dislikes de Gaulle, and Stalin has no concept of the role France has played in European affairs.'

'No idea at all,' Winston agreed. 'It is as if he has read no history books. Has he not written some books himself? Surely an author is also a reader.'

'Stalin's books are mere compilations of other people's words to suit his own purposes,' Anthony said scathingly. 'One can scarcely characterise him as an author.'

'Well, well,' said Winston, a little irritably. 'He is a busy man. The driving ideas are his. I too have made use of researchers. Indeed, Mr Bexley himself has acted in such a capacity in the past.'

'I do not think, Winston, that anyone could challenge your writing skills and style or compare them in any way with Stalin's,' Anthony said smoothly.

'Most of what appears under his name is incomprehensible to me,' Winston agreed. 'A mishmash of half-digested thoughts.

And yet he is not an unintelligent person. Crafty, yes. Unscrupulous, certainly. But he knows where he wants to go.'

'Exactly, Winston. And that is why we must divert him from negating the French position. France, after all, is a geographical necessity.'

'Well put, Anthony, very well put. She has stood between us and the might of the German lands before, and she must certainly be permitted to stand strong again. However, I dare say you will agree that France is far more than a mere geographical necessity, Anthony. Her history, her culture, her beauty, all these are of inestimable value to European civilisation.'

'Of course, Winston, you have expressed yourself, as you always do, with poetical truth.'

Winston beamed. They had forgiven each other, although each believed he had scored some telling points in the subtle denigration of the other's methods of expression.

'A geographical necessity!' Winston smirked at me after Anthony had left us. 'I respect and like Anthony, but the poor fellow has absolutely no feeling for words. A geographical necessity! And explain to me, pray, what country is not a geographical necessity?'

He didn't expect an answer, and I gave him none.

Later, as we prepared to set off for the afternoon political session at the Livadia, Anthony remarked to me:

'I hope that Winston is not going to be lyrical about the glories of France today. It is all very pretty, but it will cut no ice with hard customers like Roosevelt and Stalin. History, culture, beauty, and no doubt cuisine? Those things are deuced important in the minds of civilised men, but not for Stalin who looks only at the military and economic strength of a country, at the number of its armoured divisions, not the size of its art galleries and museums.'

The big question of the afternoon was what to do about Germany after the war. It was not enough to defeat her; no one around the table wanted her ever again to be able to wage war.

'Enough is enough!' was the unspoken consensus.

But the problem was how to ensure that Germany did not once again descend into a wasteland of bitterness where desperate men might once again choose desperate methods to disrupt the imposed peace.

Roosevelt started off by saying the discussion would be about the zones of occupation following Germany's inevitable surrender.

Stalin hauled himself to his feet and said with heavy disdain: 'I am not concerned with just the occupation zones. The question we should be discussing now is the way in which we divide Germany – for all time.'

This caught his partners on the hop. They hadn't thought much about a permanent dismemberment of Germany.

Stalin's proposal was made not merely out of vindictiveness or vengeance for the Nazi atrocities in Soviet territory. It was acquisition. Hitler had gambled for territory and lost; now the price had to be paid.

'Well,' said FDR eventually, slowly, 'I guess I understand that a kind of permanent division *could* grow out of the zones of occupation.'

Stalin shook his head impatiently at the idea of anything so hazy.

Anthony whispered something to Winston, who said ponderously: 'Dismemberment in principle, yes. But any final decision on this complicated matter will require considerable study and debate.'

Stalin stood up again. One of his negotiating methods was to stay seated, enigmatic, sardonic, taking everything in and giving nothing away. This day, even when he merely stood still behind his chair, he seemed to be stalking and prowling. When he walked about, smoking all the time, puffing out tobacco, he was monitoring his prey, out for the kill. And while he circled, Winston lounged warily in his chair and Roosevelt stared into space.

'Study and debate!' Stalin scoffed. 'Soon these criminals will be crawling out with their white flags, then we must tell them we accept only unconditional surrender and that their cursed country is going to be broken apart, yes?'

'I do not consider there is any need to discuss with *any* German *any* question about their future,' Winston growled.

'All right,' I agree,' Stalin said. 'But now is the time for us to make a decision on this.'

'Please make it absolutely clear to Marshal Stalin,' said Winston, addressing Pavlov, 'that there is simply not enough time to do that here and now. This is a problem that requires the most careful study.'

What Pavlov told Stalin in a whisper was unclear, but the leader grunted something that may have been assent or contempt. It was not translated.

Then Stalin performed his party trick: a concession followed by a demand.

'All right,' he said. 'All right. I will accept that for now we should just reach agreement in principle on dismembering Germany.'

Winston and Roosevelt nodded agreement.

'Good,' said Stalin, as if praising a class of improving children. 'But what we must do is to add to the surrender terms a clause to tell them that their country is going to be cut into pieces.'

'I share Marshal Stalin's views on this,' said Roosevelt, smiling.

Anthony again whispered into the ear of Winston, who nodded and said: 'I consider that unnecessary and even risky. Once they surrender, we can do what we like with them. What benefit, then, to tell them we are going to chop up their country? It might only stiffen their resistance, induce them to continue fighting.'

'I doubt that; don't be such a pessimist, Winston,' said Roosevelt. 'We simply will not make that public. The German *people* won't know about it.'

'Exactly,' grunted Stalin.

Winston knew he was beaten on this. It was better to retreat and summon up the strength to fight other battles.

'Very well,' he said.

Roosevelt now went into a rambling discourse on the Germany he knew as a child and young man. His moneyed, well-connected parents made annual trips to Europe in the late nineteenth century, to the capitals of the civilised world and its playgrounds and spas. He remembered a Germany in which small semi-autonomous states flourished like lush roses on the thorny vine.

'There was no word for the Reich in those days. Bavaria managed its own affairs. Our problems recently are a direct result of the way the Nazis centralised the government in Berlin.'

Anthony stared through the windows into the Italian garden, his face frozen into embarrassed boredom.

Stalin, however, listened politely and even nodded in agreement occasionally, as though some of the nostalgic utterances proclaimed universal political truths.

Winston rolled his cigar in his fingers, avoiding eye contact with anyone. Was he half pleased that his old but faithless friend was making an ass of himself?

When the President finally lapsed into silence, Winston brought up France. He wanted to give it an occupation zone in Germany. The other two were, as usual, antipathetic to France, and especially to de Gaulle. Not that Winston himself could stand that self-righteous, destiny-driven man, but he believed – and it had not needed Anthony to tell him this – that a strong France was essential for stability in western Europe.

'France must be able to help check a revived Germany,' he said.

'He means it must become strong so they can check the USSR,' Stalin whispered loudly to Molotov.

This was translated quickly by our interpreter for Winston, who chose to ignore the gibe but said, to clinch his argument, that it was not known how long the US would keep its troops in Germany to protect Europe.

Stalin leaned back in his chair and asked Roosevelt with a sly smile: 'How long?'

'Oh, I would guess two years at the most,' said the President.

Winston looked surprised, seemed about to tax Roosevelt about the sudden announcement of timing, then checked himself and said this was exactly why France had to be helped to become strong again.

'But how strong?' Stalin asked impatiently. 'What does that mean in the case of France? Was France not supposed to be strong before the war? If she had been strong in 1940 then you and I, Prime Minister, would have avoided many losses.'

Winston sighed. How often must he explain the current realities of Europe?

'My country has suffered badly in recent months from German flying bombs,' he said evenly. 'Should the Germans ever get near the Atlantic coast, we will suffer again. We have to think of the future if American forces leave our continent.'

'Okay,' Roosevelt sighed. 'Let's give them a zone carved from the US and British zones.'

'Agreed,' Stalin said.

The Russians then put forward claims for reparations from Germany. Maisky, brought in by Stalin to argue this issue, demanded: 'Eighty per cent of all German industry should be confiscated.'

Winston asked, aghast: 'Do you want Germany to starve?'

Apparently Stalin did not care whether it did or not, and the President didn't want to drag out the session.

'We've always been generous to other nations, but we can't guarantee to finance the future of Germany,' Roosevelt said. 'Of course, the German people shouldn't be starved, Winston, but we also must allow the Soviet Union to get reparations to help to rebuild it after the war. My prescription is to leave Germany with enough industry and work to prevent it from starving to death.

And so the session ended. Another day, another deal. Another prescription, perhaps, for another war.

9

Cambridge

I'd first come across Ed Brewster in early 1933, a fateful year.

Hitler had slithered into power in Germany via threats, grandiose promises and back-door dealings. He spoke the language of terror and the world listened with fear or admiration.

In America, Franklin Delano Roosevelt, inaugurated as President, told his anxious, Depression-hit countrymen: The only thing we have to fear is fear itself.

Ed and I had both gone up to Trinity in late 1932, though our paths didn't cross for several months. I'd got to know of him by repute as a loud-mouthed American lefty, and had seen him strolling confidently around the place before I finally met him in Douglas Winterton's rooms. Ed was chummy with a group of radical types who spouted pro-Bolshevik sentiments in college common rooms, or even, like the flamboyant Guy Burgess, proclaimed both their Marxism and their homosexuality from the rooftops. How different, I thought, were these privileged armchair revolutionaries to the young leftists in Berlin, who daily risked life and liberty for their beliefs. Ed's association with Cambridge Marxists was enough in itself to make him unpopular with the college Tories, who were more interested in fox-hunting, fast cars and high society than in liberal values or social justice. The fact that he was an American also counted against him. A prevalent view was that the Yanks had swaggered in to join the fighting when the Great War was all but over and then behaved as though they'd won it off their own bat before dragging the whole world down through their economic mismanagement.

I shared a few of those prejudices, but when I eventually met Ed, I found that far from being arrogant or boastful, he was amiable, open and disarmingly inquisitive. He was opinionated and knowledgeable, as keen to listen as to talk. He was athletic-looking, with thick black hair and an open, friendly face, which gazed out to the world with healthy curiosity.

'Ed Brewster, Grinnell College, Iowa,' he said giving me a hearty handshake.

He looked around Douglas's living-room, which was filling up with an assortment of students and Fellows, drinking tea and munching cucumber sandwiches. Douglas, then in his late forties, had become a highly thought of economist, a former pupil and friend of John Maynard Keynes whose influential book denouncing the Versailles Treaty as vindictive I had devoured on my return from Germany.

Douglas cultivated the best and the brightest at Cambridge, both in intellectual and sporting ability. At his Sunday soirées, you could find beefy rugger or rowing Blues arguing politics with budding poets who fancied themselves as the Cambridge riposte to Oxford's Auden. In another part of his large sitting-room, with windows overlooking Trinity Great Court and its fountain, a bright working-class scientist might be debating philosophy with one of Wittgenstein's clever students. Physicists talked to colleagues about exciting new discoveries at the Cavendish. There were usually only a handful of women – lecturers, students or wives of Fellows.

Ed found it all extremely stimulating. I said that after Iowa, I expected it was.

'Don't knock Iowa,' he said cheerfully. 'But, sure, you wouldn't find this level of ideas, serious talk, intelligent people. Doesn't it inspire you?'

'Not madly,' I said, truthfully.

He laughed.

'You Brits sure hate getting enthusiastic about things.'

'They drill that into us at school.'

'Yeah, those schools! Teaching you how to run the colonies. But still, great places for learning.'

'If you enjoy reading Homer in the original,' I said.

'I would if I could. In my high school if you asked to learn Greek or Latin they thought you were from an immigrant family. I had to cram Latin like crazy to get my scholarship.'

He'd come to Cambridge on a bursary endowed by a wealthy Iowan.

I asked how he'd met Douglas.

'I keep him supplied with the latest music from the States,' he said. 'How come he invites you?'

I said that Douglas was a friend of my father.

'The old school tie?'

'More or less. They were in the same regiment in France.'

'The old regimental tie. I suppose there's something comforting about tradition. I guess it's kind of like a protective shell against the world.'

'Exactly. We're trapped in our past.'

'Maybe, though at least you have a past. What do we have? A record of massacring Red Indians and enslaving the Negroes.'

'We taught you well.'

'Okay,' he laughed. 'Let's not compare our dirty secrets. It's a question of how we adapt to the future. I reckon you guys will do it in your usual way of compromise. Mind you, some of the people I mix with here think there's going to be a revolution, the bloodier the better. But, hell, they're wrong. It's not going to happen in England. Even Marx knew that. This isn't Russia or Germany. It's an arranged marriage between the guys who pull the strings and the nobility; you let us have our way and we'll let you keep your heads.'

'We did once behead a king.'

'Sure, and then you invited his kid back to head up the business. Things are different in the States. It's a divided country. Terrific poverty, real discrimination. Our Civil War wasn't that long ago, and nothing much has changed down South, except the Depression just made everything worse.'

I was about to say that Britain was no slouch in the poverty stakes, when Douglas came over and the talk turned to the theatre. There was nothing of much merit to be seen either on Broadway or in the West End, it seemed. Priestley's *Dangerous Corner*, a work about the circularity of time, was playing in both New York and London, and Ed and Douglas had both seen it. I hadn't. They disagreed about its merits.

I looked out of the window and watched the undergraduates, some in tweed jackets, others in baggy sweaters and long scarves, sauntering in the court, towards the town or towards the Cam with the air of self-possession so characteristic of the English upper classes. I thought Ed was right to say that no revolution would be cooked up here.

Douglas went off to join another conversation. He liked to orchestrate these get-togethers, to make everything click and meld. He saw it almost as a duty to push undergraduates on the right track, which to his mind meant a vaguely socialist morality.

Ed said to me: 'Douglas has a first-class mind, of course, but his generation doesn't go for anything really new. Not that this Priestley play is avant-garde. But it's sort of different, you know. It goes round and round in time, and there's a chance of changing things.'

'At least you agree on liking cheap music,' I said.

'I'm his pimp for musical comedy. You call it cheap, but it's an authentic American art form. Douglas's view of the States is that we're incapable of any really deep thought or art – apart from a few Anglophile characters like Henry James and Eliot. But those guys are honorary Europeans anyway. They've got good degrees in cynicism. He doesn't think much of the real American tradition – Melville, Whitman, Carl Sandburg. Do you know Sandburg?'

I didn't.

'You ought to read him. A great poet. A radical poet. But, listen, even light music can have a cultural meaning.'

He went to Douglas's gramophone and put on a record.

A clear female voice sang a new Gershwin hit:

'They're writing songs of love
But not for me...'

The lyrics were a bit self-pitying but the vocalist gave them a tough, self-deflating, almost cynical touch.

Ed asked: 'Do you know where that comes from?'

'From Broadway?'

'From suffering and survival. Of the Jews, of the Negroes.'

'And all we can boast is Gilbert and Sullivan.'

'Don't knock satire,' he laughed.

Disarmingly, he switched subjects.

'So what did your old man and Douglas do in the war?' he asked. 'Were they heroes?'

'I suppose my father was a sort of hero. He won a medal, in any case.'

'Really?' said Ed, his face lighting up. 'What did he do exactly?'

'Rescued a wounded man under fire.'
'I'd like to meet him.'
'He got killed a few weeks after that.'
'Jesus, that's tough.'
'One of the many.'
'You must hate the Germans,' he said.
'Not all of them.'

I told him I'd spent time in Berlin rather than face Cambridge right after school.

'You ran away to the country that killed your dad?'
'I suppose I went there to understand why he died.'
'You found what you were looking for?'
'In a way, I suppose. The pointlessness of war and the way in which peace gets botched up, but sometimes, perhaps, the need for war as a last resort.'
'You must've met a lot of radical guys over there?'
'I did,' I said.

He seemed to want me to go on, but sensed I wouldn't. I wasn't going to discuss Dorothy with a stranger.

'What did Douglas get up to in the war? He won't ever say.'
'Of course not,' I smiled. 'It's considered bad form to talk about things like that.'
'Stiff upper lip, and all that, eh? D'you figure Douglas has got things to hide?'
'Things?'
'Espionage, intelligence, something of that kind. He's that sort of guy. Something going on behind the façade.'
'I haven't a clue,' I said.

He seemed disappointed, then asked: 'What about your mother?'
'Not the Mata Hari type,' I said.
'Come on, Jim, You know what I meant was how has she managed after ... listen, I'm sorry. I don't go in for polite small talk. I'm interested in people's background. I know that's considered bad form too, but what the hell.'
'I don't mind,' I said. 'She seems to have coped well enough.'

As far as I knew, that was the truth. She'd never confided in me about her grief or her adjustment problems.

By now the party was beginning to thin out. People were beginning to leave, perhaps to study, more likely to cycle before dusk, play some sport or socialise.

Ed invited me to his room for a smoke and a drink.

I agreed. Despite his irritating way of rapidly switching subjects and asking pointed questions, I liked him. It was refreshing to find someone prepared to discuss things in the way he did. Most of the conversation in Trinity seemed to centre on pretentious aestheticism, convoluted Marxist theory or getting one's sporting Blue.

His room was a cramped study in a college annexe, with a tiny window. He lit a fire. We sipped tumblers of whisky while he toasted some bread, which we ate with butter and sardines. He spoke with emotion about some of the things he'd seen in America in the Depression. His own family had not been too badly hit. The farm had been in the family for three generations and there was no mortgage. A rich relative – 'in automobiles', Ed said – had tided them over the fall in hog prices.

'We had to cut back a bit,' he said. 'Had to dispense with some of the hired hands, which was terrible for them. But we haven't really suffered. Not like some of the suffering in the country. There are people out there, good people, who've worked hard all their lives, now dependent on relief or handouts, or selling shoelaces and razor blades on the streets. I've seen people who live in holes in the ground, who eat dandelions to stop themselves dying of starvation. I've seen kids malnourished, pot bellies and the like. In America! In the twentieth-century! And the worst off are the Negroes. These are the people we fought a civil war to liberate from slavery, and now they're almost worse than slaves. They can't get work, they can't get enough food.'

'At least you have a Roosevelt to rescue you, not a Hitler.'

'I don't know about Roosevelt,' said Ed. 'Still he can't be worse than Hoover, who incidentally was a man from my own state, you know. "The ship will right itself," he said. Man from Iowa, where ... you've heard of the Cow Wars, haven't you? The Farm Holiday strike?'

I shook my head. What on earth was he talking about? He took a deep swig of his drink.

'That's what they call insularity. Mind you, it's crept right into the States too, although we're a continent, not a small island. As though you can isolate yourself from the world. As though you can stick your head in the sand and ignore the sufferings in the world. China. Do you know what's happening in China?'

'Is that what the Cow Wars thing is about?' I asked.

'No,' he laughed. 'The Cow Wars were in Iowa.'

He told me how farmers in the state had resisted the government's attempt to slaughter their cows to stop the spread of tuberculosis in the bovine stock. I tried to look enthusiastic, but Ed wasn't fooled.

'Okay, so it wasn't exactly like the storming of the Winter Palace, but hell, we all got pretty worked up about it. Not as exciting as Germany, I bet.'

I shrugged.

'You reckon the Nazis could've been stopped, even in 1931?' he asked.

'Yes, but in the end, the Reds were more interested in revolution than on keeping Hitler out.'

'What sort of people were the Reds? Were they tough?'

'Tough, yes, and idealistic, some of them. I think the leadership misled them.'

'You made some good friends there,' he commented.

'Sort of,' I said, cautiously.

We agreed to cycle into the country the following Sunday, and our friendship took off from there.

I received a letter from Dr Bergsen later in the year, postmarked Berlin. I had written a cautious letter, enquiring in very non-political terms about his health and work and telling him something of life at Trinity. His reply was in English:

> My dear Mr Jimmy Bexley (if I may call you so familiarly),
> Your letter about Cambridge reached me some months before. For your life there, I am so pleased for you, and also I envy you. To do my studies there was always my dream. Everything is good here. Naturally we did wonder before what will happen when Herr Hitler becomes chancellor but so far he has done some good things even if not all. To end the danger of Communist revolution, he has been ruthless, but it had to be. Now we will have no civil war. The German people are happy and, more important,

confident. He is putting people to work, and giving the people pride in themselves again. The laws to stop Germans of Jewish faith from the civil service and the law practice we hope will not be for ever. I myself have been exempted because I fought in the war. So, loyalty and patriotism are being rewarded here still. My nephew Leo has lost his job at the university, but I hope not for ever. Some friends, who are not of the Jewish persuasion, tell me to leave Germany, but I think this will not get worse. I have seen your friend the *Fraulein* in the street once and we had a little talk. We talk about you and she asked I should tell you that she is well. But I think perhaps all is not well and I advise to her to go home.

With best greetings,
Ever yours,
Samuel Bergsen, LL.D

I tried to interpret this. I decided, sadly, that his remarks about Hitler's achievements were genuinely meant and that he was still living in a fool's paradise. But what were his real feelings about the book burnings and anti-Jewish pogroms? He had refrained from expressing any opinions about Leo's dismissal and plans for the future. This must have been a matter of anguish for both uncle and nephew. I was worried too by what he had said about Dorothy, deducing this was his way of referring to his suspicions about her activities and that he had told her to get out of Germany for her own safety.

I wished I could find out for sure that Dorothy was not in immediate danger, but she had forbidden me to write to her in Berlin because of the risks for herself, Dieter and other comrades. She had told me she would see me in England. That was all.

Tensions, mostly just below the surface, simmered at Cambridge throughout the summer. As I watched events, both there and beyond, my perplexity grew by leaps and bounds. Left-wing radicals seemed more inclined to preach pacifism than to want to fight against fascism. In London and elsewhere there was a surge in popularity for Oswald Mosley's fascist Blackshirts. Jews in the East End of London and some left-wing groups were alarmed and began resistance. The Communists were staying out of the fight, which they said was between 'fascists and social fascists'. I feared this was going to be a replay of what had happened in Germany.

My old school friend Gerald Cross was also at Cambridge, and we often met though we were in different colleges. He listened to what I said about Germany and my conviction that we had to fight against Mosley.

'I'm still a pacifist,' he said mildly.

'Surely, you've outgrown that,' I retorted impatiently.

'On the contrary,' he smiled. 'More confirmed, if anything.'

'But the fascists are out to destroy democracy. Don't you believe in democracy, Gerald?'

'I do, despite its faults, and the rise of fascism is a fault. But the way to correct those faults is through moral persuasion, passive resistance if necessary.'

'Oh, God, don't tell me you're a follower of Gandhi.'

'I admire his methods.'

'And if Britain had to fight Nazi Germany? Wouldn't you want to fight then?'

'No. Pacifism is indivisible.'

'You're sure this isn't all just an over-reaction to your militaristic family, Gerald?'

'It probably started out that way, James. Now it's a firm conviction about the right way to act.'

'And so you really believe that we ought to just lie down if Hitler attacks us. Just lie down and let him carry us all off to concentration camps.'

'That's the only way to be sure that we defeat his amorality without descending to his level.'

'And then he'd just call off his dogs and say: these people have taught me how to behave? He'd turn over a new leaf? Just like that?'

'You're oversimplifying it madly, but yes, that's the way to confront injustice. That's how the Indians will persuade us to leave their country, and that's how we can persuade Mosley – and Hitler – to stop their madness.'

'Christ, Gerald,' I said. 'You use words like amorality. How about "evil"? Doesn't your creed want to defeat evil?'

'Evil is a theological concept. But whether we call something "evil" or "amoral" isn't the point. As a pacifist, I do want to defeat that thing, but not by force – which is not only wrong, but also ultimately ineffective. We can defeat injustice by showing ourselves morally superior.'

I shook my head in frustration and bewilderment and walked away.

Oh, hell, I thought, it's not so much that the best lack conviction, but that the decent lack judgement.

One morning, as Ed and I were strolling down King's Parade, busy with cyclists and hurrying pedestrians, he suddenly stopped and gasped: 'Isn't that Chadwick?'

He nodded in the direction of a lean, ascetic-looking middle-aged man with a high forehead and a beaked nose who had paused to glance in at a shop window displaying expensive conservative clothes – the sort of place most undergraduates did not aspire to.

'Is it?' I asked.

'You idiot,' he said, amused at my attempt to cover up my ignorance. 'James Chadwick, the man who discovered the neutron.'

'Which is?'

I remembered that Leo Roth had mentioned neutrons to me once, but I retained almost nothing of what he'd said.

'You're hopeless, Bexley! It's a particle that can penetrate into the nucleus of the atom. Hell, I'd have thought you knew that!'

'I know that some Cavendish chaps were the first to split the atom last year – read it in the newspaper – but didn't think one of them was called Chadwick.'

Ed stamped the ground impatiently, watching Chadwick from afar as one would gaze at a film star or a sporting hero.

'The newspapers write a load of science fiction bullshit about things they don't understand. Anyway, it was Cockcroft and Walton, and they weren't the first to split the atom, you idiot. What they did was split the nucleus of atoms, lithium atoms.'

'With that chap's neutron?' I teased, nodding towards Chadwick who was entering the shop.

'They built an apparatus to bombard atoms with protons, and

I am not aiming to stand here and explain all that. You can read about it in the journals, not in newspapers.'

'Okay, Why don't we go and buy you a tie in that shop so you can stand next to Neutron Man?'

'Oh, buzz off! With people like you around, it beats me how the English have managed to achieve so much in physics. They've paved the way all right. God knows how many labs in the States are working on this sort of stuff right now.'

'Is it that important?' I asked.

Ed looked hard at me to see if I was still teasing and realised I wasn't.

'It really could be, Jim. Maybe more than anything to come. It could be the way to fantastic energy sources, space travel, the end of poverty, you name it.'

'Weapons?'

'Could be that too,' he shrugged. 'No one knows. The neutron entering the nucleus could – could – unleash amazing energy. The implications of what's going on are staggering. It's all just starting up. Research going on all over the place.'

'In Germany too. I met someone in Berlin...'

'Name wasn't Heisinger, was it?'

'No, who's he?'

'Guy who formulated the Uncertainty Principle in quantum mechanics. Surely you know about that?'

I remembered Leo had talked about this too, but I wasn't going to let Ed know exactly how porous my mind was when it came to scientific information.

'So the Germans are in the race too?'

'It isn't a race,' he said. 'Can't be. The whole goddam planet needs to cooperate – and it's happening. Even Russia sends people over here to learn.'

'Do you think Hitler is the sort of man to share scientific secrets?'

'Hitler won't have any say in the matter. Scientists are an international group. They value knowledge more than geography.'

'I hope you're right.'

'Wait and see! It's all going to come out okay. It's the start of a new age. That's why I admire guys like Chadwick so much.'

'Have you ever spoken to him?' I asked.

'I'd like to. Doubt if he'd see me, though. You need a Ph.D. to talk with guys like him.'

'I'm sure Douglas could arrange it. Gershwin records in exchange for atomic gossip.'

'Not even Douglas. Those physics guys live in a universe of their own.'

'Made up of uncertainty?'

'You'd better believe it,' he grinned.

Somewhat to my surprise, my mother remarried. She'd discussed it with me after taking the decision, not so much to elicit my views as to praise her fiancé to the high heavens. He was going places, she said; he was dynamic, ambitious and stimulating. I took this as an implied criticism of my father, and resented the man, Robert Massingham, even before I met him. The reality turned out to be even worse than my expectations: he was wealthy, well connected, handsome, looking for a parliamentary seat, and was what I could only describe as a reactionary.

About Hitler, he said: 'Don't entirely like the cut of his jib. He's common and he rants far too much. But he's got the right ideas and we need a strong Germany to keep the Bolshies in their place. If he gets too big for his boots, we'll cut him down to size, but for now he's knocking Germany into shape and we need that.'

When I questioned his attitude, he ignored me and said to my mother: 'Don't know what the country's coming to, Elizabeth. Young fellow like that ought to be at Sandhurst not spouting pinko propaganda.'

My mother took me aside and said she hoped I wouldn't embarrass Robert's chances at the next election by talking 'left-wing nonsense'.

'I'll try not to, but if you're really worried I'll change my name.'

'Don't be silly, James. Robert has it in his capacity to help you in life, and he will do so, I'm sure. But it would help if you were a bit more civil.'

When I told Douglas about the meeting, he said: 'I'm sure she needs a man, and if he's good to her that's the most you have the right to expect.'

I wanted to ask him what my father would have thought about it all. What I *did* ask was: 'What sort of man was my father? Was he adventurous?'

Douglas considered this, puffing on his pipe.

'That's a rather strange question.'

'I know, Douglas. Ed Brewster was asking me about him, and I realised how little I knew about his motivations. Was he the adventurous type?'

'Not particularly, no,' Douglas said.

'Well, why did he dash off to war?'

'Same reason as most of us. Duty. Obligation.'

This didn't satisfy me.

'Was he a socialist? You've implied that to me.'

Douglas thought again.

'Not a socialist. Not as such, no. I'm sorry if I put that thought in your mind.'

'You said the most important thing for him was not harming one's fellow man,' I challenged. 'And that he wanted me to believe that too.'

'That's absolutely true, but it wasn't socialism as such, except in the very broad sense. Nor was it especially religious. It was a conviction from within. At least, it was when we were together in France. Before the war we didn't discuss internal beliefs very much.'

'Did he ever tell you why he held that conviction?' I asked.

'We never really had that sort of conversation. We were usually too busy with the business of survival, or of dealing with boredom.'

'You were his closest friend out there, Douglas, and yet you've never told me very much about him.'

'I haven't consciously withheld anything you needed to know. I wasn't one of those chaps who kept a diary or wrote poetry to record events. Perhaps my memory is as selective as most people's.'

'How did he die? I know he won a medal for gallantry, and that he was shot, but how actually?'

'These things can be painful,' Douglas said.

'I'm not a child any longer, Douglas.'

'No, and you're quite right to ask. Clive would've wanted that, too. He was shot in no man's land, trying to reconnoitre enemy positions for an assault the next day. I wasn't present, you understand, so this account is based on hearsay, but very reliable hearsay.'

He looked pained but went on: 'He was badly wounded, in agony, crying out. There was heavy fire. Someone tried to get to him and was killed instantly. Clive's Calvary lasted some hours. Then he died.'

After a silence of some minutes, I asked: 'Did he say anything before?'

Douglas smiled gently.

'I could invent something, I suppose, but I won't insult your intelligence. He cried out for medical help. Frequently. He shouted that his wife should be told he died instantaneously. Nothing else that I know of. There was heavy firing. It was noisy.'

'Thanks, Douglas. Did he believe in the war?'

Douglas puffed his pipe.

'Not many of us did. Not by that time. It was a question of duty and conscience. Not the most reliable of motivations. We know that now.'

'If there were another war, say against Nazi Germany, would he have gone off to fight?'

'Most of those who fought wouldn't want another war, if at all possible. If at all possible. I'm not going to speak for your father, but I'll tell you what I feel. War is awful, but sometimes, occasionally, once in a lifetime, perhaps, it may be the only way. A lot of people – and not only in the Oxford Union – wouldn't agree.'

In February 1933, the Oxford debating society had voted two-to-one 'That this House will in no circumstances fight for King and Country.'

I'd wondered how Hitler, who'd become German Chancellor a month before, had reacted to that!

10

Cambridge and Berlin

Ed soon became my closest confidant. On one of our cycling outings to the Cambridgeshire countryside, ending up at a cosy pub for beer and cigarettes, we discussed our reactions to the world at large and to the smaller world of Cambridge and Trinity. Ed saw encouraging political signs. We had both recently attended meetings of the Cambridge Socialist Club and noted how the membership was becoming more and more impatient with social conditions. In the face of government indifference, unemployed workers staged 'hunger marches' to protest at their plight. 'Struggle or starve!' their banners proclaimed.

'You know, sometimes I reckon this is where the revolution *might* start, sooner than in the States,' Ed remarked. 'I didn't used to think that, but you can see it all around you. The best young people in the country, the future leaders, have a sort of fire in the belly. It's inspiring. Back home, most people couldn't give a shit, except about themselves.'

'What about the Cow Wars?'

'Yeah, well,' he smiled ruefully. 'But those guys in the front line were just farmers, you know – good guys, but not the intellectual elite.'

'By elite, I take it you mean Guy Burgess,' I said.

Ed pulled a face.

'He's a posturing clown,' he said. 'He's just jumping on to the bandwagon. But people like Maurice Dobb.'

Dobb, a Cambridge lecturer, was already making a name for himself as an economist and convinced Marxist.

'Are you thinking of signing up to the Party, Ed?' I asked.

'Hell, no. But I guess I would if there was no other way out. I reckon you don't see things the same way, pal.'

I drained my beer and stubbed out my cigarette.

'Do you really believe it will ever be the way out?' I asked.

'Maybe not, but who's going to stand up to Hitler if not the Soviet Union, like it or not? Certainly not the old men of the ruling classes here or in France.'

I told him about my future stepfather and his views.

'Yeah, well, that's what I mean. It leaves one with a pretty stark choice. Right?'

'It would be nice to have a cause to fight for,' I said, thinking of Dorothy and her undiluted beliefs. 'But if you can't, then maybe the only thing is to decide which enemy you have to fight against first.'

'I don't see that the Soviet Union is our enemy,' he retorted.

We decided tacitly to avoid any further travel down this conversational road, and switched to his other hobby-horse – physics.

He talked with infectious enthusiasm about research at Cambridge and elsewhere, especially into the mysteries of the atomic nucleus.

'They're aiming at the big, big questions. Know what that means?'

'The Creation?'

'C'mon, Jim, don't be so flippant. But, yes, in a way, that's what they're about. But it's not some spiritual hocus-pocus. It's physical. So guess again.'

'Energy?'

'You better believe it. I'd explain exactly how, but you couldn't begin to grasp it.'

'How can it be used?' I asked.

'That's a big question. If it can be controlled – big "if" – then it really will transform people's lives. Think of it! We're living in one of the most exciting ages ever – progress in science, progress in human affairs.'

'In human affairs?'

'Okay, not all of it. Fascism's a throwback to the Dark Ages, sure, but perhaps it's a kind of progress because it forces chaps like you and me to maybe embrace really progressive systems, even if they aren't absolutely perfect.'

He'd hit the nail on the head, as he often seemed to do. Things were moving at a breathless pace in the world, as though we were all rushing towards some climax, which might turn out to be beautiful or dreadful. One got this feeling from the words of the powerful and the actions of the masses. Hitler and Stalin, rival messiahs of the New Age, were speaking in language that was grotesquely optimistic and apocalyptic, and their subjects behaved like mesmerised sheep – not unlike the citizens of the old, pre-war Europe, rushing towards battle in 1914 under the fervent influence of blind patriotism.

Not long after this conversation, Sebastian Gosling-Jones, a final-year undergraduate whom I knew only slightly as a Marxist committee member of the Socialist Society, knocked on my door and invited himself in for a chat. Sebastian, gangling with long blond hair, was not alone. His dark, short, taciturn older companion was introduced as Gordon – no surname, no explanation. Gordon, who wore a cheaply cut black suit, may or may not have been a university man; it was not stated one way or the other.

'Is this a social call?' I asked.

Sebastian said in his languid Etonian way: 'The committee likes to keep in touch. Someone mentioned you'd spent some time in Germany recently. Is that correct old man?'

'In Berlin. I didn't see much of the rest of the country, except from the train window. I was there for about eight months.'

'And how did you assess the situation in Berlin?'

The use of the word 'assess' struck me as overblown.

'It was before the Nazis took over,' I said. 'Everything was touch and go, and just after I left, Hitler's support actually dipped a little. If the Social Democrats and Communists had stood together they could have held the balance of power and prevented him from becoming Chancellor. It was an historic mistake.'

'You use the word historic,' said Sebastian, his lip curling with sarcasm. 'We believe that it would have been an historic mistake to ally with the Social Democrats. Their leaders are traitors to the working class.'

I wondered what he knew of working-class aspirations. He turned to look at Gordon, as if for support, but Gordon merely surveyed both of us with sardonic amusement in his face.

'You asked for my assessment,' I told Sebastian. 'I've given it, for what it's worth.'

He again looked to Gordon for something – advice, perhaps, encouragement. I saw nothing in Gordon's face to suggest a message, but possibly Sebastian saw something, for he continued in a soothing way: 'You met some Communist comrades in Berlin? How did they strike you?'

'I met some wonderful people in the KPD.'

'Excellent,' beamed Sebastian.

Gordon studied his fingernails.

'Unfortunately, the whole strategy was a balls-up,' I said.

'To *your* eyes, perhaps,' Sebastian said. 'A progressive political movement has to concentrate on the greater good.'

I couldn't contain myself.

'What greater good would that be, Gosling-Jones? The socialists and the Communists are both in tatters. Those who aren't being tortured or aren't in concentration camps are in hiding, in danger. And Hitler is in power. Is that the greater good?'

Gordon spoke for the first time, in measured, even tones, as though to an intelligent but wayward pupil. He had a flat northern accent.

'My dear Bexley,' he said. 'The greater good is the victory of the proletariat. The victory of the revolution, for all countries, not just for Germany.'

'The important battle *now* is against fascism,' I protested. 'Doesn't that have to be stamped out before you can even begin to hope for the victory of the revolution, whatever that means? In Germany, all it needed was some common sense to make a united stand.'

'Your analysis strikes me as flawed,' Gordon said smoothly. 'As Gosling-Jones has correctly stated, that would have meant making common cause with the socialists, and therefore objectively aiding the reactionary fascist forces.'

His arguments made me dizzy. I had listened to Dorothy and Dieter talk in similar terms, and had believed they were wrong, though I could see how, in the heat of battle, it made some sense to be careful in choosing your allies, especially given the history of distrust. In the calmer atmosphere of Cambridge it seemed worse than bizarre.

'Excuse me for asking,' I said, 'but how would a common front against Hitler have amounted to aiding him? It might have destroyed him.'

'Even if it had,' said Gordon, 'it would merely have postponed the rise of fascism in Germany. You must understand, Bexley, that there are certain historical certainties, and one of them is that the collapse of capitalism is preceded by the temporary success of fascism. That is what has happened in Germany, which will inevitably crash like a house of cards.'

'And when on earth is that likely to happen? Before or after the Nazis have finally defeated your party and murdered all your comrades? Before or after Hitler kicks out or kills all the Jews? Before or after Germany re-arms?'

'You see it all too simplistically, Bexley,' said Gordon, still in schoolmasterly mode. 'There is no defeat involved, I assure you. The Communist Party of Germany has merely made a strategic retreat.'

I shook my head at his mental contortions.

Gordon stood up, and Sebastian immediately jumped to his feet too.

The seduction attempt, if that's what it had begun as, was over.

Gordon turned and surveyed me as he was about to leave.

'I'm not entirely against working with liberal intellectuals,' he said.

'I'll bear that in mind,' I said curtly.

I was angry more at the way they'd approached me than by their arguments. After all, I'd been pondering the pros and cons ever since my Berlin encounters with Dorothy. The courage many Communists had shown in battling Brownshirt thugs, their courage in continuing what they knew was a losing battle – because the Party opposed alliances with the SPD – filled me with admiration. Any reasonable approach to me might have tipped the scales. I wanted to fight. Mosley's Blackshirts were on the march. Ramsay MacDonald's national government was complacent and unable to combat unemployment and poverty. The labour movement was split and ineffective. Where could I go? I felt alone, in need of a home.

Ed understood my anguish but was not overly sympathetic.

'It's about choices, buddy, like we talked about before,' he said, as we sat drinking ale in a King's Street pub. 'If you need a place to go, maybe you could do worse than joining the Party.'

I raised my eyebrows.

'But then I'm hardly the right guy to consult,' he said. 'Don't even know my own direction. I've had an approach to go and work for Hopkins' outfit.'

He saw that I looked puzzled.

'Harry Hopkins. Not exactly a household name over here. He ran some big relief programmes in New York a couple of years back when Roosevelt was governor. Now he's running New Deal projects in Washington.'

'And you're tempted?'

'Right. He says the poor aren't poor because they're morally corrupt, which is how the rich see it. He says the unemployed want to work, that they want the dignity of work. Not exactly revolutionary, but that's what is needed now.'

'Sounds like a good man.'

'I think so, Jim. I went to the same college as him – Grinnell, Iowa. Methodist values, Christianity in the community, a sort of socialism, build the Kingdom of God in this world. Well, I don't go for the religious side of it – and I doubt Hopkins does – but it all makes solid, decent sense when you've got a Depression on your hands.'

'Sounds as though you've already made up your mind,' I said.

'Maybe I have. Roosevelt's America isn't exactly my heart's desire, but he's sure as hell better than the alternatives. Europe is fascinating, but it's decaying. It's the old world. It's beginning to rot.'

'Not so long ago you were saying England was the big hope for the future.'

'I think there's some great young people, but they aren't in positions of power. The system is rotten. It doesn't allow ordinary guys with good minds but no money or connections to swim to the top. Hell, why don't you go to the States too?'

I laughed.

'Mainly just because England – and Europe – *is* rotten. It wouldn't feel right to run away.'

'Jesus, that is so much romantic crap. You want to fight the good fight here, but you don't want to dirty your hands. Okay. Fine. But don't waste yourself, Jim. There's a future somewhere else.'

'That's what Gosling-Jones and his friends say too. Only they mean Russia.'

'Well, maybe there too,' said Ed. 'But they don't speak English in Russia. And they don't have Gershwin either.'

He sang in his pleasant baritone:

'I'm bidin' my time,
'Cause that's the kind of guy I'm.'

As it happened, I found a very pleasant way to bide my time for the coming months. At my mother's wedding to the ghastly Bob Massingham, who was now an MP, having won a safe Tory seat in a by-election, I was introduced to a sweet and desirable young woman by one of my new stepbrothers. Her name was Gwen Farrow. She worked as an assistant in Heffer's Bookshop in Cambridge and lived with her parents in the nearby village of Grantchester. A few days after the wedding, I went to Heffer's, spotted her walking around the shelves with a catalogue in hand, and asked her to have a drink with me.

'Why?' she smiled, surveying me.

'I need some advice about a reading list.'

It wasn't the sharpest bit of repartee I'd ever managed, but she laughed and said she thought she might manage to join me at a nearby pub after work. We hit it off well from the start and I enjoyed being with someone so uncomplicated. Like Magda in Berlin, she was blonde, but her hair was a darker shade and worn short. Unlike Magda, her eyes were alive and there was often the hint of a delightful smile on her lips and a blush of pleasure on her cheeks. She was intelligent but not ambitious about furthering her education at university.

She was uninterested in politics, yet her eyes glistened in sympathy when we stood on a pavement watching a hunger march through the Cambridge streets. A lot of students treated the march as a chance for a bit of a rag. Radicals chanted slogans, beat drums and carried banners proclaiming solidarity with the marchers. I noticed Burgess blowing a bugle with great zest, and Sebastian clutching one pole of a huge Communist Party banner. Ed, marching a little apart from any group, saw Gwen and myself and gave a cheery wave. Hearty types from some of the college rowing and rugby fraternities hurled abuse and the occasional ripe tomato at the leftists.

'Do you think this is the start of the revolution?' I asked Gwen, who was clasping my arm.

'No, but I think it's awful that those poor men can't get jobs. Of course, Daddy says they're just idle.'

I groaned, and she laughed.

At the time of the hunger march, we'd been seeing each other for a month or so, meeting at least twice a week. We'd have a drink or a meal, take a slow walk, or sometimes go dancing or to the cinema. At the end of the evening, we embraced, kissed and fondled a little. Then she'd catch the bus home, always before ten o'clock.

Ed, when I next saw him, asked bluntly: 'Have you slept with her?'

'Good Lord, Ed,' I said with mock indignation. 'One doesn't ask a chap that sort of thing.'

'Okay, so you haven't,' he said, fishing a contraceptive in a silver packet from his pocket and putting it in my hands.

'She's not that sort of girl,' I laughed.

'They're *all* that sort of girl, if you go about it the right way. Believe me.'

I didn't agree, but kept the contraceptive.

He hadn't told me any more about his possible plans to return to the US. Nor did I ask him about a rumour I'd heard that he'd become a Party member.

I decided to go to Berlin during the 1933 Christmas vacation, using a bequest from my grandmother to finance the trip. I was burning to find out what had become of Dorothy. I asked Gwen if she'd like to join me, knowing this was not a possibility. I'd not told her about Dorothy, though she seemed to have guessed there was something more than political curiosity luring me to Germany. I promised I'd be back in a few weeks, and before I left to catch a boat to Harwich, we had a very ardent farewell evening.

Travelling by train across Germany towards Berlin I noticed that despite the huge intimidating swastika flags almost everywhere, things seemed peaceful enough. Farmers in the fields waved to the train, burghers out for a stroll doffed their hats in greeting. Children whistled cheerfully. The stewards and other staff on the train were polite and deferential towards a foreigner. One of my fellow passengers, a fat merchant travelling to Berlin, on finding out that I'd been out of the country for more than a year, rubbed his hands together and said:

'You will find everything much better, very much better. We have order, stability, and we again feel we are one nation. That is all we Germans want. Just to be like every other country.'

Someone else put in: 'No, Herr Neumann, you're wrong. We Germans want only to be better than every other country.'

Everyone in the compartment laughed good-humouredly at the remark.

I had written to Frau Siegendorff a few weeks before hoping she might have a room free for me. I'd also written to Dr Bergsen telling him I'd be in Germany soon.

Frau S greeted me warmly and was delighted with my gift of a silk scarf. She said I could have her son Gregor's room, and should consider myself her guest. She wouldn't hear of accepting money. Gregor, she said, wistfully, was living in Frankfurt where he had 'a good position'.

When I asked how Dr Bergsen was she looked at me in some distress and said she had not seen him for more than a month. He was no longer a lodger, though he came every few weeks to collect his mail.

'But, for the past month, not,' she said, indicating a small pile of letters. I noticed that among them was the one I'd sent him.

'He said it could be difficult for me if I had a Jewish person as a lodger. He didn't want me to have trouble. He would find lodging with a Jewish family easily, he said. Ach, Herr Bexley, he is a real gentleman. Such a pity he is a Jew. In these times, that is not such a good thing to be. You have read in the newspapers about Germany?'

I said I had.

She shook her head, then looked around quickly to see if anyone might be in earshot.

'There is a little madness with these people,' she said quietly, drawing a swastika in the air with her hand. 'Gregor says it had to be so, and that we will soon see how much better life will be. He's a good boy, my Gregor. I thought he was up to no good, but now I see he knew the way things were going.

So he has a good position now. I think something to do with the local government. So I believe him, because he knows all these things. I hope this madness will pass and Herr Doktor Bergsen will come back here perhaps, and all will be well.'

Then she wrung her hands in a gesture of despair and asked: 'What else can I do, Herr Bexley?'

The next day I went in search of Dr Bergsen. At the law firm where he worked, a clerk told me that he was no longer practising there. He did not know why. I asked to see one of the partners and was admitted into the presence of Dr Antonius Goerdeler, an elderly man with a gaunt face. He offered me a cigarette.

'You were a client of Dr Bergsen?' he asked.

'A friend.'

'Hmm. Well all I can really say is that he no longer is employed in this firm. He left on his own account about three months ago. A great pity. He felt that because of his, ah, religious affilitation, it would not be fair for him to stay on. Of course, we had to respect his wishes and we were, I may say, very generous in an *ex gratia* payment, which we made to him in gratitude for his diligence and loyalty over the years. A great pity.'

'But I thought he was exempted from the law against Jews being lawyers because of his war service.'

'Of course. There was no question that such a man would be prevented from practising. No question. But some of the clients... Well, it was not because of any anti-Semitism exactly, but because they saw the practical difficulty of a Jewish lawyer representing them in a court where the officials might be National Socialists, you know. And we saw that difficulty too, and Dr Bergsen also. It was a practical problem.'

'And when he offered to leave, did you make any effort to persuade him to stay?' I asked.

'We respected his decision. What else could we do?'

I thanked the partner curtly and asked if he had any idea of Dr Bergsen's present whereabouts. He spread his hands wide and said: 'Berlin is a large city. But perhaps he has already left Germany.'

Next I went to Neukölln in search of Dorothy.

The building where Dieter, Dorothy's Communist boyfriend, had lived now had several Nazi flags hanging from windows. I knocked on the door of his room. A harassed young woman told me that she had never heard of Dieter and that she and her husband had moved in a few months before.

Nor was my old Social Democrat friend Klaus living in his place any more.

It was around two years since I'd last been in Berlin, but the human landscape had changed dramatically. It was like returning to the hometown of one's childhood after half a century's absence and finding that all one's old friends, relations and acquaintances had died and that no one even remembered their names; a group of total strangers now inhabited the familiar streets and buildings of the memory.

Eventually, in a narrow street where the wintry sun was hidden by a forest of swastika flags, I bumped into someone I'd once met at Klaus's room. He was extremely nervous on recognising me, but after a bit of persuasion agreed to let me buy him a beer or two. We sat in a corner in a smoky tavern and he told me in a low and shaky voice that 'our friend' – he was too scared to mention Klaus's name – had been taken to a concentration camp six months ago. He had no idea what had become of him there.

'And you?' I asked cautiously.

'I'm finished with all that shit,' he said. 'Now I just behave like every other uneducated moron of my age. I shout with the rest.'

Then he added in a whisper and with a grin: 'But, man, I didn't throw any books on the bonfire.'

This was what it had come to, I thought. Passive, secret non-compliance – daring to think for oneself – had become the height of defiance.

I decided to risk one more question. Did he remember meeting Dieter Raubel and the Englishwoman Dorothy?

He had no recollection of Dorothy but said he'd seen Dieter recently, drinking at a bar nearby. They hadn't talked.

'These days, the ones you trust the least are those you used to know before. Everyone wonders why everyone else is not under arrest.'

I wished him well and left. I found the bar easily enough

and, amazingly, saw Dieter sitting at a table on his own. It was mid-morning and there was no one else inside.

I sat down at Dieter's table without a word. He looked up blearily and didn't seem to recognise me at first. His nose had obviously been broken and he was unshaven. His eyes, which had once struck me as looking at the world in a hard and even ruthless manner, now seemed dull and defeated. We didn't talk for a long while.

Then he said: 'You've come looking for her.'

'Yes.'

'I don't know where. To Moscow, I think.'

'When?' I asked.

'I don't know. It was before they came and took me.'

I nodded and waited until, perhaps as long as several minutes later, he told me what had happened to him.

'They took me to a cell and kicked me with their boots until I blacked out, then they threw water over me, and again, kick, kick, kick, in the face, in my balls, in the back. And so on. I don't know how long. Kicked me, used truncheons, rubber straps. All over my body. Then one of them fucked me, you know, up the arse. The others watched and laughed.'

I could say nothing.

'Now I'm one of them,' he said. 'I listen. I tell them what I hear. That keeps me out of the camp. Don't tell me anything, Englishman.'

I nodded.

Then he added with a sly smile and just a touch of fire in his eyes:

'I don't mind betraying a comrade here and there if they deserve it. We were all betrayed. Some of us wanted to go on fighting, and the Party (he spat out the word) was already making plans to go underground. Now most of them have gone out of Germany. They knew we would lose. They wanted us to lose, I think.'

I shook his hand, incapable of saying a word.

'Don't tell me anything,' he repeated as I made my way out of the gloomy, empty drinking place. 'If you see her, warn her not to tell me anything.'

* * *

I renewed my search for Dr Bergsen and, more circumspectly, for Dorothy. I went for help to the British Embassy where they were distinctly unhelpful. They hadn't heard from, or ever had any contact with, a Miss Dorothy Young. That didn't surprise me. This was about the last place she'd have come for help or advice. They knew nothing about any Dr Bergsen. Oh, he was German? Oh, Jewish? Well, they'd check with the visa section to see if anyone of that name had applied. Half a mo. No, sorry, no such animal in our lists.

Then I went to see the Americans. They seemed relieved I was just a Brit seeking information rather than some German Jew desperate for a visa. I was handed to a young attaché, who tried his best to be of smiling assistance. Again, no one in the embassy had ever come across a Dr Bergsen. The attaché suggested I enquire at a Jewish community centre. He offered me a cigarette and talked about the political situation in a relaxed way that was a million miles from the angst of most of the Germans I'd been talking to. He spoke with a sort of professional admiration about the way the Nazis had handled power.

'You have to hand it to them – no messing about. Identify your enemy and rough him up, neutralise him.'

'Kill him, you mean,' I said.

'There's been a certain amount of that,' he said regretfully. 'Inevitable, really, in a revolution. And that's what this is. If you're opposed to the revolution, you generally pay the price. And, after all, most of the guys they've locked up or murdered were asking for it. You know, Reds, socialists.'

'And Jews,' I said.

'Sure, but that was expected, too,' he shrugged. 'The anti-Semitic thing has been relatively mild. We were expecting something much more drastic. Wholesale arrests, killings, mass expulsions. It didn't happen. Maybe they're scared of world opinion. Anyway, the Jews are still in Germany.'

'On sufferance. In fear.'

'Oh, yes. But that was bound to happen. Look, the Jews are not pin-ups here. Never have been. We thought things would be a lot worse. We thought it would be like the old pogroms in Russia and Poland. Hell, compared to that, this hasn't been too bad.'

I asked if a man called Leo Roth had applied for a visa. He went to a filing cabinet and came back with a smile.

'Roth, Leo, scientist?'

I nodded.

'Yes. We give priority to some of the promising ones. Left a few weeks ago.'

He couldn't say where in the US Leo was headed.

'Princeton or Columbia most likely. We treat them well once we let them in.'

I found a Jewish community centre simply by looking in an old telephone directory. A group of elderly and middle-aged men sitting on wooden chairs at a rickety table looked at me with suspicion. When they grasped I was an English student in search of a friend, the suspicion eased a little. Again, no one knew of a Dr Bergsen, though one man knew of a Bergsen family. He said he would make enquiries and inform me if he heard anything of value. I told him not to take any risks. I was invited to have some tea. They were still sizing me up. I didn't want to make them uncomfortable by intruding too long, so I declined the offer. I opened up to them about myself and about why I'd come to Germany in 1931.

'That I can understand,' one of them nodded. 'It was a homage to your father. But why come here now?'

I said I wanted to see what had happened to some friends I'd made. I omitted to mention that most of them had been radical leftists and Communists.

'You are Jewish?' I was asked.

'No.'

'As a gentile, what do you think of what is going on here?'

'I'm appalled.'

'And other gentiles, in England?'

'I think there's a lot of anger,' I said. 'But we also have a lot of anti-Semitism.'

'It's everywhere,' said an elderly man. 'Like a plague, and we are the germs.'

'You are at Cambridge University,' one of the younger men said. 'Have you met Herr Professor Dr Hans Stahl?'

As it happened, I had. At one of Douglas's tea parties. He

was a distinguished art historian, author of several books on nineteenth-century and more modern schools of painting in Germany and the Low Countries. He'd emigrated from Berlin not long before I'd met him, and was so delighted to find someone at Cambridge who'd recently visited his home city that he invited me to Sunday lunch with his wife and young family. As a result, I was able to talk in the Berlin community centre about how they were adjusting to life in Cambridge. Several of the people at the centre knew or had heard of Professor Stahl, and appeared to take my acquaintance with him as evidence of my bona fides. Even so, they were cautious in talking about their situation. Only as I was about to take my leave did the younger man, who'd asked me about the professor, say, in a low voice:

'The people in England know what is happening here, I think. You said there was anger. That is our last hope.'

'They must let the government here know that the treatment of the Jewish community is not acceptable,' another man chipped in.

A couple of the older ones looked extremely unhappy at this talk and made gestures to silence the younger people, but I was aware of a deep need of most of these people to say something. Talking to a foreigner, whatever the risks, was an affirmative act.

'We can do nothing any more,' one of the younger men said. 'Our shops are boycotted and soon we will be forced to sell them up. And perhaps our homes too. Our doctors and lawyers, our teachers, have many problems to work any more.'

'I am a dentist,' said one man. 'I had many gentile patients. Now it is not so easy for me to treat them. They say: "Herr Doktor Hecht, you were the best dentist we ever went to. Now we are forced to go to a sadist, who only knows to pull, pull, pull".'

'Our children are not allowed to the universities,' said another. 'Only a small number.'

At this stage, one of the elders said: 'Please, gentlemen. This does no good. If anyone should hear...'

'You see,' said one of the younger ones. 'Herr Reichmann is right. Nothing can help us. If the foreign newspapers write about what is happening to the Jews, then the government says it is our fault. They make the laws but if anyone talks about it, they say this is spreading lies. We must suffer but not talk. We are hostages, sir.'

An elderly man threw up his hands: 'It will pass, it will pass. Soon, you will see, they will need the Jews again. Always, it happens: when they need money they turn to the Jews.'

One of the younger ones shrugged.

'This is what it's like nowadays. We can't even agree that we're in a terrible situation. One person says the Nazis will collapse because of outside pressure and the economy. Another says if only the boycott against Germany would stop, then Hitler would forgive the Jews. Some say we should run to Palestine. Some say we should stay here and wait, because after all we are Germans.'

The last phrase was said with heavy irony.

Yet again, in Berlin, I found there was nothing I could say. I knew that people with enough money or contacts were trying desperately to get out of the country. But it was not easy. The rest were indeed hostages.

One of the younger men accompanied me into the street and hissed in my ear: 'Please, talk about it in England, write about it. That is our only hope. The older ones think it will all blow over. We know it won't. Most of the young people now are Zionists. They see no other way.'

'And you?' I asked.

He showed me his white, smooth hands with a smile and told me he was, by profession, an accountant.

'You think I could be a farmer in the desert?' he asked.

I left Berlin two days later, without tracking Dr Bergsen and without finding any more clues about Dorothy. On the morning of my departure, Gregor Siegendorff returned from whatever he'd been up to. He greeted me with a smile and with a Hitler salute, which seemed almost self-mocking. He was wearing the black uniform and black leather jackboots of the SS.

He noted that I was staring at it, and said, still smiling: 'Chic, eh? So, you are leaving us?'

I nodded.

'It is a pity you were unable to find the friends you were looking for in Berlin,' he said, shaking his head in sorrow. 'How is it possible that people can just vanish in a city like this? If you would like to leave me their names, I will do my best to locate them.'

'That's very kind, but I wasn't looking for anyone in particular.'

I had told him nothing of my quest, but was not surprised that he knew of it.

'I hope you will soon return for a more leisurely visit,' he said. 'I would be honoured to show you what we have achieved.'

'Perhaps I will return some day.'

'That is good. We will always welcome our English friends to the new Germany.'

11

Yalta, February 6, 1945

On Tuesday, in the Crimea, I woke refreshed and optimistic. Perhaps I'd meet her today. I'd go to Winston and confess all, throw myself on his mercy. Perhaps he could charm Stalin into letting her leave!

It was our fourth day here. The villa and its gardens were beginning to feel almost like home. We were becoming acclimatised to – almost friendly with – our drivers, guards, waiters and chambermaids, and they were beginning to relax a little in our presence. I wondered if it was more scary to wait on Stalin than to attend a bunch of ideologically contagious foreigners.

My hopefulness dissipated as soon as I bumped into a frowning Sarah coming out of Winston's bedroom.

She gave me a hard look and said: 'You weren't being very straight with me yesterday, darling. About this love thing of yours. It's not all over, is it? It's here and now.'

I acknowledged this, and apologised.

'It's okay,' she responded, more sympathetically. 'I've been there myself. Anyway the cat's out of the bag now. He wants you. Be careful, Jimmy. I know when it's more than just a bark. He's roaring good and proper today.'

I knocked and went into the bedroom after getting a growl of admittance.

Winston was in bed, looking pink and healthy, and, from his expression, spoiling for a scrap. He glared at me over the top of his glasses and grunted: 'You are a very foolish young man.'

'Yes, Prime Minister.'

'And that is all you can offer by explanation? I have been apprised that you are engaged in, ah, contacts with, um, unauthorised Russian citizens. This has come as a grievous shock to me. Were you not questioned by the security people? Did you not inform them of this?'

'May I offer my explanation, Prime Minister?'

'Did you not consider it a courtesy to apprise me of the fact? Do even my personal staff go about this sort of business behind my back? Why was I kept in the dark like some elderly and incapacitated relative? Have you an explanation?'

'Yes, Prime Minister.'

'Go on, go on.'

'You may recall I was a correspondent in Moscow shortly before the war, covering among other things our efforts to reach some agreement with the Soviet government before it signed a pact with Hitler.'

I was instinctively using a flack-deflecting tactic perfected at school.

'I well recall those efforts,' Winston said. 'I had been urging such a course of action upon Mr Chamberlain and his ministers for some time. Much as I have always detested the Bolshevist creed, I was not as ignorant as some of my colleagues of the need to incorporate Russia in some kind of understanding, which would deter Hitler from aggression in Europe.'

Then, instead of being sidetracked into a lengthy recollection of his anti-appeasement battles of the thirties, as I hoped might happen, he suddenly stopped himself and said, with some regret, that he must not digress and that he was awaiting my explanation.

'I was obliged to make contacts, Prime Minister. It was essential to base my reports about Soviet intentions on the knowledge and insights of well-informed Russians.'

'I am very well aware, Mr Bexley, that a journalist is often only as good as his contacts,' Winston said impatiently. 'You need not elaborate. I myself have pursued that profession, and might still be doing so if Neville had stood up to that man in Berlin. Indeed, Max Beaverbrook has been good enough to advise me that if the electorate were to turn me out of office – which is by no means beyond the bounds of probability – I might still be able to command a not inconsiderable income through my scribbling.'

'I'm sure of that, Prime Minister.'

'But this is no time to discuss my abilities in your noble profession.'

'My former profession.'

'Precisely, Mr Bexley. Your former profession, and therefore in your current vocation do you not understand that such indiscretions, such contacts are sensitive matters that must be conveyed to the security services? Whichever contacts, of whatever gender, you consorted with in 1939 was your own business, and the business of your proprietor. But the situation now is somewhat different, is it not? You are an employee of His Majesty's government on active service, as it were, of a most delicate and sensitive nature. This conference will have great repercussions for the history of our country and of the world. Therefore, I ask again, did you not understand that you needed to report such a contact, at this time and in this place, to the security personnel? And, of course, to me?'

His knowledge of my personal and professional contacts in pre-war Moscow was unsurprising. What was disturbing was that someone had got wind of, and informed him of, the gist of my talks with Podbirski and, presumably, of the note I'd received.

I felt aggrieved – I felt I was being treated like an enemy – and was tempted to say to Winston that if only he'd let me get a word in edgeways I would tell him whatever he wanted to know. However, I knew it would be silly to upset him any further, and besides, it seemed clear that he was enjoying this lecture to me.

My next remark, though, was pretty stupid.

'I did understand, Prime Minister, but in mitigation, may I say it was a personal matter, and that the Russians are now our allies.'

Winston glared at me.

'Do not be impudent, young man. I am aware of our alliances, however difficult and perhaps transient they may be, and do not need reminding of them. As to the matter of your personal affairs, I am not ignorant of the unbridled emotions of the heart. I too was young once, difficult though it is in these trying times to remember such green and salad days with any great clarity. But, whatever your ardour, you have been foolish.'

'Yes, Prime Minister.'

'There are some who wish me to ship you back to London, forthwith, and preferably in shackles. The Chief of the Imperial General Staff is among those – and Field Marshal Brooke is not an insensitive soul. There is some merit in the idea, but I have argued against such drastic measures. I have mentioned that the easiest solution might be to put you on board the SS

Franconia at Sebastopol and instruct the captain to make you walk the plank.'

His eyes were twinkling as he rambled on, and I realised that he'd already forgiven me, even though he would still deliver a stern lecture.

His expression changed to one of deep regret.

'However, I have no desire to put myself in the category of a war criminal should such an order be carried out successfully. So, while I am not entirely satisfied with your actions, I have erred on the side of generosity to you. I have said that old men should not judge too harshly the innocent indiscretions of youth. Fortunately, I have still some influence, at least among those who serve His Majesty's government, and so my views have prevailed, for the present. But pray be careful, Mr Bexley, and remember this play is set in the Soviet Union, not in Verona. You may depart.'

'Thank you very much, Prime Minister,' I said with relief.

As I reached the door, Winston said: 'Ah, one more thing, Mr Bexley. Is there any reason to believe that the, um, object of your affections would do harm to you, or indeed to us?'

'No reason at all, Prime Minister.'

'I hope your confidence is not misplaced,' he said earnestly. 'Pray tell me, if I were to forbid you to see the young woman for the duration of this conference, would you abide my decision?'

It was a tricky moment. I was going to see her, if at all possible, whenever and wherever I could, regardless of the consequences.

'Is that a hypothetical question, sir?'

'You do not wish to give me an answer?' he said in an ominous tone.

'I cannot, Prime Minister.'

'What?' he thundered. 'You would contemplate disregarding my instructions?'

'As a member of your staff, I would never disobey any order given by you, Prime Minister,' I said, choosing my words very carefully.

He looked at me, and I thought he was trying to decide whether I was a disloyal ass or a devoted lover. But when he spoke, I realised he'd made his judgement before our conversation, and that I had merely confirmed it.

'Very well,' he said sternly. 'I have, after due consideration, decided that you should not be prohibited from pursuing this, um, contact. However, I presume you can assure me that you will not allow love to blind you to your allegiances to your country and your king?'

'Yes, Prime Minister. Nothing could blind me to those allegiances. Certainly not when my country is at war.'

He gazed at me intently.

'Very well, but be careful, James. Love is an admirable, indeed a necessary emotion, but it needs to be tempered with discretion. Remember not very much at this conference goes unnoticed. Not even a flirtation. There are eyes everywhere, ours, our friends', theirs.'

I assured him I would be careful and would do nothing to embarrass him. He nodded, returned to his documents and fluttered a delicate white hand to wave me away.

As I left the room and closed the door behind me, I heard him singing:

'Daisy, Daisy, give me your answer do.
I'm half crazy, all for the love of you...'

I breathed a sigh of relief. I took up the refrain and was singing it, softly, in his lisping manner as I walked through the dining-room.

'It won't be a shtylish marriage,
I can't afford a carriage.
But you'll look shweet, upon the sheat...'

The room was almost empty but Brooke was standing, cup of tea in his hand, gazing out through the window, probably on the lookout, as he often was, for some rare species of bird life. What he saw instead, as he swung round, was me, with a music hall song dribbling unfinished from my lips. He glared at me down his long, beakish nose. I smiled sheepishly. Winston had just told me that this most senior figure in the British armed forces (part of a formidable duo with the Prime Minister that had directed our military strategy for four critical years) had wanted me shipped out and court-martialled for the folly of befriending a foreign citizen at a time of war. Despite this, I admired Brooke. He was a brilliant, cold-eyed strategist and one of the few senior people prepared to stand up to Winston's ferocious wrath, giving as good as he got within the bounds of constitutional deference to his superior.

His response to my murmured greeting took me by surprise. He had obviously seen my security file.

'You were at Tobruk, Bexley?' he said. 'Bad business. Wounded, weren't you?'

'Just a graze, sir.'

'Really?' He looked puzzled.

'A bit more seriously later on,' I explained.

'Ah, yes. Do you enjoy bird watching?'

'I wish I'd found more time for it before the war, sir,' I lied.

'Make time, make time. It soothes the soul, it comforts the heart, to observe the grace and freedom of flight. It distracts one from the deep problems of warfare and personal issues. But it requires patience; waiting for the right moment.'

Then he drained his cup, set it on the table and walked off. I realised that Winston's judgement of the man was spot on and that Alan Brooke was a much more sensitive man than I had imagined.

Later, Sarah came up to me and said: 'I'm pleased you're still with us. I don't know exactly how or what they found out, but I suppose that's their job. I doubt if they'd have been too disturbed if you hadn't happened to be on Papa's private staff. They aren't the Gestapo, after all. Was the talk with Papa very trying?'

'He was very fair. Very understanding, actually, under the circumstances.'

'It must be your charm, darling. And the fact that he's a real softie about tricky love things – as long as it's not his own children involved. You should have heard him when I told them I wanted to marry Vic. My God, you'd have thought I was doing a Unity Mitford and falling for the Führer.'

'But they gave in, in the end.'

'They had to,' Sarah said with a sad smile. 'I eloped and it was such big news that Papa could hardly have horse-whipped poor old Vic and still survived in politics.'

I'd first met Sarah in New York eight years before when I covered her marriage to Vic after the headline-making elopement. By the time of Yalta, they had been separated for several years. She'd never talked to me about the workings of her marriage, and she wasn't going to do so now.

'Sarah, I'm sorry I couldn't tell you about this business,' I said. 'You can see, from all the fuss there is now, why I couldn't tell you?'

She nodded.

'You were right to keep it from me. I would've been duty bound to tell Papa. Mind you, it might have been a good idea for you to have told him before he found out about it from the sleuths.'

'I know. When we get a quiet moment, I'll tell you about her.'

'Better not, darling. Next thing you know, we'd be exchanging confidences. And that sort of thing can destroy an easy friendship, can't it? What's her name? No, don't tell me. I'm sure it is a beautiful name, a Chekhovian name. Anya or Nina or Natasha. What parts he gave his actresses! Did you know there used to be orchards all around here? Peaches and oranges. Before the beastly revolution. You ought to have your reunion in one of those.'

I smiled at her imagination.

'Have you seen her yet?' she asked.

'No. She managed to smuggle a note to me.'

Sarah's eyes widened.

'A note! Darling, how madly romantic!'

'It was brief and prosaic.'

'Are you longing to see her? I expect you are.'

'Longing and dreading.'

12

Yalta, February 6, 1945

Oh, Lucy, Lucy, Roosevelt thinks, I dream of Lucy with the light brown hair. Why might he not spend the years left to him with her? He's done his duty to family, party and state; grand times, painful times, burdensome times – but soon it will be all over and, God willing, peace will reign, and he can get the hell out of that Oval Office and go fishing, do all the reading he's had to put off, spend absorbed hours with his stamp collection at his Warm Springs cottage, spend more time with old friends, and with Lucy, who understands him with such delicacy and sensitivity.

In so many ways, he thinks, he has been granted what he wanted from life. Not even the polio has prevented him attaining his ambitions. He's won four presidential elections, four battles against mean-spirited opponents in a name-calling, dirty ritual that was, regrettably but enjoyably, the essence of democracy. No one has done that before and no one will in the future. It wouldn't be healthy for the Union, even though it was necessary in his case. No one else has the stored knowledge and resultant prescience to round this whole damn thing off satisfactorily. He's dragged America out of the Depression, prepared her for a necessary war and is transforming her into earth's paramount power, militarily, economically, morally. His mighty armies and their amazing, awesome new weaponry are remorselessly driving the Nazi bastards back and hammering the treacherous Japs. His scientists are tinkering with the energy of the universe itself to create a frightening means of deterring future war should it ever be necessary to do so. But he's confident it won't be necessary. He's building a Council of United Nations that will ensure a future free from war, and with God's grace that will be his enduring memorial.

He turns to the doleful man slumped beside him in an armchair at the Livadia.

'I've done my bit, haven't I, Harry?' he asks. 'For the country.'

His companion, Harry Hopkins, looking more cadaverous than ever, takes his time replying. Hopkins, who should never have made this trip and who, due to doctor's decree and his own ebbing energy, is spending most of the conference in his bedroom, never rushes into giving his opinion. Not even when the answer is obvious. But when he does give it, it's to the point, honest (sometimes painfully honest) and never, not even to the President, who had raised him to influence beyond compare, obsequious.

'None more so,' he says eventually.

He has never admired anyone as much as he admires Roosevelt. He doesn't love the guy. Franklin's too elusive for love, but he would die for him.

'And you too, Harry,' says FDR. 'And I could not have done it without you. That's for sure. From the start in Washington we took on all comers, and, by heck, we've licked the lot. Those who hated the New Deal, and those who wanted us to stick our heads in the sand, Republicans, isolationists, Hitler and, let's hope soon, Tojo. That's not a bad haul, Harry.'

He chuckles.

Hopkins smiles. This is more like the old Roosevelt. As crafty a politician as ever outfoxed his opponents and manoeuvred his supporters. The President might be nearing the end – well, for fuck's sake, they both damn well might be – but he has enough steam in him for one last hurrah.

'And I want to get back home and tell everyone that we've got agreement on the world body, and kept Uncle Joe in line,' the President says, more or less to himself. 'It's going to have to be one hell of a speech. They'll be baying for my blood. You and I are going to have to draft it together. Just like the old times.'

Hopkins doesn't listen closely. He doesn't have to. He knows the man's mind better than his own sometimes. He closes his eyes and savours the sun on his gaunt face. There's no need to say anything more. If the Chief wants him to say something, he'll ask for it. He thinks of this President proclaiming victory to the nation, in a matter of months rather than years, using words that will sing to the people of their endeavours and the bravery of their troops. He thinks of the bravery of his own serving sons. He thinks of Stephen. Just another kid dying in action in the Pacific. But *his* kid. Not yet 19. At his age, I was still an Iowa boy going into college at Grinnell and beginning to see just what my worth was. And now Stephen is dead and I have only half a stomach and when Barbara died I thought life was not worth living. Then I met Louise and our marriage has been three years of joy. What did she see in me, a broken down, battered old war horse with a Sad Sack face? Whatever it was, she loves me and I wish I were back in Georgetown with her right now.

Then he realises the implications of FDR's casual mention of the speech.

Goddamit, I'm too sick for all that. This damn conference is going to just about finish me off on its own.

'I don't think I'm going to be able to help with that speech,' he mutters. 'I've got to go straight to the Mayo from here. More treatment. Maybe they can find out exactly what it is.'

The President doesn't indicate that he has heard this. His mind has by now swung back from political and military triumphs and memorials to linger again on Lucy Mercer Rutherford. Yes, of course he respects his wife Eleanor, and the children. He has a working political relationship with Eleanor. They're a team. Eleanor keeps him on the moral straight and narrow. But Lucy. That's different. She has been his ideal throughout the long years they've lived separate lives and repressed the passion between them. Now, with her husband dead, they have another chance. Why could they not have some shared happiness? Damn it, why not? As soon as he gets back from this business, he'll ask her to Warm Springs. Eleanor won't come, won't know. Oh, those lovely evenings of easy chat with Lucy, and he'll bring his cousin Laura, his dear friend Daisy, and Grace of course, who is so much more a friend than just a secretary. Why not? Oh, bliss, to be away from scheming men and the machinations of the powerful and the malevolence of the tyrants, and to be in the soft, sympathetic company of women. He dozes, and wakes to remark on Churchill's Yalta abode.

'Can you beat that, Harry? They tell me old Winston's got something fit for a caliph. Fit for the Grand Protector of the Empire. I guess it'll please his vanity.'

Hopkins grunts. He feels a touch of nausea. The drugs they push into him. He doesn't like the way the Chief sometimes treats Winston these days. Harry was in London during the Blitz in 1941. FDR had sent him to size up Churchill. Harry was cautious to begin with; he didn't like big talkers. But once he got to know the guy ... well, this man had such force about him, such drive and determination. Shit, if the Nazis had invaded Britain, Churchill would have grabbed a tommy-gun, stuck out his chin and gone to a fighting death with a song on his lips. He might have been pompous on occasion, but by God he was a fighter. It must be his American blood that made him so damn, fuck-you-all pugnacious. So when FDR these days kind of sniggered about Winston and handled him like a has-been – well, that was sad, because Winston was a great man. A great man in an age of incompetent minnows, especially in pre-war Europe when they let that sonofabitch Hitler do exactly as he liked. And even after the war was on, there were some yellow bastards in England who'd have been prepared to throw in the towel in exchange for any half decent set of peace terms, like the French had done – that difficult bugger de Gaulle excepted – in 1940. So, thank God for Winston and never mind that Roosevelt and Stalin are ganging up against him. And the President's treatment of Winston – after all they've done together, comrades in arms against the enemy, soul mates, almost – is doubly sad because FDR too was a great man and Harry, despite all he's seen and known, remains a romantic deep down and believes great men should behave chivalrously.

'Welcome, Winston,' Roosevelt says as he greets a beaming Winston, hope in the old boy's eyes that this visit will signify a great reconciliation. 'Good to have a chance for a chat. I'm told they've put you up in style.'

'It purports to some grandeur,' Churchill concedes. 'But, my dear friend, were it not for the delight of your company and for the momentous negotiations we are undertaking here, I would gladly forego all that display for a bench in the garden of Chartwell gazing at the weald of Kent.'

Roosevelt smiles thinly. Why does Winnie always have to overdo it?

Churchill greets Hopkins with warmth, placing a hand on his shoulder.

'My dear Harry.'

The eyes glisten with affection, but there is also concern in them that this wonderfully able, publicly unsung man should be in such terrible health.

Hopkins manages a grin. Unlike the Chief, he still enjoys Winston's company. And he can detect the anxiety in the Prime Minister's person. It almost makes him want to weep. Not for his health, damn it, but for Stephen. He remembers – he has never forgotten – the scroll that Churchill sent him after the boy's death. From Macbeth:

Your son, my lord, has paid a soldier's debt:
He only liv'd but till he was a man...
But like a man he died.

Jesus, how he'd wept when he got that. What would all his enemies, all those sonofabitch reactionaries who hated him more than they hated even the President, have said if they could have seen him crying over his dead US Marine kid? Would they have wept with him or would they have said: 'So what, one more boy gone? They all die too young.' And they'd have been right to say that, Hopkins thinks. Too many, and too young. Let's get this goddam war over before another million or so of our kids die. FDR is right, as always. Never mind sentiment, never mind the Poles, never mind Winston's sensibilities. Let's keep our eye on the ball. Let's make sure Stalin comes in on our side against the fucking Japs. Let's hope that goddam bomb they're working on at Los Alamos gets built and we can use it on Tokyo. He's heard encouraging things about progress on that bomb, but you can't bank on something like that working, and you can't bank on it being ready in time.

The lunch goes well, on the surface, at least. Winston tries to prod Roosevelt into some substantive agreements, but the old fox won't be drawn into any remotely detailed discussions. If Stalin got a whiff of any collusion against him, it could blow everything. Stalin is so goddam paranoid that he reckons a handshake between two of his allies means a conspiracy against him.

Hopkins watches the whole lunchtime comedy, during which he eats hardly anything and drinks some warm milk, with a sardonic interior smile. The two greatest statesmen of their time behaving like a couple of kids! Franklin Roosevelt refusing to be Winston Churchill's best buddy; and Winston so pathetically eager to be back again in Franklin's sunshine that he'll promise almost anything.

Franklin has again brought up his United Nations dream, which he wants Winston to endorse wholeheartedly. A world policed by its countries acting in democratic council. Winston is lukewarm about it all. Despite his fine words yesterday in defence of smaller powers, he is an imperialist. He has no desire to go cap in hand before a bunch of foreign rulers for permission on how to run the Empire.

FDR says that the UN is vital to maintaining peace because he doubts whether Congress would approve keeping American troops in Europe for more than two years at most after the end of the war.

Winston looks as though he's been struck a cruel blow. At the dinner last night, he'd believed this threat was uttered merely to bolster the case for making France a working power in the occupation of Germany.

Hopkins has sympathy for the rejection Winston must be feeling and for his yearning to be back in FDR's bosom. He, too, has had a spell in the cold, and although he's back in favour now, he wonders – as he has often wondered – what it is about Roosevelt that makes him need to play fast and loose even with those who love him the most, like Winston and Hopkins himself?

It's a character flaw, Hopkins thinks, perhaps going back to a lonely childhood, a desire to control stemming from an inability to believe he could be loved simply because of himself and not because of his connections and his trappings. But Harry can't help admiring the way the President is playing this whole conference in the same way as he plays politics at home: keeping colleagues and allies in separate rooms of information, each unsure of what he is telling the others, everyone kept in deliberate darkness about his grand strategy. Or is it just that the Chief is too sick to put himself to all the trouble of tough bargaining, especially with Winston? It's possible that FDR may feel he doesn't have too much time left and that it's best not to devote too much energy canoodling with burnt-out old cronies.

And, Jesus, thinks Harry, I know exactly how he feels. The carpet of time is rolling up on both of us.

13

Yalta, February 6, 1945

'Take away their troops!' Winston spluttered. 'He threatened that. Does he not realise that this would leave all of Europe at the mercy of Stalin and his armies? Will our small island once more stand alone against the military might of a voracious giant?'

He paced around his room, muttering darkly, not requiring any response from me or Sawyers – who was struggling to dress him – or Sarah who raised her eyebrows to the heavens and made some soothing sounds.

'I am sure, Papa, that the President was just having a little fun,' she said. 'It was naughty, but...'

'Naughty?' Winston shouted. 'This is not some, some schoolroom or some, some stage rehearsal. This concerns the fate of nations.'

Fortunately, Anthony arrived to calm him down. I heard the Foreign Secretary say as Sarah and I fled the room: 'I thought you understood, Winston, that it strengthens the case for a strong France.'

I travelled to the Livadia with Anthony and gathered that Winston, once he had cooled down, remained sure the President deep down believed that Britain was America's greatest and most reliable ally. The Prime Minister, in his calm moments, did not share the view of some that Roosevelt had by now decided to throw his lot in wholeheartedly with the Soviet Union as the Big Two inheritors of the earth.

'What is your assessment, Foreign Secretary?' I asked.

I wasn't sure whether he'd heard me or whether he did not deign to answer so presumptuous a question. He sat for some minutes staring out at the passing scenery.

'I would not speak in these terms in public,' he said eventually. 'However, my private estimation is that President Roosevelt has decided that the post-war world will in effect be run by America and Russia – though in the context of a workable global organisation, not an imitation of the League of Nations.'

'And where would that leave us?' I asked.

'A good question, Bexley, and one that is exercising the Prime Minister. I don't believe the President even remotely believes Britain can be discarded as an important player. As I pointed out to Winston, the Americans would in no way want us to be a weak partner in Europe. They will give us what we need to stay strong. They are not perhaps as gloomy as I am about the intentions of Stalin, but neither are they naïve in that regard.'

Then he changed the subject.

'Charming place, Yalta, is it not?' he said. 'These vistas are quite exceptional. And the Russians are excellent hosts, as they always are.'

He turned a dazzling smile on me, a broad, open smile beneath his manicured mouth-long moustache. It lit his face with honesty. I could see why women fell for him. You could trust this smile. It wouldn't let you down.

'You've been with the P.M. how long?' he asked. 'Two years?'

'Just over that.'

'Action at Tobruk and then Alamein, I gather?'

I nodded.

'Good show. Quite recovered from your wounds, I take it?'

'Yes, Foreign Secretary.'

'Terrible show Tobruk. We were all shocked, even Winston, especially Winston. The double blow, Singapore going without a fight and then Tobruk. Bad times. You managed to escape before the garrison surrendered?'

The flight from Rommel's army was one of those occasions when I found myself praying for divine assistance to rescue me from the never ending bombardment and panzer attacks. But I'd survived almost unscathed from that. The more serious wound had come later, at a time of victory in the Western Desert.

'I was lucky, Foreign Secretary.'

'Most people would call it pluck, Bexley. I knew your father, by the way. Plucky chap too.'

I was surprised. Douglas had never mentioned this connection.

'Where did you meet him, sir?' I asked deferentially.

'France,' he said vaguely. 'Fine men. We lost the flower over there. That's why we got into another shooting match, you know. The fellows who were taken in by Hitler, because they dreaded another war, weren't the chaps who'd been through it all before. Those of us who'd been through it all – who knew what war meant, all the horror – we were the ones who understood you had to be strong if you wanted to prevent another war. Baldwin, Chamberlain and the rest never grasped that.

'Once we got into it, of course, we all pulled together. More or less. And now most of the world is in it, on our side. Even Russia, for the moment. Wonderful coalition, is it not? Not without its hitches, but if we all saw eye to eye, we wouldn't need to build alliances; they would simply be there.'

He smiled again, near-perfect teeth showing. The smile we saw in the newsreels even when he was negotiating with intransigent partners like de Gaulle and Molotov. Now it was turned on me.

'One of the first things one learns in active diplomacy,' he went on, 'is that your partners never show you all their cards. Just as we don't show them ours. So we have to have ways of finding out things. To maintain that balance between support for our allies and upholding our basic principles.'

He paused, his eyes searching into mine.

'You, for instance, with all your journalistic skills, you have a nose for what is relevant. You glean things.'

This rang alarm bells with me. I nodded, but said nothing.

'Good!' he said briskly. 'As I say to my own staff: Keep your eyes and ears open, use your common sense. Standard procedure, really. Let us know if you glean things.'

I must have looked troubled, for he added in smoothly reassuring tones: 'I am merely suggesting you do what your conscience tells you. Nothing more.'

We had reached the entrance to the Livadia. Anthony glanced at his watch and out of the car window as our fleet of Packards drove through the densely patrolled gardens. Our limousine pulled up in the front courtyard. Anthony opened the door to get out, then shut it and again turned his charming smile on me, the same expression that made young girls and matrons alike swoon; the Eden touch.

'I enjoyed our little talk, Bexley. We must do it again.'

I watched him walk off, followed by three or four deferential aides, and thought: You mean, I must be sure to tell you the gist of my conversations here. I had no doubt of what was behind his approach. He and Winston had decided to handle me with kid gloves rather than put me in the grip of military intelligence, who would demand information, not simply request it. I was being given preferential treatment – presumably for as long as I played the game with them. Or perhaps I was being as paranoid as Ed.

There was time before the start of the afternoon meeting for me to walk in the gardens, a bit overgrown here and there, though that added to the grandeur, but elsewhere trimmed to perfection. I marvelled at the great, brooding cypresses. I returned to the palace and stood on the patio outside the reception room. I could see clear across to Yalta bay, its green hills dotted with villas of the pre-revolutionary great and rich. Among them was the house where Chekhov wrote *The Three Sisters* and *The Cherry Orchard*. I would have loved to stroll along the esplanade where solid nineteenth-century terraces fronted the shining blue waters of the Black Sea, but it was off-limits to us. Stalin did not allow foreigners to snoop around.

Yalta had been a fashionable spa resort of carriages, bandstands and dashing military uniforms in Tsarist times. I wondered how badly battered it was now, how many malnourished children and dogs scavenged the streets. It was impossible to tell from where I stood. From here, it seemed as splendid and tranquil as it had ever been in the imagined past. Distance lends enchantment in more than one sense.

In a story I'd been reading, 'Lady With the Toy Dog', Chekhov conveyed the ambivalent mood of two lovers sitting on a bench.

> Yalta was hardly visible through the morning mist. The tops of the hills were shrouded in motionless white clouds. The leaves of the trees never stirred, the cicadas trilled, and the monotonous dull sound of the sea, coming up from below, spoke of the rest, the eternal sleep awaiting us.

Recalling that passage, I had to shake myself out of a feeling of depression and foreboding.

* * *

In the reception hall, delegates were chatting animatedly, like country house guests arriving for a weekend of conviviality.

Podbirski waddled up and greeted me warmly.

'Ah, Jimmy, you enjoy the Crimea, yes?'

'It has its charms, Anatoly,' I said warily, wondering who was watching and listening to this exchange.

'But something is lacking?' he teased.

'Everything's just fine.'

'Your stomach has accustomed to the food? Is very rich, no?'

'It isn't what we're used to in Britain.'

This was by and large true, although the rich and powerful still dined amply back home.

'Is too rich for wartime stomachs,' he said, patting his ample tummy. 'Imagine, there is much fighting not so far from here, soldiers are dying, people are starving, and here we are eating like kings.'

'It's a sacrifice.'

'Yes,' he smiled. 'Sometimes, is too much of sacrifice. Yesterday, one of our interpreters becomes sick. Eats too much of the rich food, they say. Such agony the poor man suffers.'

'That's too bad.'

'Yes,' he said sadly. 'Too bad for the man, too bad for Valdimir Nikolayevich.'

He pointed at Pavlov, the chief interpreter.

'I hope it wasn't him? He looks well enough now.'

'No, no. One of his deputies. A man like him must have deputies, in case of long meetings, in case of ... other problems.'

'Of course,' I said. 'So they've brought on the twelfth man?'

'Excuse?'

'An English joke, Anatoly. Sorry.'

'I like how you English always can laugh. In Battle of Britain even, I believe, even when you know Germans may invade next week, you make jokes.'

'That's why we're winning the war,' I said. 'Superior sense of humour.'

'Yes. So, they need to find another, how you say, next in line, for the team of interpreters. You know, Jimmy, like for when actor is too sick to go on stage.'

'An understudy.'

The penny had begun to drop.

131

'Understudy, yes,' he smiled. 'They need understudy. But Moscow too far away. Then I remember in Odessa is interpreter visiting friend. So they send for her.'

Much as I tried to control my feelings, something must have shown in my face.

'Is interesting story, yes, Jimmy,' Podbirski said. 'Now I must go talk with some comrades in the corner behind you. You look to see.'

I turned and *did* see her, in uniform, holding a notebook, looking at the floor. After all these years, to see her again! Overcome, I could only look, stare and struggle to suppress my emotion. She must have glimpsed me as I swung round, for I noted a small flush on her cheeks, though she still looked downwards. I turned back to Podbirski.

'I go now, Jimmy,' he said. 'Have a good day, as American friends say. Tomorrow maybe I tell you about beautiful walk in Livadia gardens. You should not miss.'

Then he wandered off to join the group of his comrades.

She was not present at the session, which was the most momentous yet. The preliminaries were over. What to do with Germany, how to ransack her, whether to give France a meaningful say in the heart of Europe, how the United Nations should be run – these had been a prelude to the real business. The burning issue was Poland and, beyond Poland, all of eastern Europe at the mercy of Stalin. Nothing less than the fate of the post-war world was at stake.

This was the main show, and here I was mired in a personal problem of no relevance to the world's future, an insignificant detail blurred by the morning mist.

A log fire blazed in the huge fireplace, warming the bones of Roosevelt, as the meeting convened around the circular table. Stalin and Winston wore military uniforms. FDR did not.

Winston immediately pounced on Roosevelt's comments on how long American forces would stay in Europe, saying: 'Great Britain alone will not be strong enough to guard the western approaches to the Channel.'

Hopkins whispered something to FDR who nodded and said: 'Pulling our boys back in a few years was a thought, no more.

It's what people back home will want once the fighting in Europe is over.'

He implied that this attitude might change if the United Nations got off the ground, and said that if it *did*, there could be world peace for at least 50 years.

Winston said the UN would work if provisions were made for all countries to state their grievances frankly.

'If this is not done, it will look as if the great powers are trying to rule the world.'

'Perhaps Mr Churchill will clarify what powers he had in mind when he speaks of a desire to rule the world,' Stalin said caustically. 'Does he have the Union of Soviet Socialist Republics in mind?'

Winston reddened. Anthony pushed him a note that said 'Mollify him!'

Winston puffed out a column of aromatic smoke and said: 'I was speaking about we three great powers collectively who could place ourselves so high above the others that the world would say, These three desire to rule. Please translate that very carefully, Mr Pavlov. I was describing how a hypothetical situation might be perceived in the world.'

He swung round to Anthony and added in a stage whisper: 'Did I do that right, Anthony?'

'Perfectly,' murmured an abashed Eden.

'Listen,' said Stalin, leaning forward as though about to impart some confidential personal information, 'there is a more serious question than this so-called domination of the world. We all know that as long as the three of us live, none of us will act aggressively to the others.'

Winston and FDR nodded sagely.

'But, after all, ten years from now, none of us might be present. There will be a new generation, knowing nothing of war. We have to create, for this new generation, the kind of organisation that, as my friend the President has said, will truly secure peace for at least fifty years.'

'I agree,' said Winston.

'Well, at least we all agree on *something*,' said Roosevelt drily.

No one laughed, but his mild witticism brought the discussion round to what had always loomed as the big stumbling block – the Polish question.

We sat a little straighter in our chairs.

Stalin stared at a piece of paper in front of him, and doodled incessantly on it in red ink. He seemed to be drawing pictures of wild animals.

Roosevelt said: 'I would like to see a representative Polish government, which will have the support of all the great powers, and will, naturally, maintain friendly and cooperative relations with the Soviet Union.'

'Not only with the Soviet Union,' Stalin interjected, without looking up from his art work. 'But with the other allies as well.'

Winston said: 'Great Britain went to war in 1939 to protect Poland against German aggression. It is therefore a question of honour that we will never be content with a solution that fails to establish her as a free and independent state.'

He wanted agreement that Poland should have an interim government, including exiled leaders living in London, to function until elections could be held.

Stalin, who had already installed an interim government made up of reliable Polish Communists, stopped his doodling, leaned back in his seat and spoke with a soft, reasonable voice. 'I can understand the Prime Minister saying Poland is a question of honour for his country. But for Russia, it is a question of both honour *and* security. Throughout history Poland has been the corridor for attacks on Russia.'

Then, he suddenly became thunderously indignant.

'Twice during the last thirty years,' he rapped out, shaking his fist, 'Germany has marched through this corridor onto our Russian soil!'

'I've been through all these tricks before,' Winston whispered to Anthony. 'One minute he's all sweetness, the next hectoring and rude.'

'Now, regarding the Polish government, it must have been a slip of the tongue when Mr Churchill said we should create it at Yalta,' Stalin said with a feral smile. 'I am called a dictator, but I have enough democratic feelings to refuse to create a government without the Poles agreeing to it. So what I want to have explained is: How could it be expected that those who stayed behind in Poland to fight the Nazis will allow those who ran off to exile in London to join a government?'

He claimed that Red Army troops in Poland were being attacked by anti-Soviet 'agents'.

Winston rejected the implication that the exiled Poles were behind the attacks and said: 'I agree that anyone who attacks the Red Army must be punished, but *we* get different views of what is going on. Who knows which report is correct?'

Roosevelt called an adjournment before a heated argument could develop over this.

I had opted for the last possible vehicle to return to the Vorontsov, hoping Podbirski might appear with more news.

While I was waiting, Ed came stomping out of Roosevelt's study area where there had been a briefing for delegation staff. He caught sight of me.

'It's as bad as I said. That asshole is prepared to give everything up.'

I protested jocularly that this was no way to talk about Winston.

'Not him,' said Ed without a smile.

What had happened to the quick wit and sense of humour that Ed had possessed in our Cambridge years?

'The asshole is my President. Frankly, you guys aren't in a position to do anything much. Roosevelt *is*. So what does he say to Stalin? It would make it easier for him at home if the Ruskies could return some territory in the east that used to belong to Poland. Jesus, does he think Stalin gives a damn about public opinion, either in the US or in the USSR? Then, he's so conciliatory that I am fucking sure he's going to...'

I cut him short by putting my hand to my lips and writing on a scrap of paper: 'Do you think we're being bugged?'

'Possibly,' he said loudly.

'Then why weaken FDR's case?' I murmured.

He scribbled his reply furiously: 'Because it has to be said. Because it might do some good if they understand that we're not all feeble-minded cripples. OK?'

Then he said out loud: 'Like I said, my boss, whom I hero-worshipped once, is no longer the man he was. That's not only my view. I guess a dying man doesn't look too far beyond his own death. You think I'm disloyal, right? Well I'm not disloyal to what he stood for once upon a time. But now all he has are obsessions. The United Nations. A good thing as far as it goes, probably. A lot of guys in State, like Hiss, are big on that. First, though, we got to sort out the realities.'

'We all want some kind of new order,' I said.

'The other thing is that he's desperate for Stalin to come in against the Japs as soon as we've finished off Adolf. Okay, it would be nice to have his help, but I'm damn sure we can lick those little bastards on our own.'

'It's been a long day, Ed.'

'You can't see it, Jim. Stalin's the real enemy. You're too goddam trusting. Winston can see it – Eden certainly can – but they won't pressure Roosevelt.'

I let my eyes flicker around. Podbirski had still failed to appear.

'I have to go. Ed,' I said and began walking rapidly towards my car. 'Anyway, right now, Stalin's our ally against Hitler. We need him.'

Ed strode beside me, trying to get in as many words as possible.

'Hitler's over. He's history. Kaput! It's the next goddam war I'm talking about. The next evil bastard we have to fight. This man we call Uncle Joe, who is simply the greatest cynic of all time. Churchill knows that, I think. It may not help, but he should understand that he's got to convince Roosevelt. No one else can.'

'I'll be sure to tell him,' I said.

He frowned at me as I got into the car. Levity no longer amused him.

A few hours later, it became clear that whatever Ed might think, FDR was not ready to sell out Poland. A letter to Stalin, which the President had drafted, was brought to the Vorontsov for our consideration. It made clear that, like Winston, Roosevelt would *not* recognise Uncle Joe's stooge government.

Winston and Anthony pored over the draft. I heard Winston purr with pleasure.

Anthony said: 'It's on the right lines, yes, but the tone needs stiffening. The tone is as important as the message in these matters.'

He made some changes and the amended letter was taken back to the President.

Winston settled in an armchair, whisky in one hand, uninhaled Cuban in his mouth.

'The night is young,' he beamed. 'Let us spend a little time discussing the road ahead in Yalta, pray.'

Anthony glanced ostentatiously at his watch.

'I doubt it's going to be a long road,' he remarked, stifling a yawn. 'I gather the President intends to spend no more than five or six days here in all, Winston. We're into the fourth.'

Winston blinked in annoyance.

'Where did you hear that?' he growled. 'I cannot believe that. Even God took seven days to create the world.'

No one said anything for a few seconds. It seemed the last word had been spoken. Then Anthony drawled: 'I'm not much of a Bible student myself, but I thought the Almighty actually finished all the necessary work on the sixth day.'

Winston glared at him, and stomped off to bed.

'Or so the communiqué states,' Anthony said softly, a small smile of triumph on his lips.

14

Cambridge

I returned from my visit to Berlin full of anger, and toyed with joining the Communist Party despite all my misgivings. In 1934, many Cambridge Reds were slowly waking up to reality and spoke openly of taking an active and belligerent stand against fascism. What were my scruples weighed against the overall need to fight the greatest evil of the day? Yet I still felt unable to be blindly obedient to decrees from on high.

I would have discussed it with Ed, but he'd gone to the States and wrote that he was undecided about coming back to Cambridge – 'I'm caught up in things here.'

I went to see Douglas and explained, as best I could, my political paralysis.

He puffed at his pipe.

'You're searching for some kind of over-arching goodness to justify a moral stance. The trouble with goodness, though, is that it's so elusive. One never knows for certain whether it's there or not.'

'At times, Douglas, talking to you is like consulting the Delphic Oracle. I come for advice, and you point the way into a mist.'

'Hardly a mist,' he laughed. 'The signposts are visible. But it's not for me to choose your way. You'll find it yourself.'

'Would you be unhappy if I went all the way to the Left?'

'My unhappiness or otherwise is irrelevant. Are you a Marxist?'

'I'm not. But they're the only ones who seem to be doing anything.'

'Decent chaps, some Marxists,' he sighed. 'I can't be your guide. Your father would have told you to be guided by conscience, though he might have phrased it differently. He may have said: "Do the honourable thing." Does that help?'

'Perhaps, Douglas. I'm grateful to you for listening.'

'And I'm grateful to you for not asking what *I'd* do in your shoes.'

His comments helped settle my thoughts. The enemy was on the march in our own backyard. Mosley's fascist movement gained popularity and had influential support. The *Daily Mail* screamed 'Hurrah for the Blackshirts!' I needed to do something concrete.

Political and moral dilemmas were not the only things on my mind. I was worried about Dorothy and about Dr Bergsen. In addition, my love affair with Gwen was getting complicated. To please her, I went for a weekend visit to meet her parents. We avoided politics. Her mother spoke of gardening and of how difficult it was to teach the maid to cook properly. Her father took me golfing at his club. Gwen and I were happy whenever we were alone with each other. Sitting in the garden in a peaceful, semi-rural atmosphere, I felt relaxed enough to mention Dorothy to her for the first time, and my fears for Dorothy's safety.

'And that's why you went to Germany at Christmas,' she said. 'To find her.'

'Partly. I still don't know if she's dead or alive.'

'Are you in love with her?'

'There's never been anything between us except friendship.'

'But you'd *like* there to be something. Why don't you just go off and look for her in Russia or wherever she is,' she said, close to tears.

I took her in my arms. After a small struggle, she allowed herself to be embraced. When I kissed her, she responded with surprising passion.

'Did you kiss her like that?' she asked.

'No,' I said, grateful not to have to lie any more.

She led me to the house and up the stairs to her bedroom. I was bowled over by the femininity of it all, the pastel colours, the quilted bedspread, the teddy bear on her pillow. We sat on her bed. I kissed her neck and opened her blouse. When I put my hand on her breast, she gave a sigh of pleasure. There was a knock on the door.

'Darling, are you in there?' asked her mother's voice.

Gwen jumped up, buttoned up her blouse, straightened her hair, rolled her eyes at me and said: 'Yes, mummy. Jimmy and I are having a heart to heart.'

There was silence from outside the door. Then her mother said: 'It's lovely in the garden.'

We could hear her walking away.

'Better go outside,' said Gwen.

We kissed again.

'I think I love you,' she said, big eyes looking at me for a reciprocal avowal.

'Gwen, I love being with you,' I said.

She smiled, but I could see I'd hurt her.

'I'll go and help with lunch,' she said, leaving me sitting on her bed.

When I came down the stairs, she was standing at the living-room window looking out at the sparrows hopping on the lawn. I put my arms around her. She allowed me to do so, but stood like a statue.

I left after lunch and she waved me off with a detached smile.

That afternoon, I wrote her a letter apologising for being stupidly selfish, and saying that every moment with her was bliss and that I desperately wanted to go on seeing her. She did not reply. After a week, I phoned her.

'I'm sorry for sounding cold-hearted in your room,' I said. 'It's not really how I feel. I *do* love you.'

'You were rather beastly. I wasn't expecting you to get down on your knees and ask for my hand. All I wanted was you to say you felt the same about me.'

'I know, Gwen. And I do.'

'Is that a proposal?' she asked playfully.

When I didn't answer, she said without rancour: 'You're an idiot, Bexley. Can't you tell when I'm ribbing you? You're too young for marriage. I know that. But why does it frighten you so?'

'The responsibility. The idea of setting up a household, children, all that.'

'I bet you wouldn't mind setting up a household with Dorothy.'

'Honestly, I wouldn't mind it with *you*,' I said. 'So can we spend the next few years discussing the idea?'

'I'd like that.'

We reached a tacit agreement that we would not sleep together. In some ways I was relieved, because I feared landing in a space without an exit. I suspected that she had come to the conclusion that since I was unlikely ever to be her husband we had better avoid sex. My suspicions seemed confirmed when she said casually one evening that perhaps we should each be free to go out with other people.

'I don't want to go out with anyone else,' I protested.

'Neither do I, specifically. But I don't know what to say when mother pesters me about the future. She's always threatening to invite some man or other down for the weekend, and I've run out of excuses.'

As I couldn't provide her with the excuse she needed – an engagement ring – I had to agree to this new arrangement.

I spent more time on my own. Her parents, meanwhile, dredged up a variety of potential suitors as weekend houseguests. I was miserable, and I sensed Gwen was too.

Ed eventually returned, less ebullient than before. He professed still to be a fervent supporter of Roosevelt and the New Deal but he wondered if the Administration could – or indeed wanted to – change society in radical ways.

'I thought there *were* changes,' I said.

'There are some. Hopkins wants to do something new – making jobs for the unemployed, rather than just giving them relief.

'Sounds a pretty good idea.'

'Yeah, but it's not going to change society fundamentally. The rich will still get rich and the poor poorer. Roosevelt's a great man in many ways, but he's a compromiser and he's already more concerned with getting re-elected than with ending the problems we've got. The people don't want empty promises. They want action now. Jobs for the unemployed is a start, but we still have all the injustices of race, poverty and the like.'

'Can any politician end all the injustices?' I asked.

'That's one hell of a big question. I reckon maybe, yes, a visionary could do it, politician or not. It needs someone tough, even ruthless.'

'A dictator?'

'That's a bad word, buddy, but the sort of so-called democracy we have sure as hell ain't working.'

Though I was uneasy about the direction he was taking, our friendship remained good. We could argue intensely over politics, get drunk, laugh loudly at the foibles of our families, friends and the world around us.

* * *

'I'm going to Olympia,' I told Gwen one balmy evening in June as we walked hand-in-hand along a towpath next to the Cam. 'Would you come along?'

She looked confused. Not to Greece, I explained, but to demonstrate at a mass meeting Mosley was holding at the exhibition hall in Olympia, west London.

'Well, try not to get your fat head bashed about,' she pouted.

I said such an occurrence might improve my looks.

'It might,' she smiled. 'But I've grown to like you the way you are, Bexley.'

'Would you like to come with me?' I repeated.

'I'd love to,' she said, wrinkling her nose. 'Only, Binky Cooper-Downs is coming to stay for a few days, so I can't leave just like that.'

'Binky?'

'It's a family nickname. They can afford to do things like that. Pots of money. They're very well connected.'

'Sounds like the sort of chap you ought to marry.'

'Don't be ridiculous!'

'Half of Cambridge will be at Olympia. You could come. It's important.'

'I know it is,' she sighed.

'This is how all those blonde German maidens reacted when there was a chance of breaking up a Nazi meeting. "Ach, we have more important things to do".'

'Mosley isn't another Hitler, Jimmy. He's a clown. And this isn't Germany.'

'I'm not suggesting anything improper. I'd just like you to be in London with me.'

'Why?'

'For your company,' I said, kissing her.

'You make me want to melt, Bexley. But, honestly, I can't.'

I felt jealous and wretched.

Ed wasn't going to Olympia either.

'Can't afford to be recognised there,' he winked. 'Don't want to get deported.'

To get into the cavernous exhibition hall, one had to look like a fascist supporter. This wasn't difficult because Mosley, who'd been one of the great hopes of the Left only a few years earlier, was attracting followers from all walks of life. There must have been well over 10,000 people inside the hall. Many were working class, but others – a surprisingly large number – wore evening dress. The upper-crust swells had a class allegiance to Mosley, seeing him as someone who could help preserve their privileges against a tide of egalitarianism.

Outside the hall there were scuffles between Communist protesters and Mosleyites. I saw mounted police surround and arrest a young man in a shabby suit who continued shouting anti-fascist slogans as he was dragged off. His cloth cap lay in the street, trampled upon. Another chap ripped a fascist poster from a wall and began tearing it up until attacked by Blackshirt toughs. He got away after a short struggle.

The meeting took some time to get started. The delay heightened the tension. Union flags and fascist ones waved as a band whipped up emotions with marches and patriotic tunes. Our homemade fascists had obviously learned some stagecraft from Goebbels. Then, in strutted Mosley, trying to look authoritarian and ruthless, unable to conceal his self-satisfaction. Loud cheering, but also some booing. Finally, in the glare of spotlights, he began speaking, upper-class accent and without the hoarse passion of Hitler.

It might have been comical – this posturing former playboy of the Left trying to look like the Great British leader – except that his message held so much danger. Gwen had called him a clown, but this was an age in which murderous buffoons like Mussolini and Hitler were already ruling important countries.

Constant heckling punctuated his speech. His thugs quickly surrounded hecklers to eject them forcibly. Their brutality was met with some fairly rough responses. 'Down with fascism!' I yelled in one moment of relative quiet. I noted half a dozen Blackshirts peering in my direction and heading towards me, climbing over chairs. Near me, I heard a female yell: 'Workers unite against the Nazi menace and its capitalist stooges!' In a second, she was grabbed by two bruisers who began slapping her. No one moved to help. I saw her face twisted in pain and derision. My God, it was Dorothy! Without thinking, I dashed to her side and pushed one of her attackers. He staggered, then grinned mirthlessly, grabbed me and hit me in the face. I fell backwards on to the floor. One of his pals lifted a chair and was about to bring it down on my head, when Dorothy broke free and flew into the battle, kicking and scratching my assailants. Reinforcements from both sides arrived quickly and a general fracas broke out in the vicinity. We were outnumbered and thrown out of the building.

As I stumbled into the wintry night, Dorothy dashed to embrace me.

'My hero,' she said jovially.

Her face was already bruised, scarlet and blue.

'Are you okay?' I asked.

She kissed my rapidly closing eye.

'You're a chump, Herr Bexley,' she said. 'You ought to leave the fighting to roughnecks like me.'

'Why didn't you tell me you were back?'

'I've been meaning to. Let's get a drink somewhere.'

We found a bar close by in Hammersmith. It was Friday night and crowded and dark, but we still attracted some stares and jibes.

'You don't want to rough yourselves up like that, dearies,' exclaimed a loud woman's voice. 'Plenty of time *after* you gets hitched.'

Ribald laughter greeted this, but once we'd bought our drinks and taken them to a corner table, we were forgotten and left alone. The conversation was stilted. My euphoria at finding her was fading and I was resentful because she'd failed to write to me while away and to contact me on her return. I dismissed as irrelevant the fact that I'd been dallying with Gwen.

Then she touched my eye. I flinched with pain, but managed a smile.

'They used to hold circuses in Olympia,' she said.

'Well, nothing's changed, except it's now the animals who run the show,' I remarked.

She laughed and held my hand. The ice was broken.

She told me she'd been ordered to leave Germany by the Party in 1932, when it decided to prepare for underground work. The Communists considered the battle in Germany lost. Dorothy would be of better use elsewhere. She was to go to the Soviet Union to see how things were run in the world's only truly workers' state. She was smuggled out of Germany hidden by blankets in the back of a car, and then travelled by road and train across Europe.

'So I couldn't write, you see,' she said.

'And not from Russia?'

'Oh, *liebling*, don't be a bore about that. It would have been too risky to communicate with someone in England. I was being tested, don't you see? Becoming trusted was the most important thing. It still is.'

It struck me that she was giving the lie to her trustworthiness by blabbing to me that she was a Moscow-sponsored cadre at large in Britain. Probably she knew deep down that I was so emotionally connected to her that I would not let her down. Possibly she was making amends for her neglect of me by making me the keeper of her secrets.

'Okay,' I said. 'I understand.'

She smiled her thanks.

'And thanks for coming to my rescue tonight,' she said. 'God, I shouldn't even have been there, let alone get involved in a fight.'

'The Party would've objected?' I asked, wondering if that was also the reason for Ed's absence.

'I have to keep a low profile. But don't ask me to explain.'

As in Germany, I felt pride at the conspirational, courageous life she was living. If only I could believe as she believes, I thought.

She'd travelled a lot in the Soviet Union, looking at successful projects, talking to officials in Russia, Ukraine, Georgia and several far-flung regions of the Communist empire. It had been marvellous even though the lavatories were appalling and she went without a bath for weeks on end.

'It's a good thing that the criterion for communism isn't obsession with personal hygiene. But, *liebling*, latrines apart, they're building something exciting there.'

She sounded enthusiastic, though I noted a sadness in her eyes. Was there some Boris or Ivan in the USSR whom she'd been forced to abandon?

I asked about reports of desperate food shortages, even famine.

'Sacrifices have to be made,' she said airily. 'There are backward groups who won't understand the needs of the many. But you can't create a new kind of society without a few inconveniences. There *are* food shortages in some places, but it will get better.'

But, I persisted, was there starvation in the countryside?
Her face tightened.

'I never saw that. Of course, there's some hardship. The *kulaks*, you know, the rich peasants, are very reactionary. They won't accept that agriculture must be collectivised. The Soviet Union must industrialise quickly or die. That's Stalin's message. In the end, there'll be more food for everyone. The shortages are not significant in the long run.'

'I'll bet they're significant for the families with hungry kids.'

'The State takes care of such children,' she said impatiently. 'You really have become very bourgeois in your attitudes. What matters is not the unavoidable shortcomings of today, but the future!'

She thumped the table with her fist as she thundered the final phrase.

'If you could see the schools being built, the hydroelectric projects, the steel production, the plans for a new sort of prison system that will educate rather than punish people – if you could see all that, then you wouldn't be so cynical.'

'You mean cynical because I believe in free speech?'

'The people talk quite freely. They may be critical of some policies, yes, but they're not crippled with your negativism. If free speech means being negative and effectively sabotaging progress, then I can't see what's so very wrong in taking measures to restrict it. If free speech means allowing Mosley to stand up and preach fascism, then you can keep it. What did so-called free speech in Weimar do except allow Hitler and Goebbels to shout their lies from the rooftops?'

She glared at me. I felt I'd hit on a raw nerve. It seemed odd that we should be arguing heatedly so soon after standing together against the fascists at Olympia.

I told her I'd been in Berlin. She was visibly upset to hear what I said about Dieter, not so much about what he'd undergone in the camp but about his role as an informer. I was shocked by her lack of sympathy.

'The man has been broken completely,' I exclaimed.

'If one had a strong enough grasp of Marxism–Leninism, one wouldn't be so weak.'

After this, our conversation dried up and the pub closed. It had been a long evening. I felt deflated. Relief at seeing Dorothy again and at both of us surviving the Blackshirt assaults had been tempered by my feeling of rejection over her failure to tell me of her return, by our inability to find some common ground, by her callous attitude to the news of Dieter. We said goodbye in the street with no warmth. I found my way to the flat of a student friend and fell asleep on a sofa.

I awoke in the morning feeling awful. For more than a year, even while I'd been flirting with and wooing Gwen, I'd thought constantly about Dorothy, wondered about her, worried about her, idealised her. I'd fantasised about a reunion in which our minds, if not our bodies, met in a harmonious embrace. Now all that was dashed to the ground.

I returned to Cambridge, bruised, chastened, despondent.

The reaction to my physical wounds was mixed.

Gwen was horrified and sympathetic, but also annoyed.

'I knew you'd get into a scrap,' she said irritably.

I didn't mention that I'd met Dorothy and been manhandled because I went to help her.

'How was *your* weekend?' I asked.

'So so,' she shrugged. 'Hardly a riot.'

'And Binky?'

'Pleasant. He's a scratch golfer. *And* a crack shot, I gather.'

When I kissed her, she barely responded.

Ed was highly amused at my black eye and offered to give me boxing lessons. I told him the circumstances of the incident and something about Dorothy.

'I hope she was worth it.'

'It's not that sort of friendship,' I protested.

'Bud, it's always *that* sort of friendship.'

Left-wing students admired my wounds. Those on the right said bluntly that it served me right.

Douglas gave me a thin smile and a short homily.

'If you're going to get into a scrap for your principles, make sure you've got the heavy artillery behind you. Let's hope our government understands that, too.'

I felt more alone than ever. Dorothy had turned out to be an illusion. Ed no longer took me into his confidence. Gwen hinted that Binky was serious about her and that she was giving the matter some thought. I didn't blame her. She'd be crazy to turn down someone who was rich and eligible.

An essay I was writing about the Revolutionary Terror in France increased my pessimism. I didn't know what to do or where to turn. I couldn't talk to Douglas about my personal life – he was too much like a father. I was dangerously close to a spiral of self-pity.

Things fell into perspective when I read a letter from Dr Bergsen.

> Our former landlady has told me you were there, and looking for me. I am in deep sorrow that we did not meet. I went to visit my father in Hesse. I do not write the name of the town, you understand. Perhaps I have told you about my father. A very upstanding man in the town, very respected. But there is a madness in Germany now. I get a letter from a neighbour that my father is very sick. When I reach the town I am scared to see a sign that says: 'Jews are not wanted here.' Always, it was a good place to live. My grandfather was settled there many years and much respected and my whole family. My father, who is 80 years, has a broken skull. The neighbour, a Christian man, says a gang of people, some just children even, dragged my father from his business, shouting he charged too much money for the goods. They throw him to the ground and he just lies there. Since then he is unconscious and I hope he may recover. Soon I will go back to see him again. So that is where I was when you were in Berlin, but perhaps soon you come back, then we will talk. My nephew Leo has left for America and has work already at Princeton University.

I replied immediately saying he should go to the British Embassy and apply for a visa. I would arrange for accommodation and perhaps work. Once he was settled, he could send for his father. I hadn't the slightest idea how I could do what I had promised, but the main thing was to get him out of Germany.

His answer came a few weeks later.

> My dear Herr Bexley,
> Your letter I found at the house of our former landlady. She is well and her son is a big man now, important. How long that will all last, I don't know. Thank your for your

letter. First, there will be no need to bring my father from Germany. Last week he has died. He never woke up from his injuries, and I could not say goodbye to him. We had the funeral in the Jewish cemetery and there he is buried. I said the *Kaddish*, you know, the prayer for the dead, although I do not believe in such things, but for the other Jews still left in the town it is a nice thing I think. I followed your instructions and visited the British Embassy. A gentleman there has assured me that I will be welcome in England if I have the money to support myself or if I have a job to go to. The truth, my dear friend, is that I do not wish to leave my homeland. Here there is a madness and some difficulties for the Jews but I think it will not last. If I go to England, my qualifications as a lawyer would not be of good to me. Here I can still do some little work for Jewish people and sometimes also I am able to help some of my non-Jewish friends even if not for money. Many people have lost work and money, but they help each other. I thank you for your thoughts for me and I also think of you and your friend, the *fraulein* who also stayed with us together in Berlin. Have you received news from her?

With every best wish.
Yours respectfully,
Samuel Bergsen, LLD

When I gave the gist of this correspondence to Douglas, he adopted a pained expression.

'I think, as you obviously do, that his optimism in the future of Germany is unmerited. We're not going to get rid of Nazism by wishing it away. However, if I were a German Jew, I think I would stay put for the moment.'

I was astonished and said so, which led Douglas to add: 'If I were a German Jew I should wish things were otherwise than they are, but I would have to take into account the alternatives. The difficulty of finding a suitable country to live, the pain of being uprooted.'

'He's always wanted to study in England,' I protested. 'His English is not perfect, but it would be adequate after a few months here.'

'With what intent would he want to study? If he were a medical man, a scientist, an economist, a teacher, then, yes, perhaps, though even there ... the government has been told there will be room only for a handful of refugee doctors here. It's scandalous, but the professions are not going to welcome Jewish refugees with open arms. And certainly not middle-aged lawyers who would have to pass examinations, improve their command of English and acquire contacts. The last would be almost impossible for your man unless he has friends or relatives with legal connections over here. Does he?'

I shook my head.

'In that case, I believe you ought to respect his wishes to wait where he is for the moment.'

'I suppose I have to.'

He then added: 'There's nothing I can promise. But if he changes his mind because things become intolerable, let me know. Perhaps something could be arranged.'

Another letter arrived, a brief scrawl from Dorothy.

> Jimmy, love – I've decided to come to Cambridge. Have been accepted at Newnham next term. Your debating skills after Olympia convinced me that I have a lot to learn in the humanities area. Besides, am getting too old for street fighting. Could have gone to Oxford or LSE but your presence at Cambridge decided me, even though they won't give me a degree – well, who needs a scrap of paper? So see you in Oct. Am going on travels to old haunts before then. Hope you've forgiven me for my sins. All my love, Dorothy

I told Ed and Gwen about this.

Ed said he couldn't wait to see the wench I was so obviously besotted with.

'I'm not besotted, and I'd prefer it if you kept away from her.'

'Don't worry, I'll keep my hands to myself,' he laughed. 'Anyway, if you're not besotted, why d'you want me to stay clear of her?'

'Because you're a womaniser, Brewster.'

'Hey, I've got my hands full right now, and, hell, I would never make a pass at a pal's girl.'

'Dorothy isn't my girl,' I said. 'And you bloody well would make a pass at anyone in a skirt who took your fancy.'

Ed was in the throes of an affair with Abigail Martin, the wife of a King's Fellow. I liked her husband and didn't approve of the way Ed was potentially wrecking the marriage, especially as the Martins had two young children. But I'd never raised the issue directly with him.

'Well, yeah, maybe. But, trust me, not a skirt that belonged to you.'

When I told Gwen about Dorothy, she tossed her head haughtily and said: 'I knew she'd turn up sometime.'

'Look, I love you, you're the only girl I want, Gwen.'

I hadn't planned to say this. We'd barely seen each other in the couple of weeks since Olympia, and when we had met there'd been a definite coolness on her part.

'Am I? Who exactly are you trying to fool, Jimmy? Me, or yourself?'

'You'll see when she arrives. There's absolutely nothing between us. I swear. If anything, we're like brother and sister.'

'I bet,' she said scornfully.

We were in a café, drinking tea. I asked if she'd go out with me on Saturday night. She replied that she'd be busy.

When I'd told her that Dorothy and I were like siblings, this wasn't entirely a fabrication. I felt there was some kind of taboo about any physical relationship with Dorothy. I was sure Dorothy didn't view me as a potential lover, and I wasn't sure that I wanted us to be in that sort of relationship either. Our friendship was too valuable. What would I really like, I asked myself? The answer seemed to be sharing a bed with Gwen and an emotional intimacy with Dorothy. Some chance!

15

Cambridge

I wondered which 'old haunts' Dorothy would be revisiting. I hoped she didn't mean Germany, which would have involved danger. Equally, though, I hoped it wouldn't be the USSR where I imagined a swarthy Svengali-like comrade waiting to seduce her and lure her into espionage.

Gwen and I resumed something like our former tender togetherness – thanks to my persistence – but she wouldn't travel with me during the summer vacation. She'd accepted two invitations: one for a fortnight with family friends in St Tropez; and one for a week with unspecified people in Dorset. Clearly she was moving into the ready-to-be-married ranks and away from me.

Ed was going to south Wales with a group from the Socialist Society to investigate conditions among miners. If it had just been Ed, I might have gone too, but the idea of being trapped in a group of earnest undergraduates didn't appeal.

Douglas said someone he knew needed a bit of help with newspaper articles about political events, including European trends. He thought my interest in radical politics and my research ability might qualify me for the job.

'There won't be much pay, but the experience will be good,' he said.

'Who's the journalist?' I asked.

'Oh, didn't I mention it?' Douglas smiled. 'Winston Churchill.'

'Douglas! He's a dyed-in-the-wool imperialist.'

'Well, yes,' Douglas admitted. 'But don't let that put you off. He's surprisingly liberal in some things, and he's a man of resolve. You'll learn a lot.'

A few weeks later, I went to Churchill's flat at Morpeth Mansions in Victoria. I was surprised to find a plump little man with a benevolent smile and delicate white hands. He turned on the charm, told me he couldn't pay me anything except necessary expenses and would expect me to work all hours of the day and night if he had a deadline to meet. I agreed to the conditions.

'Very well,' he said. 'Let us proceed.'

It was the start of an interesting few months. I learned how to weather his storms, how to work to his rhythms, how to anticipate his journalistic needs. I spent time at Chartwell, his country home, and got to know the family, including arrogant young Randolph and brittle, defiant, shy Sarah. Above all, I began to understand the qualities of Winston Churchill, to admire his views on the German menace and to wonder how any democratic country could afford to consign such a vigorous force as him to the political wilderness.

Dorothy returned to England in the autumn and wired me at Cambridge. I was at the station to meet her. She was dressed in a stylish navy blue cashmere coat and wore a smart cloche hat to match her burgundy lipstick.

'To impress the natives,' she explained as I kissed her on both cheeks.

'You've impressed one already. But I like it just as much when you're in working-class disguise.'

'Not disguise, *liebling*. That's the real me. Remember?'

'Then why the bourgeois luggage?' I asked, pointing to her leather suitcases.

'I didn't want to disgrace you.'

'I bet you didn't dress like that in Moscow.'

'So, you guessed. Yes, that's where I've been. Don't spread it about, though, love.'

'Was it interesting?' I asked in the taxi.

'Was it?' she said, suddenly hugging me. 'Oh, yes! We're all on the same side now. You, me, the Labour Party.'

'You mean the social fascists?' I asked.

She smiled her wide smile.

'You can joke, *liebling*, but it's all together now. A common front against Nazism. That ought to please even an unreconstructed liberal like you.'

'Pity you didn't try for that in Germany,' I said.

She shook her head sadly.

'My love, you can't hold that grudge forever! The USSR has enemies surrounding it on all sides. They tried to strangle it at birth. How could we trust the wolves in sheep's clothing? But now, it's clear who the real enemy is.'

As we walked through the entrance gate into the porter's lodge at Newnham, she gripped my upper arm and said: 'Jimmy, will you be an absolute dear and say you're my brother?'

'Why?' I asked, stopping dead.

'It will be easier to spend time out of college if I say I'm visiting you. Besides, if you're my brother you'll be able to visit me for hours and hours.'

'I don't *want* to be your brother,' I said petulantly.

'It's just a game,' she said, caressing my hand. 'Not for real.'

'Who suggested this? Stalin or Pollitt?'

Harry Pollitt was one of the heads of the British Communist Party.

'Don't be angry, darling. I'll introduce you to some female comrades. Perhaps they're sexy enough to do what I couldn't do and seduce you into the Party.'

'You never tried. Why on earth did you have to come to this idiotic college? You could've taken digs in town like me.'

I knew all about the restrictions on the students in the women's halls. They were barely a step up from boarding schools.

'They don't allow that in the first year. Please, *liebling*. I'll be eternally grateful.'

So I became Mr Young to the porters, the dons, the staff, students and Principal of Newnham. No one thought of checking whether James Young was a student at Trinity.

To complicate matters, I was again seeing Gwen regularly. Her summer holidays had not brought her to the brink of married bliss. She didn't ask about Dorothy, and I volunteered nothing.

Dorothy had quickly plunged into a series of evening meetings, presumably with CP members or supporters. I was not included.

Ed was back from his investigative visit into Welsh mining conditions, and full of invective about the mine owners, the ruling classes and the evils of capitalism. He chastised me for working with Churchill. The workers, he said, would never forgive Winston for his role in breaking the General Strike of 1926.

'That may be so,' I said. 'But he's the only man in politics with the balls to speak the truth about Hitler's intentions.'

'He'll never live down his past.'

When I told Ed, ruefully, about pretending to be Dorothy's brother, he chuckled and said: 'Shouldn't be a problem for you, old man. Keep plugging away.'

Ed's affair with Abigail Martin continued. They were becoming quite blatant about it. They were amorous in public and seen together far more than was prudent. Ed asked if I'd mind if they used my room occasionally.

'My landlady wouldn't allow it,' I said.

'She wouldn't know. We'd sneak in and out.'

I asked him why he didn't get his own room out of the college.

'Because I like the tradition,' he said disarmingly. 'You wouldn't want to deny an ex-colonial that experience, would you? So, come on, what's the real reason you won't lend us your love nest?'

'I suppose it's because I like Donald. And I'm fond of Abigail.'

'What the hell has that got to do with anything?'

'I didn't want to get into this,' I said. 'But, well, don't you think there's a danger you're ruining a marriage?'

'Marriage? That's just a convenient institution, and I reckon it's not the issue here. There's an old-fashioned prurience about you, old man. Sex seems to bother you.'

'The issue is betrayal. You're having some fun, and it doesn't concern you in the least that you're destroying a family's unity.'

'If I am, then that unity must've been damn fragile anyway.'

'You are an arrogant, cocksure, know-it-all bastard!' I said.

We glared at each other. Then Ed smiled.

'Boy, you've got my number. Look, let's forgive each other our sins. Okay?'

'Okay,' I said, after a pause. 'I wouldn't have brought it up if you hadn't mentioned the room.'

'Forget that. That was a stupid thing to ask. Only, you know, Abby and me kind of do love each other. We need each other in a funny kind of way. And I do think about her kids, and about Don. It's not simply a bit of fun. And, believe me, it's not just my own gratification.'

We shook hands in a gesture of reconciliation. It bothered

me that he couldn't see that *he* was the reason she was prepared to put her family at risk, that if it weren't for his charm and good looks she wouldn't be tempted.

'And, by the way,' I said. 'Sex doesn't bother me.'

'I'm sorry, that was snide of me. But take some advice from an old hand: sex isn't everything between a guy and a girl.'

'This is fascinating – coming from you!'

'If the sex is good, too, that's a kind of miracle. But sex on its own? No, that's not my way. Maybe that's why I'll never be a good Communist. The comrades seem to think it's part of the revolutionary deal to fuck each other silly.'

'*Are* you?' I asked.

'What?'

'A Communist. It's the first time you've ever told me you were.'

'I didn't say that, did I?'

'You said you'd never be a *good* Communist.'

Ed regarded me with something like admiration.

'Shit, you pick up on the darndest things,' he said, but confided nothing more.

When I told Dorothy about the existence of Gwen, she was amused. I would have preferred a morsel of jealousy.

We were talking in my sitting-room in Trumpington Street. My landlady, Mrs Perkins, looked askance at all visitors, but especially women and especially women after dark, even if the woman claimed to be my sister. However, she needed a lodger and I needed a place outside the closed doors of Trinity, so we'd reached a compromise. I could have female visitors during the day – 'but just for tea, mind!'

This was the first time that Dorothy had been here. We'd met only a few times since the start of term. She'd been chatty about her academic work – she was finding her course on literature more interesting than she'd expected – but very secretive about her political activities. If I suggested an evening together, she'd say she had a meeting, or 'Party business', but nothing specific.

'So this is your love nest?' she asked.

'Not yet.'

'Ah, but it will be, *liebling*, won't it?' she smiled.

I took my time lighting the pipe I'd recently bought. Dorothy watched me, then asked: 'What sort of person is she?'

'Bright enough to have passed the Cambridge entrance, but she prefers to work. Vaguely left wing, though her parents are Tories.'

'Sounds like my kind of girl. *Sans* the vagueness and the ruling-class parents. Are you in love with her?'

'I like her. She's attractive. She's warm.'

'Ah,' said Dorothy.

'And that's all there is to it.'

'That's a lot, Jimmy dear.'

'Hold on. She's just a girl I like. It's hardly wedding bells.'

'Perhaps you ought to think about something permanent, my dear. It would give you some kind of stability, and direction.'

'Oh, my God,' I groaned. 'Bourgeois morality. What would they say in Moscow?'

'They'd probably approve. There *is* a new morality among the Russian elite these days. Family values. Bye-bye to free love. That's something the ersatz comrades here haven't quite cottoned on to yet.'

'Elite? The workers' state has an elite?'

'I meant to say leadership.'

I suspected her last trip to the Soviet Union had been an unsettling experience, despite her joy at the new common front policy. Now she was frowning. Was this because she was confronting her own doubts?

Then she brightened.

'Let's concentrate on your Gwendoline. Does she make you happy?'

'When I'm with her, yes, she does,' I said curtly.

'Have you slept with her?'

The question came unexpectedly. I looked Dorothy in the eyes and didn't reply.

'How shall I put this? There's this beautiful, desirable, intelligent young woman in your life. She probably finds you equally desirable. Why don't you just get on with it?'

'We are getting on with it,' I said irritably. 'In our own way.'

'And it's none of my business,' Dorothy smiled.

'That's irrelevant, Dorothy. Anything about me is your business – if you've got the time.'

'Oh?' She raised her eyebrows.

'Look, it doesn't matter that much, but we hardly ever get to talk, you and I. Even a bloody brother would have more access to you than I have.'

'It's those damn college rules. I'd love to see you after the business part of the night. But I have to be back in my cell by eleven o'clock. It's a bore.'

We left it at that. I walked her back to Newnham, kissed her on the cheeks outside the college and tramped back home.

One bleak and wintry morning a few days later I was walking with Gwen in King's Parade when one of the Newnham tutors passed us and said cheerily: 'Good morning, Mr Young.'

'Mr Young?' Gwen asked with a taut smile.

I told her about acting as Dorothy's brother.

'Why would you have to do that? So you can visit her in her room?'

'Nothing like that. She asked me to do it – for political reasons. I'll take you to meet Dorothy, if you like. There's absolutely nothing between us. I swear.'

She thought this over and asked: 'Have you told her about me?'

'Of course.'

'What did you tell her about me?'

'That I have a girl who messes me about something terrible.'

'Jimmy!' She stamped her foot on the pavement. 'Tell me!'

'That I see you, that I enjoy seeing you, that I sometimes feel miserable.'

'Do you?'

'You know that. I get very miserable when things aren't going well between us.'

'I'm sorry,' she said softly, dropping her head.

'It's not your fault. It's me. I just don't like it when you're with these other chaps you go out with.'

'Oh, Jimmy.'

'And you have every right to go out with whoever you want,' I said.

Suddenly, in the middle of a busy thoroughfare in mid-morning, she gave me a passionate kiss. I noticed an elderly man in a dark overcoat smile. A couple of students cycling past, academic gowns blowing in the wind, whistled furiously.

'You've never taken me to your rooms,' she said.

'I've invited you before.'

'Why not now?' she asked.

I inclined my head questioningly in the direction of the bookshop.

'I'll pop in and tell them I'm ill,' she said. 'Wait for me here.'

I had a lecture to attend, an essay to write and Mrs Perkins to deal with. But I wasn't going to miss the chance.

In a few minutes, she rejoined me, face flushed.

'Let's go,' she said, as though she, too, did not trust the moment to remain.

We walked, hand in hand, to Trumpington Street. As I'd feared, Mrs Perkins appeared in the hallway almost as soon as we entered. I introduced Gwen. Mrs Perkins sniffed disapprovingly.

'Miss Farrow attends the same lectures as I do,' I explained. 'We need to do some research work together.'

I patted the small bag of files and books I'd been carrying to the lecture. Mrs Perkins looked at her watch, as if to indicate that she was checking us in and would check us out when she thought necessary.

In my sitting-room, Gwen and I had a small, nervous giggling fit, each putting a hand over the other's mouth to stop the sounds.

'In those women's colleges, is it true they have to drag their beds into the corridor if they have male visitors?' she asked.

'How would I know?'

We kissed for a long time, then went into the bedroom, where she quickly took off her coat, shoes and dress. She stood before me in her bra and panties and allowed me to remove them. Then we made love for the first time. It was a mixed experience of too rapid ecstasy and some embarrassment on her part over the way she evidently got a lot of enjoyment out of the act. Afterwards, we dressed in silence, but her eyes were shining. We passed the landlady on our way out of the flat, but avoided looking at her. Gwen asked me not to see her back to her house.

'I'd better continue pretending to be ill in case the shop phones.'

Ed finally got to know Dorothy in the new year. He was lavish in praise of her as a woman of spirit and intelligence – though quick to add: 'Not really my type.' I was immediately jealous of his access to her.

He told me they were both part of a new non-political committee trying to organise a united anti-fascist campaign.

'When you say non-political, d'you mean you take off your political hats when you're on the committee, like when you're in church?' I asked sarcastically.

'Something like that. We want the broadest possible membership.'

'Are there any non-Communists involved?'

'Why, sure, Jim. It isn't a Party thing at all. Anyway, your Dorothy's a smart girl. A bit pushy, but so what? She gets things done. I told her that you and me were buddies, by the way.'

'I'll bet that impressed her. But she isn't *my* anything.'

'Hey, don't get mad at me, just 'cause you ain't a part of all this. She thinks the sun shines out of your posterior.'

Despite my irritation, I liked hearing this, though I couldn't help remembering, with some distaste, Gregor Siegendorff making the same comment about his mother's regard for me.

'Anyway,' Ed continued. 'I can't tell you the details of what's happening – it'll be announced soon – but she's keeping us all on the straight and narrow. If it wasn't for her we'd probably disintegrate into another squabbling talking shop. Want to know what she told me about you?'

'No.'

'She said you were the only man around that she really trusted.'

'Probably because I'm the only one she knows who's not in the Party.'

He bellowed with laughter.

'Christ, you are either genuinely a self-deprecating Limey or you're a duplicitous bastard! Why don't you make a play for her? You know you're nuts about her, and I can sort of see why. It's the energy, the ardour. Make a move, buddy, otherwise some other sod will.'

'Shut up!'

* * *

With Gwen, things had changed for the better once we'd become lovers. They had also become difficult in some ways. She refused to come to my room again because she couldn't bear to be stared at by Mrs Perkins. We managed to sneak some intimate moments when I visited her at home, but her mother was watchful and hostile, sensing me as someone likely to hamper Gwen's matrimonial prospects. Occasionally, we took a hotel room in Cambridge, but found it a bit sordid. It was also expensive. In short, something of deceit and shame had crept into what should have been happy and carefree young love. The only times we did feel relaxed and joyous were when we went away for weekends from time to time, camping or to bed and breakfast places posing as Mr and Mrs J. Bexley. But even these times had a cloud over them; Gwen had to devise elaborate stories, often involving her friends, to deceive her parents, and was always worrying they'd discover the truth.

'For a liberated woman, you sometimes seem far too concerned about what your parents think,' I said, half in jest, as we lay side by side in a Suffolk cottage.

The room was warmed by a fire. A sheet covered the bottom half of her body. I admired the rest of her, including her loose, tousled yellow hair. I kissed her hair, moist from perspiration.

'I'm not liberated, Jimmy. How can any woman be? If it's not the shackles of one's family, it's the cage of marriage. Or worse. Life on the shelf.'

'Why not study for something? You could find a career, find freedom that way.'

'Like your friend Dorothy?'

Dorothy seldom cropped up in our conversations, but she often hovered like a ghost above us.

'She's tied to her politics. Married to the Party.'

'I think I'd prefer a man to *that*,' Gwen said drily. 'Anyway, a career doesn't appeal to me that much. I suppose in the end I'll have to find some malleable chap and make the best of it.'

'I love you, Gwen. You're wonderful, you know?'

'Of course I am. Especially when you're stroking me like that.'

16

Cambridge

For a period of about six weeks before and after Christmas I barely saw Dorothy at all, except fleetingly at anti-fascist meetings or among a group of her political soul mates, usually including Ed, at a pub in Magdalene Street.

This was an uneasy time of isolation for me. I wasn't invited by Gwen's parents for the holidays. Dorothy left a note to say she was going to London 'on family duty'. Ed had been asked to a country house party in Northumberland. Douglas disappeared on a continental jaunt: he didn't specify the destinations but I suspected he would be visiting Germany, possibly at Churchill's request.

Not wishing to hang around Cambridge on my own and having no funds for travel abroad, I agreed to spend a couple of weeks with my mother and stepfather. It was a mistake. Other guests included Conservative MPs, their bored wives and various businessmen. The pomposity, condescension and prejudices of these people were matched only by their wilful misreading of political realities. I was taunted for having worked with Churchill.

'Frightful bounder, that fellow,' said one portly MP. 'Ask anyone. Only interested in feathering his nest. I'll wager you did all the work and got no pay.'

It wasn't quite the truth. What I'd learned from Winston – from the breadth of his vision – was worth more than any salary could have been. I said so.

'Vision be damned,' I was told. 'His entire career has involved one misjudgement after another. Fortunately, he'll never be anything more than a half-baked scribbler in the future.'

These people were also unanimous in thinking the rise of Hitler was the best thing to have happened in Europe for a generation – 'An iron fist,' they said admiringly.

Having to be in their company for two weeks was depressing.

My mood was made even worse by my longings for Gwen and my confusion about Dorothy. I wished Dorothy had never come to Cambridge. I found it difficult to cope with the fact that she was living only a stone's throw from me, but kept herself as remote as if she were in Moscow. It was easier, somehow, when she *had* been in Moscow.

I believed that she liked and probably did trust me, as Ed had reported her saying, but that was all. I didn't share her passionate convictions. Probably, I simply wasn't physically attractive to her. Not only was she older and more sophisticated than me, but from the start, in Berlin, she'd seen me as a chum rather than a potential partner. I was the one she could escape to for light relief when her physical and political encounters got too intense. That was the pattern we'd established, and there was no way of breaking it.

When term resumed, I decided to steer clear of her for a while. The trouble was, I kept looking out for her in the town and often found myself walking around the colleges and halls where she attended lectures. Then, late one afternoon, she appeared at my lodgings. Mrs Perkins was out so we went up to my rooms.

'What's up, *liebling*?' she asked. 'Are you avoiding me for some reason?'

'No, not at all. Tied up with this and that, and I gathered from Ed Brewster that you're pretty busy yourself.'

'What a tiresome man! Big talker, small thinker.'

'Oh, I don't know. Once you get to know him you'll find his enthusiasm is genuine enough.'

'I don't particularly *want* to get to know him. He's been telling you what he does on the committee, I suppose, but in truth he's more of a nuisance than anything else. "Oh, this is the way it would be handled in New York" or "Hopkins would suggest this" or "This is what they did in Idaho", or wherever he's from.'

'Iowa.'

'They're in the vanguard of revolution down there,' she said.

'Has he told you about the Cow Wars? A blueprint for progressive activism.'

'Oh, Jimmy,' she laughed.

I didn't join in.

'What's the matter, *liebling*? Have I offended you?'
'It's just a bad patch.'
'That girl! Gwen. Has she been messing you about?'
'Other way round, if anything.
'And she won't let go? Would you like me to claw her eyes out?'

It was my turn to laugh.

'Unfair,' I said. 'Your claws are much sharper.'
'I've had more practice.'
'Anyway, Gwen isn't the problem. It's good between us. Easygoing and good.'
'Is that why you've managed without me?'
'I haven't avoided you, Dorothy. Our paths just don't seem to cross any longer.'

She looked at me, waiting for more.

'Perhaps I've spent too long at the university,' I said. 'I'm not much of an academic. I'm not much interested. Time to move.'
'Don't be an ass. You can't go away as long as I'm stuck here too. You can't leave me in the lurch.'
'You manage well enough without me around.'
'Jimmy, love, don't be daft. I need you around. Why d'you think I came here tonight? God, I wouldn't want you to go. Who could I talk to, really talk to, if you weren't around? There are some nice women in the college – politically aware, you know – but a lot of silly girls too, not to mention the blue stockings and hockey players. And the Cambridge men! There's a clique of comrades who think a woman's place is either in their bed or in the kitchen. They hate the fact that I can run rings around them intellectually and politically. Sometimes it makes me so damn fed up. I need you to keep me sane.'
'I would if you'd let me.'

She searched my face for a hidden meaning, then said: 'We obviously miss each other, so let's make a weekly date. At least once a week we'll spend the evening together, just us two, nattering away. Okay?'

'Well, yes, all right. But I still can't promise I'll stay at Cambridge for the whole year.'
'Stay as long as I need you. Don't let little Gwen get you down. I suppose she's fallen in love with you?'

I said nothing.

'Of course, you won't discuss such intimacies. You're honourable and discreet. You don't even ask me if I'm involved with anyone.'

'Are you?'

'As it happens, I'm not. I'm not as promiscuous as you think.'

I began to protest that I had no such thoughts, but she went on quickly: 'I'm not as virginal as some, but I've never been a tart. Anyway, *liebling*, these are things we can talk about.'

'Our love lives?'

'Yes, why not? Those things ... and the revolution.'

'Spare me that,' I said.

She threw a sofa pillow at my head and began pummelling me with her fists. I grabbed her wrists and we both collapsed in laughter, which we had to stifle in case the landlady had returned. I checked to see that Mrs Perkins was not in the hall before we tiptoed out. Then we walked to Newnham, I said good-night to her just outside in Sidgwick Avenue and kissed her cheeks with the warmth of a brother.

'Thanks,' she whispered as she turned to go. A few steps later, she turned, blew me a kiss and vanished into the college. I walked back to my lodgings, feeling better than I had for weeks.

Soon afterwards, I joined the new broad-based Campaign to Aid Victims of the Nazis, which Dorothy and Ed had helped bring into existence. She was pleased to see me at their meetings, and I enjoyed being a part of her activity. We were told in speeches – some laborious, some fiery but empty of anything except slogans – that the aim was to set up a newspaper to expose atrocities, to lobby people of influence for a change in government policy, and to help mitigate the plight of political refugees. Similar groups were starting up in other centres. Soon we'd amalgamate into a national organisation, with real power. Meanwhile, we members were urged to spread the word, help in street collections.

Douglas, back from his travels, was sceptical when I told him about it.

'Fighting Mosley's hooligans is one thing but the only meaningful way to help victims of the Nazis is to defeat Nazism. And some Comintern-inspired campaign to make a noise and hope for the best is certainly not the way to defeat Hitler and Mussolini. You have to hit them where it hurts, not score propaganda points.'

'Surely it's better to make some noise than to do nothing,' I protested.

'Possibly, he smiled, 'as long as you understand the main aim is to make you feel better.'

The real way to hurt the fascist dictatorships, he said, was through trade boycotts, sanctions, collective international action and rearmament, especially rearmament.

'Sooner or later Hitler is going to overstretch himself, and we have to be ready to strike at him when that happens.'

'God, Douglas, you've become a warmonger,' I said jokingly.

'Only to preserve the peace.'

Rearmament was not a popular idea in the mid-thirties.

'Now I know what you and Churchill have in common,' I said.

Gwen declined to join the campaign. She said she had no spare time. We remained lovers, although the tempo of our relationship had slowed since Christmas. I was pretty sure she was considering getting married, to Binky or to some other chinless wonder.

This mattered to me, but the impact was lessened by the opportunities I now had for being together with Dorothy.

After one meeting, I was standing talking to Dorothy when Sebastian Gosling-Jones, who'd tried to recruit me into the CP a year before, butted in rudely and said to her: 'Why are you being so nice to the social fascists, Comrade Young?'

'What a quaint and outdated way of putting it, comrade,' she replied sweetly. 'Surely you know the Party regards anyone who opposes the real fascists as a potential ally?'

'I have never had any directive to that effect,' Gosling-Jones said pompously.

'Then perhaps, comrade, you require education on how to understand what is meant by a changed policy to meet the changed political situation.'

'Oh, and you of course have been educated to do that,' he sneered. 'You've been to Moscow.'

'That helped.'

'And, of course, Comrade Stalin himself outlined the correct way to look at things,' he said.

'Don't be juvenile, comrade,' she said.

His face lit up as he perceived his gibe hitting home.

But his expression changed to apprehension when she added sternly: 'Let me assure you that you will be informed of the Party's policy.'

Gosling-Jones stalked off.

'Why don't they know what the new line is?' I asked Dorothy.

'It isn't written in stone yet. These things are not settled by one person; they're the outcome of collective thought and debate. There's confusion. One has to take a step into the darkness, a leap of faith until then.'

'It sounds to me as though you're faltering.'

'Does it?' She sounded wistful. 'I hope not, Jimmy. I believe we'll reach the correct end.'

I found myself – to my surprise – disturbed by her reaction. I knew how much the Party mattered to Dorothy. It was her religion, and the way in which she defined herself. Much as I couldn't share her beliefs, they were important to me because they were a part of her. I felt vaguely and uneasily that she wouldn't be the same Dorothy without the revolutionary ardour.

But serious soul searching played only a minor part in our times together. Apart from the chats we had at the campaign meetings, we kept to our agreement for a weekly rendezvous, usually spending an afternoon together and then going to a film, play or concert. Afterwards we'd stroll back to her college, holding hands like childhood friends, kiss each other chastely and have a good-night hug.

We discussed books, paintings and music, as well as politics. We gossiped. I told her about my late father, and my mother and stepfather. She didn't talk much about her family. Her father was a tailor who'd migrated from Lithuania around the turn of the century. Her mother was a seamstress, the daughter of Dorothy's Latvian grandmother. They had a constant financial struggle, which dominated their lives. She was part protective of, and part scathing about, her family.

'All they worry about is "Earn enough to live on, keep your nose clean, don't get into trouble." Never mind other people who can't escape their poverty!'

Dorothy had been bright enough to win bursaries. Her two younger, less gifted sisters were doomed, she said, to nothing better than mundane marriages.

'And then they'll be trapped with dreary men scratching a

living in dreary jobs – if they can get work! – and hordes of children. Poverty is just bloody dreary. It's the worst trap of all. That's one reason we have to change the world.'

We discussed world affairs, expecially opposition to colonialism in India and elsewhere, the way in which Hitler and Mussolini were intent on military build-ups and adventures – and the failure of the democracies to respond to this threat.

Dorothy didn't care for Churchill despite his loud warnings about the growing military power of Nazi Germany. This was mainly because of his strike-breaking history and his opposition to self-rule for India.

'It irks me that he gets newspaper space to air his opinions,' she said.

'And that I helped him as a researcher?'

'No, she laughed. 'You merely joined the ranks of the exploited.'

I told her the latest news of Dr Bergsen, and of the attitude of people in the Jewish communities I'd met in Berlin. Dorothy said she'd once been a Zionist.

'It was at school. God, you wouldn't believe the amount of anti-Semitism some of the kids had in their hearts. So I joined a young Zionist group in the East End. My father was furious. He said: "We Jews are guests here; we shouldn't get involved in politics." That made me all the more ardent. Then one of my uncles, a black sheep because he was a founder member of the CP, took me aside and said he disliked his favourite niece being a nationalist. I said Jews were always persecuted because they didn't have a homeland. He said: Why fight just for one group that is persecuted? Why not fight for a homeland for all the oppressed? I came to see he was right, that Communism is Zionism writ large – not merely a state for persecuted Jews, but a state for all the exploited of the world. It hasn't come yet, Jimmy, but it will.'

We'd managed to get hold of a board game called Monopoly, which had just gone on sale in the US. Our games were played with a ferocity that would have delighted Wall Street, usually ending in a dispute followed by a cushion fight until we dissolved into laughter.

We poked fun at people. Dorothy could be wickedly amusing, even about those who shared her political ideology. One target of her butts was a Trinity Red called Martin Onslow, who was often to be seen in the common rooms haranguing bored students about fighting the class war. Her name for him was the Lady with the Lamp. 'I'm sure he has wet dreams about fighting at the barricades.'

In the privacy of my room, she let her hair down about some of the male comrades whose attitudes appalled her.

'The Lady and his clique can't stop posturing. When they aren't showing off, they're going at it like little rabbits with each other. They come out of the burrow and can't stop spouting Marx and Stalin. Was I ever like them, love?'

'A rabbit?'

'No, idiot. A spouter.'

'I bet you bored your way across the socialist homeland.'

'Beast!'

One afternoon I found a note on the hall table in my lodgings from Gwen: 'Must see you as soon as possible.'

I phoned her and we arranged to meet at a pub. She sounded agitated. She was waiting outside when I arrived, standing in the rain. When I went to kiss her, she offered me her cheek.

I feared she might be ill, or pregnant, or that she'd heard gossip about Dorothy and me. It wasn't any of those things. Binky Cooper-Downs had proposed and after long consideration she'd decided to accept him. The wedding was set for June.

'Well,' I said, stunned. 'Congratulations and all that ... oh, hell, Gwen!'

She put her hand on mine across the table.

'It can't be that much of a surprise, Jimmy. I told you marriage might be my escape, or whatever you like to call it. And you know I've been seeing Binky.'

'Yes. But I love you, Gwen.'

'You don't,' she said matter-of-factly. 'And even if you did, you don't love me enough to marry me.'

'I would if...'

'I know, Jimmy dear. If you were ten years older and getting a bit desperate yourself, and had some money – and if you loved me a lot more than you say you do.'

'We have good times together. They must mean something.'

'They do, very much. And you know I've loved you. But we

couldn't go on like this for much longer. You'll have left Cambridge soon, and what then? Occasional meetings in London or somewhere – if I'm lucky. Or would I be your kept woman?'

'Things can happen. I don't know the future. Perhaps I *will* be able to marry you in a year or two.'

'Perhaps, but unlikely. Look, Jimmy dear, don't be so glum about it. We've had some great times, and I've loved them. But the time has come.'

'Why?'

'Because Binky's popped the question, and because I need to escape.'

'Escape from me?'

'In a way, I suppose so. Because we're not going anywhere. But it's escape from what I am, really: a woman who's still living in a little girl's room at her parents' home. You turned me into a woman, and yet I'm stuck in that room at home.'

I found it hard to say anything.

'And you have Dorothy,' she added.

'I don't, as it happens, *have* Dorothy. She's a friend, that's all.'

'Jimmy, dear,' she laughed. 'I've known all along that you are mad about Dorothy, so don't even try to deny it. I was jealous. I'll admit that. In fact, I still am jealous of her. And I probably will be when I'm eighty-five.'

'Promise?' I managed to smile. 'Anyway why should you be jealous when you have Binky to keep you warm?'

'Why indeed?'

'I hope he's nice.'

'Oh, yes,' she said.

'And stinking rich?'

'Definitely,' she said. 'And even more so when he comes into the title and gets the stately home. Once his ancient bachelor uncle dies.'

'You're joking.'

'No. I shall be Lady Harding in due course. My Lady, to the likes of you. His family aren't thrilled that he's only marrying into the middle classes, but he's been a bit wild in his time and they know I'll be a safe wife and mother.'

'I'm pleased for you, Gwen. Are you happy?'

'Who wouldn't be?'

Outside the pub, we kissed tenderly.

'Shall I see you again?' I asked.

'I don't think that would be a good idea. I might be tempted.'

'If I drop into Heffer's?'

'You won't,' she said. 'You're an honourable chap. Besides, I shall have to stop working soon. To prepare for married life and all that.'

'Will you ask me to the wedding?'

'No, Jimmy. Not a good idea either. Let's just say goodbye.'

We shook hands like a couple of strangers who'd spent some time together, pleasantly, by chance, but didn't expect to meet again.

It's a bit thick being called an honourable chap by the two important women in your life, I thought glumly.

After our breakup, I felt low and full of regrets. Why had I let Gwen slip? I allowed myself to day-dream of married life with her – me working, she bringing up a family. Given that it was an impossible outcome, it didn't seem such a trap after all. The tender thought of her carrying my babies arrived simultaneously with the knowledge that she never would. I never seriously considered asking her to give up Binky and marry me. Gwen's way of escape was not mine.

What surprised me was the depth of my feeling for her, and the fact that my friendship with Dorothy could not compensate for the loss.

That friendship was something of a haven for both of us, even though as winter turned to a drizzly early spring Dorothy seemed to become more careworn by the week. I put it down to her political doubts – increased, I assumed, by the fact that the campaign had attracted few new members and little public attention.

One week, she was more depressed than usual, and weepy, but wouldn't say why. I suspected it might be something to do with a man. She said she was feeling a bit under the weather, but that was all. I saw her walking in the town, head bowed, and dragged her off to a tea room.

'Come on, Dorothy,' I urged. 'What's the bloody problem?'

She gave me a wan smile.

'You're not often this masterful,' she said.

'Whatever it is, it's making you ill. I promise I won't be jealous.'

'Jealous?' She looked surprised.

'If it's a love problem.'

Her eyes sparkled, but only for an instant.

'Oh, Jimmy, *liebling*, would that it were. Except that I've long been immune to that sort of thing. Can we go to your place? I'll tell you there.'

What she told me was that she was being attacked by a group in the Party – a cabal, she called it – for all kinds of imaginary crimes against Communist orthodoxy. The group was led by a man from London, who had suddenly appeared, joined the campaign and gathered a group of comrades, including Martin Onslow and Gosling-Jones, who were spreading lies about her among Party members.

'And why? Because I'm trying to promote the common front with other groups. They accuse me of revisionism, selling out to enemies of the Party. "Capitalist lackey deviationist whore" is one of the more polite insults.'

I was amazed.

'Where does the man from London come into it?'

'Arthur Ford. He was sent here to cut me down to size.'

'But surely London accepts the official line from Moscow?'

'There is no official line yet. Things are never quite that clear cut in the CP, especially when we aren't being force fed by Moscow. No one knows which way to jump and so they stay on the fence and find scapegoats. In this case, it's me.'

'Is this Arthur man an official representative?'

She shrugged her shoulders.

'I don't know who or what faction may have sent him. All I know is that what comes out of his mouth are slogans and rhetoric. He'll say: "We must continue to confront the enemies of revolution." Then everyone looks at me with hatred as though I'm the one who's not doing this because I want to make common cause in the real war of today – against Nazism.

'It also rankles with them that I was in Berlin, in the heat of battle, and – this may surprise you, *liebling* – I've learned from that episode that you can't just shout at the Nazis and expect them to vanish. You have to plan, prepare for the future, even for the eventuality of accepting that in any war you have to suffer some defeats. The people in the cabal are political adolescents. They behave as though the whole thing was a game, as though it's something they'll grow out of once they leave here for the real world. What they don't understand is that this *is* the real world, that we're in a real war. Part of my work here was to persuade them to behave with gravitas, not as though the Party was a secret society, to become real revolutionaries, to work for change, to do things that make people take the Party seriously. I told them they should try to be actors in a script by Karl Marx, not by Oscar Wilde. They just sniggered.'

She stopped, exhausted by her outpourings, and looked washed out.

She hadn't told me who'd ordered her to undertake her work in Cambridge but I guessed it was some organ of the Comintern, the Communist International, which was run from Moscow.

'Can't you complain to the Party leadership?' I asked.

'In London, you mean?' She gave a hollow laugh. 'They wouldn't intervene unless there was a formal denunciation. If I protested, it would be seen as a sign of womanly weakness. Even in the Soviet Union, women aren't much valued.'

There was much more along these lines. I let her go on partly because I thought it good for her to talk it out, and because she seldom stopped for long enough to give me a chance to say anything. She became, in turn, angry, weepy, despondent.

Finally, she told me shamefacedly that she'd been accused of counter-revolutionary activity because of her friendship with me.

'They must be desperate,' I said.

'You think so?' she asked tremulously, unable to smile at – perhaps even to take in – my attempt at humour. This was a new, unconfident, unsure Dorothy.

'Look, Dorothy, my advice, for what it's worth is: don't let them get at you. You've got a job to do. You hold all the cards, which is probably why they're behaving like that. They can't hurt you. So, counter-attack.'

'Do you really think so?'

'Stick to your guns and they'll collapse. Even revolutionaries have human weaknesses.'

'Real revolutionaries don't, actually. But I'm sure you're right about these toads. That man Ford is an absolute idiot. Almost illiterate.'

'Play them at their own game. Get some allies and attack them.'

'I'll try,' she said, bursting into tears.

For long minutes, she cried bitterly, her body heaving. I sensed that it was a release of emotions that she'd been trying to keep under control. I embraced her and held her tight until the sobbing began to subside.

'Thank you,' she breathed.

Then she kissed me on the lips with great intensity. I responded. We clung to each other passionately. I had no time to think about what was happening. It was like being caught up in a strong current and swept out to sea. We'd drunk quite a bit during the evening and it removed all inhibitions.

'Jimmy, please take me to bed,' she pleaded.

Her body was whiter than I'd imagined and thinner, her breasts as fulsome as I'd expected, her pubic hair as copper coloured as the curls on her head. This was a dance of fire rather than an unexpected coupling. She was desperate, hungry, greedy. And I too. Her responses were loud and wild, and I didn't care if Mrs Perkins and all Cambridge heard us.

We lay in each other's arms afterwards, in silence.

Then she said, with something like her usual voice of authority: 'It was lovely, Jimmy, but probably not very wise.'

'I don't see why not. A lot of people seem to think we're lovers – probably even Newnham thinks we've got something incestuous going.'

'This changes things,' she said.

'I can't see why.'

'Because you might fall in love with me.'

'I *am* in love with you, woman.'

'Oh, Jimmy,' she groaned sadly.

'I shouldn't have said that. Forget I said it. All I'm trying to say is that nothing has changed for me except…'

'That's what worries me. You'll expect things from me from now on. And I can't give them to you, Jimmy. I'm not a loving sort of person.'

'I'm not asking for your love, Dorothy. I'd like it, of course, but I don't expect it.'

We argued back and forth along these lines for a while until we again both felt desire and she said: 'Just fuck me again, *liebling*, and let's not worry about the future.'

* * *

She followed my advice about confronting the cabal, and gained the upper hand. Arthur Ford was shown to be a man of straw once Dorothy rallied support for her efforts. He faded away. Whenever I saw Onslow or Gosling-Jones I had to suppress a smile, remembering that their efforts to undermine Dorothy had driven her into my arms and my bed. I gathered that Ed was one of her allies in routing her opponents, although neither he nor Dorothy spoke about it to me.

Summer came and Dorothy and I began to think of finding a place where we could live together. It seemed the right and convenient thing to do. We were in that first flush of desire when we could not keep our hands off each other. We were virtually penniless, but Douglas came up with a solution when I mentioned our financial plight.

He hadn't met Dorothy – and I could tell that what he'd heard of her didn't impress him. But, as always, he was ready to help me on my way through life.

He knew the editor of a new London left-wing magazine who was eager to develop readership in the universities and was looking for a Cambridge correspondent. I went to London to see the editor, Tom Rathbone. He was impressed by the fact that I'd worked, albeit briefly, with Churchill. He didn't like Churchill but admired his way with words, and agreed with him about the dangers posed by Hitler.

I got the job, which involved writing a weekly column of analysis of the way students and staff were thinking about the issues of the day combined with interviews, titbits of news and gossip. I was paid on a lineage basis, which was sufficient to pay the rent on a modest flat. I enjoyed it. My academic work didn't suffer much. Dorothy pursued her efforts to make the Victims of the Nazis Campaign into a major movement, but it failed to ignite. The public attitude to events in Europe was apathetic.

Dorothy and I agreed tacitly that we wouldn't have to meet each other's families, much less inform them of our liaison.

My mother, however, had got to hear of it.

'I don't approve of you living in sin,' she said loftily when I visited her. 'But since the girl is a Jewess it's just as well things stay as they are. You couldn't possibly marry one of that tribe.'

'Of course I could, but we haven't any intention of marrying.'

'Praise God for that!'

'Thanks for your blessing, mother,' I said caustically.

When I told Dorothy, she exploded: 'Bitch!'

She added: 'If that's her attitude, we ought to get married – out of spite.'

'Suits me,' I said.

'Or maybe not. I can't imagine being a respectable married woman.'

'You couldn't ever be respectable, Dorothy,' I smiled.

'Thank you, *liebling*. That's the best compliment I've had in years.'

Ed told me he'd decided to return to the United States for good. He'd been offered a job in a government welfare agency and was going to take it despite his reservations about the New Deal.

'It'll look good on my résumé. It might even be a good experience for me.'

'Even though you'll be working with social fascists?'

'Maybe I can shake up a few ideas. Hopkins has a genius for getting things going. Maybe I can help him in the WPA.'

This was the powerful Works Progress Administration, a vast relief programme which Harry Hopkins had been appointed to head.

'You'll be that senior?' I asked.

'Not to start with,' he smiled. 'No, I don't have the experience to be senior. I'm going in a very lowly capacity – they're taking me on trust on account of they think I have some knowledge of European welfare systems.'

'And do you?'

'I've been around a bit,' he shrugged. 'Talked to people, read a lot of things.'

He wasn't sorry to be escaping his entanglement with Abigail Martin.

'She's been getting kind of possessive. Wonders if she should get a divorce and live with me. I don't think I could handle that sort of closeness, Jim.'

I made no comment.

'Yeah, I know you warned me, but what the hell, it was fun

while it lasted. But something's happened with you, pal. I can tell. You and Dorothy sleeping with each other?'

'Don't ask stupid questions, Ed.'

'Hey, nothing wrong with it. I reckon both of you need it. She's quite a girl, Dot, but I wouldn't get in too deeply, old man. She'll hurt you in the end.'

'Since when did hurting or getting hurt come into your morality?'

'Okay, and, yeah, I fancy her like hell myself, but one thing I would never do is let a dame come between a good friendship.'

'I suppose it's useless to tell you that this whole thing is a figment of your fevered imagination.'

'Oh, really? Well, in that case, maybe I ought to make a play for her.'

'I don't think so, Brewster.'

'Just kidding, Bexley.'

In mid-summer, Dorothy and I went on holiday to southern Spain. We hiked along the coast and to the mountains where we found a cottage to rent. It was primitive and without electricity or running water, but who cared? I had never felt as close to anyone as I did to her during those five weeks. The differences in political beliefs seemed to have little effect on our relationship, based as it was on physical attraction and easy friendship. We discussed politics, of course, along with almost every subject under the sun, but there was never any rancour when we disagreed.

When I suggested she read some exceptional lyric love poems written by a well-known rightist, she replied she'd as soon plough through *Mein Kampf*.

'That's absurd,' I said.

'Art has a social role. Reactionary art is by definition bad.'

'But if you read a poem, or listened to a piece of music, and enjoyed it, would it matter if you discovered it was created by a reactionary?'

'The question shows just how much time I need to spend on educating you along the right lines,' she said smugly, and we both laughed – at ourselves and at the madness of ideological dogma.

After making love, we often discussed politics. It seemed almost to provide light relief after the intensity of our passion.

'God,' she sighed one glorious afternoon. 'The Party never instructed me about the delights of the multiple orgasm.'

'Of course not. It would distract hot-blooded animals from their dialectical duties.'

'Am I hot-blooded? I think of myself as cold-blooded, calculating.'

'You could have fooled me. Are all the comrades like this? Automatons on the outside, volcanoes beneath the surface?'

'I can't speak for the females. The males vary. Mostly, though, they're awfully domineering towards women.'

'Well I can be as domineering as the next comrade. So, why don't you be a good little mistress and make me some coffee?'

'Get lost, my love,' she said, ruffling my hair. 'I will honour you, but I won't obey you.'

'You'll never have to. Save your obedience for the Party.'

'I don't obey the Party,' she said with a slight frown. 'I try to advance its aims. But I don't accept orders without thought.'

A week or so after this exchange, she woke me late at night by gently shaking my shoulder.

'I have to confess something,' she said.

'I'm not a priest,' I mumbled, coming slowly out of slumber.

I sat up. The moon shone through our window and I could see her face was serious. She lit a cigarette.

'You're not pregnant?' I said. 'If you are, that's wonderful.'

She allowed herself a little smile.

'No, I'm not, and it wouldn't be wonderful,' she said. 'The last thing either of us need is a child. What I want to say is about the way I feel. All my talk about the Party. You know, it's been my life, really, for years.'

'I know.'

'But, oh, Jimmy, it's complicated.'

'Try me.'

'Remember I told you my work at Cambridge was to galvanise the Party members, or something like that? Well, it was a half-truth. If I tell you the other half, will you promise to keep it to yourself?'

I nodded.

She hesitated for a long while.

'I should have told you right away, and certainly as soon as we became lovers. I suppose I was too ashamed of it. The Party *did* instruct me to go to Cambridge, but not for routine activity. I was told to persuade likely people that they could serve the Party better if they hid their allegiance. They should pursue careers, and gain influence without anyone suspecting they were Communists.'

'Why?'

'Use your imagination, *liebling*. If you became, say, a Cabinet minister, and were a secret Party member, wouldn't that be of immense importance?'

'My God, you're recruiting spies,' I said.

'Don't be silly, Jimmy. The Party is internationalist. If I recruited someone to the Labour Party, say, would that be seen as treason just because, say, France had a socialist government?'

'You wouldn't ask him to keep it secret. Why instruct your recruits to deceive the world?'

'It was a question of being discreet about their beliefs,' she said, a little impatiently. 'Very discreet. Most of the ruling class here regards the Party as an enemy. Moscow's view is that this will take time to change, and in the meantime some of its ablest members would be debarred from public life if they professed their beliefs openly.'

'In that case, why are you ashamed, Dorothy?'

'Because I kept it from you. As if I couldn't rely on your discretion.'

'It's a small thing,' I said with a casualness I did not feel.

'And because I found out that the Politburo, or whoever takes the real decisions on things like this, didn't fully trust a non-Soviet person to do the job. I had to report to ... well, it doesn't matter exactly who. You can guess.'

I knew it could only be a Soviet agent, either in the embassy or working here under another cover.

'They didn't trust me,' she said.

Her expression told me that this was the biggest betrayal she'd ever faced. She looked bereft.

'In that case, it's their loss,' was all I could say.

'The Party is a part of my life, Jimmy.'

'I know.'

'I still believe in it,' she added hurriedly. 'It's our only hope.'

I knew now what this late night confession was about. It wasn't about keeping the truth from me. It was about her own crisis of faith. I supposed she wanted me to reassure her that her god was testing her, that she should continue to believe. But I was the wrong person to ask.

I could only try to comfort her by holding her tight. She wept a little, then said, with forced brightness: 'Anyway, *liebling*, I'm sorry I didn't tell you everything at the time.'

'Your St Peter project,' I said lightly. 'Fishing for men. How many poor fools have you managed to reel in?'

'None,' she said. 'I was settling into Cambridge, looking around to see how the land lay. And then I was told to report to ... never mind the name. I did. Even though they didn't trust me enough to do the thing myself, I would still have been willing to work under someone else's direction. Then I was told to abandon the whole project.'

'Why?'

'They don't give reasons. I suspect it was because they felt a woman might more easily be tricked into believing promises. Or it may have been because of you.'

'Me?'

'When we became involved with each other they may have felt I would blab something on the pillow to you, and that you might be, um, unreliable.'

'Ye gods! So I've saved the kingdom from revolution.'

'Do you have to joke about it?'

She looked uncertain, vulnerable, miserable.

'I could never be unreliable as far as you're concerned,' I said, kissing her.

'You won't tell a soul? I mean, I know you won't.'

'It's your business, and that of the idiots you might have seduced into it. Why should you even think I'd tell anyone?'

'Because you know very well that someone else is probably doing the work, and because you have a damn conscience,' she said.

'A damn bourgeois conscience.'

'Yes, the very worst kind,' she laughed.

I kissed her and said: 'I promise never to tell. And my conscience doesn't allow me to break promises.'

She stuck her tongue out at me, mockingly. Then we made long and strenuous love until the sun began to rise and we could go back to sleep, exhausted, satiated.

17

Yalta, February 7, 1945

Winston summoned me to his room at around 2 a.m. He was in his pyjamas but not yet ready for sleep. The news he had been given by Anthony about the President's resolve to leave within a day or two had unsettled him.

'I want Harry,' he growled at me.

I must have had too much to drink that night, for I could do nothing but look blank and perplexed.

'Mr Harry Hopkins!' he said. 'I assume you know of him.'

'Of course, Prime Minister. Do you mean I should seek him out now?'

'Don't be a bloody fool!' he snarled. 'If I wanted him now I'd have sent a detachment of hussars to fetch him. I want you to collect him and convey him here early tomorrow morning.'

He was in an ugly mood, so I didn't dare point out that it was already tomorrow, or that Hopkins was obviously a very ill man who could not simply be yanked out of his bed in the early morning and driven 25 miles to and fro along a mountain road at Winston's whim, or that President Roosevelt might take a dim view at having his close aide whisked off, without his consent, for a conversation with the British Prime Minister. I tried to prevaricate.

'What reason shall I give, Prime Minister?' I asked.

'Reason? Simply tell him that his friend Winston Churchill requests the pleasure of his company for a private discussion over breakfast.'

I nodded.

'Of course, if you think that protocol demands it, you might take along an embossed invitation,' he added with great sarcasm. 'But I believe that Harry and I are of sufficiently the same mind to render such ceremony unnecessary. I should like to see him at ten o'clock, if possible, or at his earliest convenience. Now I'm going to sleep. Good-night.'

He switched off his bedside lamp.

Outside his room, I glanced at my watch and winced. If lucky, I'd have three or four hours' troubled sleep before heading off on what I was sure would be a wild goose chase. Hopkins would scoff at the idea or – at the very best – seek permission from Roosevelt. If he *did* ask permission, I had no doubt the President would refuse it.

It was not only Winston's strange errand that kept me from restful, dreamless slumber. Perhaps it was my conversation with Anthony, perhaps all the secrets and deceptions and intrigues – personal and diplomatic – swirling around my mind, that made me dream of Dorothy. She and I were together, laughing, but the sheets were unwashed, and I was ashamed of this. She didn't mind and kept reassuring me: 'It's okay, *liebling*, it's okay.'

When I opened my eyes at seven o'clock and then dropped back into a dozy state of semi-sleep for a few minutes I couldn't help my mind running rapidly over the events at Cambridge in the 1930s and of the love affairs of those and later days. Then I remembered what had to be done this morning and put aside my memories, along with my dream. I hopped out of bed and commandeered a vehicle to take me to the Livadia. A mist lay over the Black Sea, but it was going to be another brilliantly sunny day.

I was well enough known to the military guards to get access to Hopkins' quarters on the basis of carrying a message from Winston.

Hopkins was awake but still in bed, looking worn out. He recognised me as one of Winston's entourage and sighed.

'A message from my old friend so early in the day? It must be serious.'

'He wants to talk to you, Mr Hopkins.'

'That's okay with me. We'll find some time later in the day.'

I coughed apologetically: 'He'd like you to visit him this morning.'

'What's happened? Is he ill?'

'No, he's well enough.'

'I'm pleased to hear that. So why the hell can't he come to see me?'

'I don't think I should speculate on that, sir.'

He eyed me.

'That's pretty good, young man. The trick of this business is never to put words into the boss's mouth. Only gets you into hot water. I learned that early on. So, my guess is he doesn't want the President to know about this.'

'I think that's probably right,' I said.

'Well, now, that puts me in a bit of a spot, because I didn't get where I am – wherever that is – by going behind my boss's back. Can't this business wait?'

'The Prime Minister seemed quite ... agitated about seeing you this morning, privately.'

'He told you to come and grab me?' he asked, amused.

'Yes.'

'To kidnap me, if necessary?'

'He didn't go that far.'

'Don't tell me the old boy's going so soft that he'd stop short of abduction.'

I didn't respond.

He looked down at his bony hands, then slowly climbed out of bed, walked stiffly to the wardrobe and began dressing.

'I'd sure put you on the spot if I declined this invitation,' he said.

'Yes.'

'Okay, I'll come quietly. It's the least I can do for Winston.'

I waited while he put on a wrinkled suit. It hung loosely around his gaunt frame, accentuating the way he had seemed to shrink in size even since the start of the conference. He winked at me and said: 'Right, let's see if we can avoid the presidential nursemaids.'

He put on a coat and a battered hat and we went to the waiting car.

During the journey, he mostly slumped with closed eyes, but it was hard to tell if he was dozing, or just reflecting.

He is reflecting. He's ruminating about Winston Churchill and their unusual relationship, so important, he thinks proudly, to the cementing of the Atlantic alliance.

He remembers the beginning – the phone ringing in his second-floor suite in the White House one crisp day in Washington in January 1941.

'Yeah?'

'Harry?'

'Steve. What's up?'

The caller is Stephen Early, the President's press spokesman.

'Congratulations, Harry.'

'Well, thanks. But on what?'

'On your trip.'

'What trip?'

'To England. Poppa's just announced it to the press. You're going as his special representative.'

'That's great, but goddamit, Steve, he told me I was too valuable to him here.'

Early chuckles.

'Well, no doubt, Harry, he thinks you're much more fucking valuable in London dodging Kraut bombs.'

'Thanks for that, Steve, and a happy New Year to you too.'

Harry, wearing a shabby old dressing-gown though it is past noon, puts the phone down, hunts around for a letter from a former Cabinet member seeking a meeting with the President. He eventually finds it, beneath a pile of newspapers, and scribbles a reply, to be typed later in the day. The reply turns down the request politely because of the President's pressing current business.

He won't show the reply to the President – just as he hasn't shown him the original letter. He doesn't have to. He knows Roosevelt's mind on these things, and Roosevelt trusts him to know and to act accordingly. That's his role. He has no official title. He is FDR's most trusted friend, the repository of his secrets and his schemes. It doesn't annoy Hopkins that the Chief gets enjoyment from keeping him in the dark on occasions.

Still in his dressing-gown and slippers, he shuffles in to see the President.

'Ah, Harry,' Roosevelt says with a broad smile. 'You've heard?'

'Steve called me.'

'Sorry I didn't have the chance to inform you beforehand. It just came out at the press conference. The boys were pressing me on lend-lease and I suddenly thought well we'd better have someone over there at this critical time, so I told them I was sending you.'

Harry sits down and nods. He doesn't believe a word of how

it all came out just like that. He knows Roosevelt needs a bit of harmless, mischievous fun.

'I want you to find out if the British can hang on and win the war, Harry. Kennedy doesn't give much for their chances. I want you to be my eyes and ears. Find out what they need to keep going – if they really do intend to keep going.'

'Churchill *says* they do.'

'I want to be sure. If he's ready to fight to the death, then I want to meet him. You're going to fish all that out for me, Harry. I wouldn't trust anyone else to do it.'

In London, Brendan Bracken hurries to tell Churchill the news. Bracken, Churchill's long-time supporter and crony, is currently his parliamentary Private Secretary.

'Roosevelt's sending Harry Hopkins to see you,' he says breathlessly.

'Harry who?' booms Churchill.

'Winston, this man is the President's closest friend and confidant.'

'I would prefer to be meeting the President himself.'

'The first thing, Winston, is to convince his emissary that such a meeting is vital to you both.'

'Hopkins, you say? Not the New Deal man?'

'Yes, and very successful at that.'

'Well, well. Is he, do you think, Brendan, coming here to lecture us on how to increase employment in these grave times, perhaps on how to pay the poor to construct better air raid shelters?'

'Trust me, Winston. This is important.'

'Very well. In that case, we will roll out every red carpet that we can muster to welcome this Mr Hopkins.'

The two men meet a few days later at 10 Downing Street. They approach each other warily, like two stags about to battle it out.

Harry, weary of being told by everyone in the know in Washington that the only person who counts for anything in the British government is Churchill, wonders if the fellow is a great man or merely a grandiloquent one.

Churchill, for his part, doesn't like being fobbed off with a mere aide, no matter how loyal to his master.

'Welcome to England, Mr Hopkins.'

'It's good to be here at last, Prime Minister.'

'Your journey was not too arduous, I hope?'

'To tell you the truth, I hated every minute of it. There is nothing I dislike more than flying – unless it be Adolf Hitler and his gang.'

'Ah, I see we already have some common ground. However, while I too abominate that man in Berlin above all other creatures, I find air travel enjoyable, even stimulating. Did you know that I piloted biplanes in those days before aeroplanes were used for more diabolical aims?'

'They may be diabolical but from what I hear you guys are doing pretty well in retaliation. And I hope we may soon be able to help you to do even more diabolical things against Germany.'

Ah, thinks Churchill, there is more to this man than meets the eye. He isn't much to look at, at first sight – thin, wispy-haired, crumpled clothes, untidy on the surface, but with bright eyes and piercing gaze.

Over lunch in a basement room – cold beef, green salad, cheese and biscuits, coffee – they begin to warm to each other.

Harry says: 'I've had a few glimpses of the bomb damage, and admire the amazing resilience of you all. I fancy that much of it is thanks to your speeches, Prime Minister.'

'No, Mr Hopkins. I hardly knew what I said. All I knew was that the people felt, as I did, that it would be better for our country to be destroyed than to see the triumph of such an impostor as Hitler.'

Harry perceives there is a genuine emotion in the way Churchill speaks about England and its people and about how he has merely been the vehicle for voicing the nation's will to resist. Harry is not a blind lover of the British, and certainly not of their Empire and their class system, but he admires courage and respect for democracy. Already, his doubts about Churchill's greatness have begun to evaporate. Above all, he senses that this is an inspiring leader who will fight to the bitter end.

'Your speeches have produced a most remarkable and stirring effect on all classes in America. You know, at one Cabinet meeting, the President had a wireless set brought in so we could listen to you broadcast.'

'I am gratified, Mr Hopkins.'

'Please, call me Harry. Just Harry, son of a saddle-maker from Sioux City, Iowa.'

'Here, take some more jelly with your beef, Harry,' Churchill urges, much impressed with the man and his manner.

'One of the messages I have for you from the President is that he is very eager to meet with you soon.'

'I too think a meeting is essential, and at the earliest possible time. But pray tell me if there are other reasons for your visit?'

'I'm here to find out what you need, and to see that you get it – and then some.'

'We shall tell you, Harry. We shall show you what we have and what we desperately need. Of course, we cannot immediately pay you for your deliveries. Our reserves are low, nay worse than low. But we will not be shy in listing our needs.'

'I hope not. The President hopes not. And payment is not an issue, Prime Minister. You will see very soon when the Lend-Lease Bill is published, exactly how we aim to do this.'

'That programme, my dear Harry, is one of the most unsordid acts in the history of friendship between nations. But will it pass Congress?'

'I believe it will. The President had to be very cautious in what he said during the election campaign. Now, he's free to say what he pleases and he will mobilise opinion and Congress to pass this measure.'

'What a wonderful democracy is the United States of America!'

'It is,' says Harry. 'Of course, there have been divergent views about this war. The President knows, though, and I know, that we have to be involved, that we *are* involved, that your fight is our fight.'

'Bless you, Harry.'

'I should tell you, though, that there are a lot of people back home – Irish zealots, German and Italian fascist sympathisers, the Communists who follow Moscow's line, you name it – who can't stand the British and actually hope you're going to lose.'

'We must face such hostility with as much fortitude as we can manage,' says Churchill with a smile.

Harry's face cracks into a rare grin.

'Well, yes, that's exactly what the President thinks about it.'

Then he says, more seriously: 'But these sort of characters

have spread the word that deep down you don't like America or Franklin Roosevelt.'

Churchill looks pained.

'I hardly know how to answer such a despicable canard, Harry.'

'Naturally, I do not believe such rumours – and neither does the President,' Harry puts in quickly.

'My dear mother was an American,' says Churchill. 'I am half-American. The United States is the great hope of the free world. And as for President Roosevelt, there is no one in the world I admire more than him.'

'The President has no doubt whatever that you are the best friend we have in the world.'

'And I never had any doubt that he would become our great ally,' Churchill smiles. 'Although he did appear to be a little hesitant before, um, taking the plunge. We understood the reasons for that.'

'He had to bide his time. There were people – influential people – telling him that giving armaments to you might be a waste of weapons. They said you people might not be able to fight on, that you might try to negotiate.'

Churchill starts to protest, but Harry blithely waves him to silence.

'The President never bought into that kind of thinking, but what convinced him that you meant business was when you attacked the French navy after the surrender.'

'It was a heartbreaking thing to do, Harry, but we couldn't allow those ships to fall into German hands.'

Both men are moved by the memory of a tragic necessity. Battleships of a recent ally sent to the bottom of the sea, along with more than a thousand French sailors.

Churchill takes some snuff. Harry lights a Chesterfield.

C'est la guerre. It is time to move on.

'Is there anything, Harry, that I can do to assist you in your mission?'

'I would like to see as much as I can with my own eyes, and to talk to people who count, which I guess includes just about everybody in Britain.'

'I will personally conduct you in some of these ventures, and ensure you have the opportunity for others.'

No red tape for this man, thinks Harry. We're two of a kind.

No obfuscation with this man, thinks Churchill with gratitude.

In the next month, the bond becomes stronger. Churchill, so impressed by Hopkins' ability to cut through difficult details and get to the heart of the issue, refers to him as Lord Root of the Matter. And Harry is moved and uplifted by what he sees and hears during his visit – especially of what he sees and hears of Churchill.

In mid-January, Churchill takes his guest to shivering Scotland, where snow lies deep and blizzards rage. It is here, at a reception in Glasgow, that Harry rises to give a short speech, turns towards Churchill and says:

'I suppose you wish to know what I am going to say to President Roosevelt on my return. It would be impolitic to tell you the exact words I plan to use, but I am going to quote to you a verse from the Book of Ruth: "Whither thou goest, I will go; and where thou lodgest I will lodge: thy people shall be my people, and thy God my God."'

Then he pauses, and adds, quietly: 'Even to the End.'

Churchill has tears in his eyes.

There are no reporters present and nothing is published, but the word gets out, and Britain knows – as Churchill knows – that this means it is now certain that the war will be won.

Four years on, with the war nearing its end and peace – of a kind – looming, Churchill clasps Hopkins' hand in greeting at Yalta and asks with tender solicitude: 'Harry, how are you, my dear friend?'

'Not so damn hot, Winston. I shouldn't be here at all.'

'Forgive me, Harry, for dragging you all the way to see me this morning, but we have not had an opportunity to talk.'

'I meant I shouldn't be at this goddam conference in this goddam place. All I have the strength for is to sit in on some of the sessions and try to keep Franklin focused.'

'Ah, yes. Now, Harry, what the devil is he up to?'

'Who knows? He has his way of doing things, always did.'

'He has been cold and abrupt towards me. He appears to ridicule me, to reject my arguments with disdain.'

'From what I've observed, he's just the same old Franklin, doing what he has to do.'

'He offers Stalin whatever the man wants, he gives me nothing. It's treachery, Harry – treachery to an old friend.'

'No, Winston, just practical politics, what he's best at. Besides, didn't we help you out over the French? And, you know, Stalin's made a hell of a lot of concessions here, Winston.'

'Concessions, bah! Don't tell me you trust that man? Are we that far apart, Harry?'

'So help me God, it's been a long time since I really trusted anyone besides my family, Winston. We have to take our allies as we find them. I wouldn't go fishing with the guy – not for pleasure – but I can't say I distrust him any more than a lot of other so-called friends we're lumbered with.'

'Sometimes, and with great sadness, I wonder whether *I* am trusted, Harry. I fear the President does not have full confidence in me. Why else, at a time when I am still struggling for sensible and workable agreements, does he decide to take premature leave of us?'

'I guess he reckons we've all got as much as we can out of this junket.'

'You would defend him, then? You would agree that he must appease this man in the Kremlin at my expense?'

Hopkins thinks carefully about his response. He can see both sides of the question. Winston, he knows, feels deeply betrayed and saddened, but then Winston is sometimes a little blinkered in his thinking these days.

'Both of you know that Stalin is going to be a mighty big player from now on. We can't just sideline him.'

'Hitler too was a big player, as you put it, Harry, and did we not sideline him?'

Hopkins chuckles.

'We sure did. But there is no way either the United States or Great Britain is going to get into another world war just yet. You asked me a question about the President's intentions, Winston, and I have to say that I don't know for sure, but he's fixed on a way of the world living together without war. And if that means we have to be nice to Joe Stalin, then so be it.'

'But, but,' Churchill splutters. 'We cannot give in to that Bolshevik blackguard's every whim. He will gobble up all of Europe if we don't put a stop to him. And all the President wants to do is – what is the word? – sideline me and be nice to Stalin, whatever the cost? Is that why he is cutting and running from this conference before we have fully discussed the big issues?'

'They've been given an airing, Winston, and the unresolved matters will be discussed further.'

'I have been fobbed off. Stalin gloats, and the President sails off. But the President will not have to live with that man as his greedy neighbour.'

Hopkins sighs.

'One of the things this war has done, Winston, is to shrink the world. We're all neighbours now.'

'But *you* don't have Stalin breathing down your neck. Franklin says he plans to pull your troops out of Europe in a few years. The Red Army is about to take Berlin. Are we to allow them to control Germany?'

'No, and that's why we've got to tie him into the United Nations.'

'Pshaw,' says Churchill.

'Didn't you once say that jaw-jaw is better than war-war?'

'It is attributed to me but I cannot recall the occasion. Nevertheless, the sentiment is valid in so far as all the parties wanting to jaw-jaw are genuinely interested in resolving problems through negotiations.'

'And you don't think Stalin has such an interest?'

'My dear Harry, his interest is only in advancing his own interests, regardless of the cost to others. If only I could have one more meeting with Franklin here, to make him understand.'

'Once he's set on something, he'll see it through.'

'Ah, Harry, Harry. I wanted some light from you, and all I get is a dark tunnel. You can influence him.'

'Not any more, Winston. I'm sorry. I really am. But you know I've always given things to you straight. And that's the way it is.'

Churchill nods sadly.

Hopkins glances at his wrist-watch, and says: 'I'm not feeling that chipper these days. I'd better get back and rest.'

'Of course you must, Harry. You must take care of yourself. You and I have always been true friends and will remain so.'

'You have no truer friend than me, Prime Minister.'

'I know, Harry, I know.'

Churchill escorts his visitor to the entrance of the palace. They shake hands.

'Harry, one last thing before I leave you in peace to rest. They tell me little these days. Is this Tube Alloys project going to come to fruition sooner or later?'

Tube Alloys is the code name for the huge research programme under way in America in the atomic field.

'I'm no longer in on it,' says Hopkins. 'I can't tell you anything you don't know.'

'But surely Franklin confides in you. You're his right hand, Harry.'

'Not to the same extent. I'm worn out, and he knows it. I damn well hope he knows it. And to tell the truth, I don't figure he knows too much about Tube Alloys either. They're a law unto themselves, the guys running the project.'

'No whispers, Harry?'

'All I've heard,' says Hopkins wearily, 'and it was just a throwaway line from someone vaguely in the know, is that they could begin trials in the Fall but it isn't likely to have any impact on the Pacific War.'

'But we could bluff on it, though, couldn't we? Tell Stalin that if he doesn't, um, fall into line, then we could, in theory of course, use some of these new weapons against him.'

Oh, God, thinks Hopkins, Winston *has* lost the plot. Threaten our most necessary ally with an atomic bomb!

'I don't believe we can count on it for at least a couple of years, and I don't think we could begin to fool Stalin about that.'

'Oh,' says Churchill, crestfallen.

'Goodbye, Winston.' Hopkins touches his hat in a gesture of affectionate homage.

Winston raises a paw in a parting salute. 'Godspeed, Harry.'

18

London

'It's no use,' Dorothy said on a summer evening at our little flat in Bloomsbury in 1936, her eyes reddened by weeping. 'I have to go away.'

I protested, though not as vehemently as once I would have done. Our relationship had begun to turn sour about a year after we set up home together, first in Cambridge and then in London.

She was going through a deepening crisis of faith. She still believed Marxism was the only path to greater happiness in the world though she choked on the lies, manipulations and crimes that the Stalinist system was using to achieve its aims. Her experiences in Germany, Russia and England disturbed her deeply, though she clung to her basic creed. Even when no impartial person could ignore the reports of millions dying in Russia and Ukraine through a policy-induced famine, and when it was clear that Stalin had unleashed a reign of terror against his real and imagined critics in the Party, she lived in the hope that all would be well in the dream future.

Her inner turmoil made her depressed, neurotic and hell to live with – and I wasn't much good at providing her with the support she could have got only from someone who'd been through an experience similar to her. I tried to help her through what I hoped was a bad patch, but gradually began to lose patience. My view, expressed often to her in more restrained language, was: 'Communisim is fraud on a gigantic scale – let go of it and get on with your life, doing what you think is right.'

This was tactless and catastrophically misguided advice to someone as devoted as she had been for so long to a living faith. However, I was young and unable to cope with her moods and the withdrawal of her love, which happened when she felt that I was trying to destroy the last few hopes she had. Despite everything – perhaps because of everything – I remained in love with her and desperately sought to believe that she would get over her depression and become again the determined, sparkling, audacious person I'd fallen for in Berlin.

'It's no use,' she said on that evening in Bloomsbury. 'I have to go.'

'Is this because of the paper? I'll quit, find something else.'

I had managed to land a full-time journalistic post – but on a newspaper whose editorial line offended both of us.

'It's not just that. It's that we're harming each other. I'm dragging you down with me.'

'You're not. I'll try to be more patient.'

'It's not patience I need, or sympathy, Jimmy. Whatever I need, it can't come from you. You're understanding, but you *don't* understand. Does that make sense?'

'Is there somebody else?'

'There's the Party. You can't understand that.'

So she left, and I was miserably lonely for weeks, then angry at her and the whole corrupt system that had built up her faith and then destroyed it but would not let her be free of it. I had no idea where she was living. She wrote a few short notes saying she was well and I was not to worry about her. No regrets about leaving me, no expression of worry about how *I* might be taking it!

Sometimes, I felt relief at being free from her anguish; at other times, I was bitter at her selfishness and at my failure to preserve this first great love of my life, guilty about my inability to cope with her troubled needs.

The job on a right-wing paper had come about because my stepfather introduced me to the proprietor. I thought a spell on it would count as a step on the way to something better. Dorothy disagreed. As a favour to Bob, I was given a trial, and then a job. The week after Dorothy left me, I had a row with a sub-editor who removed background material in a story I'd written on Britain's refugee policy. The material listed the long catalogue of anti-Semitic laws enacted in Germany. When I asked why he'd taken that out, he said it was 'unnecessarily inflammatory'.

'For God's sake, it's factual,' I exclaimed. 'Do you think Jews are fleeing because they're being well treated over there?'

I was hauled before the editor who said: 'We have to live with the new reality of Europe, my lad. We don't want to antagonise Germany. The proprietor says so, and that's the way it is. Better the Nazis than the Bolsheviks. If you want to write sob stories about the Jews, join the *News Chronicle* or the *Manchester Guardian*.'

I told him, briefly but pertinently, what I thought about the paper and its proprietor, and my employment was promptly terminated.

My first thought was – Dorothy will be proud of me. Then I told myself: no she won't; she's gone, she won't even know.

Word of my stand, however, did the rounds in Fleet Street, where dog loved nothing better than eating dog. Someone suggested I try my luck at the *Review*, a new weekly paper becoming known for espousing left-wing causes. I was hired as a junior reporter. Not long afterwards, to add to my good fortune, Tom Rathbone, for whom I'd worked while at Cambridge, was appointed the *Review*'s editor.

My stepfather was furious not so much because I'd messed up the chance he'd given me, but because I'd joined a paper that was highly critical of the government.

'You're going to have to learn,' he said pompously, 'that the policies of England are made in Downing Street and *The Times*, not by the leftist rags.'

I enjoyed working at the *Review*. My colleagues were congenial and I was learning my trade, dreaming of a big story that might come my way but not fretting about advancement. I was also beginning, just a little, to enjoy being a bachelor in London. I wasn't earning a great deal, but the big city offered much, even to someone on my salary, in the way of decent food, good entertainment and attractive young women eager for male friendship and, on occasion, uncomplicated sex. I missed Dorothy, and was angry about our parting, but didn't pine for her.

One morning I got a phone call in the office.

'My dear Herr Bexley, how happy that I can hear your voice again.'

It was Dr Bergsen. I'd had a letter forwarded from Trinity a few weeks before asking if I'd be his sponsor so he could get a visa for Britain. I replied that I'd be happy to do so, and advised the British Passport Control Office in Berlin. Nevertheless,

I was surprised to hear his voice so soon. I knew that acquiring a visa was only one obstacle to be cleared. The Germans wanted to get rid of the Jews but weren't going to make it easy for them to leave. One of the hurdles for would-be emigrants was a hefty flight tax.

Dr Bergsen explained that though my reply had not been delivered to him, he'd assumed I would agree and had gone to the British Embassy where he was swiftly given his visa. Then he paid a middleman to bribe a Nazi official who issued a pass with permission to leave Germany.

'So here I am where I long dreamed to be, in England. And thanks to you, also, my dear friend, for sponsoring me. I hope you do not mind that I bother you like this. And now I phone to say thank you in my voice. I did not know where to find you, so I went to Trinity. It is so beautiful, peaceful, civilised, exactly as I imagine, exactly as some of our great German universities were before this madness came.'

He'd been told by a hall porter that I'd left the college but Mr Winterton might know where I could be reached. Douglas had received him kindly and given him my telephone number at the *Review*.

'He is a great gentleman, Herr Professor Winterton,' said Dr Bergsen reverentially.

'Where are you now?' I asked.

'In London. Might be one day we drink tea together, Herr Bexley.'

He was lodging with a family in the East End.

'Is not as *gemütlich* as Frau Siegendorff's residence,' he said wistfully. 'But this family is good people.'

I said he should come and stay with me. He demurred. It would be inconvenient to me, it would be a burden, he had not yet found a job so could not afford to pay rent, he wanted us to stay friends and not to cause me trouble.

'Herr Dr Bergsen,' I said firmly. 'It would be an honour if you would be my guest until you find your feet.'

'Thank you, dear Herr Bexley, but I cannot...'

'I should feel hurt if you refuse my invitation.'

In the end, I extracted his address, asked him to pack his suitcases and said I would pick him up that evening.

'I will write to tell my nephew Leo of your kindness,' he said.

'Is he well?'

'I believe, but he is too much a European to live so far away.'

'And still at Princeton?'

'*Ja, ja,*' said Dr Bergsen with pride.

'What sort of things is he working on?'

'About that, he has not told me. He has become very secret – is that the right word? – in his letters.'

'Secretive.'

'*Ja*, secretive. Nothing he writes, except that he has a job, and that he worries about his mother, his sisters and the others in our family. They still cannot have the money to leave Germany, and also they are not so much wanting to leave. Me and Leo, we will have to try to help them.'

That night, after settling Dr Bergsen in his room, making dinner and reassuring him a hundred times that he was not imposing on me, I heard more about life under the Nazis. My various letters to him had not been delivered to Frau Siegendorff's house. They must have been opened by the police and thrown away, or put into a file by the Gestapo.

'Do they do that to all mail for Jews?'

'They do it to me, yes, because I am a Jew and also maybe because I write a lot of letters that do not get answered.'

'Letters to whom?'

'Ach, someone like me with much time to do nothing, I write all the day, to Goering, to Hess, to the law societies, to ministries, I write to everyone. I say how unjust that even frontline fighters – men like me who fought in the last war – now cannot properly practise their professions. The Gestapo come to see me. They say I should be thankful I am not already in a concentration camp and that I will be in one quickly if I go on complaining. They threaten me like that, Herr Bexley.'

'Did you stop writing?'

'*Naturlich*, no,' he said. 'No, I write more even than before. They come again and say they will take me away. I tell them: "Show me the law that says I cannot write letters." They say, they use terrible language, Herr Bexley, that they care nothing for the law. So they put me in the Dachau camp – it is near München, Munich, yes? – for a month. There I see things.'

He blinked.

'Inside there is Communists, socialists, all they call "enemies of the State", like good Christians who say murder is bad, and of course Jews already. We have to do work, never mind how old you are. "Work makes you *free*" is motto of camp.'

He laughed briefly and shook his head from side to side as he emphasised the word 'free'.

'They make rules that even if you criticise what goes on, even if you write anything about the camp, they can hang you. I see prisoners hanged. They make us to watch. Terrible. I see people who cannot finish their work being beaten. Ach, there is nothing more to tell.'

He paused.

'Is that when you decided to leave?' I asked.

'When the month is over, and they take me out from the camp and say: "You can go home, but next time you will stay here until you die." Then one tells me I will be free to leave Germany if I hand over all my property to the State. I laugh, Herr Bexley. What property do I have? A small house that my father had where he lived and is now, how do we say in English – *verfallen?*'

'Derelict,' I suggested.

'Derelict, *ja*. A good word for so much things. Broken windows, walls damaged. Inside is furniture stolen or broken. All is worth nothing. So I laugh at that policeman and he hits me across my face and says I am telling lies, all Jews are rich. Bad times, my dear Herr Bexley. Bad times. So I return to Berlin, and still I say to myself: "This is your country also, Samuel Bergsen. Why should you leave your country?"'

He spread his arms wide to indicate the ridiculous idea that anyone should want to leave their homeland.

'But then one day I find out it is not my country any more. They make a law, the Nuremberg laws, that mean Jews are no longer Germans. So then I think it is finally time for me to leave my beloved Germany.'

He smiled ruefully.

A lawyer to his fingertips! Only when they legislated to deprive him of his citizenship did he accept the final reality of his status.

'One day I will go back,' he said. 'When this madness is over, one day. They cannot get rid of all the Jews in Germany.'

Later, I told him about how Dorothy and I had lived together and recently broken up. He expressed sympathy and concern and then added: 'You do not look like someone who dies from a broken up heart.'

I agreed that heartbroken wasn't the way I'd describe my feelings.

'Fraulein Jung – excuse, Young – has very big feelings about things, but maybe not about persons. *Naturlich*, naturally, I say nothing against her, but I do not think you could change her.'

'You think that's what was behind it all?' I asked, surprised.

'Perhaps. Perhaps you want to save her. But is not a good formel – how you say in English? – for loving.'

'Formula.'

'Formula. For love, should be something not so from the mind. I cannot express well.'

'I didn't know you were such an expert on love,' I teased.

'An expert, I do not believe so,' he said, smiling modestly. 'Once, after I come back from the war, in 1918, I fall in love with a woman. I think about how to marry her, but I am only a poor soldier. Her family is among the most rich in Berlin, with a big home on the Tiergartenstrasse. For them, I am not good enough for their daughter. So, she marries later an important man who owns theatres, kinemas, all kinds of businesses. He is older than her by much, but richer than me by much. So I study law and about love I only think.'

'Did she return your love, Herr Dr Bergsen?'

'I think, yes. But not so much that she would go against the wishes of her family. And that, also, I would not have expected she should do.'

I tried to find him work that might utilise his legal knowledge, but it was difficult to know where to turn. England had little use, it appeared, for a virtually penniless, ageing German lawyer with rudimentary linguistic skills in English.

Much as I disliked doing it, I approached my stepfather.

'All these people, flooding us out,' he snorted. 'No one I know has anything for another useless Jew. Tell him to go to America or one of the colonies, if they'll have him. He should have stayed in Germany.'

'Bob! For God's sake, you're supposed to be a bloody Member of Parliament. You're supposed to know what's going on in Germany.'

'I do,' he said angrily. 'And it's not at all like your wretched rag paints it. Hitler has done a lot for Germany, and the Jews have only themselves to blame. All that's happening is they're being weeded out from business, law, medicine, the press – all the things they've dominated for years.'

'And, really, Jimmy,' my mother put in. 'Why you choose to let such a person share your flat, I don't know. First that ghastly woman, and now this, this *refugee*. As you know, neither Bob nor I are against the Jewish people, but a lot of them come here with the most awful diseases.'

'Don't worry, mother, I've had the place fumigated,' I said, stomping off in disgust.

One evening, I got home to find Dr Bergsen preparing a mutton stew and wearing a broad smile. He had a job, he told me. As a travelling salesman for a wine company. My face must have shown my surprise.

'You wonder what a German lawyer knows about wine, eh? Answer is, not anything much, but I will learn. And I will learn English well and study for my law degree in England, and make money enough to send to my relations in Germany so they will all come to England, and all will be good, my dear Jimmy.'

I had insisted he call me by my first name, even though I continued, German fashion, to address him as Herr Doktor Bergsen. He hoped soon to be earning enough to rent a place of his own, 'so no longer will I be a burden upon you'.

'Maybe I will prosper like the new Reich ambassador to the Court of St James,' he chuckled in a reference to the absurdly pompous and devious Ribbentrop. 'Also, he sold wine, you know?'

I told him yet again that he was not a burden, that he was welcome to stay as long as he liked, and that I enjoyed his company. This was true. I did not mind at all having him around. It reminded me, in a small way, of my happy early friendship with Dorothy at Frau Siegendorff's house in Berlin when even the growing menace of Nazism could not dim, indeed probably had helped to stimulate, my budding love.

The only times when his presence was a bit irksome was when I brought a young lady home and he, instead of retiring to his room, would insist on being gallant and engaging her in lengthy conversations, mainly one-sided, to make her feel at home, tell her what a jolly good chap I was and hone his English language skills. Most of the girls took this in their stride and showed no lessening of ardour when he eventually bade us good-night and left us to ourselves.

The only one who showed her displeasure – a hazel-eyed beauty called Sally – turned out to be as latently anti-Semitic as my mother. Dr Bergsen seemed oblivious to this as he prattled about my virtues and the pleasure he got from persuading liquor shops in southern England of the qualities of hocks and Moselles.

Next morning, he asked me if I'd had a good evening after he went to bed.

'Very pleasant,' I said. 'A good book and a concert from the Wigmore Hall on the radio.'

'And the beautiful Miss Sally?' he asked.

'Oh she left rather early. Had a headache or something.'

'I hope I did not give a headache with all my talk.'

'I rather hope you did, Herr Dr Bergsen.'

A few months later I had a chance meeting in Fleet Street with Ed. I'd no idea he was back in England. The last I'd heard was that he was teaching underprivileged children in Washington after losing patience with the New Deal's palliative efforts to deal with the root causes of poverty and discrimination. He seemed embarrassed at bumping into me.

'Been meaning to get in contact,' he said. 'How you doing, pal?'

I told him a bit about my work, then asked: 'What about you?'

'Up and down, you know. I enjoyed working with Hopkins in relief. He's some guy, a real go-getter. Gets things done. Cuts red tape. But he's too tied to the Roosevelt theme. Uplift the poor, create jobs, but don't rock the boat of society. America needs something one hell of a lot more radical. America needs anger. It needs solidarity. Has the name Odets filtered across the Atlantic yet?'

'I read a review of that play of his.'

'*Waiting for Lefty*? What did it say?'

'That it's powerful, but strident. That he rants.'

'Rants!' exclaimed Ed. 'Any goddam writer worth his salt

ought to rant. There's a whole lousy world to rant about. Shaw rants. Shakespeare rants.'

'Their characters do.'

'Yeah, well Odets' characters are the working people. They sure as hell need someone to holler about them.'

'Theatre-going apart, how are things on a personal level?' I asked.

'It's all a bit delicate, old man. Let's go get ourselves a drink.'

It was mid-morning, before the bars opened, but I belonged to a private club, which was only too happy to provide us with cocktails in a dingy basement setting.

'I couldn't tell you,' Ed said. 'I shouldn't be telling you now. I knew I should've stayed low.'

'Sorry that happened along,' I said tartly. 'You don't have to tell me anything. I'm used to living with paranoia and imagined conspiracies.'

'Yeah, I heard,' he muttered. 'Sorry it had to happen.'

I didn't really feel like discussing my breakup with Dorothy, so I repeated: 'Look, Ed, you don't have to tell me anything.'

'I know, but...'

He downed his cocktail and signalled for another, which arrived while we were both still sitting in silence. Then he straightened his shoulders and said: 'You know this Spanish thing isn't going to be over by Christmas?'

I nodded. Fears were growing that Spain would be engulfed in a lengthy civil war, with Nazi Germany aiding the right-wing General Franco and the Soviet Union likely to come in on the left-wing republican government's side.

'Okay,' Ed went on. 'Thing is, I'm over here to help in any way I can, and right now I'm involved in the Congress.'

I'd read newspaper stories about the Solidarity with Republican Spain Congress, which was backed by practically every left-wing organisation in Europe. I'd gathered that much of the impetus came from the Communists.

'Okay,' he said. 'It's just a talking shop for now, but we've got some real hotshot people in on it. Better than doing nothing, don't you think?

'Maybe not,' he muttered, in answer to his own question. 'Maybe we should all be fighting there. Anyway, it's bringing together a lot of folk who wouldn't know what to do on their own. But I think you're right to stay away. As a journalist, it's better to appear as impartial as possible.'

'Objective, you mean.'

'Sure, that's what I mean. You could get your paper to send you to Spain. Then you could dig around, tell the world what's going on.'

I laughed: 'I wish it was as easy as that. The *Review*'s already got a man in Madrid.'

'Then quit the job and get some other paper to accredit you. It's real important stuff, Jimmy. Dig up the dirt on German involvement.'

It crossed my mind that if he regarded the task as so important he might have got in touch with me before.

'I'm sure you'll find some other reliable reporter to do that for you,' I said drily. 'I'd go like a shot if sent but I'm not leaving the *Review* on a wild goose chase.'

I got to my feet since I needed to get back to the office, but Ed patted me into a chair, ordered himself another cocktail and regarded it thoughtfully.

'I came across Dorothy at the Congress office first time I went there.'

This didn't surprise me. I'd surmised that Dorothy, desperately in search of something to revive her faith, would rush to the first decent cause that offered itself.

'She told me about what happened to you two. I'm real sorry about that, pal. I want you to remember that I'm sorry it happened. Everything.'

'These things happen,' I said.

'So?' he asked eventually. 'Found anyone else?'

I didn't reply.

'No,' he said. 'No, you wouldn't. Mind you,' he added chuckling, 'I remember you running Dorothy and that other babe in tandem at Cambridge.'

'In my green and salad days.'

'Well look...' he began. 'No, maybe Dot had better tell you.'

'About what?'

But I knew from his eyes.

'Come for dinner tomorrow,' he said. 'She'll explain.'

'She wouldn't want to see me.'

'Sure she would,' he said, gulping his glass. 'I guarantee that.'

He scribbled his address on a beer mat.
'About eight o'clock,' he said. 'If you're free.'

Apprehensive but curious, I rang the bell at Ed's flat in a street of Victorian terraces close to Regent's Park. Dorothy opened the door, smiling nervously though looking much more relaxed than she'd been when we'd parted. We kissed each other on the cheeks, like old friends. The flat was spacious and well furnished. There was money, somewhere, behind this. I guessed it must be the Party. Dorothy apologised for Ed's absence, saying he'd arrive shortly. She asked about my work. I said things were going well. Was I on my own? I said that in a sense I wasn't. She raised her eyebrows.

'I have a house guest,' I said. 'Dr Bergsen.'

'Oh, Jimmy, you have a thing for strays,' she laughed. 'First me, and now him. How many others will there be?'

We talked for a while about Dr Bergsen and she said she'd keep her ears open in case she heard of some more appropriate employment for him.

Then she got to the point: 'You've probably guessed. Ed and I are together now. It just sort of happened. Not planned.'

I said these things usually weren't planned.

'I knew you'd understand, Jimmy. You and I had good times together and it wasn't your fault that we couldn't make it. I was going through a hell of a bad spell – and it had nothing to do with you.'

'You look as though you're over it now. You look happy, Dorothy.'

'I think I am. Spain has put everything into perspective. No political system is perfect, but some are incredibly better than others. No, it's more than that, even. I don't believe there's any alternative to the whole damn mess the world's in except the Party, with all its faults.'

'You must be relieved.'

'Exactly,' she said. 'Relieved that I don't have to examine every bit of doctrine and practice.'

'Good,' I said smiling.

'I knew you'd be pleased for me, Jimmy. I kept meaning to write and tell you about Ed. Our ideas are so much in tune. I love you, *liebling*, but we didn't exactly see eye to eye, did we? In the end there were going to be too many strains.'

'You mean you need yes-men,' I said, and didn't like myself for saying it.

She gave me a sad-that-you-have-to-think-like-that look.

'Sorry,' I said. 'Should have expressed it differently.'

'I suppose I deserve that. It's not even half the truth but you're probably right in some ways. It's not that I can't put up with disagreement, but it's different if you disagree from a common base – which you and I never had.'

'We didn't,' I agreed. But I knew that the emotional gap was even more vast. Dorothy embraced absolutes; I didn't trust them. Not even the absolute of love.

'Still, I'd hoped you might come back,' I said.

'Don't be angry with me, love. Ever since I left school, maybe before, I've loved the Party above everything else. That's why I was devastated when I couldn't agree with some issues. And as long as I loved the Party, how was it ever going to be possible for me to settle down with someone who didn't feel the same?'

'Did you leave me because of Ed?' I asked.

'You and I broke up because of...' she hesitated. 'Because of incompatible attitudes. You tried damn hard with me, Jimmy. But we came at my problems from different angles.'

'And Ed comes from the right angle?'

'He knows the Party from inside. He can feel what I'm feeling.'

'And was he back in London when you left me?' I persisted.

She clenched her jaw.

'He was, yes.'

This unsettled me. I was prepared to be civilised about the whole business, but it was weird to find that all the while I was trying to patch matters up, things had been going on behind my back. Dr Bergsen had observed that she had stronger feelings about ideas than about people.

'Thanks for telling me,' I said.

'I was going to leave you anyway. Ed wanted me to go back and give it another try.'

'He's always been a very principled guy when it comes to affairs of the heart,' I said.

'Don't be bitter, Jimmy. It wasn't anyone's fault but mine.'

I thought it would be better if I left the flat before Ed returned. Dorothy made no great effort to dissuade me.

'I loved you for a long time,' I said.

'And I, you.'

Walking in the wholesome night air, I felt angry and aggrieved. I'd been betrayed by the two people who, in different ways, had meant more to me than almost any other living person.

For several weeks, I suffered in silence and solitude until one day I woke up feeling almost liberated. They deserve each other, I said to myself – and believed that I meant it. Then I dithered about making contact with them. One couldn't just write off one's past, I felt. Finally, I wrote a card to say I wished both of them well, and that we should get together for old time's sake. A few months later I received a short letter from Dorothy explaining that they were in Spain.

> Ed is with the International Brigades in the south – I can't be more specific. I'm in Barcelona doing what's probably best described as liaison work. *Liebling*, thank you for writing and for forgiving.
>
> Lots of love, Dorothy
>
> PS Ed and I got married in Barcelona last month. Who'd ever have imagined me as a wife?

The Brigades, made up of foreign volunteers, symbolised the great hopes of many on the Left that at last democracy was standing up to fascist aggression. I shared those hopes. When I'd told Ed that I wasn't prepared to give up my job and go to Spain as a freelance journalist, I'd been speaking the truth. Since then, however, I'd begun to wonder if the right thing to do was to go there and fight. What was holding me back was the strong suspicion that the main backing for the Republicans came from the Soviet Union.

The fact that Moscow was beginning to pull the strings was confirmed by Douglas who'd been on a month-long trip to Spain with a group of academics.

'This isn't a war for democracy any longer, James. It looks a bit like that from the outside, but the truth is it's Germany versus Russia, for national interests and prestige. The Nazis want to give their troops battle experience. Russia want to make sure the Spanish Communists come out as the winners.'

'If you were younger, would you go out as a volunteer?' I asked.

'If I were younger, I wouldn't have the experience and caution of age,' he smiled.

I was spared having to make a decision. While I was still turning over the pros and cons of heading off to fight in Spain, I was given an assignment – get to New York pronto and cover the marriage of Sarah Churchill and Vic Oliver.

'Ye gods,' I complained to a colleague. 'Madrid is burning, and I'm being sent on a *Woman's Own* jaunt.'

'Don't knock it, old boy,' he said. 'It's a big story. Churchill's daughter eloping. Randolph chasing after her. Great fun. It's what sells papers – even a left-wing rag like ours. It's what readers want. They'll take the blood and guts and the politics if you give them a bit of romance on the side.'

I wasn't convinced, but it was an opportunity I couldn't afford to miss. Do a good job and, who knows, I might be sent to Spain next time round.

In New York, I sent Sarah a message saying she might remember me from the brief time I'd worked for her father and that my newspaper felt obliged to report on the wedding but that I had no intention of being intrusive. She invited me for a drink at the Waldorf. She was nervous of me, to start with. She needed press people she could trust, but didn't know whether I was simply another damn reporter who would twist everything she said and make her parents more upset than ever. Luckily, we hit it off immediately. She could see I wasn't relishing the assignment and that we were, in a way, kindred spirits. We were both working our way in the world – she from out of her father's shadow, I towards a career that I felt mattered. We laughed at the same things, and we both, in our own ways, were rebels from family situations.

Once she was sure I wasn't going to pry and wouldn't write sensational or sentimental rubbish, she began to open out to me, pleased to have an English chum to chat and gossip with. She told me how much her parents disapproved of Vic.

'Is it because he's Jewish?' I asked.

'I don't think so. Papa has a lot of prejudices, but not that one. It's more that they see him as a sort of itinerant foreign fiddler without two pennies to knock together. Vic's the son of an Austrian baron, you know, but really they think no one lower than an English duke would be good enough for me.'

There was no doubt that she loved her family despite all the pressures, and looked sadly at me with her kittenish eyes when she gleaned my own history.

'Gosh, Jimmy, you're practically an orphan. Is that difficult?'

We were walking down Fifth Avenue in search of Christmas presents for Vic: she thought I'd be helpful if it came down to choosing a tie or some gloves.

'Not really. Except it might explain why I fall in love so often.'

She laughed: 'Believe me, that has nothing to do with it. I have the most wonderfully embracing family, and look at me. Dozens of crushes.'

She paused for thought, then hurried on.

'But nothing at all serious until Vic.'

She was tall, attractive and walked in a jaunty way that seemed designed to mask a deep uncertainty. One wanted to protect her, perhaps to hold her, but one did not dare. She lacked confidence, not in her status but in herself. Her hair was auburn, inherited from Winston. She had her mother's sharp patrician nose.

'You won't write that, will you?' she asked anxiously. 'About my crushes.'

'Every word. I'll paint you as a wanton, pleasure-seeking playgirl.'

'You wouldn't be far off the truth,' she laughed.

'You're desperately keen not to hurt your parents, aren't you?' I said.

She stopped in the middle of the throng of shoppers. It was snowing lightly. Franklin Roosevelt had just been re-elected as President. The Depression wasn't yet over and there were still beggars and food queues and anger in the streets, but to the affluent shoppers of Fifth Avenue good times seemed just around the corner.

'I love them dearly, but I can't let them decide whom I should marry. That would be the end of me as a person.'

'Parents can't see that,' I said.

I told her about my mother's attitude to Dorothy.

'Bloody cheek!' she said. 'Why can't they let one be? And

why do they say they only want what's best for one? How can they know what's best for me?'

As we went into Saks, she added: 'In my family, when we were children, their way of punishing us was usually to banish us – to our room. Oh, dear, I hope I shan't be banished from their lives now!'

'Well, you've done what they asked: Vic's got his American citizenship. So you can enjoy the wedding with a clear conscience. And, please smile for the occasion, Sarah. I've roughed out my story in advance and said you were smiling radiantly.'

A few days later, I attended the wedding and Sarah did smile. I wrote a low-key story, and received, after getting back to London, a note from her which ended by saying: 'I'm sure our paths will cross again, Jimmy, either in Blighty or some romantic, faraway place.'

It was signed 'Mule', which touched me because it was a family nickname.

Dr Bergsen left my flat and rented a room on his own. He seemed happy to have attained some independence again. We met for a meal at least once a week. He was making an adequate income and his English was improving by leaps and bounds.

Not long after my return from New York, he came to the *Review* office and said: 'Come, Jimmy, I want to give you a slap-up meal. I want to thank you for all your goodness to me.'

He hailed a cab in Fleet Street and told the driver with obvious delight: 'The Ivy, please, cabbie.'

As we drove towards the West End, I tried to think of ways to spare him the hideous expense of dining at this fashionable restaurant, but could think of nothing that would not embarrass him. Finally, I said: 'This will be a treat, Dr Bergsen. I only hope I can do it justice.'

I had by now dropped the 'Herr' in addressing him, at his request.

'I am English now, my dear Jimmy – no more a German,' he'd explained. 'The Aryans don't want me, so I say: It is your loss, you Boche swine.'

This was said jocularly, but he was becoming increasingly hostile and aggressive towards Germany. He'd begun writing letters to MPs and others demanding a tougher attitude towards Hitler. One letter had gone to my stepfather who, in response, asked me to come and see him at the House of Commons.

'How dare he, your friend, write to me in such a vein? These people have been here for five minutes and they're telling us how to run the country.'

'We've given the refugees asylum, Bob. That doesn't mean they're here on sufferance. They have rights as well as duties.'

'I'd send them all packing, if I had my way,' he stormed. 'Back to where they came from.'

'Luckily you're not the Home Secretary.'

The Ivy was full of its usual theatrical types – impresarios, actors, playwrights. Dr Bergsen had booked a table. Already seated there was a woman of about 30, not a beauty but with a strong, shrewd face.

'Allow me to present, my dear Jimmy, a friend of mine, Dinah Woolf.'

I took her hand. She gave me a cursory look and sent him a slight smile.

'And, Dinah,' said Dr Bergsen. 'This is my very dear friend, Mr James Bexley, of whom I have told you so much.'

'How d'you do,' she said. 'Sit down, both of you. I'm not Lady Astor, you know. Sam, I'm dry as dust. Get me a Tom Collins will you?'

Dr Bergsen flushed and promptly hailed a waiter. I suspected he flushed more because of being called Sam in my company than because of her peremptory manner or vulgarity of speech. Indeed, as the evening progressed, he appeared to be rather proud of her bossiness.

I discovered that Dinah was an ardent Zionist. I was more surprised that Dr Bergsen had apparently taken up with someone holding such views than with the fact that she was at least 20 years younger than him. She was quite definite that the only hope for the Jews was a state in Palestine.

Dr Bergsen disagreed mildly.

'Yes, yes, perhaps it's true, but who will want to go to Palestine, apart from you, Dinah? And how is it to be achieved?'

'Every Jew in Europe. It's a matter of survival. Don't you agree, Mr Bexley?'

'I believe that Jewish refugees should be allowed into Palestine.'

'Yes, yes, but how many cultured people will want to live in the desert?' asked Dr Bergsen. 'And also there will be such problems with the Arabs, no?'

'Of course, there'll be problems,' Dinah said scornfully. 'But what's that compared to what's facing the Jews of Europe? Everyone says to the Jews: "You don't belong here, go to your own country." And when we go to our country, they throw up their hands: "Oh, you can't stay in Palestine, that belongs to the Arabs".'

'But, Dinah, in some countries, in England, there is no such difficulties for us. Everyone helps, everyone is kind.'

'Sam, you're such an innocent,' she smiled. 'The only difference here is that they're too polite to show their anti-Semitism. Isn't that the case, Mr Bexley?'

She turned a look of complicity on me. She wanted us to be in league against Dr Bergsen in this matter. I didn't like that, but I couldn't disagree with her.

'I'm afraid you're right,' I said. 'Whatever one calls it – anti-Semitism, general xenophobia – a lot of people here hide their prejudices under a sort of façade of good manners. Our inability to confront even our own worst aspects is amazing.'

'Let alone the worst aspects of others,' Dinah said drily.

'That too,' I agreed.

'It is good to see that my two dear friends get on together so well,' beamed Dr Bergsen.

I met Dorothy in London later in 1937. She had aged considerably. There were lines of despair in her face. She told me she'd been deployed in administering the work of political commissars with the Brigades. She'd found it difficult, and then impossible, to do her job once she became aware of the extent to which the Communists were determined to crush their allies even if that meant Franco might win the war.

'I thought this was going to be a good war. I was prepared to forget all my doubts for the sake of the greater good. But I was being forced to justify to members of genuinely revolutionary groups that they needed to be disbanded or destroyed in the interests of the greater good. Destroyed, Jimmy, meant arrested, tortured, killed. Because the Stalinists wanted it that way!'

She was horrified too at the flood of trials and purges in the Soviet Union.

'In short,' she said, trying to smile but looking like a sad and embittered older version of the Dorothy I'd known in Berlin and later, 'I'm considering leaving the Party. Finally. It's like having to decide whether you want to cut off a couple of your limbs, but I'm not sure I can go on.'

Then she stared at me, anguish in her eyes, and said: 'The problem is: no one else really opposes Hitler. That's what stops me from taking the plunge.'

'And Ed?' I asked.

'Ed was only ever an ersatz comrade. He never really believed in it all. He's an idealist. He got disillusioned pretty quickly in Spain. He was wounded fighting fascists, and was then ordered into street fighting against anarchist militia – not against the fascists but against soldiers who we should have been standing shoulder to shoulder with. He's quit the Party. He went back to the States last month. I'm on my way to join him there.'

'The citadel of capitalism?' I smiled.

'Ah, *liebling*,' she said, giving me a glimpse of an earlier Dorothy, 'citadels are made to be breached, *n'est-ce pas?*'

19

London and Moscow

I had come to the middle of nowhere with my life. My career was going fairly well and my personal affairs not always unpleasantly, but I had no sense of momentum. My father had died for no real purpose, and as Europe rattled towards a general war I wondered how soon I'd follow him to oblivion.

Then things began to change for me. In 1939, the *Review* offered me a posting as correspondent in the Soviet Union, a plum job and an extremely sensitive one. The Russians had expelled our last correspondent two years before, and had refused until now to allow a replacement. I was chosen, apparently, because Tom Rathbone wanted a young, enthusiastic and ideologically untainted eye looking at a country, which, despite the flaws of its system, was still the hope of many on the Left.

One bleak February morning, a few weeks before I was due to go to Moscow, Ed appeared at the newspaper. It was the first time I'd seen him since his marriage to Dorothy. He said she sent her love. I nodded my thanks.

He had joined the European section of the State Department in Washington and this visit was, in his words, 'to poke my nose around a bit'.

He insisted on taking me to lunch at the Savoy Grill and, over a lavish meal, picked my brains about European politics. I did what I could to help.

We talked for a few hours though it wasn't the same free and easy give and take of our Cambridge days. He was scathing about Britain's policy of appeasing the fascist dictators. In his view, as in mine, it had brought war closer than at any time since 1918. He'd had a chat with the American ambassador, Joe Kennedy, and been appalled by what he felt were the man's appeasement sympathies.

'FDR has this weakness of not being able to say no to his old political cronies,' Ed said, suggesting how Kennedy had got, and would keep, the posting.

'Does he have any other weaknesses?' I asked mischievously, recalling Ed's complaints about the Administration's lack of radicalism.

'He's kind of improved. Now that I'm working for him.'

He added seriously: 'One thing, though, he's got a much better handle on what's going on in Europe than your leaders. And he's way ahead of the mass of Americans, who don't give a damn about what happens over here. As if we can turn our back on the rest of the world!'

We had just finished the meal when a small party bustled into the restaurant: Winston Churchill, with Randolph, Brendan Bracken and one or two others whom I did not recognise. Churchill seemed to be fizzing with energy.

'Now that's a guy I need to meet,' said Ed. 'Will you introduce me?'

'If he remembers me, I will.'

'I was going to try and get to see him anyway. They'll have to bring him into the government now, won't they?'

'If they do, it won't be generally popular in the Conservative Party.'

Ed told me he was going to Germany in a few days time.

'I want a look-see at where things are heading.'

'You know exactly where they're heading,' I said. 'We all know. Hitler's going to push for whatever he wants, and if he can't get it by threats, he'll go to war. The military build-up tells you all you need to know.'

'There are other things too. Fucking frightening, buddy.' He lowered his voice. 'A couple of physicists in Berlin have shown that uranium atoms can be split by neutrons. Know what that means?'

'Remind me.'

I still had a blind spot about nuclear physics. It seemed so speculative; first came the theory, and then the attempt to prove it. I couldn't get excited about this. Even in my lifetime, there'd been dramatic concrete technological advances – in aeroplanes, motor cars, radio, even television, which was just becoming a feasible medium. But what had nuclear physics ever achieved, apart from some vaunted, but barely comprehensible, laboratory experiments? Where were the tangible results? Because of my attitude, almost the only knowledge of this arcane science that I'd acquired had been poured into my mind by Leo Roth, Ed and a few others.

'It may mean scientists will be able to produce a chain reaction, set off unbelievable amounts of energy,' Ed hissed. 'The energy of the stars.'

'What exactly is a chain reaction? I mean, how does it work?'

'Look it up,' he grinned. 'I have to catch my boat to Germany in forty-eight hours. Not enough time to explain.'

'And the significance?'

'Weapons. The likes of which nobody ever dreamed of.'

'I thought the best scientific minds believe those sorts of weapons aren't possible,' I ventured.

'Some of them do. Lots of professional jealousy around. Sometimes that clouds the judgement.'

'Are you saying the Germans might have the knowledge to build some kind of ultimate bomb with all this energy?'

'Yup. That's what's so frightening.'

'And *only* the Germans have the knowledge?'

'Not only the Krauts. Information of this sort gets around pretty damn quickly. Only thing is: knowledge ain't everything. You've still got to be able to build the thing.'

'Are your people working on something?' I asked.

'How the heck d'you think I'd know about it if they were? I'm with State, not Defense.'

'Still, you're going to check on what the Germans are doing.'

'Not to check, Jim. This isn't official and I'm no scientist. But it's still peacetime – sort of – so I'll keep my ears open. You never know. A lot of those guys in Germany hate Hitler's guts. They don't want him ruling the world.'

He paid the bill and asked again if I'd introduce him to Churchill.

'They're eating,' I said.

'Yeah, I know it's bad form, but it'll only take a minute and I'll arrange to see him.'

With some diffidence, I moved to Churchill's table. He looked up, saw me, waved a pudgy paw and said: 'My dear Bexley, good to see you again. Come to the flat in Victoria and we'll have a chat sometime, eh?'

'Sir, I'd like to introduce...' I began, indicating Ed beside me.

'Yes, but not now, not now. These gentlemen and I are engaged in weighty business.'

With that, he returned to his steak and cut into it with relish. Randolph gave me a curt, ill-tempered glance. Bracken said jocularly to the table: 'Putting *on* weight, eh, Winston?'

Despite feeling that I may have done my own tenuous relationship with Churchill some damage by intruding on his luncheon, I was pleased that I hadn't been able to do Ed a favour by making the introduction.

'Don't worry about it,' said Ed genially. 'I'll get to see him some day soon when I come back to London. Maybe next year. I'll write him beforehand.'

Before leaving for Moscow, I had some long talks with my predecessor as correspondent there, Crompton-Smythe, who'd had his visa revoked in 1937 because of something he'd written about a show trial.

His offending passage was: 'On hearing the sentence of death imposed on him, the accused looked to the ceiling as though willing Stalin to reach down and pat him on the head. There was a greater probability of this happening than of the fact that his "confession" was genuine.'

'I put in the last bit as a joke,' Crompton-Smythe, a florid-faced man in his seventies, told me. 'Thought the censors would automatically scrub it out. They didn't. Probably wanted a cast-iron reason to get rid of me.'

He said he'd gone to Moscow in the 1920s as a 'devout Bolshie'.

'Thought this was going to be heaven on earth. Then, when I saw it wasn't, I invented all sorts of excuses for the shortcomings. Sabotage by imperialist countries, counter-revolutionary Trotskyite plots, you name it, I invented it. Took a long time to open my eyes, old boy.'

When he heard I'd been at Trinity in the mid-thirties, he looked at me with a crooked grin and leered: 'Ah, one of those.'

I said, mildly, that I was neither a member of the Party nor a sympathiser, although I'd known plenty of both groups at Cambridge.

'Rum bunch,' he said. 'You were lucky to escape – if you really did. The state security comrades were behind it all, you know. They were looking to impregnate our ruling classes with Marxist semen. Fathered a crowd of little Bolshies. Some of them still in hiding, gravitating to senior posts. Perhaps you're one of them.'

I asked if he'd mentioned his thesis to Scotland Yard.

'No one would believe me. They don't believe our upper class chaps could ever stoop to treachery. A few revolutionary pranks, yes. But treason – never!'

Crompton-Smythe warned me that the Russians would assign me a female interpreter and secretary, who would certainly be a secret police informant.

'If she's pretty and you fancy her, try to resist copulating with her. Once you do that, she's really got you by the balls, so to speak. Just be pleasant and impersonal, and don't ever, ever tell her anything of significance, either about yourself or about what you've heard from others.'

An important part of my brief was to cover the efforts by Britain and France to get a treaty with the Soviet Union. Rathbone said the *Review*'s editorial line would continue to be that Britain needed a pact, not because we liked or trusted Stalin, but because we had to prevent him striking a deal with Hitler.

'I'm not asking you to tailor your reporting to our line – but be aware that if those two jackals team up Europe's going to go up in flames damn quickly.'

I found it hard to swallow the view that such implacable foes as the Nazis and the Communists could embrace. Then I recalled how the German Communists in 1931 had preferred to bash the socialists rather than the Nazis. In a mad world of amoral dictators, anything might happen.

A few days before my departure, Dr Bergsen invited me to lunch with Leo Roth, who had recently arrived from the US for unspecified work in Britain.

'I think already he has been asked by the government to do some research,' Dr Bergsen told me. He added mischievously: 'We will ask questions to find out exactly.'

Leo looked fit but exhausted.

'You have been working too hard,' said his uncle. 'What are they making you do to tire you out, those government people?'

Leo smiled: 'It was quite a long journey. We're based some way from London.'

'You see, my dear Jimmy, he will tell us nothing,' said Dr Bergsen.

That much was obvious. Leo wouldn't say – presumably was forbidden, anyway, from disclosing on pain of imprisonment or deportation – what his work was about.

His uncle, as innocent as always, continued to probe him.

'Come, come, Leo! What can it be that is so secret you are doing? You are hiding it, so that someone will not steal the ideas and win the Nobel Prize instead of you, no?'

'Nothing escapes you, Uncle,' Leo smiled. 'But, honestly, my job is not very important in the long scheme of things.'

However, I suspected it must be extremely important. He would not give Dr Bergsen even a clue about where he was living and working. All we knew was that he had come to see his uncle for two days. At the end of the meal, Dr Bergsen suggested that I show him the town.

'You must instruct him in how the young people live in London. It is very different from Göttingen.'

Leo looked pained at the mention of his old university town. I didn't need to ask to know how much he must have been hurt and humiliated when the Nazi racial laws brought the termination of his research work. Nor would I ask him about the family members he'd left behind. He'd probably been recruited by the British because with war more than just a possibility, someone with his knowledge of nuclear physics and of German progress in that field was worth netting.

He implied as much to me when we spent the evening walking around the streets of London and talking.

Had he been in touch with his old colleagues in Germany, I asked?

'Every few months, some scientist or other manages to get out of Germany, and one is soon in touch with them. We're quite a little club in the States and here. It's a bit like one of your school networks. Everyone knows someone who knows someone. We get the gossip. Sometimes, even some real information.'

'A friend of mine told me that in Germany they'd managed to split the atom with neutrons – hope I've got it right – and this could release untold energy.'

'It's called fission. Your friend's right, Jimmy, up to a point. It has been discovered but not achieved yet in practice. When an atom of uranium 235 absorbs a neutron, it becomes unstable and the nucleus splits into parts, giving off energy and neutrons. Other atoms then absorb the neutrons and release energy and more neutrons, and so on, and so on. A chain reaction. Then, God knows.'

'And you think this will be achieved?'

'Oh, for sure it will be done. But when and by who – those are the questions.'

'Are we working on it?'

'What do you think?' He smiled. 'Naturally, I have no knowledge of this.'

'Naturally. And the Germans?'

'You may assume that,' he said, not smiling.

'And who will get there first? Will Germany do it first?'

'God forbid!' he said.

'And all this research and planning...' I began.

'It is more than just research,' he said.

'All of it could lead to a bomb being built?'

He looked long and hard at me, as if weighing up what to disclose, then said: 'That is a reasonable assumption.'

'Exactly how powerful?'

'My dear fellow,' he sighed, 'this is not a good thing to talk about. And you understand I am not involved. All I do is speculate.'

'Of course, Leo.'

'Such a weapon, if and when it is built, will be of such immense force that it would destroy all of central London and kill millions. One bomb will do that.'

'Then let's hope we get it first.'

'Precisely.'

'Even so,' I said. 'Do you think it's right that we should make the first one – if we can – or just let the enemy know that we are capable of building it?'

'If the enemy is Hitler, then we have to make it. Otherwise, *he* will make it, and he will not miss the opportunity of blowing us all to bits.'

'And if we manage to build it, Leo, should we use it?'

He considered this for some moments. I wondered how often he had put the same question to himself.

'If there is a danger of Germany getting their hands on such a weapon and using it against England, then I don't think there is any alternative,' he replied.

'Even so,' I said, 'how many civilians will have to die along with the Nazis and the military?'

'My mother is in Germany, my sisters too. Other members of my family. But, Jimmy, in this world, we have no choice. There is going to be a war, for sure. Either we have to defeat the Nazis, or they will defeat us. There is no middle way. The way to make the weapon must be found, and before Hitler makes it. If the world were otherwise, I would say no, such a bomb should never be created.'

I nodded. Morality had already moved into the shadows. Most sensible people believed war was inevitable. Best to have the strongest weapons in our hands.

Could he get his relations out of Germany, I asked?

His face clouded.

'The gates are closing everywhere.'

I arrived in Moscow on a gloomy March day in 1939 and was allotted a hotel room. An official in the Foreign Commissariat's press office said he would let me know if an apartment became available.

'They are scarce, but sometimes they become free, for some reason or other,' he said without a touch of irony.

I wondered if I would ever sink so low as to accept a flat whose previous occupant had disappeared into a labour camp or a shallow grave.

As Crompton-Smythe prophesied, I was assigned an interpreter-secretary, who was female and attractive in an onion-smelling sort of way. Her name was Vera and she always seemed to be staring greedily at my few possessions, including a camera and a gold watch that had belonged to my grandfather, as she read me the generally stupefying articles in *Pravda* and other newspapers.

Most of the news concerned the menace posed by Germany and what Moscow saw as the weak-kneed response by the western powers to Hitler. In the week I arrived, Stalin said in a speech: 'The Soviet Union will stay out of a war of imperialists.' At the end of the month, the British worm turned, finally, and we, and the French, guaranteed Poland that we'd come to her help if Germany attacked her.

'At last we're taking a stand,' I said to a British colleague.

'True, but we've tossed away the last bargaining counter for a treaty with Stalin. There's nothing now to make him want to climb into bed with the West.'

Vera, on the other hand, did try to get into bed with me. One evening, perhaps pushed into it by her bosses, she managed to manouevre into a physical closeness and touched my cheek with her lips. I was tempted briefly to return the kiss on her voluptuous lips, but remembered Crompton-Smythe's warning even as I noticed that she'd undone the top buttons of her blouse to reveal a heavily hanging, and not unalluring, pair of breasts.

'*Nyet*,' I said with an apologetic smile. 'Thank you, but *nyet*.'

Poor Vera. Soon after this, she told me glumly that she was being assigned to a 'very important' Amerikanski and that some other secretary would be sent to me. I got a bored, drab, overweight woman called Nina, who had a persistently drooping mouth and lifeless eyes. I deduced that she'd been badly beaten up by life and had no interest in fighting back. We got along quite well.

Moscow early in 1939 had two faces. One was a drab, unsmiling, depressing city, enveloped by a fog of fear that covered everyone and everything. Fear had crept into the very smell of the place. The smell of Russia had hit my nostrils as soon as I crossed the border. It was an amalgam of body odour, sheepskin, vodka, disinfectant and the pungency of sweated terror. Fear seemed to put a grey, even greenish, colour into the faces of every visible stratum of people: apprehensive women queuing for food or whatever was available in the shops; anxious minor bureaucrats; worried hotel staff – everyone who had survived the purges and the bullet in the back of the head, but anticipated an arrest at any moment. Even senior officials in the foreign ministry and the NKVD, the secret police, showed the unmistakable hue of extreme dread. I say 'even', but in fact they had as much reason as any to be fearful: the Stalinist Terror had cut down the top echelons of Soviet power. The army had been decapitated, old guard Bolsheviks eliminated, secret police chiefs executed, and God knew how many officials killed, jailed or exiled to terrains that were death traps.

The other face of Moscow, of which I caught only glimpses, was a capital that drew in young people from all, ethnically diverse, parts of the empire: Asiatic as well as European features, floral dresses and open smiles giving a cosmopolitan lightness to the student areas and the springtime parks. Young love flourished, I noted with envy, even when surrounded by the grotesque reality of constraint and control in a police state. That reality appalled and sickened me. Despite all the knowledge I had gleaned beforehand of the Soviet system, from reading, discussion and my life with Dorothy, the reality shocked me to the core. I never saw the torture cells or the executions, but could not avoid imagining, sensing, feeling the hopelessness of the individual and the massive malevolence of the central power that ordered and directed this orgy of blood and suffering.

What came home to me in Moscow, as I lay awake at nights, was the agony of our times. I was by nature positive, but how could one retain any sort of hope in a world contested by the twin monsters of fascist and Marxist dictatorships, while the democracies dithered and dallied? The Anglo-French guarantees to Poland gave me little cause for hope; it was too late to deter Hitler and, besides, we could – and indeed might – still funk out of fighting in the end.

I had witnessed the violence of the Nazi storm-troopers in Germany and knew of the brutality and death meted out to Jews, Communists, socialists and others. Hitler's proclaimed belief was that might was right, and that the extermination of human beings was a valid method of securing his own power and the ultimate supremacy of the 'Aryan' race. His intentions were clear – the German peoples would inherit the earth.

The Soviet system, for its sake, claimed to be acting for the benefit of all humanity. And if thousands, or even millions, had to suffer in the interim, this was justified because the ultimate future would be a paradise on earth.

By 1939, the major purges were over, but the fear lingered. No one knew if, or when, the terror would restart. People lived in dread of the late night knock on the door, which might come because of some real or some manufactured disloyalty. Their only defence was to stay silent, to be as invisible as possible, and to avoid foreigners. We were the plague bacillus. Contact with any foreigner could lead to a fatal infection of outside ideas; in other words, to allegations of espionage. The show trials had been littered with such allegations. No one in their right mind would dare get too friendly with an outsider like myself. The exceptions were those whose job it was to work with, observe, or inform on foreigners. And even these privileged few approached their jobs with fear, based on the hard experience that innocence, in the Soviet Union, was never a bar to accusation and liquidation.

All this made it difficult to report on the country's internal affairs and its policies. I couldn't talk to ordinary people so all I could do was read between the lines of the official media, interpret the blank looks and hunched movements of the citizens and exchange rumours with fellow journalists and diplomats.

It wasn't as tough when it came to covering the diplomatic manoeuvring, for which I could tap into western sources. However, even in this reporting I was at a big disadvantage: I had not the remotest access to any Russian prepared to speak freely on how Stalin might be thinking about foreign alliances.

That was before Anatoly Podbirski entered my life.

I met him in May at one of Vyacheslav Molotov's first diplomatic receptions. The pragmatic Molotov had just taken over as Commissar for Foreign Affairs, and this was interpreted as a signal that Stalin was abandoning any strong anti-German stance. The previous commissar, Litvinov, was a Jew, and his demotion, together with the rumoured removal of other Jews from high foreign affairs positions, took on an added sinister significance. Could this be smoothing the way for a deal with Hitler?

The foreign press corps in the main thought it was probably no more than a coincidence. Anyway, Molotov's wife, it was whispered, was Jewish.

Podbirski, a large, jovial man with a shock of brown hair and wide nostrils that gave him an almost comical porcine look, introduced himself with a smile but without telling me where he worked. I deduced from the bonhomie he exuded that he had authorisation from on high to associate with foreigners and that this meant he had some kind of lofty rank, probably in the NKVD. His English was understandable though heavily accented and error-strewn. He seemed to know a fair bit about me and said he was a regular reader of the *Review*.

'When it comes to my desk, I read,' he laughed. 'My department get only one copy and many people higher up like also to read. I think sometimes they enjoy so much, they keep. So not always do I read, and when I read always I do not understand everything.'

He asked how I was enjoying life in Moscow and listened intently when I talked about my frustrations.

'I regret,' he said. 'If I was in Politburo, I would allow such things that you want to do. How could correspondent of the *Review* be a spy, eh?'

I was startled by such critical levity, but knew there must be a reason why he had the licence to talk in such a way. It seemed likely that his task might be to gain some kind of rapport with me and then entrap me into espionage or something similar. That feeling was strengthened when he asked if he could visit my office.

'Do you have to ask for an invitation?' I said.

'But of course,' he laughed. 'In England, no one visits without invitation. It is because your home is your mansion, no?'

'Castle.'

'Excuse me, I get wrong. Please may I visit castle?'

I assured him I'd be delighted to see him.

'You see, I am fascinated by the press,' he said. 'Not the kind of newspapers we have in my country – they all give the same news, which we know anyhow. So, I see you tomorrow, Mr James Bexley. May I be to call you James?'

'Make it Jimmy,' I said.

'Ah, thank you,' he beamed. 'And please to call me Anatoly.'

I asked some colleagues if they knew him. None did, but they confirmed my suspicions that he was a goon assigned to oversee my activities.

'We all have them, but we don't always get to meet them, thank God,' said one correspondent. 'Just assume that whatever you say to him gets back to his immediate boss and probably right to Beria's desk.'

Podbirski's visit to the office scared the local staff rigid, though he conducted himself with good humour. He asked me questions about the way British papers covered politics, culture and sport and seemed intrigued by what I told him.

'Ah, I wish I have your job, Jimmy. Instead mine.'

'What is yours, Anatoly?'

'Is dull job with Foreign Commissariat.'

'But perhaps they'll send you somewhere interesting,' I suggested.

'Maybe yes, maybe Siberia,' he said jocularly.

As he took his leave, he asked whether I was satisfied with Nina, the middle-aged frump who was my interpreter, translator and secretary. I had no real complaints about her except that she was incredibly ill-informed about almost everything, or pretended to be. I didn't want to get her into trouble, though, so I told him I was very happy with her.

'Cannot be,' he smiled. 'She is ugly, she never smiles. She is not for young man like you interested in everything. I try to find some other one.'

I protested there was no need, but a few days later Nina had gone and her replacement was seated at her desk when I arrived at the office. She was young, small and had black, curly hair. She had a pleasant, intelligent face. Her eyes were big. Her name, she told me in perfect English, was Natasha Khazan.

'What happened to Nina?' I asked.

'She had to leave Moscow to look after her old mother.'

'For how long?' I asked.

'I am to be her replacement,' she said. 'I will do my best, comrade.'

'Please, just call me Jimmy.'

'No,' she said firmly. 'If "comrade" does not please you, I will call you Mr Bexley.'

But within a few weeks we were calling each other by our first names. Natasha was good humoured, without being either overly familiar or obsequious. She kept her distance, which suited me perfectly. All I wanted was someone intelligent and able to understand the needs of my job. Natasha fulfilled both functions. She was efficient and an excellent translator, who quickly came to understand what I needed to know in the controlled media. She'd been sent by Podbirski, so I assumed she was controlled by the NKVD.

Every so often, Podbirski would drop into the office or phone me to ask how I was getting on and, sometimes, how Natasha was doing. But he never pumped me for information. On the other hand, if I asked him anything, he seemed to try and give a response that went beyond the stock bureaucratic answers I was used to getting.

On one occasion, almost as a joke, I asked him if he knew how Stalin was thinking about the current world situation.

'Diplomacy means you never must trust anyone, is not?' he said.

'Never?' I asked.

'You ask question, I answer true as I can, not what I think should be.'

I had by this time become attuned to looking and listening for nuances and coded meanings in any statement, public or private, so I was surprised that he was implying that Stalin would never make alliances in good faith. This, in itself, would scarcely have been an earth-shattering observation if made by an outsider. But Podbirski was a Soviet official, and his remarks were made at a time when both Britain and Germany were seeking to reach an understanding with Stalin. What surprised me even more was that he seemed to be telling me he disagreed with Stalin. No Soviet official I'd yet met had ever dared to be even fractionally as candid.

'But, Jimmy, we talk like friends. No story you write. Is understood?'

I nodded. As a reporter in a place like Moscow one's ability was only as good as one's sources. I wasn't going to risk losing Podbirski. He was worth cultivating, even if he was part of the secret police system. I knew he'd feed me misinformation from time to time, but he might occasionally put something worthwhile my way.

This, in fact, was how things developed between us. He did his job, and I did mine, which was to decide what was propaganda and what might just be fact. Sometimes, a cynical smile on his face would suggest that, sorry, Jimmy, my superiors have told me to tell you this nonsense, and could you somehow fit it into an article and cover yourself by conveying your scepticism. I managed to oblige on occasions, without feeling that I was compromising my integrity. On other occasions, when he requested it, I was happy to treat our talks as strictly off the record and, sometimes, as strictly unprintable in any form. My task was to report as best I could on this strange, controlled society, and the insights I got from Podbirski were often invaluable in increasing my understanding.

Natasha, I believed, was a protégé of his. To start with, I was content to believe that like Vera and Nina before her, she'd been planted on me to observe and report back to her superiors. That was normal practice even for staff of the pro-Soviet toadies in the foreign press corps. So I was wary of her for some months. However, I couldn't help warming to her obvious sensitivity once she'd got over her initial nervousness.

By this time, I'd been allotted an apartment to use as office and residence. I wasn't told who'd arranged this but suspected Podbirski had a hand in it.

I gave Natasha a key. She arrived early, seven days a week, and would have tea brewing even before I was awake. In the small office area, separated from my living quarters by a wooden partition with a little door, she was mainly responsible for translating significant items in the media, usually official statements or speeches praising the achievements of the workers or the wisdom of the rulers, and especially of Stalin who was referred to as though he were a combination of divinity, prophet and monarch. She also acted as my secretary, taking my articles to the censors and then to the post office for transmission if there were no censorship problems. She would accompany me, as translator, to press conferences and for any conversations I might have with ordinary people in Moscow – which were hardly ever possible.

At first, she did her press translations without comment, but gradually as we began to trust each other a little, I would let a snort of contempt or a laugh of incredulity escape my lips, and she would try very hard not to smile.

One morning, she was reading out a story in *Pravda*, which began: 'Members of the Politburo yesterday sent their congratulations to Comrade Stalin, the beloved leader of the Nation, on the outstanding achievements in uniting and building the Soviet state, which is the constant envy of the whole world.'

At this point, she stopped reading and looked at me sadly.

'So the whole world envies us? So you are very lucky to be living here for a short time?'

'I suppose I am – as a journalist.'

'But surely, Jimmy, you would like to live here for always, in this great socialist paradise?'

I looked pointedly at the telephone, which almost certainly had a microphone installed with a direct line to Podbirski or whoever monitored me. Natasha followed my eyes and smiled.

'You nod your head. Good. This afternoon we will finish reading *Pravda* and then I will take you to see some more sights of Moscow.'

I agreed, and as soon as we'd finished some routine business, we put on our coats and went into the streets. I had, of course, already seen most of the authorised sites, including Lenin's tomb housing his embalmed corpse, Red Square, the St Basilius Church, the GUM department store and the outside of the surrealistic Kremlin with its forbidding walls, steeples and glinting onion domes, the highest by far atop the soaring white stone Ivan the Great bell tower.

'Have you visited the Tretyakov?' she asked.

When I told her I hadn't, her face lit up. There were some paintings she'd like to show me, she said. As we walked to the art gallery, close to the Kremlin, I asked her what she'd done before her current assignment. In the office itself, I'd been careful of asking her anything remotely personal.

'I graduated at the university where I studied English and then went to work as a translator. Sometimes for government business, sometimes for state-run enterprises.'

'Am I the first westerner you've worked with?' I asked.

'Yes. But not the last one, I hope.'

'Isn't that a risky thing to say?'

'Perhaps. Everything is risky.'

'Is that why you made that provocative comment in the office about the socialist paradise?'

'I am expected to provoke you,' she smiled.

I hadn't often seen her smile before, not like this, with her eyes as much as her generous mouth, delicate teeth. The smile lit up her whole face, and all of Moscow, too.

In the Tretyakov, she took me to see paintings of various eras and types, including propagandist pictures of workers and soldiers and of Stalin himself. These works of Social Realism were mostly giant static cartoons without any of the inner truths of great art. She talked about each in an official monotone.

Then she stood on tiptoes and whispered in my ear: 'Now I will show you something that will tell you all about my country.'

Her soft breath on my ear and the way she gripped my arm to lift herself on to her toes were a breath of summer flowers in that musty museum. When she was close to me, I could smell her delightful, unscented essence.

I'd better be very careful, I thought.

She stood close to me after she'd led me to a medium size canvas, which had a disturbing, mysterious quality. Under a heavily clouded sky, a brown dirt road, little more than a track, ran between drab fields into the distant horizon. The road was without end and the landscape enlivened only by a far-off clump of green trees. There were no human figures. Where was the road going?

'It is called the *Vladimirka Road*,' she said, reverting to the monotone she'd used for the earlier descriptions. 'The painter was Isaak Levitan who lived from 1860 to 1900.'

'I'm ashamed to say I've never heard of him.'

'He studied at the Moscow School of Painting and Sculpture from 1873 till 1883. One of his teachers was the great Russian landscape painter Alexey Savrasov. Levitan was a friend of Anton Chekhov. He paints in a very realistic style.'

After a few more paintings, I said I had to get back to the office.

In the street, I asked: 'Why did you show me that landscape, the one with the road? You said it would tell me about Russia.'

'Yes. What does it tell you?'

'I don't know. The space, I suppose. The cloudiness, the road to nowhere.'

She clapped her hands.

'Jimmy, you are clever for a foreigner. It *is* the road to nowhere.'

'Thanks. But there's something you aren't telling me.'

'Two things,' she said seriously. 'One: the Vladimirka Road is where everyone going to Siberia has to travel. Two: Levitan was a poor Jewish painter.'

'A revolutionary?'

'No. Just a poor Jew with a soul, who could see into the future.'

We walked on in silence.

'Thank you, Natasha,' I said eventually.

She smiled at me with her mouth and her big brown eyes.

20

Moscow and Kharkov

By the early summer, the diplomatic game had begun to hot up. It was like the mating season, with everyone vying for everyone else's hand. Podbirski had given me a clue as to Stalin's thinking – or his idea of the way Stalin was thinking – but no one could be sure. Molotov lambasted Britain and France for hesitating over a proposed pact, and hinted the Soviet Union might favour lining up with Germany.

It seemed unthinkable that the Bolshevik state would sign a treaty with its deadly Nazi enemy. Nevertheless, Podbirski had told me – perhaps as a warning I should discreetly pass on to the British Embassy – that Stalin trusted no country above another, and was guaranteed to strike a deal with whoever offered him the best short-term prospects.

I'd become friends with a German diplomat, Guenter Wolf, who made no secret to me of his intense dislike of Hitler. One evening he said sardonically: 'Our far-sighted Führer knows he cannot fight a war on two fronts. It's as simple as that. You won't go far wrong predicting that he will reach a non-aggression pact with Stalin soon. Then he'll be able to invade Poland. He already knows that Chamberlain and the French have no stomach for war – but even if they do make some sort of military gesture, he won't have to worry about Russia fighting us as well.'

I felt obliged to say that Germany should not underestimate Britain, adding: 'We don't want war, but we've never shirked it if we're pushed to the brink.'

'In that case,' he shrugged, 'Europe will be in flames soon.'

'What will you do if there's a war?' I asked.

'Same as you,' he smiled. 'Get into uniform. It's the only thing one can do. And hope that the army will have the balls to throw out the little Adolf. Then maybe we can have some real settlement.'

'What I find very hard to understand is how Hitler can contemplate a deal with Stalin. He's always made out that he hates Bolsheviks and Slavs almost as much as he hates Jews. How can he hope to do such a deal and still emerge with credibility among the Germans?'

'My friend, how little you know the Germans,' he laughed. 'We are a nation of diligent sheep. We follow blindly. And the few people still prepared to think for themselves will see the reality behind everything – our beloved Führer will attack Russia one day soon, not only because of the hatred he has, but also because he needs the food the Ukraine can produce. He remembers how we were starved in the last war. But before he can start on Russia, he must take Poland, and then be free to fight in the west. He can only do this if Stalin guarantees to do nothing.'

'Do you think Stalin understands all this?' I asked.

Again Guenter laughed.

'Of course he understands. But he needs to buy some time, and he wants a piece of Poland also, and I think it probably tickles him to think of the Germans and the Anglo-French armies tearing each other to bits. Doesn't it tickle you too my friend? You and I will be shooting at each other so that Stalin can laugh into his bortsch and his vodka. It's a good joke, eh?'

I wrote the story he'd suggested, but it didn't seem to alarm anyone in dozing England. Almost the only reaction I got was a note from Douglas to say: 'Your analysis is quite perceptive. Our diplomatic efforts are paltry and half-hearted.'

And so it seemed.

'Your people moving too slowly, much too slowly,' Podbirski told me, shaking his head.

'Tell it to the ambassador,' I said.

We were in my office. I assumed microphones were picking up our words.

'Ambassador not listen to me, my friend. Maybe he listen to you, eh?'

'I think the British government *is* serious, Anatoly.'

I wasn't being truthful. The government had sent a team to Moscow to negotiate with the Russians, but it was low-level.

Podbirski laughed.

'You think it is, how you say, a big deal, for Comrades Stalin and Molotov, that they must talk with such a delegation? They want to know why Chamberlain not come to Moscow. He crawls to Hitler, but does not even visit us.'

Molotov eventually rejected the proposals for a treaty by Britain and France, telling them: 'You must think we are nitwits and nincompoops.'

He'd spelled out the words in English, so Natasha, reading me his comments, didn't have to translate them.

She scribbled on a scrap of paper: 'Stalin/Molotov – nitwits, but dangerous ones. Snakes.'

She showed this to me with a smile, then tore the paper into tiny bits and nodded towards the toilet, indicating that I should flush them away quickly.

I was becoming intensely attracted to her though I still didn't trust her completely. I was sure she was reporting on me to some NKVD officer, probably Podbirski. Yet I felt that this was forced upon her and anyway it was secondary to my physical longing for her. When I was near her – and I was near her for most of every day – I longed to put my arms about her, to kiss her, to stroke her hair.

This was partly, I told myself, because I'd been starved of close contact with any desirable female. Apart from some of the wives of fellow correspondents and diplomats, I met no one in Moscow – until Natasha – with whom I could contemplate falling in love. The city itself offered few distractions for a lonely bachelor. The diplomatic receptions and dinners were a big bore. The Bolshoi doing *Swan Lake* was a wonderful experience the first time round, but made stale by repetition. The long evenings and nights were difficult. Natasha went home promptly at five o'clock unless there was a late press conference.

One evening, as she prepared to leave as usual, I said, casually: 'If this were London, I'd suggest we went out for a meal.'

'I cannot,' she said. 'I visit my cousin Olga and her husband.'

Then she grabbed a piece of paper, scribbled on it and handed it to me. It read: 'Meet me in one hour this side of Crimean Bridge.'

I nodded.

'Well perhaps another night, Natasha,' I said.

'Perhaps,' she muttered, putting on her coat and leaving the office without a glance at me.

It was with a mixture of anticipation and some trepidation that I made my way to the newly constructed bridge across the Moskva. I was worried because I knew that this was a probable scenario that would lead to an entrapment attempt. On the other hand, I desperately wanted to spend some hours alone with Natasha, out of earshot of other staff members and hidden microphones. It was dark when we met each other along the embankment, but there was no mist and the stars were sharp and bright in the black sky, pinpoints of light in the vast space of the universe. We walked in silence for half a mile or so, then she said: 'Jimmy, this is exactly what they want me to do.'

'I guessed that. I don't care. Let's enjoy ourselves, Natasha.'

She laughed bitterly.

'How can I enjoy myself in such a situation?'

'If we can meet sometimes, like this, as friends, I can't see the harm.'

'Why do you want such things?' she asked. 'You have many foreign friends in Moscow. You have many things to do.'

'I'd like to do them with you sometimes.'

'In the daytime, it's okay. Part of my job is to show you the culture of Moscow.'

'But that's during the day and with everyone watching.'

'Here, they watch all the time. You think now there is no one following us?'

I glanced all around. There was not a hint of anything suspicious.

'No one at all,' I said.

'Maybe not, but if not now, then next time they will see.'

'I understand your problems, Natasha. If it makes things difficult for you, I won't suggest anything again.'

'What makes it difficult is that this is what they want. And I do not like doing what they want, Jimmy.'

'If they didn't want you to do it, would you like to see more of me?' I asked.

'Of course. I like you. Of course.'

'Then let's pretend they don't want it to happen.'

'No, Jimmy. It's not fair to you. There must be other women

you have met in Moscow. Diplomatic staff and other foreign women.'

'I have met other women,' I said.

I sensed her tense up.

'Then you can take some of them to the restaurants and to drink wine in your apartment,' she said.

'Their husbands might not like that.'

'Ah, you are a nice man, Jimmy,' she said without irony.

'Besides, I'd like to spend some evenings just with you.'

'Why?' she asked.

'Because the only alternative is the Bolshoi or the theatre where I can never understand the dialogue.'

'I see,' she said seriously.

'And because I think you're lovely,' I said.

'No, I am unattractive Soviet woman, without lipstick and lovely clothes and make-up.'

'I don't care about the clothes and the make-up.'

'But you agree I am ugly.'

'Natasha,' I said, 'you are lovely.'

'But not beautiful. Lovely is not beautiful.'

'You're beautiful.'

I wanted to kiss her, but knew she was going through agonies of indecision.

'Thank you, Jimmy. I like you too. But I cannot just be their puppet. They will clap their hands and say to me: Well done, comrade, you have done your duty. Now you can find out from this man all the secrets he knows about what the diplomats are really saying, and maybe even better, some secrets of British arms production. Ask him about their aeroplanes.'

'And if I don't tell you anything?' I asked.

'Then they will *not* say: Well done, comrade.'

'Is there no way we can meet secretly?' I asked.

She shook her head. 'No,' she said.

We walked a little further, then she added: 'Let me think some more. Now, I had better go to see my cousin Olga.'

She held out her hand and I shook it, but did not let it go right away.

'You may kiss me good-night, if you wish to,' she said. 'I do not think anyone is watching us.'

So I kissed her and her warm lips responded. To anyone

watching, we must have looked like local lovers enjoying the relative privacy of the banks of the Moskva. Eventually, with a sigh, she drew apart.

'Let me think some more,' she whispered, then disappeared into the night.

The next day, she was strained, distant, formal. She didn't take off her coat. When I asked why, she replied that she was cold. I tried smiling at her, but she looked away. After a tense hour or so of press translations, I scribbled a short message: 'If you like, forget what I said about us meeting secretly.'

She read it and wrote underneath: 'Yes, it is better we should.'

Then she gave me a cold stare, so uncharacteristic that it scared me.

'I'm sorry I put you in an awkward position,' I wrote.

'I, too,' she scrawled.

I suggested eventually, out loud, that since it was a quiet news day she should go home. She agreed in a monotone. I wanted to hold and kiss her, but didn't.

The day after that, she failed to appear. I was upset and angry with myself for pushing her into an untenable situation. Clearly she liked me enough to find it distasteful to have to report on any advances I made to her, but not enough to respond to my attentions. I borrowed a colleague's translator to get through my day's work and felt sure that I would not see Natasha again.

Twenty-four hours later, though, she came back. She didn't smile at me as she took off her coat.

'I am sorry that yesterday I was not well,' she said.

'Are you feeling better today?'

'Very much, she said briskly. 'And I also have some news. If you like, we will go on a journey to outside Moscow.'

Even if the prospect of a trip with her hadn't been on offer, I'd have been delighted to get away from Moscow and see something of the country.

'That's wonderful,' I said. 'Where will we go?'

'You want to see Ukraine?'

'Yes, I do.'

'Then I will advise tomorrow when we can depart.'

With this, she picked up *Izvestia* and said: 'Here is an interesting article by Ilya Ehrenburg. He is quite famous writer. You have heard of him?'

'I met him in Paris a few years ago.'

'Ah, I did not know that; so you also are quite famous.'

'No. I'm as lacking in fame as anyone you're ever likely to meet.'

'This is your English modesty?' she asked.

'No, I'm not even famous for my modesty.'

Suddenly, she smiled at me and my heart felt warm.

'So, here is what Ilya Ehrenburg says about the international situation,' she said, getting back to business, but still smiling.

The next day, she told me: 'I have got our papers in order, and our tickets for the train. Tomorrow we leave for Kharkov.'

It was an overnight trip. I had a first-class compartment to myself. When I asked her in the dining saloon that night, Natasha said her accommodation was comfortable too. But, I persisted, was it first class, like mine? The dining car was full of self-important officials and Red Army officers. The smell of Makhorka tobacco, cheap and pungent, enveloped everything.

'Don't worry, it's quite comfortable,' Natasha replied with a twinkle in her eyes. 'I am sharing with a very nice lady commissar.'

I was irritated that we were travelling in different classes, but didn't want to put her under pressure and suspicion by showing it. Because we were surrounded by other travellers, we talked of the weather, the excitement of the Moscow circus and the construction of the metro, and went to bed early. There seemed no point in staying up for the Russian supper, which began at around midnight. I would have loved to ask Natasha to my compartment, but it was clearly impossible to do so.

I awoke in a better frame of mind. She and I were on the same train, and soon we'd be in the same city, far from Moscow. The conductor arrived with a glass of steaming tea, which he refreshed at hourly intervals. I sat reading and looking out of the window. The Ukrainian countryside – the envied bread basket of Europe – looked fertile and abundant, but my mind dwelt on the Stalinist policies that had induced two devastating famines here in the past 20 years.

My sixth-floor room in the Kharkov Hotel was large. I suspected Natasha's was much smaller. We met as arranged in the cavernous lobby, high ceilinged and marble floored, 15 minutes after arriving, and walked through the glass entrance doors into the city.

At last we were alone – or felt alone – walking in the streets in the late afternoon, but she seemed nervous, unwilling to talk.

'Is Kharkov your home town?' I asked.

'It was.'

'And your parents? Do they still live here?'

'No,' she said, quickly, harshly.

I tried to take her hand, but she pulled it away.

'Are we being watched?' I asked.

I looked around. The streets were busy, people keeping to themselves. No one appeared to be following us. She didn't answer but strode at a brisk pace.

'Where are we going?' I asked.

'I will show you.'

She took me to some city landmarks, giving me information in stilted tones. We came to an interesting, almost oriental building whose dome might have been inspired by cinematic versions of a spacecraft, bulbous and curving concavely to a sharp point.

'Ottoman?' I asked. 'What is it?'

'Now it is the Kharkov sports centre. Since ten years our young people train here to be athletic and strong. The pride of our country.'

'What was it before?'

For the first time that morning a spark of expression, sardonic, angry, came to her face.

'The Great Synagogue,' she said. 'The biggest in Europe. And now it is a sports centre. Wonderful progress, yes?'

'Natasha,' was all I could say.

'It is the same with the churches and the mosques. We put them to good use. Storage rooms, factories, gymnasiums.'

'But people still pray?'

'Oh, yes. They pray – somewhere, in their heads, maybe at home, they find some place to pray – and what good is that?'

'You are not religious?' I asked.

'I do not know what that means. I don't believe in gods and angels. I believe in devils though. I see them in this world. I see them here.'

'Be careful, Natasha,' I said looking around.

'Careful of what? No one can hurt me.'

'I don't understand.'

'No,' she said in a quieter voice. 'It is difficult to understand. Maybe I exaggerate. Maybe I just have a bad day. Let us say that, Jimmy.'

Her anger had passed but so too had the earlier flatness of manner. She seemed almost without care. When I tried, again, to hold her hand, she said, quite gently: 'Not yet, Jimmy. When it gets dark, maybe.'

Kharkov was an industrial city, scarcely beautiful. Many of the new buildings were functional but ugly. Natasha pointed to one of them.

'In that building, until five years ago, lived my grandparents in a room. Before that, since 1870, they lived in a small town near here. My grandfather was a big grain merchant in those days. Later, in the famine in the 1920s, not so big. That was when they moved from the small town – the *shtetl*, as they called it – to Kharkov. My grandfather worked in some little jobs but he was not an educated man. Just a Jew who had a nose for business when he was young. You have guessed I am Jewish?'

'I guessed.'

'How? My nose? Is it too big? My hair is too black?'

'No,' I smiled. 'Something ... sensitive in your character.'

'My name is Khazan. You know what that means?'

'A cantor.'

'Ah, Jimmy Bexley, you know a lot of things. My great grandfather and before him, his father and grandfather. All were famous cantors.'

'Really?'

'No,' she laughed. 'I don't know. My great grandfather was a cantor, yes. But famous? Who can say? There were no cultural journals with operatic experts to describe his singing.'

'Your grandparents? Are they still alive?'

'They died five years ago. The last famine, Stalin's famine, made life very hard in the Ukraine, even in the big towns. They had only a little money by then, and the food in Kharkov was very expensive, believe me. So they had to eat less and then they could not resist sickness.'

After we had walked a little way further in silence among people hurrying on their way, clambering on to trams, she added:

'My parents and I, at that time, were living in Moscow. My father got a letter finally from his parents asking for some help, so he sent money before they died. That was the first time in years they had written to each other.'

'Why?'

'Because of madness. Like everything here. My grandparents believed in God who was strong but merciful. As long as you worship him, he looks after you, that god. My father's god was the Communist future. When he was a young man, he was jailed by the Tsarists, deported. He despised his parents. They hated him because he abandoned their religion for another one, and because to them he was criminal. They had enough trouble with Ukrainian anti-Semites without a son who was a Communist. Later on they had more troubles from their other sons, my uncles. One was killed by the Reds in the civil war, the other died from diphtheria.'

It was getting dark, so I was able to hold her hand as we walked.

'My parents were both Communists,' she said. 'My father had a quite high position in the Party. His god changed names: first Lenin, who he admired; then Stalin, who he did not admire but was better than no god at all. And like with my grandfather's god, you had to praise and obey.

'I don't believe my parents ever lost completely their faith even though they knew what happened in Ukraine and then elsewhere when the purges started. But then they were caught in the net also. They were denounced as Trotskyites and saboteurs and all sorts of things. It's a wonder the Soviet Union has survived with so many traitors around! But they still believed. They confessed their sins, that in their hearts they had been critical of Comrade Stalin, that they had doubted his supreme wisdom. My father was sentenced to jail, and there he died two years ago. How he died, I don't know.'

'Natasha, I'm sorry.'

'I think probably he did some agreement with the NKVD. He would confess if they were not sentenced to death and if I was left alone, maybe even helped. My mother was sent to a labour camp in Siberia – sent on the Vladimirka Road. Once I had a letter saying she worked hard but was well. Then nothing more. Me? I have been given a reward for my parents' deep faith, which made them confess to sins they had never imagined they committed. I am a trusted translator, who also must spy on foreigners I work for. And that is all you have to know about me.'

After a while, she said: 'And all I know about you, Jimmy, is that you studied at Cambridge University and you work for an important English newspaper.'

'There's not that much to tell.'

'No famines, no torture, no betrayals? Life must be very boring in your England,' she said with a slight smile.

'Very boring,' I agreed. 'But here goes.'

So, as we walked a long route back to the hotel, I told her about my father dying in France, about going to Berlin, about Cambridge and Dorothy and Ed. She listened quietly, said nothing, but seemed to imbibe with pleasure the rhythms of a non-totalitarian twentieth-century life: war, ideals, education, love, travel, work.

'I am sorry about Dorothy,' was her only comment.

Later that evening, after we'd had something to eat in the soulless hotel dining-room and then gone to our separate rooms, there was a knock at my door. It was Natasha. She asked in a small voice if she could come in. I was reading and hadn't gone to bed. She asked if she could have some vodka, seeing a bottle on my table.

'I never knew you drank.' I smiled.

'I don't. I want to say sorry.'

'For what, Natasha? You don't need to apologise for anything.'

'It was very boring for you today. To listen to all my family stories and to be with me when I was in such a bad mood.'

'You don't need to apologise. I wasn't exactly chirpy myself.'

'Chirpy? I like that. Like a bird?'

'Exactly.'

'Do you think I was in a bad mood because I did not like being with you?' she asked staring at her glass.

'I didn't know.'

'It was not that. And it was not because I was upset by memories.'

She gulped down the vodka, pulled a face, then said: 'I will let you kiss me, Jimmy.'

The abruptness of this and her businesslike tone made me laugh. She frowned. 'I knew it,' she said. 'You don't want to kiss me again.'

I embraced and held her and then we kissed. Eventually, she broke away, put her finger on her lips to command me to silence, switched off the light and undressed, with swift movements. I took off my clothes too and we climbed into bed. She was almost desperate in her lust, as was I, and we grappled our way to separate moments of ecstasy. Then we fell asleep in each other's arms. Not a word had been said since before we kissed. Early in the morning we made love again, but this time slowly, deeply, calmly, until we climaxed in mutual wonderment. A few hours later she kissed me on the forehead and said: 'I go to put on clean clothes in my room, then I will take you to see Gorky Park. You will like it.'

In the park, we sat on a bench, a little apart.

'Thank you for being with me,' I said.

'Jimmy,' she said in a quiet voice. 'Jimmy, I want nothing more than to share your bed. Nothing more. That is why yesterday I was in such a bad mood. I was upset because that is exactly what *they* want. That is part of my job for you.'

I winced and she noticed this.

'Yes, it is not nice. Do you think I would like to do that because they want it? But then I could not help myself.'

'I'm glad you couldn't stop yourself,' I said.

'I too. But now we are both in their power.'

'No, I won't let that happen,' I said.

'Jimmy, we are in their power. Already, you are thinking: How can I save Natasha? How can I get her out of Russia?'

'Yes.'

'You see? That is what they want. You are in their power. If you fall in love, you will do anything to get me out, yes?'

'Yes,' I said.

'Oh, Jimmy. How can you think you will fall in love with me? I am ugly and not a very good mistress. All you know of me is that I am a good translator.'

'You are everything I need,' I said.

'Because we spent one night together?'

'That was only the icing on the cake.'

'That is a funny thing to say. I am like icing, or I am like cake?'

'It's an expression. It means that I love you, in bed and out of it. Equally.'

'Jimmy, that is a very nice thing, a lovely thing, to say. But now we must be serious. We must say this is the end. When we get back to Moscow, I will tell them I have failed. That you slept with me and didn't like. That you do not love me. That they should find you another translator.'

'I will absolutely refuse to let you go,' I said, half jesting. I couldn't take this conversation seriously, and I thought she wasn't being very serious herself. But I was wrong.

'Don't joke with me, Jimmy,' she pleaded. 'I mean what I say. I cannot be their pawn, and I cannot let you be their pawn. You know what is a pawn?'

'I know,' I said. 'And we're not.'

'How can you say that?'

'The fact that you're telling me all this,' I said, clutching at straws. 'The fact that they can't manipulate our feelings.'

'Oh, yes, that they can do; they can manipulate,' she said.

'You haven't said how you feel about me.'

'What can I say? How can I say I love you? That's what you want. But how can I say it? We can talk properly only in the street, in parks. We have passion for each other, yes. But is there anything more, Jimmy? What do you know about me, except what I have told you?'

'It's enough for me.'

'No, it cannot be,' she said. 'And, Jimmy, what do I know of you? You have told me about events in your life, and I loved to listen to that. But, inside you – what do I know of that?'

'That sort of thing comes later,' I said.

'In England, perhaps it does.'

'Everywhere. Look, already, now, we're talking about inside us.'

'I suppose.'

'A few more sessions and I'll be able to predict your every word.'

She looked at me in surprise, saw I was trying to be humorous, and then smiled: 'Jimmy, Jimmy, Jimmy. So what am I going to say next?'

'That you're dying of hunger,' I ventured.

She laughed loudly.

'You see, I already know that you have a sense of humour,' I said.

'And I know that you are very bad at making jokes,' she teased.

'Exceedingly bad.'

'And you know that I like to laugh at bad jokes. That is the Soviet way.'

'It's your way, Natasha.'

'Maybe the Jewish way?' she mused.

'Why, yes. You have that sad, sympathetic humanity of Jewry.'

'And what do you know of that?' she asked, smiling. 'Even I do not know. I know nothing of Jewishness.'

'I know a bit about it. Remember, I told you about Dorothy yesterday?'

She nodded.

'Already I hate the woman,' she said. 'Because you love her, and because she has hurt you.'

'I did love her, and she did hurt me, but she's not a rival to you.'

'No,' Natasha said, suddenly becoming glum again. 'Stalin is my rival. He gets in the way of what I feel about you.'

'Which is what, exactly?'

'You were telling me about Dorothy,' she smiled.

'Only that she also had that sympathetic humanity. Once.'

'Now I hate her even more,' Natasha said. 'But she is a Communist, so how can she be like that – to have humanity and also to believe in Communism?'

'I'm not sure she had much choice, given her character and the times we've lived in. Once she'd rejected a divine meaning, she had to find something to believe in. Marxism seemed the way at the time. It seemed the right thing for humanity.'

'She *thought*.'

'Yes,' I said. 'She thought so.'

'Like my father and my mother,' Natasha said. 'They also thought so.'

We were both grimly silent.

'But you, Jimmy, you never chose that way,' she said after a while.

'Probably because I never had that sharp need to look for some explanation of things. For a long time I wanted to find out why my father died. Then I came to understand it was due to the way things were bungled. It was stupidity rather than malevolence that killed him. Stupid beliefs, like patriotism.'

'So, you believe in nothing, Jimmy?'

'I wish I could find something. I suppose I believe in love.'

'Yes, I also believe in love,' she said sadly. 'Only in my country you are allowed to love only what they permit.'

We appeared to be heading for another bout of gloom, but suddenly she said quite cheerfully, tossing her head as though to toss the bad things away: 'But now I think I know you a little better. You fall easily in love with women, but not with ideas. And also I am hungry.'

We were in Kharkov for a week, and spent every harmonious night in my bedroom and every glorious day walking and talking. I didn't want to see more of the Ukraine. I didn't want to see anything except Natasha. And I became aware that she felt the same about me. Was it the cliché of opposites attracting: the passionate, impulsive Natasha, freed suddenly from the strait-jacket of the Soviet system, encountering the unemotional would-be rationalist Jimmy, adrift in a deep sea of feeling? I knew I shouldn't tarry longer than a week. Things were happening in Moscow and the world, and it was my job to report on what I could. We were both reluctant even to glance at the newspaper headlines, but we had to. And what they showed was that war was getting closer, that tensions were rising, and that one key factor was the question of whether it was Hitler or the western allies who would come to an understanding with Stalin. On that, it seemed to me, depended the future of Europe. I imagined Stalin sitting in his office putting the pros and cons of each suitor into columns on a large piece of paper and wondering which would be the best bet. I imagined the British and French governments at last waking up to the realisation that it was vital to have an alliance with the Soviet Union, however distasteful.

Natasha found it hard to see the logic.

'If I was the Prime Minister of England, Mr Chamberlain, I

would not want to make my hands dirty by shaking the hand of that man in the Kremlin,' she grimaced.

'The danger *now* is that man in Berlin. He wants war, he would like to enslave the world, kill the Jews. The only way to stop him is to gang up against him.'

'That is how you see it, Jimmy. And of course you are right that someone must stand up to him. But all I see is that England and France will shake Stalin's hand and dance around him and make him into the great statesman – and then we, in this country, will never be rid of him. He will go on forever.'

A few rambling political arguments of this sort did not tarnish our happiness. Europe might be on the brink of war, an apocalypse might be imminent, but Natasha and I were together, and we didn't want to think beyond being together.

Only as our train got closer to Moscow and reality did we each become self-absorbed and irritable. My mind was beginning to focus on that unstoppable future and on my work. Natasha read the papers to me, her face bleak. Moscow meant being watched, being exposed to a heartless power.

'Jimmy, in Moscow, we have to be careful again,' she sighed.

We were in my compartment. We'd had to risk her coming there for one more night of togetherness.

'They already know we're lovers,' I said. 'Let's just pretend they don't exist. Why does it have to be different from Kharkov?'

We'd been over this scenario several times.

'Because in Moscow they can put pressure on both of us,' she said wearily. 'Because in Moscow they are there, just behind the door. If we make love together in Moscow it will not be the same like in Kharkov. It will be awful.'

I hugged her.

'It will never be awful between us,' I said. 'You're right that it will be difficult, but we can survive that.'

'I hope,' she sighed.

We decided on a series of silent hand movement signals we could use in the office to arrange meetings where we might be unobserved.

'I will have to report,' she said sadly. 'You understand that, Jimmy?'

'Yes,' I said. 'Tell them I'm a lousy lover.'

She laughed.

'I think even they, even those vile men, will see in my eyes that you are not.'

'Is Podbirski one of them?' I asked.

'Please, Jimmy, you promised never to ask about them. If I tell you names, you may try to do something and get us into more trouble.'

'I know. I'm sorry. I don't give a damn *who* they are. One day, they'll get their due.'

'You believe?' she asked, hope in her eyes.

'Yes, I do,' I lied.

Back in Moscow it was sweltering. A joint British and French military team arrived for talks on a treaty. The delegation was treated with disdain by Molotov.

Tom Housegow of the British Embassy – a man fiercely opposed to appeasement of Hitler – felt that at the very least the Foreign Secretary, Lord Halifax, should have come to Moscow.

'Chamberlain and Halifax are going through the motions because of the pressure being put on them at home. The very last thing they want is a pact with Stalin. It's only the pressure from Churchill and the press that's forced them to send this token delegation. It's half-baked and too late. Meanwhile, the Germans have been dangling very tempting carrots in front of Stalin.'

My German Embassy friend Guenter confirmed that Berlin and Moscow were hurtling towards an alliance.

'Adolf is worried that perhaps you *will* fight in the end. He's got to finish Poland off quickly, before you fight and before the winter, and he won't be able to do that if the Russians are unfriendly. So, he's desperate to sign something with Stalin, and soon.'

My first article after returning from Kharkov reflected these views as well as Podbirski's confirmation that Stalin and Molotov were increasingly attracted by the benefits of a deal with Germany – a share of the spoils of war and breathing space to prepare for any eventual German onslaught against Russia.

The *Review* put a headline on the story saying 'Britain Missing the Boat for Russian Alliance'. I was delighted to learn that government speakers, including Chamberlain, had attacked my story in the Commons as ill-informed scaremongering. Their attacks increased the article's credibility.

Churchill spoke in support of the article:

'The *Review* has hit this particular nail right on the head. It is not a question of whether we must cease to trust the good faith of Herr Hitler – heaven forbid that we should do that after all the evidence of recent months and years. It is a simple question of whether we have any alternative but to stand up to him. In these dark days, the answer is "No". When you are dealing with a brigand, strength flows from the forces you have at your disposal to encircle and strangle him. We must ensure we have those forces at our disposal – from whatever source, from whatever alliance – so we can prevail.'

Moscow's heatwave continued until relief came. Thunderstorms, frightening in their ferocity and heralded by huge flashes of lightning above the Kremlin, began to cool things down.

And then, with the smell of autumn in the air, Ribbentrop arrived to sign a non-aggression treaty with Molotov. I felt sick at heart and in my stomach. At the ceremony, Stalin stood behind the two functionaries, grinning like a sated forest beast.

It was done. What we had feared was signed and sealed. David Low's cartoon in the *London Evening Standard* summed it up: the two dictators, blood enemies, bowing greetings to each other over the corpse of Poland.

Of all the reactions I encountered in Moscow to the pact – mainly gloomy and resigned, whether from diplomats, correspondents and even, to judge by their countenances rather than their words, some Soviet officials – the most surprising was Natasha's.

'I am happy,' she whispered fiercely, as we walked in the cool of a late August evening, careful to keep an innocent distance between us. 'I am happy because now there will be a war and now there will be an end to both these monsters. They join together, so let them die together.'

'But, Natasha, a world war will be awful. Millions will die.'

'I know, dear Jimmy, and also maybe I and you will die, but also millions will die if there is no war. It is terrible thing to say, but perhaps if there is no war then people in England and

France and America will stay alive. But believe me, millions will die in the empires of Hitler and Stalin – and eventually anyway they will turn on you, and your peoples will be killed too.'

'If there is a war, I will have to go and fight,' I said.

'I know. That is only thing that makes me very sad about this treaty.'

'Will you come with me to England?' I asked.

'They will not let me go.'

'I will marry you, and then they'll have to let you leave.'

'Even if I am married to you, they will not let me leave.'

'The embassy...' I began.

'Jimmy, they will not allow me to go.'

'I want to marry you anyway,' I said. 'Then we'll see.'

'No, Jimmy,' she said firmly.

'Don't you want to?'

'Of course, I want, if it will be the best thing for us both. But it will not. It will make it difficult for you if there is a war between our countries – and for me. Also, it will be difficult for you if we cannot be together and you want to marry someone else.'

'Darling Natasha, this is ridiculous,' I protested.

'Jimmy, marriage is for civilised people in civilised countries like yours. If I am your wife, and in Soviet Union...'

She passed her finger across her throat.

I couldn't budge her, and later found out at the embassy, when I asked what would happen if a British friend of mine married a Soviet citizen, that Natasha was right in all she said.

'Sorry, old man,' I was told. 'Tell your friend we could try for a visa for a wife, I suppose, but doubt if we'd get it, not even if the King were to ask. We're not very much loved in these parts at the moment, but even if we were I doubt we'd be able to swing it. Unless, of course, your friend was a high-ranking Party member or a Soviet spy – but then you wouldn't have had to ask us, would you?'

On September 1, Germany invaded Poland and two days later Britain declared war on Germany. I got a message from the *Review* that they wanted me to stay on and report from Moscow as long as possible, but I knew I had to go back to England. I knew that even if Natasha had wanted me to stay in the Soviet

Union, I would not have been able to do so, much as I loved her. But she didn't ask me to stay.

'Jimmy, darling, I understand. You must go back. Your country is in danger, and I love your country as much as you love it. I love it because it is your country and because it is fighting against the monsters. I understand also that you must go back and join the army because of your father.'

'I suppose it's what he would have expected of me. Not to avenge him. Just to do my duty.'

'Yes,' she said fiercely. 'To do your duty. And I will always love you because you want to do your duty.'

'I'll get you out,' I said. 'I promise.'

'I will wait. Who knows?'

21

London

We were sitting, uncomfortably but contentedly, on a wooden floor inside a makeshift concert hall in the National Gallery in central London. I was in army uniform, my companion in a grey striped suit. In front of us, a dumpy, dark-haired, middle-aged woman walked confidently on to the stage, smiled at the applause, sat down at a piano and began to play with precise, gently pumping hands. We were in a city at war and the music warmed our hearts. Schumann, Bach, Beethoven. Outside it was a grey December day at the fag end of 1939. On the other side of Europe, the Nazis had finished off west and central Poland with military efficiency and methodical cruelty. The bombardment and bombing of Warsaw was a foretaste of what modern aerial warfare would mean to civilians in the other great cities of Europe. In the east, the Russians had moved in, under the agreement reached by Ribbentrop and Molotov, to complete the conquest of Poland. The Red Army had also invaded Finland. Europe was ablaze and being enslaved. We might be next on the list. Would our defences, like those of Poland, be crushed in weeks, or even days, our towns bombed to pieces, our citizens humiliated, worked to death or made to dig their own graves before being shot in the head?

Those were the new realities of our world, and there were few of us who were blind to them. We knew what would happen if Hitler invaded us. We knew the price of defeat. We'd declared war and we'd better be prepared for the consequences. That was the underlying feeling, and yet there was no mood of despair. We've beaten the Boche before, and we'll do it again, was one refrain. You can't compare us – or the French – to the isolated, unprepared Poles. Hitler's built up his forces, sure, but we've woken up now and we'll be ready for them if they dare to come.

In September there'd been real fear that the Luftwaffe would begin air raids on London from Day One. It hadn't happened. In fact, very little had happened, apart from the blackouts, the temporary evacuation of women and children to the countryside, the brief closure of cinemas and theatres, the sandbags, the rationing of petrol, the uniforms proliferating in the streets and the stress of waiting for the unknown.

London, when I'd reached it from Moscow a week after the declaration of war, was a city preparing for the worst, but without panic or very great urgency.

What struck me right away was the grumbling, often good humoured, at the bureaucracy of new wartime organisations rather than any signs of mass fear. The first weeks of war produced air raid sirens but no bombing raids.

'They bombed us in the last war, it were bloody 'orrible,' a greengrocer told me cheerfully. 'Killed a lot of kids, an' all. But they lost the war just the same, didn't they?'

Londoners feared gas attacks more than high-explosive or incendiary bombs. It was a city at war, but without any real idea of what modern war entailed. Perhaps because of my awareness of German technological efficiency – gleaned from Leo and Douglas, among others – I had greater concern than most about the devastation London might suffer if and when the Luftwaffe began to target us. The barrage balloons were supposed to be deterrents against low-flying bombers, but I felt they would be a puny defence if the Heinkels came in force.

This was the period that came to be called, courtesy of American newspapers, the Phoney War. Hitler was too busy in the east to consider attacking us just yet, and there was simply no way our troops could rush across the vast tracts of Europe to the defence of Poland. In London, there was not much danger in the streets apart from vehicles speeding blindly without headlights in the blackout; only boredom and frustration at the restrictions on normal life, and griping about the rise in crime during the unlit nights and about petrol rationing.

I enlisted in the army as soon as I got back. Douglas, now installed in a London flat and working, he said vaguely, in a War Office desk job – 'boring, but I'm told necessary' – implied he could arrange for me to work in information or propaganda.

'Pretty vital stuff,' he said. 'They need people with your

background and knowledge. It could lead to something a lot more exciting.'

I said I'd think about it, but all I wanted to do was to get into the war as a soldier, do something physical in the fight against the Nazis and get Natasha out of Russia. It didn't seem all that difficult at the time.

Churchill had been brought back into the government on the outbreak of war, as head of the Admiralty. Chamberlain had no choice but to invite him in. The British public demanded it. They divined that our only hope of survival was to fight Hitler to the death, and Winston was the man who'd do it.

The outside world, apparently, didn't give much for our chances. While waiting to start army training, I received a letter from Ed in Washington.

'I have to tell you, Jim, we're pessimistic. The fact is that you guys are outgunned and have been outsmarted by Hitler. I hate the evil bastard as much as you do but it doesn't look good for you. And even if you manage to avoid losing the war, it would simply mean Stalin would take over – not only Germany, but all Europe. So what's the point? America isn't going to pull your chestnuts out of the fire this time round. No one in the US wants to get involved in Europe, believe me. Except Roosevelt, and since he can't run for a third term he's a lame duck politically. If for some reason Chamberlain and Co. don't negotiate a decent peace with the Krauts, then it's going to get real bad for you. So, for what it's worth, my advice for you personally is to stay out of it. Get a desk job. Don't sacrifice yourself for nothing. Deep down, though, I know you're probably not going to pay one damn bit of notice to me. So, good luck.'

A decent peace! A desk job! I didn't bother to reply.

Now it was winter and Londoners could still joke, complain, bicker, fall in and out of love, worry about money – and find refuge in the music of the same German nation that was raping Poland, as it had raped Czechoslovakia before, and would rape us too if it got the chance.

I glanced at Dr Bergsen, sitting next to me on the floor at the lunchtime recital, clasping his knees to his chin, listening, rapt, as Myra Hess gave us the sublime sounds of Germany's majestic composers. What a schizophrenic country, I reflected, to produce the *Appassionata* and Goethe but also the Kristallnacht and Goebbels!

The National Gallery was shorn of its masterpieces, which were in storage beneath the ground somewhere in Wales. Ornate frames still hung on the walls, but there was nothing in them. The music, on the other hand, filled the vast space, and poured into our hearts. Strange times!

I thought incessantly about Natasha, but had heard nothing from her since our parting in September. Did she go to concerts in Moscow, or was her spirit too damaged to permit herself moments of happiness? Had she been punished because we'd fallen in love? Had the NKVD tried to force her into seducing another foreigner? I was consumed with jealousy at the last prospect – though I believed she would refuse to comply, no matter what they threatened her with.

The vast recital room was crowded, every chair taken, every bit of space on the floor filled with office workers, servicemen and women, off-duty fire wardens, ambulance drivers and others, gas masks beside them, all devoutly drinking in the beautiful side of the nation that was at war with them.

Stories were filtering through about Nazi barbarity in Poland. Civilians murdered in cold blood, random bombings, executions of the 'racially impure'. Some of my colleagues at the *Review*, especially those recalling the false atrocity stories coming from Belgium early in the last war, treated the reports with scepticism. I did not. I knew what the Nazis were capable of and what they wanted to achieve.

After the concert we filed out into the cold London afternoon. The statues of Trafalgar Square were boarded up, except for Nelson, who had saved England from Napoleon, and who gazed from on high down Whitehall towards the Houses of Parliament. In the skies above, the dirty silver barrage balloons prodded into the clouds.

Dr Bergsen said to me: 'Nothing ever can destroy such creations as we have just heard, my dear Jimmy. Not bombs, not the Gestapo. Such a message does this concert send to the world.'

We walked in silence for a while, and then he added: 'They called me to a tribunal.'

I knew what this meant. The government was considering ways of dealing with so-called enemy aliens.

'What happened?' I asked.

'They ask questions. Who I am? Why I come to England? Nothing bad.'

'If you'd told me, I'd have gone with you,' I said.

'I know, but I could not trouble you, and there was no need. As you can see, I am still a free man. They do not think I threaten the security of England.'

'You're a refugee. How could they think otherwise?'

'Many people think any German may support the Nazis and give to them information.'

'Only people who read the right-wing rags think like that,' I said.

'Also others,' Dr Bergsen said. 'But, Jimmy, is a small matter. There are bad people everywhere. Even here, in England, they call us refuJews. But is a small matter. This is a good country. Where else, in a country at war, can you go off the streets at lunchtime and hear Myra Hess play the Beethoven sonatas?'

I smiled at him. 'So you think we'll survive, Dr Bergsen?'

'Of course. Me and you, Jimmy, maybe we won't survive, but civilisation in the end will survive. I think...'

His voice tailed off.

I was pleased that the recital had cheered him up. When he'd phoned me to suggest attending it, he'd sounded as downcast as I'd ever heard him. Dinah Woolf, on whom he had apparently pinned hopes for his future happiness, had managed to get to Palestine just before the outbreak of war. Dr Bergsen, I surmised, was pining for her, even if not for Palestine. To him, it was a country far, far from the European culture that he still romanticised despite its descent into barbarism. His job as a wine salesman had collapsed because of government restrictions and the shortage of foreign alcohol. Some wine was still trickling in from France, and some from South America, but that was about all. His employers had cut their staff sharply.

When I asked him after the concert, in a roundabout way, about how he was managing to survive, he said with a smile: 'Ach, my dear Jimmy, you do not have to worry for me. I have saved a little money. Also, as a travelling salesman, I built up many contacts. Together, we have stocks. I cannot say more.'

I knew that his great ambition was to join the war effort. Some refugees had managed this, but there were difficulties in his case; he was too old to fight, and had no special skills to employ.

My face must have shown my concern, for he suddenly said, with great cheerfulness: 'Come, Jimmy. The soul has been satisfied, now it is time for the body. We will drink a cup of tea and eat some fish and chips, yes?'

I agreed. He'd adapted well to English ways.

Winter passed slowly. The reports from Poland grew ever more gruesome. Jews locked inside a synagogue for days without food, water or sanitation, then forced to clean up their excrement with prayer shawls and holy scrolls, then murdered. Polish civilians rounded up in hundreds as reprisals for anti-German actions and shot dead. In Finland, the Red Army suffered a humiliating set-back. Stalin had shot himself in the foot by purging the best people in the armed forces. I was delighted that a small democracy could stand up to a giant and voracious dictatorship. I was sure that Natasha would be equally happy if the true news was known to her. Perhaps, I thought for a while, this would be the end of Stalin. Perhaps the army would get rid of him. Fat chance! The Russians launched a mammoth new offensive and forced the Finns into surrender.

We continued to suffer great shipping losses, many of them caused by a new magnetic mine developed by the Germans. If they were such good scientific inventors, I thought, remembering Ed's glowing report on their advances in 1939, how far could they be from making an atomic weapon? It was a chilling thought.

By spring I had finished my army training and was with my unit waiting to be posted abroad or to take up arms on the coast against any invading force. I wanted to get to Europe, where I imagined we'd soon be slugging it out with the enemy. I had no idea how ridiculously under-prepared we were, in terms of men, equipment and tactics compared to the Germans.

In April we suffered our first real defeat of the war. Churchill's plans to invade Norway and block raw materials vital for Hitler's war effort were thwarted by a swift German occupation of the country. Reports that the Germans were aided by a fifth column of Norwegian Nazis fuelled fresh suspicion of aliens living in Britain.

Chamberlain, trying to calm nerves (or perhaps really believing his own words), said: 'One thing is certain. Hitler has missed the bus.'

The next day, I overhead a conversation between two middle-aged women in the street: 'Missed the bus, 'as 'e? 'E bleeding well would 'ave if 'e'd been trying to catch one this morning, ducks. Queues as long as me old man's aspidistra.'

'Lucky you, Doris, to 'ave an old man like that. Who'd believe anything old Chamberpot said anyway. Don't matter if 'Itler's missed the bus, 'e'll come in an aeroplane if he wants.'

'Winnie'll stand up to him if 'e gets the chance.'

'High time Winnie was in charge.'

'Mind you, my George don't like Winnie. Says 'e broke the General Strike.'

'Maybe 'e did. But mark my words, Doris, 'e's the only one who can break 'Itler's 'ead. You tell that to your George and his bleeding great aspidistra.'

The chance came Churchill's way sooner than expected. Hitler attacked western Europe in May. The Führer hadn't missed the bus, after all. The German tanks burst through with a speed none of our defence experts had foreseen. It was the blitzkrieg, the lightning war. Holland and Belgium were overrun, France was invaded. We knew for certain now – we would be next on the list. Disaster piled on disaster. For Chamberlain, the game was up. He was forced to resign.

On a day's leave from my unit, I bumped into Douglas walking in St James's Park at lunchtime.

'Who's it going to be?' I asked.

'Our friend,' he smiled.

I knew Douglas had his fingers on the pulse, and I was relieved. I'd feared along with many others that the British establishment would keep Winston out of 10 Downing Street and bring in Halifax, one of the leading pre-war appeasers. Common sense prevailed. There was going to be no more crawling to Hitler.

Churchill became Prime Minister on May 10, 1940, as things went from bad to worse across the Channel. The French weren't going to put up much of a fight. Our expeditionary army was under-cooked and under-armed for the Nazi onslaught.

Winston's first message was: 'I have nothing to offer but blood, toil, tears and sweat.'

That was what we wanted to hear. No more obfuscations, no more platitudes. And, above all, no more pious hopes of peace. We hadn't started this war, but now that we were in it, we'd have to win it, whatever the cost. We knew there'd have to be great sacrifices, and now Winston had told us in plain words exactly how elemental those sacrifices would be.

To my chagrin, my unit was kept back in England for the time being.

In Europe, our troops were trapped and forced to retreat to the French port of Dunkirk, exposed to artillery and air attacks. We didn't dare hope the army could survive in any strength.

Douglas phoned. 'Glad I found you. I heard you had a few days' leave. I've arranged for some more. Can you get hold of Robert's boat?'

I was puzzled. I realised that Douglas could easily find out my movements, and just as easily arrange furlough, but why was he suggesting I borrow my stepfather's motor yacht? I knew better, however, than to question him.

'I should think so.'

'Then get it to Dover and wait for orders.'

I knew then that something big was up. I drove to my mother's house to ask Bob's permission.

'I'm coming too,' he said instantly. 'You can crew.'

He'd had word that small boats were required to help evacuate troops from the beaches at Dunkirk and nearby areas. His vessel, the *Burgundy*, was a well-appointed 70-foot pleasure craft. I surmised it could carry a couple of dozen passengers at a pinch.

My mother hugged both of us and wished us good luck. According to Bob she hadn't been told about the mission, but she must have guessed. She whispered to me: 'Come back!'

She sounded as though she meant it desperately.

War, as I knew from what had happened to my parents and from my own experience, forces families and loved ones apart. It does so physically and emotionally. But, as I now saw, the over-arching peril can also forge a common resolve that brings families closer together.

My own family was surprising me.

On the way to Dover, Bob – he was no longer an MP – talked frankly about being one of a group that had been keen to negotiate with the Germans even after the invasion of Poland.

'We thought we could do business with them. It wasn't treachery, more like myopia. We wanted to avoid our own involvement, but weren't looking at the whole picture. We'd been sure that Hitler, whatever his faults, was out to save Europe from Bolshevism. Now he's shown his true colours. It's *our* values that he hates above all.'

This wasn't the time for gloating, so I simply nodded and said: 'Well, we're all in it together now.'

'Right. Whatever's happened before is old hat now. We're in a real war and we have to smash the Hun once and for all. I've written to Winston giving him my full backing. Got a reply thanking me. Never much cared for the blighter but I have no doubts that he's the man for the job. So let's go and pick our chaps off the beaches.'

From Dover, with a couple of young naval ratings on board, we set out for France in the dark. Flames from burning oil tanks guided us towards Dunkirk. What we saw, in the morning, was total confusion. I doubted whether we could accomplish anything. Thousands and thousands of troops were stranded on the beaches, many of them wounded, dying, under fire. German Stukas screamed down to dive-bomb our vessels as well as the men on shore. Soldiers waded out to jetties or blindly towards boats. We managed to load about 50, some close to death, and make our way back to Dover, half submerged, it seemed, by the weight of humanity. Then we did it twice more. On the last trip, as we neared Dunkirk, a shell seemed to be whistling straight for us, and smacked into the water close by. I was flung across the yacht, crashing against the side. I couldn't walk and sat helplessly between exhausted soldiers on the way back. I'd broken my ankle.

The entire operation brought back more than 300,000 troops to fight another day. People called it a miracle, but Winston put it into perspective:

'Wars are not won by evacuations.'

Still, it boosted morale. We now had an army to defend us against an expected invasion, even if they'd had to leave most of their weapons in France. I brooded because I wasn't going to be one of that army just yet. My ankle would take a couple of months to heal, but I had my rifle and some ammunition to use on the invaders if they came. Churchill said we would fight to the death, and that was what I intended to do.

The fall of France was the last straw. Our main ally defeated, almost without a fight. Things looked bleak indeed, though I seldom heard a word of defeatism.

Winston captured the mood in speech after stirring speech. He kept us going, reinforced our bloody-mindedness. Even his overblown rhetoric sounded just right to us. He said what we would have said if we'd had his command of language.

We spoke of our resolve in more prosaic terms.

'Fuck you, Adolf,' I heard someone say in a pub – its windows painted black – one night as the radio brought more grim news from Europe. No one laughed.

Churchill let the world know that if Hitler conquered us then we all would sink into a new Dark Age. He summoned Britons to steel themselves for the battle ahead: 'Let us brace ourselves to our duties, and so bear ourselves that, if the British Empire and its Commonwealth last for a thousand years, men will still say – This was their finest hour.'

As I write these words, years later, I find my eyes moistening. I remember every syllable, as if they still flow hot in my blood stream. Even those of us who longed for the end of colonialism were ready to forgive him (for the time being) his imperial foibles. His words sustained us as we stood alone and prepared for an unequal struggle.

Nevertheless, united as we were against a common enemy, bigotry continued to divide opinions. Feelings against so-called enemy aliens intensified – in the right-wing press at least, and also inside government.

Douglas told me that all male Germans and Austrians between the ages of 16 and 70 were going to be interned indefinitely.

'You'd better warn your friend to be prepared,' he said.

'Can anything be done for him, Douglas?' I asked. 'He's been in a concentration camp already. He was categorised as no risk to security over here. All he wants to do is help in the fight against Hitler.'

'I can't promise anything.'

'He'd enlist if they'd let him; and learn to pilot a plane if he was younger. Surely it's worth something that he speaks German and good English.'

'So do ten thousand others,' said Douglas drily. 'I'll do what I can, but it may amount to nothing.'

'His nephew is trusted enough to be allowed to help our government in scientific research.'

'The nephew undoubtedly has more to contribute than the uncle.'

Our talk turned to the war. Douglas said the Germans had to bring us to our knees if they wanted an easy road to victory.

'If they can invade or force us into negotiations before then, Hitler will have a free hand to turn on Russia. And if he can overrun the Soviet Union, he'll get everything he needs – food, land, oil and raw materials – to keep him going indefinitely.'

'When does he plan to invade us?' I asked.

'Set for September. But first they have to win air supremacy, and that won't be so easy.'

I didn't ask where he'd got the raw information on which to base his conclusions. It had to be pretty good. Douglas had never gone in for guesswork.

'Can we hold out, Douglas?'

'I believe so, but it may be touch and go.'

'And if the Americans came in?' I asked.

'Ah, that would tilt the balance, but it's a very big "if". Roosevelt might want to if he could, but we still don't know if he's going to run again or not.'

'And if he doesn't?'

'With luck and guts, we'll get through it on our own. It will be a desperately close run thing.'

'Then the sooner I get back into the fight the better.'

'Has the foot mended?' he asked with a smile.

'Almost. A bit of a limp won't prevent me from using a machine-gun.'

'It may come to that,' he said. 'But don't worry that you're going to miss the action. Whatever happens here, there'll be plenty of fighting to follow.'

I tried to persuade Dr Bergsen to stay in my flat in Pimlico, where I was living until I could be declared fully fit again for training. I felt he might be less vulnerable there almost under my protection. I didn't expect to be able to prevent his internment, but perhaps I could postpone it until Douglas came up with something. I knew, though, that personal connections were unlikely to help the case. For some reason I remembered the rationale given by a Nazi bigwig about why there could be no exceptions for the treatment of Jews in Germany: 'Everyone has his favourite Jew. And if everyone asks for special treatment for a favourite Jew, we might as well allow them all to live like ordinary Germans.'

Who had said this? Himmler, Goering, Goebbels? Who was saying something similar in England?

Dr Bergsen dismissed my pessimism about my own country, and said he wasn't going to impose on me in any way. He did not feel threatened.

'My dear Jimmy, they will only need to speak to me a few minutes and they will see there is no need to lock me away. This is not the Third Reich. There are laws here, there is justice.'

'Laws have been suspended, Dr Bergsen.'

'And for a good reason. Why should England let supporters of Hitler wander around like everyone else?'

'I'd feel better if you moved into my place,' I said.

'Thank you, thank you, Jimmy. But I will stay where I am.'

I asked if he'd heard from Leo.

'Since the war started, no. That is good. He is working on secret weapons, I am sure. He will help to win the war.'

In truth, I was not entirely disappointed that Dr Bergsen had declined my invitation to move in. There'd been an unexpected development in my life.

Stumbling towards my flat in the black-out one evening, I'd bumped into someone and heard a vexed female cry and then a thud as she hit the ground. I felt my way to her side and began to help her up, apologising profusely.

'It's all right, I'm not hurt,' she said. 'No thanks to you, though. I can't make out your face, but do I know you from somewhere?'

I recognised her voice.

'Not unless you sold books in Cambridge and had a Trinity boyfriend.'

'Jimmy? My God, Jimmy Bexley.'

It was Gwen. I gave her a big hug.

'If I could've chosen anyone to knock me down tonight, it would've been you,' she said.

I'd not seen her since we said goodbye at Cambridge, when she went off to marry Binky Cooper-Downs and I began living with Dorothy.

She came to my flat for a drink and we talked late into the night. She was as pretty as ever, but something had changed. She was more secure, more conscious of her allure, more sophisticated. I'll be damned, I thought. Sweet Gwen Farrow of Cambridge has become a glamorous lady about town.

As she'd predicted six years before, Binky had come into his title – Lord Harding. The grand aristocratic life suited her and had moulded her.

'I was such a little mouse when I knew you,' she said. 'No wonder you ran off with that Communist creature.'

'You were the one who ditched me,' I protested.

She was missing Binky. He was in Cairo, an aide-de-camp to one of our generals.

'Hardly any action in North Africa, so far, thank God. The only danger he's in is from excessive gin and syphilis.'

She said this lightly, but I could tell there was a deeper emotion underneath. She was scared of losing him.

'I have grown rather fond of the old boy,' she admitted. 'Donford isn't the same without him. That's why I spend so much time at the London place.'

Donford was the stately home in Wiltshire, and the London place was a town house in Mayfair, which had also come into Binky's possession when the previous Lord Harding died without issue.

We were still talking when we heard Big Ben chime midnight. She'd listened avidly to all I'd told her about my life with Dorothy and my love for Natasha.

'You poor boy,' she said gently, touching my hand. 'Have faith. It will all work out some day.'

Then she said, shaking her head: 'Christ, Bexley, you do go looking for trouble, don't you. Exotic, mixed-up women. And all the time you could have had me for the asking. I wouldn't have caused you trouble. You deflowered me, after all. Rather deliciously, I seem to remember.'

She was fiddling with some diamond earrings as she said this.

'Why are you laughing?' she demanded.

'Because you've grown up. You're a society lady. You're poised and gorgeous, Lady Gwendoline.'

'So you didn't find me gorgeous before, you beast!'

She said this with a smile that was mostly in her eyes and in a slight twitch of her lips. Her smiles were deep within her, not, I realised, mere reflexes to what amused her or caused her pleasure. She looked at the whole of life with an interior smile. That was how much she'd changed from the unsure, rather timorous girl I'd known in Cambridge.

She asked me to walk her home, which I did. We'd both drunk quite a bit and clung to each other as we walked. Her home was a large Georgian terrace. At the front door, she seemed about to invite me in, then thought better of it. I had no idea how I would have reacted. She invited me to dinner later in the week.

'There's a butler called Stowcroft – terrifyingly stuffy until you get to know him – and a rather dear cook, Mrs Beech, who scurries around town and manages to find all sorts of goodies to dish up for me and my guests.'

She giggled with pleasure.

For a few weeks we saw each other intermittently, kissed chastely to greet and part, and enjoyed each other's company. On my side, it was delightful to be able to spend time with a woman I liked in an uncomplicated, easy sort of way. I hoped things would continue on the same level. I was in love with Natasha and I didn't want another passion.

However, these were times of high emotion on all levels. In the blue skies over southern England, the crucial battle between the RAF and the Luftwaffe was going on every day. We could see the distant, curving white vapour trails of the planes, but could only imagine the frenzy, panic, rage, terror of the crews inside. Everything hung in the balance – our lives, our families' lives, the future of our islands. I knew I'd be involved in the fight, sooner or later, either in Britain or somewhere far away. I didn't think much about dying, but I felt a great need to make the most of life while I could. Gwen too was caught up in the intensity of living on the brink. The inevitable might have been forestalled if Binky had come home on leave. But there was no chance of that. Things were brewing in the North African desert.

Finally, on a humid summer evening, with all the news dark and the outlook dubious, Gwen and I threw our doubts to one side, along with our clothes, and became lovers again.

I might have suffered from a stricken conscience next morning (was I any better, after all, than Ed Brewster whom I'd berated at Cambridge for womanising?) but any guilt feelings – of disloyalty to Natasha, of potential hurt to Binky – were diverted by a letter from Dr Bergsen to say that he'd been interned as an enemy alien in a camp in the north west of England. I borrowed Gwen's two-seater, and drove to Huyton, on the outskirts of Liverpool. The camp was located on a newly built housing estate surrounded by barbed wire.

When I was eventually allowed to see him – through a mixture of pleading, persuasion and reckless hinting of my importance to internal security – he seemed like a broken man. It was not so much the conditions, which were not gruesome, but the feelings of being let down about Britain.

'My dear Jimmy, not in my wildest nightmares did I ever think that in Britain I would be in a camp with guards carrying guns and behind barbed wire.'

At first he'd been put into a category deemed to be of no risk to security and was not detained. But when he was questioned later he'd divulged his business contacts. It turned out that some of them were, unbeknown to him, of dubious character and, even, political allegiance. No officials in these times were prepared to accept his pleas of personal innocence and he was netted along with thousands of others. I promised I'd do what I could to get his case reviewed.

He said he'd tried to contact Leo but he appeared to have vanished from the face of the earth. I too had no luck in getting in touch with Leo, who was presumably sealed off in some secret scientific establishment.

I approached Douglas for help. He sighed and said he'd do his best, but I had to remember that there were more important things at stake than the individual freedoms of a small minority of refugees.

'I thought one of the things we're fighting for is the right of individual freedom,' I protested.

'We're fighting for survival,' Douglas said brusquely.

'That's exactly what Hitler and Stalin would say.'

'Perhaps.' Douglas permitted himself a smile. 'But would you rather your friend were in our hands – however uncomfortable he might find it – or in theirs?'

In the end Douglas was unable to help, and it was some months before the government relented on its internment policy and began to release innocent refugees like Dr Bergsen.

'I knew your fair play would set me free in the end,' he told me on the day I went to Huyton to pick him up.

My ankle was healed and I was back doing army training.

By now, we'd effectively won the air war against the Luftwaffe and begun to build up a formidable armed force again inside Britain. Douglas was convinced Hitler had given up all thoughts of invading us.

'He'll still move against Russia, even if it means that they'll face a two-front war. They've no alternative now; they need the resources.'

I shuddered, thinking of what might await Natasha if the Nazi armies sliced through the Soviet Union.

22

London and North Africa

A few weeks later, the Luftwaffe's bombing Blitz of London began, massive raids, devastation and death. But it didn't break morale. My mother, doing relief work in the East End and dock areas, was full of tales of the courage and humour of people amid all the hardships of the times. Homes were obliterated, people smashed to bits or buried under the rubble.

'I used to think that the working classes hated us,' she told me, 'but when I see what these people have gone through, and how they keep smiling through all the horrors, then I understand that they are the real backbone of England.'

'So, you and Bob will be giving up your privileged existence soon?' I teased.

'Yes,' she said seriously. 'We're all in this together, so we should all be prepared to share.'

I wondered how long she'd stick to this resolve if we managed to win the war, and when the shared struggle became nothing more than a nostalgic memory.

I helped out in rescue work, mostly at night, digging for survivors, or bodies, in the ruins, taking survivors to first aid units. I'd rather have been fighting, doing something aggressive, but this was a necessary, if gruesome, task.

My mother was delighted, as most people were, when the RAF retaliated by bombing Berlin and other German sites. At last we were starting to pay them back.

Dr Bergsen was ecstatic.

'Another raid on Berlin!' he exclaimed over coffee. 'This is the medicine they will hate to be taking. They will soon give up. The Germans are basically cowards. I am sad when my beloved Berlin is bombed, but from the ruins something better may one day come.'

'Let's hope so,' I said, though I doubted whether the end was even remotely in sight.

'You think I am foolish,' said Dr Bergsen. 'Before, in Berlin, I was wrong about many things. But I know the Germans. They follow Hitler because they think he is winning the war, but if they come to believe they are losing, they will quickly change their minds.'

'And how many raids on Berlin will that require?'

Dr Bergsen looked hurt at my sceptical tone and my lack of faith.

'Ach, Jimmy, it is true they are indoctrinated but when America joins in the war, then they will know all is over for them.'

'*If* America joins in, Dr Bergsen. At the moment all they're prepared to do is trade us some old destroyers.'

'Those destroyers we need so badly.'

'We need a hell of a lot more than that, and the Yanks simply aren't prepared to go all the way for us.'

'Of course, at the moment. But when President Roosevelt is again elected President, everything will change. You will see, Jimmy.'

He was right. We began to get small, but certain, intimations that the United States would come into the war eventually, or at least help us significantly. Roosevelt *was* re-elected and devised the Lend-Lease programme to get supplies to us without payment. He also introduced conscription. All it needed was an act of war against the US – and we wondered if Hitler was crazy enough to launch one.

I was given orders to sail on a troopship, and I suspected – rightly, as it turned out – I was bound for North Africa. The Italians invaded Egypt from Libya, and we would have to respond in kind. At stake were the Suez Canal, the Middle East oilfields and control of huge swathes of African territory almost in lobbing distance of occupied Europe. I was excited, apprehensive and relieved – relieved that my waiting was over, and to be extricated from my entanglement with Gwen. Not that either of us had become too emotionally involved with the other. We enjoyed the friendship and the sex, but I loved Natasha, and Gwen was devoted to Binky.

'It's not the title and all this,' she'd said, waving her hand around the large drawing-room of their opulent town house, after I'd gently teased her for becoming such an affectionate wife. 'He's a kind, decent chap. Not as brainy as you, thank goodness...'

'Lucky for you.'

'But a much better lover.'

'I'll pass that on when I see him in Cairo,' I said.

'You'd never do anything like that, Jimmy,' she laughed. 'You're not such a bad chap yourself and you only hurt other people when you're thoughtless. That Russian gold digger is very lucky to be loved by you.'

'It takes another gold digger to say that.'

'Beast!' she said, kicking my ankle with a sharp-pointed shoe.

Another reason why I was far from unhappy to say goodbye to this pleasant interlude with Gwen was that I'd begun to feel uncomfortable with the luxurious lifestyle. I yearned for a Spartan existence, and to share the hardships of others. My mother might talk airily of this; I needed to do it.

It wasn't long, however, before I looked back with longing to those lazy days and nights in Gwen's bed and at her table.

For a while, the North African campaign meant sheer boredom in the pitiless desert, interspersed with action and jubilation as we thrashed the Italians. Then Hitler sent in Rommel and his Afrika Korps, and the real Desert War began. We were quickly on the back foot and the going was tough and dispiriting. It was no real consolation to the soldiers fighting against superior tanks that both the Russians and the Americans were now our allies – thanks to Hitler's invasion of the Soviet Union (which both Douglas and my German diplomat friend Guenter Wolf had predicted) and the Japanese attack on Pearl Harbor.

'If I had three wishes, the first would be for a night in Mayfair, and the second for a hot bath there,' I wrote to Gwen. 'I leave the third to your imagination.'

In August 1942 I was in a tent in North Africa trying to ignore the heat and the flies so I could take a brief nap when a sudden wave of cheering outside jolted me from afternoon torpor into wakefulness. Good Lord, I wondered, have the Germans surrendered? I dashed into the dazzling sunshine to see a pink-faced figure wearing a pith helmet and a boiler suit striding around in the sand, cigar in mouth, shaking hands with bemused but happy soldiers. I blinked. Winston Churchill had arrived in the desert! As he walked towards a waiting jeep, his eyes moved across the cheering throng and lingered on my face. He recognised me and at once approached with a huge grin.

'Well, well,' he said. '*Lieutenant* Bexley, I see.'

'Sir,' I replied stiffly.

He turned to Alan Brooke beside him.

'I have had dealings with this young man, Brookie. A fine fellow. Eager for a scrap, I'll be bound. Shall we offer him a command?'

Brooke allowed himself a thin smile.

'I will have a private talk with him,' Churchill said. 'I must take the pulse of the, um, thinking Eighth Army man. I will obtain some first-hand knowledge from this young fellow, who once worked for me and was, may I say, seldom as argumentative as you.'

'It is my job to put arguments, Prime Minister,' said Brooke stiffly.

'Indeed it is,' said Churchill.

He steered me away from the crowd of disapproving brass and their aides and goggle-eyed troops until we were out of earshot.

'You're a lucky chap, Lieutenant Bexley,' he said. 'Been in the thick of things, I don't doubt. I wish devoutly that I could be out here enjoying the simple cut and thrust of battle rather than having to struggle against endless argumentation with brainless subordinates. I hasten to say that I do not, of course, include General Brooke in the brainless category. But I must not burden you with my cares. Pray tell me of your adventures.'

I gave him a brief account of my service. It had won me no medals. Until recently it had largely been a chapter of military set-backs and retreats. I'd been lightly wounded in the arm while leading a night patrol just before the fall of Tobruk a few months previously. Then came the mad dash to escape from Rommel's panzer-led attacks and live to fight another day. We'd been strafed by the Luftwaffe, pounded by artillery and chased by tanks. It was a retreat but not as bad as being a prisoner of the Afrika Korps, which was the fate of more than 30,000 men after the surrender of Tobruk. Back we scrambled to El Alamein where the Eighth Army, under General Auchinleck, finally stopped the rot and prevented the Germans from taking all Egypt and the Persian Gulf.

'Well, well, and now the time has surely come to put an end to all this turning tail, has it not?' Churchill said.

'But, sir, I think it has,' I said. 'We've managed to stall Rommel.'

Churchill's eyes narrowed.

'That is your considered strategic assessment? As a lieutenant?'

I bit my lip.

Churchill smiled forgivingly.

'I am being too harsh on you, Bexley. I did not mean to be, for it is *I* who am seeking your insights. Tell me, pray, how low is morale, in your estimation?'

'I don't believe it is low, sir. No one likes being chased, but we've made a stand and I think the chaps are in good heart, and ready to strike back.'

'Ah, and that is the nub of the issue. To strike back, to hit the enemy. They are eager to do so at the earliest opportunity?'

'Yes, but...' I began.

I wanted to stress that we were eager to fight again, but also happy to have some rest, more preparation, more equipment. I had just returned from a few weeks of leave in Cairo with all its attractions of good beer, cricket at the Gezira Club and tender expatriate women. For me, to be in the company of, and to converse with, women remained one of the greatest pleasures and privileges of life. In Egypt, it was also a reminder that the old charms and civilised habits were not yet dead.

These friendships – for they were never more than that – didn't mean that I ever forgot Natasha. The German invasion of the Soviet Union made me worry intensely about her fate. I had no illusions about what the Nazis would have in mind for Jews and anyone working for the Russian regime. In a safe, comfortable bed at Shepheard's Hotel, I stayed awake at night, trying to face up to the worst possibilities. In all that time, there were no letters or messages from her.

Nor did I forget Gwen, though I told myself that between us it was nothing more than old playmates finding a bit of necessary diversion at a time of global conflagration. I made no effort to contact her husband in Egypt, and was pleased that our paths never crossed.

Cairo had, all in all, acted like a restorative for me after long months of deprivation amid the sand, insects, remorseless sun and thirst of the North African desert in the company of none but leathery, weary comrades and the littered – often charred – remains of friends and enemies that you could be sure to encounter after every engagement. Everyone in the army, I guessed, needed the same chance of rest and exuberant pleasure to recover their strength and lust for victory.

I didn't get a chance to say anything of this to Churchill, who was answering his own query about morale.

'But, you were about to say, they smart at any delay. The loss of Tobruk was a terrible thing for all the Allies. It was a humiliation, which we must rapidly undo, or all the prestige and honour of Britain may be lost.'

I was rendered speechless by the way he jumped so quickly from his own assumptions of army morale to the big political picture of Allied strategy. I decided to let him know that we all had faith in Auchinleck – 'the Auk'. I told him that from the viewpoint of the ordinary Tommy, things had begun to change. We had wounded and stalled Rommel's army, which only months before had seemed likely to overrun Egypt.

However, Churchill, by now wrapped in his own thoughts, seemed not to hear me and abruptly walked back towards his waiting jeep with a nod of dismissal.

One of the visiting military aides then descended on me and shook my hand.

'Congratulations, old boy. I hear you're taking over from the Auk.'

It was Gerald Cross. I was delighted to see him.

'You're surprised to see me in uniform?' He smiled.

'Good Lord, no, Gerald. I'd heard you joined up right at the start.'

'Yes, I suppose the army owes a great deal to Hitler – turned a lot of pacifists into militarists almost overnight. I threw off my Ghandi loincloth after Munich and couldn't wait to start shooting at the Nazis. I still hate the concept of war, but sometimes it's the only way.'

We exchanged titbits of anodyne news about each other and he briefed me on some of the things happening in the great world beyond the Western Desert.

'Winston's in a bind. Stalin's clamouring for a second front in Europe to take the heat off him. The Yanks think it's a good idea – as though you just sail across the Channel and then slug it out with the Germans. In fact, it needs years of preparation if we don't want to be massacred on the beaches. It's a tricky situation, though. We don't want the Americans to give up on Europe and concentrate on the Pacific. Anyway, Winston has to go from here to Moscow to give the bad news to Stalin – no second front just yet. He's dreading it, I shouldn't wonder.'

'You mentioned the Auk?'

'I did,' said Gerald. 'The PM thinks it's time for a change here.'

'Who will he bring in?'

'No idea, but you're in for a lot of action, old boy. I envy you.'

I knew Gerald had never been one for shirking danger. Like so many in this war, though, he was found to be more useful as an aide than as cannon fodder. I was determined I wouldn't end up like him.

A few days later it was announced that General Montgomery was to lead the Eighth Army. Monty was cocky and infected us with his enthusiasm and confidence. He told us that we'd knock Rommel for six out of Egypt, and so we did, beginning with the second battle of El Alamein.

During this battle I was again wounded, much more seriously than before, and invalided out of Egypt with a badly broken leg and internal injuries. I had been manning a machine-gun until in one blinding, deafening moment of exploding sand, smoke and intense light an artillery shell knocked out our position. Though I didn't know it at the time, I was one of the lucky ones. Five of our chaps were killed there and then.

Back in England, first in hospital and then in my flat, I fretted about getting back into the war, and about Natasha, while Gwen visited, tended, provided and consoled.

In the desert, where one seemed always to be on the move – forward, backward or sideways – and to be constantly exhausted, one seldom had the luxury of worrying about anything other than survival, sleep and water. Now, restricted in movement, I found terrible apprehensions about Natasha flooding my mind. The Germans had penetrated deep into the Ukraine. I was concerned that she might have gone there, but I knew that even if she were in Moscow she would not be safe. The way things were going Hitler might soon be reviewing a military march past in Red Square.

In the absence of any news from her, all I wanted to do was to get back to North Africa. I began to feel much better. My stomach injuries were healing quicker than the doctors expected, thanks to my general fitness. The plaster was off my leg, and I no longer used crutches. It had been a bad break, but I was able to walk with only the slightest of limps.

Gwen divined that my mind was constantly on Natasha, and was wonderfully sympathetic. She had her own preoccupations. Binky came back on leave, and then returned to Egypt. Who knew where he'd be posted next? By tacit agreement, I had not contacted her while he was home and she did not invite me to meet him.

After he'd gone, we assured each other that both he and Natasha would survive the war. But deep down our fears for them made us desperate. Our easygoing sex turned into a demanding, hungry passion, which neither of us had wanted but which neither of us wanted to end. Time was short, the future opaque. My desire to get back into the war wasn't heroic. On one level, it was simply a need to do something to help defeat an enemy I hated and to make my reunion with Natasha – if it ever was to take place – a little nearer to achieving. Whether there was some other deep need – patriotism, or to avenge my father or to assuage my guilt over leaving Natasha – I did not know.

Apart from Gwen, there were few people in London I could really talk to. Friends came and went, usually on short, pleasure-seeking leave, with little time available for decent conversation. Douglas was seldom free; he was obviously working under great pressure somewhere in the secret bowels of government. Dr Bergsen had managed to get a passage to Palestine, from where he wrote me a letter full of enthusiasm about the way the Jews were making the desert bloom and about how wonderful it was to be together again with Dinah Woolf.

My mother and stepfather had thrown themselves body and soul into the war effort. They seemed to have completely forgotten about their earlier sympathies for Germany and distrust of

Winston. They had become Churchillian to the core. My mother had ceased her voluntary relief efforts and was working full-time, helping to administer a rest centre for recuperating war wounded. Bob had a regional command in the Home Guard. They were proud of me – and, despite myself, I was pleased that they were.

One morning, as I waited impatiently for a letter ordering me back to Egypt or another theatre of war, I had a phone call from Douglas asking me to lunch.

We met at his club, which, despite wartime austerity and its boarded-up exterior, managed to provide its members with surprisingly good fare. We had vegetable soup and – though eggs were a rarity in London – omelettes. The wine was acceptable, probably of better quality than the cellar accumulated by Dr Bergsen.

'You do yourself proud here, Douglas,' I said.

'No more than we deserve,' he smiled. 'I see you can consume as well as ever. That's a good sign. How's that leg of yours?'

'Much better,' I said enthusiastically. 'Good as new. I'm waiting for orders to get going again.'

'Ah. The doctors say you're ready?'

'You know what doctors are like, Douglas: ultra-cautious. If we had to depend on them, we'd never have any armies in the field. Lots of chaps out there have injuries and old wounds but they've had the sense not to get too involved with the quacks. Anyway, I take it you haven't invited me for lunch merely to enquire about my health?'

'No. But it might have some bearing,' he said, looking serious. 'You're probably not going to like this. And I'm partly to blame.'

'For what, Douglas?' I broke in. 'Please don't tell me you've been trying to stop me from getting back to the army.'

'Don't be an ass, James. You know I wouldn't ever do that. I happened to be with the PM a couple of days ago and he asked, quite innocently, about you, said he'd had a chat with you in Egypt, wanted to know if you were still out there. I told him you'd been hurt and were back here. His eyes lit up; that usually means trouble, so I said you were okay and itching to get back to your unit.'

'I wouldn't have called it a chat, actually. He did most of the talking.'

'The sort of conversation he most likes.' Douglas smiled. 'Anyway, for some reason he has a high opinion of you. He said he felt your talents might be better employed elsewhere.'

'And you agreed?' I burst out. 'That's why you're feeling guilty. Douglas, I respect you more than any other man I know, but for God's sake I do not want to be employed elsewhere. I'm a soldier.'

'No, you misunderstand. I did not agree. But I do blame myself for having told him you were in England and temporarily out of action. I should have omitted the latter part, and he might never have found out. Nothing I could say after that seemed to get through to him. He's like that. Once he gets an idea in his head ... well, it's very difficult to change his mind, as I've found out, as the chiefs of staff have found out, painfully. I couldn't sway him, I'm afraid. He's insisted.'

'Insisted on what?'

'He wants you as one of his private secretaries. He says he likes your steadfastness when confronted with shaky arguments. I believe him. He's a tyrant, of course, but he likes people who speak their minds. He'll give you a blast for doing it, but he prefers a bit of independent thinking to some of the sycophants that gather around great men. Funny chap, Winston! Likes to get his own way, but he needs a bit of opposition along the route. That's why he and Brooke make such a great team.'

'Sorry, Douglas,' I said. 'I won't do it.'

'Won't?' He raised his eyebrows.

'Can't. Don't want to. I'm too young to sit out the war in some cushy job with Winston Churchill.'

'Hardly cushy. After a week with Winston, you'll remember Rommel's artillery with affection.'

'I already do, Douglas. I have to get back into action. Please thank Mr Churchill for thinking of me, but I'm sure there are plenty of willing and better equipped people for the job. Please thank him and say I can't do it.'

'I'm afraid, James, that he's made up his mind. He likes to have people he trusts. He wants you, and he can be rather stubborn. As Mr Hitler has already discovered. Anyway, I'm afraid that in wartime you can't refuse the orders of your Prime Minister any more than you can refuse those of your superior officer.'

'I'd refuse even if the King ordered me to do this.'

Douglas smiled again.

'It might be easier to persuade His Majesty than his first minister.'

'What can they do if I refuse? Throw me in irons? Firing squad?'

'Don't be silly, James. If you were serious about persisting, then I dare say your views would be respected. But it wouldn't do your cause much good. Someone might decide to transfer you to some deadly dull desk job in Whitehall or the colonies. Look, James, this could be the making of you.'

'Douglas, do you really think I worry very much about what might or might not be the making of me? All I want to do is to fight in this bloody war, not be a nursemaid to Mr Winston bloody Churchill.'

Douglas sighed.

'I'm going to say a few more words and leave it at that. Wanting to be in the front line is a noble sentiment. Your father would have approved. It's what he would have wanted to do. But there are more ways of helping us win the war than shooting up or blowing up Germans. Easing our war leader's burden is one of those ways. It's not a nursemaid's job. It's ensuring he can follow an uncluttered path in making the decisions that matter in the long term. His private secretaries protect him from trivialities and diversions, they see he has access to people and papers that are important, they get to know the workings of his mind so that they can anticipate and interpret his needs. They bar the way to fools, and are a buffer to some of his excesses, especially when the stress is close to intolerable. I don't want to exaggerate the job's importance. It does not involve making decisions on political strategy or on sending vast armies across the globe. But it is of crucial help to the person who has to make those decisions. Someone has to do it. It's a duty not a sinecure.'

'Then let someone else do it,' I said sulkily. 'Why not someone who's too old to fight?'

'I'm quite sure there are tens of thousands of people who would be willing to take it on, and that there are thousands of young men – for the pace and the energy required mean it is a young man's job – who would be perfectly fitted. But the PM wants *you*. He gets bees in his bonnet sometimes, and this is one of them.'

'And if you can't swing it with me, he'll make you pay,' I said unkindly. 'Just for a whim. Like he did to Auchinleck.'

'I think it most unlikely that he'll risk replacing me with Montgomery,' Douglas said drily. 'Well, you've had my last word, James. I'll convey your deep reservations to Winston when I see him next week. I doubt if it will be of much help.'

After lunch, I regretted the way I'd talked to Douglas. It was unfair and I wrote him a note apologising for implying he might have been motivated because he feared the Prime Minister's ire. But I knew I'd made the right decision in refusing to accept a job with Churchill, no matter how vital. It was important to me to get out in the desert, or wherever I was needed, and kill some Germans.

Gwen was initially delighted when I told her about the suggestion, after a torrid session of love which helped to remove some of my irritation at Winston Churchill and his whims. She clapped her hands with pleasure and said:

'That's top-hole, darling. Now you can hold my hand until Binky comes home.'

'That would help the war effort. But, sorry, I've said I won't do it, and I mean that.'

'Of course you do, Bexley, but you know as well as I do that it won't help. If Mr Churchill needs you and wants you, he's going to get you.'

She kissed me. 'And I shall not be lonely again, worrying about Binky and about you all night long.'

'Dear Gwen,' I laughed. 'I can't somehow imagine you being lonely for any length of time, especially not with all those Yank officers coming over here.'

'You rotter!' she said, but without acrimony.

Then she became thoughtful. She sat up in bed without a stitch on and I thought: What a gorgeous woman she is!

'Having two men to worry about is more than enough for this lady,' she said lightly, but added: 'Actually, Jimmy, perhaps you're right to want to get away. It wouldn't be so marvellous for us to be together for all that time. It could become uncomfortable.'

'I'm not trying to run from you, Gwen.'

'We'd get too damn close if you stayed around. We'd get absolutely hooked on each other. And then what would happen when Binky got back? I'd have to choose. I love you both in different ways – like you care for me and Natasha in different ways – and I'd hate to have to choose. Oh dear!'

'So, you'd rather I was in some trench a long way away?' I smiled.

'You know exactly what I mean,' she said seriously. 'What we have – this delicious fun – is beautiful, but it can't go on for ever, can it? Not for either of us.'

'No, it can't,' I replied, looking at her with great affection. 'You're right, dear Lady Gwendoline, as usual. You know, I love the way you've grown into such a wise and beautiful woman from the mousy little Gwen I knew in Cambridge.'

'Mousy!' she said indignantly. 'You rat!'

We both laughed and lit another cigarette.

Then I said: 'Anyway, neither of us is going to have to make choices about lovers. I'm going to be out of your gorgeous clutches soon, shooting at some poor sod of a Boche and not sitting at a desk in Whitehall.'

I was wrong. I went to the hospital for what I believed was a routine visit to give me clearance for a return to the Eighth Army. Instead, the surgeon told me my leg had not recovered as it should have done. He showed me the X-rays. He couldn't certify that I was yet fit for an active role. He must have seen the acute disappointment in my face, for he said, kindly: 'I dare say they'll want you back in Cairo in some capacity, but not in the infantry.'

'But if I have more treatment?' I asked. 'Surely it will knit properly in time. I can get about pretty well already. I'll manage.'

He shook his head.

'Not for a while, old man. Come and see me again in a year or so.'

'I'll drive a tank then, or an ambulance,' I said. 'Something any old cripple can do.'

'That will be up to the medical board,' he shrugged.

I knew from his tone that I would not be passed fit for active service. I wondered bitterly, for a moment, if he was acting on orders from above; but I soon dismissed this thought – even Winston Churchill would not intervene in such a way merely because he needed another secretary! Or would he?

A week later, following a period of heavy gloom, I received a telephone call from the Prime Minister's office. It was from one of the private secretaries.

'I hear you're coming aboard,' he said. 'Drop around and see me later today and I'll brief you.'

'I never agreed...' I began.

'Bad luck about the medical news. Still, could be worse. The PM is, of course, upset for your sake. He understands better than most what that sort of thing means to someone like you, but he's very happy that you'll be working with us. Look forward to seeing you at three o'clock if that's all right with you. Winston would like a word with you too. Cheerio then.'

Obviously, I thought, Churchill must have asked for my medical files, and probably every other file about my life.

'Blast him,' I said aloud.

I decided to tell him point blank that I would rather become an air raid warden than shuffle papers in his outer office.

But when I was summoned to his office, he greeted me with great geniality, smothered me with charm and persuaded me that I could do no greater service to the nation than work side-by-side with him.

'I know that I have required some, um, personal sacrifice from you. Like myself, when I was younger, you would far rather be charging into the cannon's fire than engaging in less obviously vital tasks. However, just as I saw that I could be of more service to the nation by entering a life of politics, so should you realise that you can do more good for our great cause here, at the still eye of the storm, than in the muddle of battle. Thus it is in modern warfare. The glorious days of the infantry charge are no more. Planning and supply routes are all important today, and it is my lot to oversee the strategy and the logistics by which we can win this war in as swift a time as possible. You will be of assistance to me in this task, whatever your personal feeling. We must all bend our shoulders to the wheel in whatever capacity we are required. The burden must be borne, whatever the cost.'

You old humbug, I wanted to say. But there was no way out. I told him, summoning up an expression of gratitude, that it would be an honour to serve him.

A flicker of a smile crossed his face, then he glared down at the paper on his desk and growled: 'Damn and blast the bastard!'

I had no idea who he was talking about. He looked up, seemed surprised to see me still in the room, and waved me impatiently away.

It took me a while to adjust to life with Winston. The job involved long hours and some drudgery, but there was much stimulation in working so close to the centre of power and under such a man. It was sometimes difficult to put up with his moods and his tirades. His verbal abuse could be cruel and caustic, and often unjustified, but he never held a grudge and his moments of kindness made one forgive everything. One minute he would be calling me a bloody fool, and the next praising me for some underdone bit of work. Given that he was under unbelievable stress, it was a miracle that he was ever able to be polite to underlings like me. But he managed it from time to time, and I grew to enjoy even the insults, knowing they meant little beyond a moment of pique, and that the next time I saw him he would be pink and elephantine in a hot bath expounding on one of his hobby horses, elaborating on some impossible plan.

The work itself was far more interesting than I'd envisaged. I always felt close to the centre of things even though I and my colleagues had no overt decision-making duties. However, we could influence decisions in minor ways: by seeing that the Prime Minister was always kept up to date on things he needed to know; by ensuring the right papers and messages and memos were on hand at the right time; by drafting letters and memos for him to sign and sometimes even parts of his speeches; by toning down the language of some of the more intemperate memos he scribbled out himself; by quietly suggesting where a letter of commendation or reproof or sympathy might be sent. Of course, we were always careful to see that the spirit of his intention was maintained. Woe betide anyone who went too far or tried to outflank his views. In those cases, the barrage of abuse was indeed as bad as most things I'd faced in the Western Desert, as Douglas had correctly prophesied.

Gwen, meanwhile, had been thinking deeply about the dangers of our situation. She looked quite crestfallen when I told her that Winston had roped me in for the duration of the war.

'Well, that expression tells me everything,' I laughed.

'It's not like that, Jimmy. Only, the longer we're together, the harder it's going to be when we have to part.'

'Shall we call it a day?' I teased.

'Don't be horrid.'

I held her close and tried to explain that the best way of dealing with this dilemma was to treat it as lightly as we could.

'You're right,' she sighed. 'Anyway, we could be blown to smithereens at any time. So we won't call it a day just yet, Bexley. I'll let you know when.'

The truth was there was nothing either of us could do. We were still hungry for one another, and decided, tacitly, to make the most of the times we shared.

Leaving Winston in the early hours after a gruelling day of 18 hours of work, I would head for Mayfair and flop into bed beside Gwen, falling instantly into a deep sleep – and being woken hours later by her, dreamily desirable, for lunch and bliss.

This was my war routine: long, hard, stressful work for Winston, and joyous respite with Gwen. I was much, much luckier than most. I had Gwen and my job was engrossing. I had little time or energy for worrying about the future.

I felt in my bones that Natasha was dead, and had forced myself to accept this. Gwen understood, and was tolerant of my depressions. She got news that Binky had been captured during the campaign in Italy and was in a German POW camp. She was briefly elated that he was alive and then deflated with the realisation that he might not survive camp conditions and barbaric treatment.

'He'll try to escape and they'll shoot him. I know Binky. He'll do everything he can to find a way out. They shoot our chaps if they try to escape, don't they, Jimmy?'

'No,' I lied. 'Even *they* don't flout the Geneva Conventions when it comes to prisoners of war.'

She refused to believe me, and then, with the mature resilience that had become a part of her emotional make-up, she said: 'Still, knowing my man, he'll probably have half the camp searching for scraps of food so he can stay healthy.'

So the months and then years went by. The long-awaited second front opened in June 1944, with the invasion of Normandy. Successes on the continent and elsewhere made people believe that we were heading towards victory. But we had become inured to disappointment. It was tempting fate to ask: 'When will the war end?'

By New Year's Day 1945, for the luckier ones, it was satisfaction enough to know that one had survived yet another year, and, for Gwen and I, that we hadn't yet had the worst possible news about the people we loved most in the world.

23

Yalta, February 7, 1945

Driving to the afternoon session along the coastal road, pure Mediterranean sunshine and shade, flashes of bright white light reflected by the sea, Winston growled to Sarah: 'It's the bloody Riviera of Hades!'

She was delighted by her dear Papa's spontaneous wit. I felt it was due to his irritation at Roosevelt's decision to make a quick exit from Yalta.

At the Livadia, Podbirski bumped, deliberately, into me in the reception hall, which as usual was crowded enough – uniforms, suits, grey heads and fresh-faced young men all milling around – for such minor incidents not to attract attention. Instead of apologising, he asked: 'You go into meeting?'

'No,' I said.

'Good. Outside of terrace here, just when meeting begins, you walk until stairs go downhill. Walk steps until no more, then go right up path. There is stone bench. Is lovely place to see view. Also is in the middle of big path that go round like this (he drew a quick curve in the air with his finger), so easy to see if someone coming.'

'Anatoly, why are you doing this?'

'Favours. Not good time to talk now, Jimmy. Eyes are everywhere. Joseph Vissarionovich watches, and all around him watch. Just you go.'

He moved off into the room.

I felt myself being snared. If Podbirski was playing Pander, then someone must have written the script. That was the way it was in the Soviet Union. On the other hand, if he was still a friend and employer of Natasha, and assuming the food poisoning of the first interpreter was arranged by him, then might it not be merely a personal favour to be repaid by another favour – to *him* rather than to the system? What the favour would be, and when it would be demanded, was not something of very great concern to me at that moment despite my assurances to Winston that I would not compromise myself or the government. I was not thinking clearly. What was overriding was that I talk to Natasha.

If I say that nothing else mattered but talking to her again, what does that mean? Was the winning of the war not more important? Were the fates of Poles, Jews, Filipinos not more important? I couldn't answer that – not then, not now! If someone had said to me, at that moment, when I was thinking only of holding Natasha in my arms again, that I would have to make a choice between being with her and being on Winston's staff, it would have been an easy decision. I had concerns, but they were not about losing my job, or my freedom. My fear was, as it had been for five and a half years of being parted, that things might not be the same between us; that time – the ultimate enemy – might have eroded feelings and memories; that emotions and events might have altered the Moscow morning of mutual love.

As soon as the delegates had stepped into the conference hall and the doors to the reception room were closed and the guards stood nervously alert, fingers on triggers – because anyone breaking in with a machine-gun, bomb or grenade could have decapitated the Allied leadership at a stroke – I strolled the length of the palace exterior unti I came to the stone stairs Podbirski had mentioned. I went down, often stopping to show my official pass to a hard-faced guard. Eventually, a little way down a gently curving gravel path, I came to a stone bench as directed.

I waited for perhaps ten minutes, listening to the birds and the slight fluttering of leaves in the breeze, catching glimpses of a very blue, shimmering sea a few hundred feet below. Then, as if from a dream, she appeared, walking briskly towards me, expressionless. Before I could stand, she was sitting beside me. I took her hand. For a second or two we looked at each other, each placing changes in the other's face over the remembered original, like a palimpsest. I touched her face, as though to measure it against the past. She seemed barely to have aged although her hair was cut shorter. Perhaps she noticed lines of stress on my forehead or the questions in my eyes.

My two hands were holding her two hands.

'I got only one message all the time,' she said gravely. 'That you were in the army. I was so scared for you.'

'It was okay,' I said lightly. 'We got beaten. I escaped. Now things are really hard.'

'What?' she asked, wide-eyed.

'Working for Mr Churchill. I'd rather be a prisoner of war.'

'Don't make jokes like that, please. Time is too short.'

'I know. I'm sorry. All I want to do is tell you how much you mean to me and to find out what you've been through.'

'Don't waste words,' she interrupted, quite brusquely. 'We must try to discuss things. When will we have the chance again?'

'As soon as the war's over, maybe before. What is there to discuss except that I want to be with you?'

'You think it will be easier when the war is over? It's going to get worse, believe me, in this country.'

'I'll work something out.'

I embraced her. She stayed for a moment, then pulled away.

'Jimmy, there is not time for such things now. I don't know if I can see you again. We must discuss things.'

'I don't understand.'

'It is not possible, just like this,' she snapped her fingers, 'to say that it is like before. We don't know. It was wonderful six years ago in Kharkov, in Moscow. But six years ... how much has happened? So much, that I don't know.'

'You don't know if you still care for me?'

'I don't know what I feel. What you feel. Everything is awful. I don't know if I can feel anything.'

'I know what I feel for you, Natasha.'

'You say so. You think so. Maybe you do, maybe not. We cannot just wipe out the years like that. We both have changed. Everyone has changed.'

'I haven't changed in that respect,' I said. 'Have you?'

'So many things have happened,' she said sadly. 'But my feelings? For you? No. They have not changed, I think.'

'Then, nothing else matters. I'll work things out.'

For the first time, she smiled.

'Oh, Jimmy, you do not change at all, in that way. You are always optimist. But how will you work something out? Will Mr Churchill discuss you and me with Stalin?'

'He might.'

'There's no time for jokes; I told you,' she admonished, but not roughly. 'How can you work out things?'

'We'll get married. You can come to England with me, as my bride.'

'They would not let me go,' she said seriously, then suddenly seemed to relax, and added: 'Anyway, who said I would want to marry you? You have not gone on your knees and proposed.'

'I'll do it right now,' I said, standing up and preparing to kneel.

She pulled me back on to the bench.

'Jimmy, that is another thing,' she said, serious again. 'Everything that has happened, to all of us. What has happened in the war – what the Germans have done. Everything has changed. All of us have changed because of that.'

'The Germans are gone,' I began.

'No,' she said harshly. 'They are still here because of what they did. I have been in Kiev, I have been to Babi Yar. You have heard of the places where they pile bodies on top of bodies?'

'I know about the mass graves.'

I had heard about the Nazi atrocities in eastern Europe, from refugeee reports, from Dr Bergsen and, in some cases, from the lips of the killers themselves – our Ultra intercepts had given us access to boastful descriptions from German Einsatzgruppen, the mobile killing units, relayed to Berlin about what they were doing with such enthusiasm in occupied territories. I had deduced, from various intelligence reports, that a campaign of extermination was under way too in various concentration camps. At Auschwitz, liberated only a few days before the start of this conference, there was evidence that the Nazis had murdered more than a million people, mostly Jews.

'You know, yes,' she said flatly. 'But if you went there, Jimmy, to Babi Yar, you would *see* the fear, you would *hear* the screams, you would be able to be inside the heads of the victims. That is why the Nazis are still here. They have won. They killed 50,000 Jews in a few days in the forests outside Kiev, and they have got away with it. No punishment, no courts, no justice.'

'It will come,' I said. 'They'll be hunted down.'

'Who will hunt them down? Mr Churchill? He has other grand designs.'

'This very conference has decided that war criminals will be caught and punished. Churchill, Roosevelt and Stalin all agree on that.'

'Stalin?' She laughed bitterly. 'You think he cares what is done to the Jews? All these killings – yes, many were killings of non-Jews; of course, the Nazis hate Slavs, they hate Communists, but most of those who were slaughtered were murdered just because they were Jews. And has our great Stalin ever said so? No. And why? Because he hates the Jews the same as Hitler hates the Jews. And, by the way, you have heard of Katyn?'

I had heard of the Katyn forest massacre of thousands of Polish army officers. German troops had uncovered mass graves a couple of years before in western Russia and blamed the atrocity on Moscow. The Kremlin claimed the Nazis were responsible. We had stood aside thus far – for we knew what the Germans were capable of, and Stalin was our ally, was he not?

'Natasha, I understand you, but you mustn't say these things here, now.'

She laughed.

'You think there are microphones in this tree?' She shook the trunk of the overhanging tree. 'And if there were, why should I care? I want to say what I have to say.'

I knew there might indeed be listening devices in the trees around, in the bushes, perhaps even under the stone bench, perhaps directed at us from considerable distances away. Was that why Podbirski had been so helpful, to the point of arranging this particular place for our rendezvous? But I didn't want to move yet, didn't want to break up this meeting, however painful.

'Yes, but don't be reckless,' I said. 'What's important is survival.'

'Nothing survived at Babi Yar! All right, I will survive. But let me tell you one thing, Jimmy, and this you must tell Mr Churchill. This man – his name is not Stalin, even, it is Djugashvili – he is not what he seems, so genial, so gracious, even, as I have seen a little at these meetings with Mr Churchill and President Roosevelt, so reasonable, so casual. He is not that, Jimmy, believe me. He is premeditated mass murderer.'

'I know about him, Natasha. Remember, I lived in Moscow. I think Mr Churchill also has no illusions. Let's not waste time on him. Not now.'

She touched my arm.

'I believe, Jimmy, that you know what sort of man he is, but exactly how much evil he has done ... there is no time, yes, to tell everything. He was Tsarist spy, you know. Never a true Bolshevik. Always, he only wanted power. Because Trotsky was a rival, he had to devour Trotsky. And because Trotsky was a Jew – like my parents were Jews – he has to devour all Jews. That is what he does, Jimmy. After this war, when he has finished his foreign enemies, he will start again on anyone he thinks is enemy to him at home, and when there is no one else, he will start on the Jews, maybe not like Hitler, with so much shouting, but on Jewish people because they are Jews. Believe me, Jimmy. And that is why – because of this hatred – that he will not say those victims of the Nazis at Babi Yar and other places in Ukraine were all Jews. I knew many who died, I know...'

Just then we heard the scrunching of boots on the gravel path. We hastily stood up and I gave Natasha a cigarette. I was lighting it for her when the Soviet guard appeared. It was an innocent enough sight, a man lighting a woman's cigarette after they had bumped into each other while on a walk. And even if it was two lovers meeting, so what? On a glorious day in a beautiful setting, what could be wrong with that? He almost averted his eyes as he passed us. But did he wink at me?

However, I was sure that the meeting would be reported to someone.

When the guard had disappeared from view, Natasha whispered: 'We go separately now, Jimmy. I will see you perhaps tomorrow at Vorontsov if they want me to translate at foreign ministers' meeting. After talks, I may be able to meet you.'

We embraced quickly, kissed tentatively, and went off in different directions along the path.

I felt flat. While I'd been nervous at how this reunion might turn out, I had often imagined – so often –a scene of undiluted tenderness and of whispered love. Instead, we had discussed atrocities, ruthlessness, the politics of war. Not the best subjects for a lovers' tryst. Still, I had seen her again, at last, had held her in my arms, kissed her sweet lips, even if only for an instant. And I knew I had to ensure that I would not leave the Soviet Union this time without some plan to get her out as well.

How had she changed, and had her changes altered my feelings? She was more obsessive than ever. Yet her obsessions, as I'd known in Moscow and Kharkov in 1939, were an indivisible part of Natasha.

'Love is not love which alters when it alteration finds,' I recited to myself.

I had loved her all those years ago at least partly because of her passions and rages. I had loved her fire and her anger as much as I did the flashes of tender intuition and humour. Now, the obsessions raged like a forest fire out of control. But who could blame her? I could not deny that I found her outpourings uncomfortable, even though true. Perhaps I had become too used to the delicacy of English friends and lovers, to the understated or entombed emotions of our settled island, protected by inhibitions from external obsessions – except, of course, when they threatened our survival. And yet, I told myself, I did not love Natasha any less because she raged so compulsively. I would need to tell myself that over and over again if necesssary. I could not let her go merely because I found her scorn uncomfortable.

At the plenary session an obstacle over the United Nations appeared to be getting resolved. The Soviets had been arguing for 18 seats in the assembly, and the Americans had responded that in that case they ought to have several seats too. The whole thing seemed so ridiculous and trivial to me. One might imagine the Ukraine or Byelorussia being members – especially as we actually wanted them to be independent countries – but not every single constituent part of the USSR. And the idea of California or Texas having separate seats was absurd.

Winston, seeing a threat to six prospective British Commonwealth seats if we didn't give Stalin something, suggested membership for two or three of the larger Soviet republics. Roosevelt probably thought it was just another imperial ploy, but was even more keen than Winston to conciliate on this.

There was the possibility too of some kind of breakthrough on the provisional Polish government. Molotov said it might be possible to add some leaders 'from Polish émigré circles' to the Soviet-backed government.

FDR and Winston didn't like the word 'émigré'. Stalin agreed to the wordage 'Poles abroad'. It was all semantics. The real question was: Would the Soviet Union permit anything other than a puppet regime to be installed in Poland?

That evening Winston sent a short message carrying little optimism to the War Cabinet, saying Britain and America still planned to wrestle with Stalin for a Polish government that they could recognise.

He looked bleak and tired.

I felt a pang at the long age of difference between his roar of defiance to Hitler in 1940 and the war of attrition he was waging against a master schemer who knew he could get his way by playing on our exhausted resolve – playing for time against a Prime Minister who would soon face an election and a President who would soon face his Maker. In 1940, there had been a simple moral choice. We could fight to the death against Hitler, or witness the end of Britain. Now the issues were complex. Yes, we wanted Poland to be free, and, no, we did not trust Stalin; but there was no question, no means of fighting to the death over Poland, no easy way of defying a powerful ally, no way of coming out of it with honour. Certainly not without American resolve – and there seemed precious little of that on this matter.

I was on duty and spent some time with Winston after dinner. I'd been pondering whether I should enlist his help over Natasha's situation, but decided it would be inexcusable and inadvisable to ask him to devote his mind to something so cosmically insignificant compared to the sufferings of Europe and the problems of its future contours.

'I am very weary,' he said.

I thought for a moment, with surprise, that he was contemplating an early night, but it was a more general, almost metaphysical, fatigue he was talking about.

'All the battles I've fought, all the wars, the Sudan, India, South Africa, Flanders, against Hitler – and still it never ends.'

But did he want it to end, I thought? What on earth would this warrior do if it did end?

'And now another conflict looms,' he went on, oblivious to

my presence, as though addressing Parliament or the nation. 'I do not refer to the final battle for Germany, or the great struggle in the Pacific, but to the next war, which I fear will be unlike any before, a war not of dynasties or nation states, but of ideas. Ours against theirs. Democracy, human liberties against the philosophy of State socialism, the uncontrolled authority of the secret police.'

He looked at me and frowned. All these words wasted on a private secretary.

'Ultimately, it must come to such a conflict,' he went on. 'Unless they change – or unless we change, which could only be for the worse. Thank goodness, the British people, after all they have been through, will not be inclined to vote in a socialist government.'

I did not care for a discussion on this. My view was that Britain could do with a government that would try to change the inequalities of the present system and build a new society, but I didn't want a conversation in which I would have to say that to Winston of all people, the upholder of privilege and traditional values.

'But if – if, as seems likely – there are no changes, then can another possible war be averted, sir?' I asked.

He thought. He looked glum. Then he perked up a bit and said, virtually contradicting his earlier gloomy forecasts:

'As long as Stalin is alive, I do not think it will come to a war. He is not unfriendly towards us, I believe. He has his own interests, but he respects our position. All may still be well if we make concessions but retain our honour.'

Then he waved a hand to signal an end to the conversation.

Walking away from his rooms, I encountered Sarah.

'You look worried, Jimmy. Problems of the heart? Believe me, I know what it's like. Absence does not always make the heart grow fonder.'

'No, no,' I said hurriedly. 'No such problems. The Prime Minister seems a bit depressed tonight. Careworn. Wavering. Contradictory.'

She didn't seem surprised or upset by my parade of negative adjectives, but was quick to find excuses for her father.

'He's fed up with the President's attitude,' she said. 'We can all see that poor Mr Roosevelt is very sick, but he ought not to be so ... so casual with Papa. Perhaps his mental powers are declining at the same rate as his physical ones. Anyway, Papa is also getting a bit homesick. He's missing Mama. He always does when he's away.'

I muttered something sympathetic.

Sarah studied me shrewdly. She sensed there were deep internal pressures lurking behind my uncharacteristic criticisms of Winston's mood.

'You needn't talk if you don't want to, Jimmy, but it's sometimes better to get things off one's chest. I know I told you before that we oughtn't to get into exchanging confidences and all that, but this place is so remote from reality that personal things can get badly out of perspective. And I don't like seeing you in pain, darling.'

'There's nothing I need to get off my chest,' I said, but smiled to show I was grateful for her concern.

'That's all right then, Jimmy.'

'Is this why they call you "Mule"?' I asked. 'You never give up, do you, Sarah?'

'Don't be cheeky, darling. But if you do need a sympathetic ear...'

'Thanks, Sarah,' I said. 'Her name, by the way, is Natasha.'

'I love that name,' said Sarah.

24

Yalta, February 8, 1945

In the late morning, carrying a mass of work from Winston's bedroom, I passed the Orangery and saw Anthony and Stettinius in conversation. The Orangery was a pleasant, spacious glass-fronted area of plants, Grecian busts and wicker chairs, between Winston's rooms and the hall where the foreign ministers' meetings took place. Today's meeting had just finished and I could see, through the glass doors, the unsmiling Russian party departing in their cars. I couldn't spot Natasha among them. Anthony noticed me and quickly drew Stettinius out on to the patio. Deep discussions about Poland, I did not doubt.

They had just withdrawn, when Natasha, to my astonishment, peered cautiously into the Orangery, checked that I was alone and motioned me to go down towards the sea. I indicated the papers I was carrying, pointed to my watch and mouthed 'In half an hour, no, twenty minutes?' She nodded, but with a frown, as though it was unreasonable of me to let a world war intervene in our personal affairs.

In the office, I managed to plough through some of the urgent work quickly, delegated other routine stuff and left a small pile that could safely be handled later. Then I rushed down steps and paths, past stately cypresses and cedars, through overhanging branches thick with green leaves. I passed a number of guards, vigilant but unquestioning. In contrast to the Livadia security, our delegation was seldom challenged in the grounds of our own residence.

Natasha was waiting, standing alone on the shingle beach, looking out across the azure sea in the general direction of Turkey.

'I told them I had headache and wanted to rest before returning,' she explained. 'A driver will come to fetch me in an hour.'

'And they believed you?'
'I don't know.'
'Natasha, this is a big risk.'
'Everything is a big risk. We must talk, or what is it all for?'
'But they'll suspect...'
'Of course they suspect,' she said impatiently. 'In that way they are not fools. Maybe they want me to talk to you. What does it matter? Come, we walk.'

We strolled along the beach, where a couple of Red Army guards lolled casually, smoking, gazing out to sea in case a German U-boat should suddenly appear and disgorge an assassination squad to get Churchill, Brooke and the rest. All that sort of thing seemed distant and improbable to me. This meeting was my reality, yet I was still finding it hard to grasp the moment.

'The guards?' I asked. 'What will they think?'
'They do not think, Jimmy. They are just peasant boys. If someone tells them to shoot us, they shoot. If no one tells them, they do nothing. They do not think.'
'You may be right, but if they see a Russian woman and a British man walking together, one of them is going to tell someone – whoever it is they tell things to.'
'Of course, someone will tell someone. So what? I say that you and I are friends from Moscow. That is the truth, isn't it?'
'Even that is a dangerous truth,' I said.
'Oh, Jimmy,' she sighed. 'Everything here is danger. Each word, look, movement. It doesn't matter whether it is innocent or guilty. If Stalin thinks so, then everything is guilty. If Beria wants to please Stalin, then everything is guilty.'

She walked a few paces further, then stopped and looked at me.

'An hour?' I asked.
'It's enough.'
'I love you, Natasha.'
She looked at me as though she wanted to weep, then her face hardened and she said angrily: 'Why do you have to say that when you know nothing will come of it?'
'Something will come of it,' I said.
'Like the way you are winning the war?'
She looked at me fiercely. I didn't respond. I felt no hurt

that she was blaming me for the shortcomings of the Allied war effort.

'Why don't you end it quick?' she demanded. 'Sometimes I think your leaders have not enough desire to kill off the Nazi Germans.'

'Of course they have the desire,' I said. 'Everyone has.'

'Everyone? Like your mother and stepfather you told me about before the war. How they admire Hitler, how they don't want to fight against him?'

'Those opinions don't count any more. Now, everyone wants to win the war. But we're fighting on two fronts, against the Japanese as well as the Germans. You must be realistic, Natasha.'

'And also I must be realistic about the way the Nazis are murdering the Jews? Why don't you bomb concentration camps?'

It was a question I'd asked myself. I didn't agree with the stock western military argument that the best way to save lives, all round, including the Jews, was to win the war in Europe quickly, and that diverting forces to bomb or capture concentration camps would dilute the concerted effort needed to end the conflict.

'The argument is that if we bombed them, we'd kill the people inside as well as the guards,' I said.

'So what is the difference?' she said bitterly. 'They are all dead people, anyhow. You can bomb them or the SS can kill them. Is it different?'

I couldn't dispute this.

'No different,' I said.

Only an hour, and I wanted, desperately, to talk about us now, not about the evils of our age.

'Is it because there are so many anti-Semites also in England and America?' she demanded.

'There *is* anti-Semitism,' I said. 'I don't know why it exists, I don't understand how it can exist when everyone knows what is going on in Europe.'

'I tell you why. Because it means they can blame the Jews for everything. Someone is a failure, he blames it on the Jews. He can't get a job, it's the fault of the Jews. A woman sneezes, it's because the Jews are spreading germs. Oh, Jimmy, Jimmy, why can't you see what is happening in the world? And even when they've managed to kill off every Jew in the world, they will still blame every bad thing on the Jews. They will blame the war on the Jews.'

She looked at me pathetically.

There was so much truth in what she said that it hurt; but I couldn't allow her to despair.

'After the war, it'll be different, Natasha. You'll see. The good guys will see to that.'

'The good guys!' she snorted.

'The main thing is to win the war and make sure things get better.'

'Then why don't you stand up for the Poles?' she demanded.

'I thought you hated the Poles,' I said, trying a touch of lightness.

'Not as much as I hate him,' she said, tilting her head in the direction of Stalin's residence. 'I only hate the Poles who are anti-Semites.'

'He holds all the cards. He holds Poland.'

'And you think he would be prepared to fight for that?' she sneered.

'I don't know.'

'So why could you good guys not fight?' she asked.

The question made me suspicious, in spite of my love for her. Was she being used to get information? I couldn't believe it, but I had to stay on guard.

This was such a wasted conversation, as obsessive as the earlier one, taking over our precious hour together.

'Natasha, let's make the most of this time.' I urged her. 'Let's not spend it arguing.'

'Has the war taken away your will to fight?' she demanded.

This was said with such contempt that I felt bound to reply: 'Of course the Allies could fight.'

'But *will* they?' she persisted.

'They could.'

'Threaten him, then! Don't you know, the bully is always a coward? That you have to meet threats with threats.'

'I don't think that's how our diplomacy works,' I said.

'Then your diplomacy is stupid. That is how *our* diplomacy works.'

'Possibly,' I agreed.

'Your diplomacy! That is what allowed Hitler to make war.'

I felt I must not get sucked into her rage and a dispute over the causes of the war. All I wanted was for her to come back to me.

'Why do you say nothing?' she asked severely. 'In Moscow, and now in Yalta after six years, and always it is James the silent Englishman. I hate silent Englishmen. You never can believe them.'

I put my hands on her shoulders and squeezed them. I didn't care if the whole damn Soviet apparatus was watching us. She was so angry, beyond any anger I had known in her before, and I wanted to soothe that fury, not argue it away, or dismiss it, but calm her with love. I was gripping her hard, and she moved her head to my chest. I took my hands from her shoulders and put them around her.

'I hate silent Englishmen,' she repeated but when she looked up to my face there was no anger in her eyes, only doubt.

I kissed her and told her that I loved her. She let herself sink into my embrace, then pulled away and looked at me with an expression I could not fathom.

'How can I believe you?' she asked dispassionately. 'You are an English diplomat. How can I believe you?'

'I mean it, Natasha. I mean to marry you.'

She laughed, but without humour or rancour.

'Now you are telling me a fairy-tale,' she said. 'It's like your Mr Churchill. Always some sentimental story.'

'But not as long-winded, I hope.'

She didn't smile.

I said: 'In Moscow, we agreed that I had to go back to England to fight but that I'd come back, when the war was over, to marry you.'

'Agreed?' She laughed scornfully. 'Who believes in agreements? Only you English, I think. You are like Mr Chamberlain with his umbrella who believes in agreements which mean nothing.'

'Natasha, we have to stop playing these games. The war is something out of our control. Do you love me? As you told me in Moscow? Or was that an agreement I should not believe in?'

'I do not break agreements,' she said hotly.

I kissed her before she could go off on another tangent. She didn't respond and drew away quickly. Then she looked at me, perhaps saw the misery in my eyes, and came back to me, put her lips to mine, kissed me with warmth.

After a while, she said: 'I didn't doubt that you loved me, Jimmy. But everything...'

'It's okay now,' I said.

'No, not okay.'

She took a step away from me.

'In the war,' she said, 'things happen. Everyone is parted from who they love. Me from you. I knew you would be with other women, Jimmy. No, say nothing! I knew, because you are a man and you need women, and you are fighting a war and I knew you loved me and that if we survived you would still love me, because that is the sort of man you are.'

'Natasha, I never stopped loving you,' I said.

'And I knew it was different for women. I thought it was different. But then we all grow older and are going to die. Jimmy, I met this boy and we were lovers.'

'Boy?' was all I could say, though I had always known something like this might happen.

'Just a boy. From Kharkov.'

That hurt me. Kharkov was the city where she and I had first really found each other.

'You don't have to tell me about it, Natasha,' I managed to say.

'I have to tell you all,' she said, staring hard into my eyes.

She'd rejoiced when Germany attacked the Soviet Union on June 22, 1941. Now these two monsters could fight each other to a standstill. She felt not the slightest twinge of patriotism. Thereafter, her feelings swung, like a conductor's baton, to the brutal rhythms of the war. The speed and ferocity of the German onslaught and the barbarity of the Nazis, murdering anyone suspected of being a commissar, a partisan or a Jew, frightened her. She was sickened by the horrors of the German occupation of her native Ukraine. For a time, her heart beat with pride at the Red Army's resistance. Then she heard of her mother's death in the Siberian gulag and she hated Stalin with all the old ferocity. The news was brought to her by a young Jewish soldier stationed outside Moscow.

'He was eighteen years old. Leonid was his name, from Kharkov. His family knew my grandparents. They heard from a relative in the gulag that my mother is dead. That's all. This boy, Leonid, looks for me in Moscow to tell me. Also he tells me what the Germans are doing to the Jews in Kharkov and other places, like in Babi Yar. They force them leave their houses and live all together in a camp on the outskirts of the city. Then they take them out – thousands, Jimmy, thousands of them – and stand them up near open pits in the ground and shoot them so they just fall into this big grave, whether they are already dead or still alive. This boy's own parents were taken and murdered at a village a few miles from Kharkov.'

I listened in horror. I knew such terrible things had happened, but that didn't muffle the horror. I felt as bloodthirsty as Roosevelt had professed to be after seeing the wastage of warfare on the drive from Saki.

Natasha was talking in a flat and unemotional voice, almost in the official tones she used when she first showed me the sights of Moscow. She hurried on, not waiting for me to say anything.

'So Leonid comes to see me and tells me everything, and we cry together, and cry, and cry, and then we go together to bed. He was a boy, Jimmy, and I wanted to give him something from life, and I too wanted something.'

She looked at the ground. I took her hand.

'It was that night, and then some more times, and then he was sent to fight in Stalingrad.'

She looked into my eyes, defiantly.

'After that I don't hear from him for many months. Until I go to Kharkov myself. One night in those dark streets, I meet him again. In the dark, and he has a beard now and has shaved his head. He is fighting together with some comrades, partisans, in the forests. He tells me he has deserted from Stalingrad and is now with a band of Jewish boys and girls in the forests. Their enemies are not only the Germans but Ukrainian nationalists and Communist partisans. All these enemies have one thing common: they hate the Jews. He is in Kharkov this night on some kind of secret mission, to get information about where they can make an attack next. He comes to me for love again that night, and I give it to him, and I am glad to give to him and take from him. A few weeks later, one of his group brings me a message. Leonid was caught by the Germans, and they hanged him, with a notice around his neck to warn other partisans of same fate. He was hanged with a notice around his neck. He was eighteen years old. A boy.'

She wept.

I held her in my arms and tried to soothe her.

'I'm so sorry, Natasha,' I said. 'So sorry.'

'So now you know. Now he is dead, and now you know. All is terrible.'

'It's all right, Natasha,' I said.

'No, not all right. Nothing is right. He is hanged. You hate me.'

I kissed her cheek, tasted her tears on it.

'I don't, and it's all going to be okay.' I said. 'There is nothing wrong about what happened between you and the boy, between you and Leonid.'

'I know there was nothing wrong,' she said fiercely. 'I would do it again. I was proud to do it.'

'I know,' I said.

'You forgive me?' she asked, surprised.

'There is nothing to forgive. I love you, Natasha. There was nothing wrong. I know that. It was the right thing to do. To do for him.'

'Jimmy.' She shook her head. 'How can you still love me?'

'How could I not? You know I do.'

She looked at me in silence. But there was no time for silence, so she said: 'I know. And I always love you, Jimmy. But I am so worried what you will think. I am not ashamed that I went to bed with the boy. It was something for both our lives in those days. Such terrible times. I love Leonid, and I cry when I think what they did to him. Still, now, in the night time, I cry. Still. But I never did not love you.'

'I know that too. Do you still want me? Do you still want us to belong together?'

'Yes,' she said, 'of course. Why do you think I pestered Podbirski, begged him, to let me come to Yalta. To confess to you, yes. But more. To see you again. To share with you. To see if you still can care for me, Jimmy.'

'I still care, Natasha.'

She wiped her eyes.

'And for you, also, there is no one else?' she asked.

I hesitated. She pounced on this.

'Ha, there is someone else! You listen to my confessions and you say nothing.'

Her flared anger cheered me. It was human and natural.

'There is no one else, Natasha. Not now. But there was someone in London, for a time.'

'Ha!'

'It was a wartime thing. It's over now.'

'So you say!'

'Her husband was a prisoner of war. He's probably coming home soon. We both agreed that it's over. She loves her husband.'

'And what was this woman's name? I must know so I can scratch out her eyes.'

'I'm not going to tell you because I don't want my wife – you – to be imprisoned for assault.'

'Okay, I will not scratch out her eyes if I find her. Only I will bite her arm. And why does she prefer her husband to you, huh? Because only he is very powerful or very rich? I hate this woman because she prefers her husband to you.'

'And I love you for hating her, and I'm going to get you out so we can be together, you and I. I'm going to try to sort things out. I don't know how, yet.'

'Yes, you *will*. I know now that you will if you can.'

We hugged each other.

A thought struck her.

'Jimmy, why don't we steal a boat?'

The absurd desperation of this idea made us both laugh.

'Do you know how to sail?' I asked.

'You will teach me.'

Footsteps sounded on the shingle. A guard walked to within a few feet of us. Expressionless. But could he have been remembering – with or without envy of us – some sweetheart in the Steppes of Russia?

He said something in Russian. Natasha had stayed in my embrace until this point. Now she took a small step away, though she smiled at me, before replying to him. Then she took my hand and we trudged back towards the path that would take us upwards to the reality of the Crimean Conference.

'What did he want?' I asked her.

'Someone brought him a message that there was a car waiting for me.'

'It's not yet an hour.'

'Don't worry, Jimmy. The driver probably is in hurry to get off duty.'

'I don't like putting you in danger.'

'The danger, my Jimmy, is that you stop loving me because of these problems. I am sorry I was angry today. It was not with you; you understand now. It was with me, and with everything else.'

'I won't stop loving you, Natasha.'

She squeezed my hand, then let it go as we walked along narrow paths up to the Vorontsov.

'I hope not, for your sake. Soviet women, you know, are trained to be deadly soldiers. We are told: If someone betrays you, then show no mercy.'

'I would not expect any.'

As we neared the villa, she asked: 'How long you will stay in Crimea?'

'The way things are going, it could be a few days before this conference ends.'

'I wish it could go on for years,' she sighed. 'But at least even a few days is a good thing. We may meet again, Jimmy.'

'Whatever happens, we will meet again.'

'And I promise, no more attacking you because Churchill and Roosevelt are such ... help me, Jimmy, how do you say it?'

'Statesmen?'

'No! Like you told me Mr Chamberlain is.'

'Appeasers. And Chamberlain is dead.'

'I am sorry for his wife and children, but, yes, they are like that towards Stalin. It is a bad policy towards such men like him and Hitler.'

We had reached the path at the bottom of the steps that led up to the entrance past the stone lions. Natasha went off to her car, and I climbed slowly upwards. I noticed two figures examining a large marble urn in one of the alcoves. They were Field Marshal Brooke and Sarah. They must have seen us. As I approached, Brooke looked at his watch and moved off into the front hall.

Sarah smiled at me and said it was a lovely morning, wasn't it?

'Yes, Sarah, that was she,' I said.

'Rather beautiful,' she commented.

I nodded.

'It's not my business, I know, darling,' she said solicitously. 'But do be careful. For both your sakes.'

I nodded again and said: 'Of course.'

'You know, the other day, a group of us - including Brooke and Alex (Alexander, the Supreme Allied Commander in the Mediterranean) - were standing here and saw some schools of fish being attacked by, would you believe it, porpoises and sea gulls, a sort of combined sea and air operation. We were looking down from the terrace. An amazing sight. I thought the fish should have scattered and dispersed. Brookie said it was much better for them to stick together. Papa said I was right and the Field Marshal wrong. He said that either tactic was a gamble, but that he'd bet the fish had more chance if they went their own ways.'

'Your father's always enjoyed gambling,' I said.

'At the tables, and in politics,' she agreed, then added thoughtfully: 'But he's lost more times than he's won.'

'Are you advising me not to gamble?' I smiled.

'Don't read things into my girlish chatter. It's not my business to interfere. I wouldn't presume to offer advice.'

'Nevertheless, you're going to.'

'Let's take a hypothetical situation,' she said. 'Imagine it on stage. Boy and girl in love. Family of each against marriage. What happens if caution is thrown to the winds, and things go wrong?'

'Corpses on stage?'

'Exactly. So weigh up the consequences. Try to negotiate with the family. Prevent it from becoming a tragedy.'

'Family?'

'So to speak,' she smiled.

'Negotiate with your father?'

'You could ask him what he thinks. Ask him what he suggests.'

I shook my head.

'I couldn't do that,' I said seriously. 'I wouldn't.'

'He wouldn't bite your head off. Well, he might, but he'd offer some way out, perhaps.'

'I would never presume to ask him about something so trivial, but if I did, he'd tell me to give her up. For both our sakes.'

'Trivial?' said Sarah. 'You think it's that?'

I did not, but I couldn't say so.

'Compared to the war, yes,' I said. 'Don't you?'

'That's what wars are about, Jimmy. Giving people the right to love and live as they please.'

'But you agree that he would tell me to give her up?' I asked.

'I don't know what he'd say, Jimmy. He's a great man but he was pretty beastly to me when I wanted to marry Vic. However, in the end, he was prepared to offer a compromise. He was against the marriage – strongly against it – and he used every argument he could: Vic was an itinerant; Vic was an Austrian and so might become an enemy alien; he was "common", "common as dirt"; I was throwing away my career. Then he compromised. He'd withdraw his objections if I promised not to marry until Vic had American citizenship.'

'And, as we know, you promised,' I said.

She nodded.

'*After* you eloped,' I said.

She nodded again.

'One has to take chances, sometimes. Although, strictly speaking, it wasn't really an elopement. We married in the full glare of publicity. Remember?'

'Radiant bride,' I said.

We both smiled at our memories of flash bulbs, microphones and a rather startled Sarah as the world's press moved in on the happy couple.

'Anyway, I somehow doubt whether the Prime Minister is going to suggest that I bide my time until Natasha is allowed to have a British passport,' I said. 'That could be considered a commitment on his part, which he couldn't ever guarantee.'

'He might be able to persuade Uncle Joe,' she said. 'Papa is at heart a big romantic, you know. Don't be fooled by all that belligerent armour, he's a real softie underneath.'

'I'll take your word, Sarah.'

'Why do you think he sided with Edward? It wasn't that he particularly liked the man, or the Simpson woman, but he loved the romance of it all – lonely king just wanting a bit of personal happiness with the woman he loves. He was reviled for that, and Mama thought he was wrong to take a stand that would damage his political career and his reputation. She was right, but he stuck to his guns.'

'He always does, but I don't think he and Stalin are going to sit down and work out a happy ending for Natasha and me. We'll have to play the waiting game, I suppose. Disperse like your fish until the predators have gone away.'

'The war's coming to an end,' she said.

'This war is,' I said.

'Natasha is a lovely name,' said Sarah wistfully.

With that, we walked into the villa, each with our own thoughts.

I had been hurt by Natasha's affair with Leonid – someone I would never meet, and whose grisly end I wished had never happened – but it was only a small wound to my self-esteem rather than to my feelings for her. In a way, the desperation of both their needs made me feel closer to her than ever. I had never expected us to survive unscathed. I had not been a monk myself. And in some ways it was far easier to accept her human frailty – if one could even call it that – than her cosmic rages at fate. She was still the person I had known in 1939, not someone propelled to unreachable territories of irrationality by grief and guilt and hatred.

There were, anyway, more pressing issues than recriminations over times past and the indulgence of self-analysis. Despite the optimism I'd voiced to Natasha, the hopelessness of our situation had already begun to creep in on me. Short of managing to smuggle her away on one of our planes, or myself defecting to the Russians, no solution seemed possible. Stalin was bolting the doors of his own house even as he seized the property of his neighbours. I knew that no one – not Winston, nor Eden, nor Roosevelt or Hopkins in their heart of hearts – would paint a dramatically different future. We were all of us heading for a world of parallel cages, which was the tragic irony of this war, and not only for Natasha and me. We'd fought it for freedom, and we'd surely had to fight it. But here we were – our troops poised to cross the Rhine, Stalin's closing in on Berlin, the Yanks beginning to obliterate the Japanese – and what sort of freedom was in store for us?

I tried to work myself out of this pessimism. I told myself we were putting an end to the horrors of Nazi domination, the brutalities and mass murders. I recalled the joy of liberated Paris. Remember the flowers of liberation, no matter how fast they may fade, I told myself; nothing is ever perfect. No victory in history ever meant more than simply the conquest of one side by another. That was the way the world worked. I thought of the crumbled ideals of Dorothy and of Ed's festering disillusionment. I thought of how Dr Bergsen had come in stages to accept the fact that one could never cocoon oneself from reality. I thought of the selfishness of my mother's early life, of the short and pointless duration of my father's, of Douglas's unashamed pragmatism, of Podbirski's apparently shaky amorality. None of these thoughts, it was true, could drive from my mind the fate of Natasha and me. But duty preserved me from sliding into self-pity. I had a job to do still, however small. I was not indispensable, but I was in the position of being one man – however insignificant – in a small army of aides helping Winston Churchill to concentrate his energies on winning the war and trying to forge the peace. History, I was sure, would forgive his brusqueness, his pettiness, his foibles, his egoism and all the other human flaws, and would define him as a giant among his contemporaries who had, fortunately for us all, come to office at a point in time when no other man could have done the job. History, I was also sure, would define various other European rulers of the time as being of immense significance too in their own ways – but it would not forgive them their flaws. And it would not forget their inhumanity.

It's early afternoon at the Livadia, and Roosevelt and Stalin are meeting, secretly closing a deal.

'Well, Marshal, it looks like I lost my bet,' FDR begins jovially. 'General MacArthur says he's captured Manila. Still, I'm sure your generals will soon be raising the Red Flag in Berlin.'

'It is very bitter fighting, but they will be there soon,' Stalin agrees.

Both men know it could be some months, at least, before Berlin finally capitulates.

Roosevelt has already begun to turn his focus away from Europe. He has done all he can to try and allow the Poles in Poland to decide their own government, and he hopes the Poles in America will appreciate his efforts. He is concentrating on the Pacific. Now is the time to agree on the price for Soviet assistance there.

'We have to decide whether to invade the mainland Japanese islands, with all the heavy losses that will entail, or bomb them to smithereens,' he says. 'I favour the latter course.'

Stalin grunts, whether with approval or not it's difficult to say, but he readily agrees to the US using bases in the Soviet Far East and in Hungary for its aircraft. In return, he says he understands that the US may have some surplus shipping at the end of the war.

'If this is for sale, we would like to buy.'

'They won't be for sale, Marshal. We'll let you *have* them on long term credit, which in twenty years will be extinguished. How about that?'

Stalin nods with satisfaction. He praises the Lend-Lease programme, which supplied Britain in its darkest days and also the Soviet Union.

Roosevelt – like an old man wandering in childhood memories – recalls the times when everything was straightforward in this war. Democracy threatened by Nazi aggression? So help the guys fighting the dictators. Your country doesn't want to be dragged into a European war yet? Figure out a way to arm the guys doing the fighting. It was a time when the good guys were your friends and the bad guys your enemies. Mind you, he tells himself, I always felt the Russians were going to end up as our pals in this business. Not that I trust them totally. Certainly, not that I trust Uncle Joe totally. But, hell, I've learned to work with all sorts in my career, even – sometimes especially – with people I neither like nor trust in the Democratic Party.

He describes to Stalin how he sold the Lend-Lease idea to the American public.

'I said it was like lending your neighbour a garden hose to put out a fire that could burn down your house as well as his. You wouldn't ask him for the cost of the hose while he was battling the fire. You'd lend it to him on the understanding that you'd get it back once he'd put out the blaze.

'And then we got it through Congress with a clause giving me powers to aid any country whose defence was vital to the defence of America. Now, you may not know this, Marshal, but a lot of folk who grudgingly agreed we should give help to

Britain, Greece, China, and so on – to our allies – felt pretty sore at the idea of giving aid to the Soviet Union, which was a co-signatory to a pact with Germany.'

Stalin shows no embarrassment at this reminder. He whispers to Molotov, beside him: 'Any world leader would have wanted such a pact. That fool Chamberlain was only too happy to do deals with Hitler when it was in his interests.'

'Well we had quite a battle on that bill,' FDR says. 'But we were able to come to your help when you were invaded.'

Stalin looks at his nicotine-stained fingers and says, yes, Lend-Lease was an extraordinary idea.

Roosevelt thinks he had better give some credit where it's due.

'Anyway, I put Harry in charge of managing it, and, being Harry, he did it magnificently, and without any thought of glory.'

'Mr Hopkins is a good friend to you, a good advisor,' says Stalin. 'I wish that he may very soon be well again.'

'So do I, Marshal. He would have been with me today, but he's feeling just too damn ill to do so. God knows how he's managed to go on for so long without most of his stomach.'

'I think because he believes in his work.'

Roosevelt nods agreement. I thought Harry was at death's door in 1940, he ruminates. Then the Nazi blitzkrieg began and it was like the strongest medicine in the world to that guy. It got him going for years – knowing what raw materials we desperately needed, how to get industry mobilised, missions to Winston and to Uncle Joe. I know all about that sort of medicine. After the polio, my whole body would have withered away if it hadn't been for politics.

Stalin thinks: I wish I had such a man as Hopkins to be at my side. He glances at the stolid figure beside him. This Molotov is not a friend to me. He obeys because he fears. The realisation that he can trust no one in the way Roosevelt trusts Hopkins makes Stalin uneasy. He changes the subject to the conditions on which he will enter the war against Japan after Germany surrenders.

Roosevelt nods. 'There's no problem in Russia getting back those places snatched by the Japs, the southern half of Sakhalin and the Kurile islands.'

Stalin realises he's put one over FDR without even trying. Roosevelt has not read his history, or forgotten it. The Kuriles were not taken from Russia by force; they were granted to Japan under a treaty in 1875.

He whispers to Molotov: 'Churchill would never make such a mistake. I am almost ashamed to take advantage of this man. What do you say, Molotov, shall we tell him he's wrong?'

'With all due respect, Joseph Vissarionovich, we should perhaps first discuss very carefully whether to take such a decision,' says Molotov nervously.

'Don't be such an idiot, Molotov! Can you not understand a joke? Is it possible the Soviet Union should continue to put up with a Commissar of Foreign Affairs who does not have a sense of humour?'

Molotov blanches.

It is also agreed that the Soviet Union will get the use of two ports in the Far East, one as a naval base and one to be internationalised, and will be allowed to operate jointly with China two railways in the Chinese region of Manchuria, which since the early 1930s has been occupied by Japan. China – which is not present at these discussions – is to be informed of the decisions later.

I was present at the afternoon plenary session, at which Winston warned: 'Failure to agree on a Polish government will stamp this conference with the seal of failure. The world will see this as a breach between us with lamentable consequences for the future.'

If Stalin cared, even in the slightest, about how the world viewed this conference, or his future reputation, it did not show in his face. He smiled genially.

Molotov said the Soviet-installed government was backed by the majority of Poles. The only question now was whether this body should be expanded to include some people from the government in exile in London.

Winston said portentously: 'I have no special feeling for the Polish government in London, but to break with a government that we have recognised during all the years of war would create the most severe criticism in England.'

Roosevelt stared into space and stayed silent. He knew the Poles in America – not to mention his political foes – would also be furious, but they'd come round.

Then Stalin, smiling, stepped into the discussion: 'I can assure you that the men running the provisional government inside Poland are popular with the people. They did not flee from Poland. They stayed and fought in the underground.'

Around the table flickered the thought that Stalin had refused to help an underground uprising by Poles against the Germans in Warsaw just a few months ago.

He paused, then added: 'What is important is the feeling of the people in Poland towards the Red Army. They have hated Russians for many years – maybe with good reason – but when the Russian army liberated them they rejoiced.'

Confronted with an amiable, pipe-puffing Stalin speaking so calmly and reasonably, Winston and FDR were reduced to appealing for free elections in Poland. They didn't *demand* this; they just asked, almost pleaded.

'Of course, there will be no problems in having elections once the fighting is over,' Stalin beamed. 'I think it should be possible within a month.'

With that, all seemed settled. Uncle Joe had promised elections soon, and there was no option but to accept the promise without guarantees.

Clearly, neither of the two western leaders was going to thump the table and say: 'We want free elections, or else.' There was no 'or else' available. British forces were depleted, the Americans overstretched in two theatres. We couldn't threaten Stalin (as Natasha had suggested we do) because we had nothing to back up the threat. Besides, it seemed evident that Roosevelt had no real desire to challenge Stalin on this issue, or perhaps on any other issue.

I looked across to where Ed was seated, like myself, a little behind the senior delegates at the round table. He was scribbling something, his brow furrowed.

A few hours later, I wangled myself a journey to the Yusupov Palace, where Stalin was hosting a dinner. I hoped I might get a chance to see Natasha.

The villa, which looked more like a solid pre-revolutionary hotel than a palace, had the most overtly high level of security of the three conference residences. It suggested to me that Uncle Joe remained as fearful as ever of enemies even within his own camp. The Supreme Hero of the Great War of Liberation slept as uneasily as any threatened, tottering monarch.

The banquet started at nine o'clock and went on till one. I, and other uninvited aides, were given lavish refreshments as we waited and talked. The hours dragged. I became worried that Natasha might already have been arrested because of her meetings with me.

Around midnight I was lounging in an armchair when Podbirski appeared, suddenly, stealthily. He sat down next to me. No one else was close by.

'Jimmy, even in Moscow, when you pose as journalist, I believe you have other irons in the fire,' he said with a smile. 'That is good English saying, no? Now you work in very important job for Mr Churchill, our very distinguished guest.'

'Hardly important, Anatoly. In a very junior capacity.'

'Of course.' He spread his hands with a wide grin to indicate he didn't believe me in the least, then chortled. 'In very junior capacity. I like. I too am in very junior capacity. So we are allies, no? Like Mr Churchill and Mr Stalin.'

'There's nothing worthwhile I could tell you, Anatoly, if that's what you're after,' I said, smiling back at him. 'Not even if I wanted to. And I was a correspondent in Moscow. It wasn't a pose. So what are you insinuating?'

'Jimmy, everything with you people is about suspicion. You don't even trust old friend Podbirski.'

'Especially not old friend Podbirski,' I said, still smiling.

He laughed, then asked: 'You have met your friend?'

'Who?'

'Jimmy, again sense of humour! You are in love? You want to marry?'

I didn't answer.

'Jimmy, you must trust me. She is always in difficult position. Because of her father. Always something bad could happen. If you want to help her...'

He shrugged. I said nothing.

'You think is hopeless?' he said. 'But maybe there is way.'

I closed my eyes.

'Information is our currency more than dollars,' he said in a very low voice. 'It can buy you anything.'

I'd been expecting something like this, but was still shocked when it came in such a blunt and crude way. However, I wasn't going to reveal anything of my feelings to Podbirski.

'Perhaps,' I said, opening my eyes, 'but I'm short of hard cash in that case, Anatoly.'

He raised his eyebrows in a query.

'I don't have worthwhile information,' I explained. 'It doesn't come my way. But even if I knew some great secret, I certainly wouldn't pass it to you.'

'But why not? Mr Churchill, Mr Roosevelt, Mr Hopkins, Field Marshal Brooke – all of them share secrets with us, and we share secrets with them.'

'You are talking about the mighty people. They can do things that the rest of us can't. Put it out of your mind, Anatoly.'

'Is pity,' he said sadly.

Just then, to my relief, the guests from the banquet began to appear. The dinner was over. Faces were flushed, some from alcohol, some from exhaustion, some with euphoria. I judged everything had gone well.

Podbirski wandered off, and I put aside the implications of our conversation, not least because they were too ugly to think about.

At least on the social level, I reflected, the Yalta Conference was a success already – and wasn't the building of friendships as important as the cementing of alliances? Perhaps the friendships could preserve the peace, as Winston seemed to believe. Perhaps all problems could be solved through friendship. Perhaps.

Sarah, looking happy, put her arm through mine and said we should ride back together. I found myself in a car, sitting between her and Brooke. He seemed a little put out to have me, rather than an admiral or air chief marshal, as his neighbour, but was polite. Sarah's eyes were dancing.

'It was great fun,' she said.

Some of the dinners at the conference resembled male macho drinking sessions. This one apparently had more class. Apart from Sarah, the guest list included two other women: Roosevelt's daughter Anna and American Ambassador Averell Harriman's daughter Kathleen.

'All three of us were toasted,' Sarah said. 'Kathy replied on our behalf – in Russian. Uncle Joe was in great form, so friendly and courteous, wasn't he, Sir Alan?'

Brooke would probably rather not have responded, but he was the sort of man who could never appear rude in the presence of a woman.

'Stalin was in good form,' he conceded.

'I sat next to Vyshinsky,' Sarah said. 'We both watered our vodka. I stuck to the bubbly.'

I couldn't help but think of how Vyshinsky, as prosecutor, had taunted his victims with vicious cruelty during the Soviet show trials of the thirties.

'And I met the head of their security service,' Sarah went on. 'What's his name, Jimmy? I've drunk too much to remember it.'

'Lavrenty Beria,' I said.

'Yes, him. I tried out one of my Russian sentences on him. "Can I have a hot water bottle, please?"'

She giggled and added: 'Guess what he said? "I cannot believe that you need one. Surely there is enough fire in you."'

Neither Brooke nor I made any comment on this. It would have seemed churlish to enlighten Sarah, in her innocent pleasure, of the nastiness of Stalin's fellow Georgian with his prissy face and reputedly coarse methods of obtaining and discarding mistresses, not to mention his aptitude for disposing of his master's enemies and rivals, real or perceived or invented.

'There were so many toasts drunk,' said Sarah. 'More than thirty.'

'It seemed more like three hundred to me,' said Brooke. 'Interminable, insincere, undistinguished.'

'Oh, but some were jolly good. Didn't you think Papa's toast to Marshal Stalin was good?'

'Better than most,' said Brooke grudgingly. 'It had wit and humour, at least. However, I think even your father would agree it was not one of his more memorable speeches.'

'What did the Prime Minister say?' I asked.

She looked at Brooke, who pulled some notepaper from the pocket of his crisp uniform and peered at it in the dim interior lighting of the car.

'He mentioned that Marshal Stalin was precious in the hopes

and hearts of all of us,' Brooke said with a sardonic smile. 'Is Marshal Stalin precious in *your* heart, Bexley?'

'Papa said some other things that were very clever, only I can't remember any,' Sarah mumbled.

Back at the Vorontsov, I was on duty, which meant a very late night.

'Stalin proposed a gracious toast to our alliance and its, um, free expression of views,' Winston remarked, sipping a whisky. 'It bodes well, though we cannot relax our vigilance. We cannot trust such a man to deliver what he promises.'

His report to the War Cabinet said: 'Today has been much better. In spite of our gloomy warning and forebodings Yalta has turned out very well so far.'

I suspected he'd been infected by some of the euphoric 'Yalta Spirit' that senior American officials were spouting about, and was being overly optimistic. However, I wasn't prepared to make these criticisms to the Prime Minister, and certainly not at three in the morning.

25

Yalta, February 9, 1945

The overall strategy is simple: finish off the Germans, and then throw everything into forcing Japan to surrender by blockades, bombings and invasion of the mainland. With Stalin's help, the whole thing can be done quite quickly.

This plan for the end-game of World War Two is put forward by the British and American military Chiefs of Staff for Churchill and Roosevelt to consider.

It does not mention one detail – while German soldiers, apart from the most fanatical, might give themselves up when the battle is clearly lost, the Japanese mentality is to die rather than endure defeat, no matter how certain. The Japanese believe surrender is a disgrace and that it's more honourable to kill yourself, preferably by disembowelling or hurling yourself on to an enemy bayonet, than to be taken captive.

The Combined Chiefs say the allies should plan for a German defeat between July and December of 1945, and for the conquest of Japan 18 months later. This suggests it will take around two years more to end the Pacific War. The unspoken question is how many deaths, traumas, broken bodies and broken families will this mean?

At the meeting, Churchill wonders if the hard slog is the only way. He suggests the Japanese might agree to an ultimatum to lay down their arms if they get some assurance that they would be spared a totally rigorous unconditional surrender.

Roosevelt – who first introduced the concept of unconditional surrender – sighs wearily.

'Okay, Winston, we can mention this to Uncle Joe if you insist. But the Japs aren't going to respond to any ultimatum. They still reckon they can get some compromise peace if they fight us to a standstill. They're not going to wake up to reality until every island is bombed into the Stone Age.'

'But, Mr President, air attacks thus far have not induced the Japanese to accept that they must lose the war. Surely they might accept the inevitable if threatened with the full weight of our destructive power – the obliteration of their cities – unless they agree to immediate capitulation on terms which I...'

'We're going to give them the full weight all right,' says Roosevelt. 'And damn soon too. We've just sent Curtiss LeMay to organise the new precision bombing. He'll give 'em hell.'

Churchill, having no option, nods his acceptance. There will be no ultimatum on the road to Tokyo. The enemy will be bombed into submission.

In the afternoon, Ed and I walked in the Livadia gardens. I said I thought the presence of three women at Stalin's dinner had lightened the conference atmosphere.

'Yeah, nothing like the feminine touch,' he said. 'Being over here without Dorothy, you know, without any female softness, makes me realise how much she counts for in my life. We're one hell of a team, Jim. She's still the most intellectually stimulating person in my life. I shouldn't say this, but your loss was my gain. I can say it now though because, after all, you've got your Russian girl. Have you seen her yet?'

I wasn't surprised that Ed knew about Natasha, and knew she was at Yalta. Nothing in this fish bowl of modern wartime intrigue could be hidden from prying eyes. Still, when he actually mentioned her to me it was another reminder that my personal life had ceased to be private.

'Has it been written up in *Stars and Stripes*?' I asked caustically.

He laughed this off: 'C'mon, Jimmy, Yalta's a small place.'

'Then why the pretence? You obviously know I've seen her here. But please don't call her my Russian girl. She doesn't belong to me. We met in Moscow years ago, and met again here. That's all there is to it.'

'Hey, don't get so sore, fellow.'

'It's no one's damn business. How would you like your private life being spied on?'

'I get it. This is about Dorothy, isn't it?'

'You always were self-centred, Ed. Why the hell should it be about her?'

'Probably because you're still mad at me over what happened.'
'Not any more. It's water under the bridge.'
'I hope so, because, you know, we both care a lot about you.'
'Don't pile it on.'
'I didn't think you still had it in for us. I thought there was some residual fondness.'
'I'm pleased everything's going well for you both,' I said grudgingly.

Why on earth couldn't I keep from showing my lingering anger? It was all so much in the past, in another life. Besides, for all his faults, I was fond of Ed. And my life with Dorothy had given me as much joy as pain.

I smiled at him and repeated: 'I'm really pleased it's going well, Ed.'

'That's a big-hearted thing to say. Thanks.'
'You were obviously made for each other.'

He looked at me suspiciously, as though there were some underlying accusation in my words, but then seemed to decide it didn't matter.

'Yeah,' he said. 'Her mind and my earning power. What's so great is that she's become so really integrated into American life, but without losing her independent streak. All that energy! She still has it; just it's channelled differently.'

I nodded. Whenever I thought about Dorothy, I could still marvel at the drive and determination of her youth. But I wondered at Ed's blindness about her character. What had always made me a little wary of her – even at the height of my adoration – was precisely that she *lacked* any independent streak. She lived by putting the ideas of others into practice with much more vigour than if they'd been her own. And she did so without much concern for any individuals, even those close to her. She was ruthless on the surface, but fragile beneath. Any concerted opposition – as had happened with the 'cabal' at Cambridge – and the veneer of certitude could fall away.

'What she's doing in civil rights is terrific,' Ed went on. 'Campaigns against the internment of Japanese Americans and for integrating Negroes into the armed services. You know how deep-seated those prejudices are? Even when we're fighting a world war, the southern racists won't hear of arming black people. It was only the Ardennes attack that got the military to form a few integrated companies because we were suddenly short of men.'

'It's good that she's so involved again. I wondered if she'd be dragged into domesticity.'

'Not a chance! She's amazingly active. Not that she's one of those born-again liberals. She's still plenty radical, but not in the way she once was. That all went out of the window with the Ribbentrop–Molotov pact. We suspected, after Spain, that something of that kind could happen, but it was still a shock to the system. Don't know if she's more scornful these days of the commies or of Roosevelt. The American Reds don't give a shit about civil rights; all that concerned them was FDR's re-election. They figure he'll be soft on Stalin. They reckon a strong Soviet Union is more important than equal rights in the United States. Is it the same in Britain?'

'Stalin is a big favourite in England,' I said. 'A lot of people see him as a kindly father figure who can be trusted. It's not a view I share.'

Ed steered me to a gravel path circling the palace. We passed what appeared to be a store room, linked to the Italian garden by a covered, columned pathway. The building was boarded up, no longer in use.

'Know what that is?' he said. 'Used to be the chapel of the Tsar and his family. Nobody prays there these days. There's a lot of old history that isn't talked about around this place.'

'But it doesn't just go away.'

'Right. Nothing does. Memories are like matter: indestructible and convertible into energy. Some day these memories will destroy Stalinism.'

'Some day, they might,' I said.

Not in time for Natasha and me.

'So, Dorothy is on this two-pronged campaign: for civil rights and against Communism,' Ed went on. 'She's so passionate she'll vote for anyone, Democrat or Republican, who opposes Roosevelt.'

He fished an envelope out of his jacket pocket and handed it to me.

'I don't know what she's written, and I wasn't convinced I should give it to you if you were still so mad at us. But I reckon it's okay. Read it later.'

I put it in my pocket.

He led the way along a sandy uphill route towards the hills overlooking the palace. We went upwards and away from the great white edifice of the Livadia.

'It's a better route to walk,' he said, stomping upwards. 'Not so many guards, and not so nosy either. They've got the whole perimeter of this place sealed – but it's to stop people getting out, not to stop some Nazi commando squad getting in.'

We passed a group of parked black limousines, each with the flag to show which delegation it transported. The drivers, in the uniforms of their countries, were smoking and relaxing with each other. They paid not the slightest attention as we walked by. I heard them laughing and joking – an international fraternity.

'Gives one a bit of hope for the future,' I remarked.

'Don't believe it, buddy. The ordinary Joes aren't the ones who start shooting wars. It's the great peacemakers back in the palace. You ought to know where appeasement always leads.'

As we trudged uphill, though, I wasn't thinking about the great issues of war and peace. Perhaps because of Ed's eulogising of Dorothy, my mind went to the important women in my life. I'd been in love in utterly different ways with three creatures of utterly different characters.

Dorothy had a Byzantine mind but I loved her even when I'd mistrusted her passionate beliefs and her capacity for convenient U-turns. Gwen was wonderfully, unabashedly open and uncomplicated, like a garden flower in the spring. And Natasha was diamond pure of mind and body. The fierce clarity of her obsessions was a necessary ingredient of her character. Even her affair with Leonid seemed to me, this Sunday morning, to be pure and necessary and good.

Ed broke into my reverie.

'Know what Roosevelt's done? So desperate to get the Ruskies into the war against Japan that he gave away some islands as part of the deal.'

'You mean he offered to give back what the Japs seized in 1904.'

'Some weren't war booty; they're legally leased by Japan. He just gave them away. Maybe he doesn't know what he's doing. Either that, or he thinks he can buy Stalin like he was some big city boss in the States. He should've sent someone else to do business here. Even Truman, for Christ's sake, could do better.'

'You don't like Truman?'

'Like him? You've got to be kidding. Two-bit little senator from Missouri, all puffed up, and now he's just a heart beat from President. Roosevelt will be remembered as the guy who screwed up the peace, handed the Soviets all they want, and chose Harry fucking Truman as his running mate.'

'At least Truman's been in a war before,' I said.

'Some kind of captain in France,' Ed said dismissively.

We continued to climb upwards, past ruined outhouses, through foliage that almost cut off the sunshine. Finally we reached a clearing with a rotting old wooden bench. Ed glanced around and said we could talk freely here.

'I thought we had been talking freely,' I said. 'And my father was a kind of captain in France too.'

He shook his head. 'Sorry. That was thoughtless.'

I nodded, in acceptance of his apology.

'But listen,' he said, speaking in a low voice despite his confidence we could not be overheard. 'Do you reckon we had to go to those lengths to get the Reds into the Pacific War? They'd have come in anyway. They got interests there too.'

'The Japs won't surrender until they're beaten into the ground,' I said. I didn't agree with Winston's view that an ultimatum could succeed. 'Soviet help *will* shorten things. So, yes, it's probably worth going to those lengths. God knows, we're prepared to swap populations in Europe as though they're chess pieces.'

'We don't need Stalin to help us shorten the war,' Ed said.

'Bombing alone?' I shook my head. 'I'm not sure it's going to do the job, either against Germany or over there. Even if you reduce Tokyo to rubble, you're still going to have to invade the home islands sometime.'

Ed looked sombre.

'We're developing something that will do the job on its own. You don't need precision bombing if you're going to dump one of these babies on a city. One of them explodes over Tokyo and millions will be dead. Then Hirohito is gonna *have* to surrender. You can't fight against this thunder, buddy.'

'Tube Alloys?' I asked.

'Almost there,' he said confidently.

I was astounded. I knew a little bit about Tube Alloys – as much as I'd been allowed to know. Enough to believe that building an atomic bomb was something for future wars, though not, thank goodness, this one. British experts were involved. I'd heard, from Leo and others, in a general way, about the huge problems – scientific and engineering – in the way of turning the research into weapons.

Now, Ed was suggesting the Americans were overcoming the obstacles. I knew of his deep interest in nuclear physics. He had constantly talked over the years of the progress and practicalities of unleashing the power of the atom. I'd deduced he had cultivated excellent links to experts who were in the know.

'What if we were going to be ready to test a bomb – an atomic bomb – in the next couple of months, maybe even weeks?' he said in a low voice. 'If it worked, we could hit Tokyo with one in March or April.'

This ran counter to all predictions I'd heard. It was clear that the Yanks were going flat out trying to make a bomb, even though the threat of Germany getting one had receded. However, this didn't mean they were close to final success. I wasn't privy to secret information, but it was plain from all the talk and military decisions at Yalta that production of an atomic weapon wasn't imminent.

If it *was*, then why bother with bringing the Russians into the Pacific War? For that matter, why bother with crossing the Rhine? We could blast the enemy into surrendering, and let Stalin know we held all the cards.

Was it possible, though, that Ed had access to such highly classified and sensitive knowledge?

I knew Winston was kept informed about the research but I had no idea whether he was right up to date about the actual development of a workable weapon. Surely, he must be, I thought. Could Ed Brewster be better informed than Winston Churchill?

'Don't ask me too many questions on the technical data,' Ed went on after watching me digest his words. 'I wouldn't answer them even if I could. What I *can* tell you is that there are a couple of different techniques for exploding a bomb. It has to be a bomb containing an element called uranium-235 or one with plutonium, which is produced when you bombard uranium with neutrons. Follow me? The point is that both these elements fission easily. I remember telling you about fission once. It leads to a chain reaction, and the scientists now know how to keep that going until – boom! To start with, they couldn't get enough uranium-235 or plutonium to make a bomb, but now the stuff's rolling in. We got factories turning it out by the ton. And you can take it from me that the actual method of triggering the chain reaction in a weapon is in the hands of the engineers and it's progressing pretty damn fast.'

He outlined rapidly, and in layman's language, some of the basic problems still facing the bomb makers, but implied these would soon be overcome. He talked about the lead casings of bombs, about one possible gun-type method to start a chain reaction, about another in which a laboratory-induced implosion of plutonium would cause the reaction.

'How do you know all this?' I asked. 'Why tell me?'

He peered at me with a vexed expression.

'Jesus, Jim, you know the way I work. I've always made it my business to know the right sort of people.'

I nodded. Ever since I'd known him, he'd had an uncanny ability to strike and maintain contact with people who were specialists in their field – economists, trade unionists, politicians, artists, scientists. He prided himself on his ability to win trust and acquire facts. As a journalist, I'd often envied his insatiable appetite for digging in the fertile fields of human knowledge.

'But why tell me?' I asked.

'You're an old buddy and maybe I trust your discretion. Okay, okay, don't look so sceptical. Maybe the reason is that it's so big I need to get it off my chest. And it's so goddam crucial now that Roosevelt is grovelling to Stalin. And there's no one else here to talk to. And you never gossip.'

'Does Dorothy know?'

'No,' he said, looking hard at me. 'Not from me. I've never taken my work home since we got into the war. Once you start talking about national security to your wife, you have to swear her to secrecy. I never wanted to impose that on her.'

I asked him if FDR had told Winston about it.

'Perhaps. And then again, maybe not. Depends how much Roosevelt himself knows of the actual progress. He's been told there'll be real tests before September – but that's a long way off in this war. My informants say things could go a lot quicker. Maybe Roosevelt's got that dope too but isn't taking anything for granted until he's got hard information. This is all informed speculation, if you follow me, but I reckon he hasn't passed on a lot even to guys in his inner circle like Hopkins, let alone to Churchill. Roosevelt plays things close to the chest. Especially military secrets that he doesn't want to share, not even with his allies. Hell, and don't forget that Stalin is an ally too. I don't know exactly what's going on, but maybe Roosevelt just doesn't want your boss in on this at the moment.'

We both stayed silent for long minutes, thinking it over.

Then he said: 'Oh, shit, I shouldn't have said anything. This was all in confidence. I was speculating aloud to an old and trusted buddy. I guess it wouldn't do much good if I asked you not to shoot your mouth off to Winston?'

'You haven't told me enough of anything to repeat. You must know more than you're letting on.'

'I've told you just about all I've got – in simple language, of course. It isn't much anyway, is it? So you better forget what I said, or you could land up with egg on your face. I'm not a scientist.'

'If it *were* true, though, it could mean a quick end to the war,' I said trying to probe him for something more specific.

'And it would mean we wouldn't have to pal up with the Russians,' he said. 'But there'd be damn big risks too. The world's going to be an even more dangerous place after the war. We might be the first, but we won't be the last. Some of the scientists would like to share everything we've got with Stalin. It's taken billions of dollars, best brains in the world, and *they'd* like to hand it to him on a plate. For all I know, they're already doing that. Imagine if he had a bomb too.'

Then he looked at his watch and said: 'Hey, we'd better get back before the FBI come to pick us up.'

I decided there would be no point passing on what I'd heard to either Winston or Anthony. Possibly, they already knew. If they didn't, they'd want to be told – and the security services would certainly want to be told – where I got the information. Even if I refused to say, they'd deduce it was from Ed. That would be the end of his career, and maybe his liberty too. I decided to say nothing. It was all just guesswork, I reasoned, useless to anyone, spouted by Ed to impress me.

Just before the afternoon session, the Big Three went into the Italian garden for official photographs. They sat on straight-backed chairs in the central area of the courtyard. Persian carpets were spread around the chairs. Roosevelt, his naval cape spread over a dark suit, sat in the middle, looking tired and bewildered. A beaming Winston, in a cashmere coat and Astrakhan hat, was on his right. Stalin, wearing a grey, red-braided Marshal's greatcoat and red-crested military hat, and smiling like someone who has just dined well and wisely, was on FDR's left. Behind them stood the senior advisors – the well-dressed diplomats and the smart military brass. Flashed around the world, the photographs defined the conference as a united front of determined allies. In some ways, this is what it was – a final handshake of resolve before the last phase of the onslaught on Germany. But the reality was a mosaic of patched-up differences, hidden motives and secret deals.

The plenary session starts with a skirmish. A report by the foreign ministers says the United Nations charter should set out ways for dealing with 'territorial trusteeship and dependent areas'.

Churchill bristles, sees this as a threat to Britain's colonial possessions.

'Under no circumstances will I ever consent to forty or fifty nations thrusting interfering fingers into the existence of the British Empire,' he blusters.

Red-faced with anger he glares at Eden whom he assumes has been a party to this conniving. Eden studies his fingernails. It is not his place to contradict his Prime Minister, even though he believes it is a storm in a tea cup: in the end, in practice, Britain will do whatever it wants to do in its colonies.

Roosevelt smiles at Stalin, as if to say: 'You see. This fellow Churchill remains an old-fashioned, unreconstructed imperialist of the worst kind.'

Stalin busies himself with a whispered consultation with

Molotov. He knows it is best to steer clear of disputes between other parties.

Churchill won't let this thing die. He's like a dog with a bone.

'After all that we – England, the Dominions – have undertaken in this war, I will never consent to any representative of the Empire to go to any conference where we will be placed in the dock and asked to defend ourselves. Never, never, never!'

Stettinius, flustered at this barrage, says: 'Prime Minister, let me clear this up. No reference was intended to the British Empire. What we had in mind particularly were dependent areas taken from the enemy. That is all.'

Churchill is mollified, though he still glowers at Eden. He is determined to make his point that no one can rob the victors of their possessions.

He asks: 'I wonder how Marshal Stalin would feel if the suggestion was made that the Crimea should be internationalised for use as a summer resort?'

Stalin takes a moment to consider this, then replies with a straight face: 'Well, if it were requested of me, I would be glad to give the Crimea as a place to be used for meetings of the three Powers.'

He glances over to Roosevelt and comes as close as ever he can to winking. There is general good-natured, low-keyed chuckling and coughing, except among the British delegation.

'Let's break up for a few minutes now,' says Roosevelt with a kindly smile towards Churchill who still has thunder on his brow. 'Time for a smoke in the garden, eh, Winston?'

The two of them sit together outside in the sunshine.

'Winston, we're not going to take away your Empire,' says the President. 'We both know you can't hold on to it for ever, but I am the last man to want to prise it from your grip.'

'You are my old friend, Mr President,' says Churchill. 'And we have been through thick and thin together. I have every trust in your assurances.'

'You can, Winston, you can,' Roosevelt chuckles. 'If I was going to fight another election, then anti-imperialism might be a good campaign issue. The American people are sick of the old pre-war order of things. But I won't run again. I'll see this war out and lay some foundations for the future – some democratic foundations – then I'll go into the night. I deserve a rest. We both deserve one.'

'I can contemplate for myself a short holiday, a cruise, perhaps, some painting in the sun, but not the long rest you envisage,' Churchill smiles. 'Politics are in my blood. I could not live without the cut and thrust.'

'And in mine too, Winston, but I can't sustain the interest in the way I once did. That's gone. I'm going to leave it to younger men when my term runs out.'

'By that time, Mr President, I too may be grazing in the pastures. It is not improbable that I will have been booted out of office by then.'

'Well, I guess they'll just have to get along without us.'

'A disagreeable thought,' says Churchill, dropping his cigar into a rose bush.

Not for me, thinks Roosevelt, not if I can spend time with Lucy, and my other dear friends, and my stamp collection. Why, with Harry's help I might even write my memoirs if I can take the time off from relaxation.

After the break, Roosevelt asks for assurances that the elections promised in Poland will be free and honest. This is important for him, he says, because of the concerns of the six million Poles in the United States.

'What does it matter to him what the Poles in America think?' Stalin whispers to Molotov.

'They voted for him,' explains Molotov.

Churchill leans forward, palms on the table, to emphasise his point: 'I *must* be able to tell Parliament that the elections will be held in a fair way.'

Stalin slowly lights his Dunhill pipe – a gift from Churchill – and seeks to make the real issue disappear into the smoke of his Georgian philosophy.

'There are some good people among the Poles,' he emits as he puffs. 'They are good fighters and there have been good scientists. Copernicus was a Pole. But they are very quarrelsome.'

Churchill slumps backwards in despair at the obfuscation.

'All I want is to ensure that all parties get a fair hearing,' he mutters.

Stalin looks at the block-faced commissar beside him and nods gravely, as if to say: 'See to it, Molotov, let it be done as my good friends want!'

But there is no spoken commitment.

The Big Three have greater common ground when it comes to the question of war criminals.

Churchill says he personally feels that the 'grand criminals' should be shot as soon as they are caught and identified. To his evident surprise, Stalin appears to disagree, shaking his head.

'Is it Marshal Stalin's view that grand criminals should be tried before being shot?' Churchill asks. 'In other words, that it should be a judicial rather than a political act?'

Stalin knows full well the value of staging trials. He has been doing so with theatrical success in Russia for more than a decade.

'That is so,' he grunts.

Roosevelt finds a grisly middle ground between his two allies.

'It should not be too judicial,' he drawls. 'We should keep out the newspapers and photographers until the criminals are dead.'

Much later, in bed, I was at last able to read Dorothy's letter.

> I'm sure Ed has told you of the sort of things I busy myself with these days. It's a far cry from recruiting Cambridge comrades to be the backbone of revolution. You always teased me about my rosy spectacles. But I really do want you to know some of the things I couldn't tell you when we were friends and lovers. When I rejected the values of my family as a young girl, it was out of deep shame at their helplessness. They accepted with such docility everything that had been done to them and their ancestors. I wanted to become something as distant from them as possible. Assimilation might have been the way; but I knew I would despise English society even if I could have become 'accepted'. Religion was never on the cards. Zionism appealed greatly, at first. Then my uncle introduced me to Marx and all that. The Russian Revolution was being defended against overwhelming odds, and foreign intervention. I was hooked to the cause.
>
> When I went to Russia for the first time it was a bit of a let down. Nothing much worked, or looked like working,

but still this was our only hope. I had a lover in Russia – did I tell you? He made me see that all was well, and all would be well, if we trusted Comrade Stalin. I rejected reason in favour of faith. England seemed so banal after all that, but I was given a task. Then something you said at Cambridge – you were exasperated and made me see how utterly wrong the Communists had been about allowing the Nazis to seize power in Germany. Perhaps I saw that because I loved you in my own way. I began to doubt – but in the way of religious doubters this made me all the more determined to redeem myself by ferocious belief in the teeth of the doubts. In the end, that's probably why I left you, Jimmy. It was too uncomfortable to be with someone who reminded me of my hypocrisy and double standards. I needed a more malleable lover. Not that I don't love Ed. I do, and he's so much easier to live with than you were.

There was no Damascene revelation on my road – just a steady erosion of false belief and a slow realisation that the Stalinism Menace had to be defeated. Naturally, this was secondary to killing off Nazism. I was delighted when Hitler invaded Russia because I believed the might of Russia was necessary to defeat Germany. And so it has proved. So here I am. America's not perfect, but don't let anyone tell you it's a fascist state. Perhaps it's going to lead the world into some new way. I hope this all helps you bury the past.

With love, Dorothy.

I folded the letter and put it away. I didn't get to sleep for some time.

26

Yalta, February 10, 1945

I'd had troubled dreams after falling asleep. In them, Natasha pleaded, Podbirksi smirked, Ed pontificated. Then I woke and immediately the events of the previous day coalesced in my mind into a glowing solution, like the dawn. It struck me that I might have currency to rescue Natasha, if I were bold enough. But would the Russians accept it? They'd demand more than just my say-so, more than just the flimsy information I'd got from Ed. Perhaps, though, I could use that information as bait for something more. But for what? I couldn't start working the whole thing out yet. Then, awareness of the terrible risks involved flooded in. What had seemed a bright plan became clouded with indecision.

I drank several cups of coffee and prepared for my duties, hoping my face wouldn't reflect my inner turmoil. Something must have shown, though. Sarah looked at me with concern. Anthony asked if anything was bothering me.

'Nothing at all, Foreign Secretary,' I said.

'If there is, you'd do best to get it off your chest,' he said casually.

Winston's doctor Charles Moran offered to take my temperature. Moran nodded in agreement when I said it was probably just stress and exhaustion brought on by long days and Winston's late nights.

'We're all feeling it. Even Winston. Eyes giving him hell, poor devil.'

Winston, however, was in bristling form. In bed, in crimson dressing-gown, papers strewn around, he brushed aside the eye irritation.

'It's nothing, damn it,' he said in response to my enquiry. 'A minor visionary fatigue brought on, no doubt, by the Polish problem.'

I handed him a minute from Anthony setting out a formula for Poland's future, agreed by the three foreign ministers. The loopholes were obvious to Winston.

'Can they be trusted?' he muttered, shaking his head sadly.

The document talked about the provisional government being reorganised on a 'broader democratic basis'. This implied that an element of democracy already existed in Stalin's puppet body. And it failed to indicate how many non-Communists would be included.

'Nevertheless, it's the best we could get,' Winston mused aloud. 'Nothing could be worse than that we should leave this conference seeming to be in dispute with each other while the war is still being waged.'

This was the time, perhaps, when I should have suggested to him that a fully developed atomic bomb might be ready for use in a matter of weeks, and could be used to deter Stalin from imposing his regime over eastern Europe.

I said nothing. If he already knew of the bomb developments, my comment would be pointless. If he didn't know – and in the unlikely event that he took me seriously – I would have to face a security inquisition.

He looked up at me, his gaze piercing.

'Are you quite well, young man?' he asked solicitously.

'Quite well, Prime Minister.'

'Perhaps it is the tedious argumentation that afflicts you. I too have found this conference to be full of sound and empty fury, and of less consequence than I had hoped. We have made some points, won some concessions, but it has not been our finest hour. I have done my best, yet fear the ultimate result. We will put on a brave face, and talk of broad agreement, and in a matter of months, perhaps weeks, the world will know the agreements are minimal, nay worthless.'

I listened in silence. One never interrupted Winston in full flow.

Then, suddenly, he asked me: 'But is this black dog look of yours perhaps connected to the, um, attachment formed with the young lady on the other side of the fence? With your Juliet, your Grecian Helen in the clutches of Troy?'

'I wouldn't describe it as an attachment, Prime Minister.'

He did not hear, or chose to ignore my comment.

'Ah, yes,' he sighed. 'I can recall the exhilaration of youthful ardour, the belief that nothing else matters but to please the beloved. Of course, to a degree, this pertains even when one is past the first, or indeed the second, flush of youth.'

His eyes moistened and he added: 'How I wish I was at my dear wife's side at this very moment.'

Then he remembered himself and his audience.

'Mind you, James, I myself have never been totally carried away by such feelings. I was ardent, yes. But there was always duty to bring one back from the brink of self-absorption. My dear mother taught me that, even if she herself seldom seemed able to live up to it. She was an American, you know?'

I nodded. He knew that I knew; who didn't know of his American pedigree?

'Wonderful people the Americans, despite a certain naïveté. They may irritate one, indeed at times disappoint one, but in the end they are our greatest friends and, I believe, the greatest hope for mankind. I am sorry that your liaison with this Russian lady is causing you such anguish. I am possibly the last man on earth to be able to offer sensible advice to the lovelorn – you may obtain confirmation of that from my daughter Sarah – but I do know something of the affairs of nations. In the final analysis, what is important, what is vital, is the well-being of one's own country, and in the case of Britain, its Empire as well – its alliances, its security, its popular will. All else is of much lesser consequence. I caution you to remember that, James.'

'E.M. Forster said that if he had to choose between his friend and his country he hoped he would have the courage to choose his friend,' I responded rashly.

'Ah, yes. Mr Forster,' Winston said, shaking his head. 'A foolish man in a foolish place of learning. A novelist of no small ability, I am told, but writing fiction is at best a flight from the mundane complexities of real life. It may amuse, entertain, divert, even educate, but it is not reality. A writer of fiction is a player of games, not an actor in the drama of great events. I dare say that Mr Forster would feel somewhat differently about the order of loyalties if his own, um, beloved, um, comrades in the front lines were betrayed by someone with sentiments similar to his own. The world is changing, young man, and it will change with ever greater rapidity in the future, but the basic values will remain: courage, self-denial, faith. And, of course, glowing in bright letters above all else, loyalty to one's heritage.'

At that, he replaced his reading glasses and went back to his papers.

He was warning me, firmly, if not unkindly, of the consequences of choosing love for Natasha above love of my country. Did he know, intuitively, that somewhere along the line I would probably have to make a choice of some kind, and that this might lead me into possible indiscretions?

When he talked of self-denial, though the implication was that one should give up personal happiness for the sake of the greater good. There was an irony! There was the clarion cry of all the Communists I had ever known!

As I left his bedroom and shut the door, I could hear him singing 'Keep Right on to the End of the Road'.

I resented his warnings to me, but how could one not be loyal to such a man?

A little later in the morning, we went to the Yusupov Palace where Winston and Stalin were having a meeting. While this was going on, I was cornered by Podbirski. He took me into a small side room. I put my fingers to my lips to indicate we had better not talk.

'Jimmy,' he said. 'I have influence, a little, in matters like here.'

He swept his arm around the room to indicate possible sites of eavesdropping devices, and said: 'Empty. No microphones. This is private conversation, you and me. Like Mr Churchill and Mr Stalin in another room.'

'Sure, Anatoly,' I said, unconvinced.

'So, Mr Churchill is happy about conference? Always he is in his bed, I believe.'

'He works there, Anatoly. What about your great leader.'

'He sleeps on sofa, with his boots on.'

'Is that some old Bolshevik custom?'

'I think, no,' he laughed. 'Some old Bolsheviks like very comfortable beds. Especially when they have drunk too much. They like snore in comfort.'

'So why does Stalin sleep with his boots on?'

'Now, Jimmy, I convince you that room is safe one to talk in. I tell you secret things that I could be shot for telling.'

I still didn't believe this. If he was going to tell me anything of interest, then he was authorised to do so.

'I wouldn't want you to risk that, Anatoly.'

'What is life but risk? Joseph Vissarionovich is great man but he trusts no one. You know last Tsar also feared he would be killed, so every night he slept in a different room. Joseph Vissarionovich sleeps on sofa with his boots on. Just in case.'

'And does he have good reasons to distrust everyone?'

Podbirski shrugged. 'Maybe. Who knows for real? But he knows he is only one who can run Soviet Union. Lenin also knew this about Stalin. Lenin knew Stalin can manage peoples like no one else. This was the talent – is right word, yes? – that Joseph Vissarionovich showed in civil war.'

'In the end, though, Lenin didn't trust him,' I ventured.

'Who can say? Lenin was sick and dying. Who else could run our country? Is country of madmen, poets and peasants. Trotsky was clever, yes, an intellectual, but nothing he knew about reality of power. You notice, Jimmy, I do not say Trotsky was traitor or that he plotted against our government.'

He was desperate to let me know he could say dangerous things without fear of reprisal. To speak of Trotsky, who'd been murdered in Mexico in 1940, as anything but a treasonous snake in the grass was to risk a death sentence.

'Surely he must trust someone,' I said. 'What about Beria and Molotov?'

Podbirski smiled. I noticed there was sweat on his brow.

'Ah, Jimmy, I see how clever you are. You are not caring about the past. But you should be, my friend. From the past you can learn about the present. The past can tell you what to expect. I do not know how Comrade Stalin exactly thinks about his closest colleagues. Molotov, he trusts. Molotov has no ambition to become leader. And Molotov has, like you say in English, Achilles' foot.'

I waited for him to go on. But he didn't add anything about Beria. Perhaps his very silence was an answer to my question. Perhaps he was too scared to answer even if he had authorisation to do so.

I knew Beria was ambitious. But he was aware that his

predecessors were destroyed because they knew too much and wanted too much. Beria probably feared that Stalin might have the same treatment in store for him once he'd served his purpose. Perhaps he had it in mind to strike first. Perhaps this was at the bottom of Podbirski's licence to talk.

'Achilles' heel,' I said. 'Molotov?'

'Yes. Weakness. The commissar has Jewish wife.'

Eavesdrop-free zone or not, this was as far as he would go. I knew Molotov's wife had impeccable Party credentials, but these hadn't been enough to save thousands of others, including Natasha's parents.

I took into account that Podbirski might be warning me of my own Achilles' heel, cautioning me that the NKVD had Natasha and me in its power, and that I had better act quickly.

They could arrest Natasha any time they wanted to. And they could advise British intelligence that I was a spy, whether I gave them information or not.

'Are you trying to tell me, Anatoly, that I have a lot to lose?'

He looked puzzled.

'You? Jimmy, this is nothing personal. This is building bridge. I tell you some things to show how much we must trust each other. We are allies, no?'

'I'd better get back to my delegation unless there's some point to this all.'

'Jimmy, I am friend. I want to show you I am friend.'

'Why would you want to do that, Anatoly? What's the point of friendship in these times anyway? Let's leave it to our masters to be friends.'

Suddenly his eyes flashed angrily. He grabbed me roughly and whispered harshly into my ear.

'Sometimes you big fool, Jimmy. Sometimes you see everything like in official document. I am Russian. I have heart. I am friend with you because of *her*. Yes, her father was good man, was good to me. I tell you this. This was *my* Achilles' heel. They let me to survive. Now maybe you understand. Everyone must take risks, otherwise we die anyway on our knees.'

He let me go. He looked exhausted.

I didn't know what to think. I said nothing.

'Go back to your British friends, Jimmy,' he said in a flat voice. 'See how much they can help you.'

'Are you okay, Anatoly?'

'Okay?' he laughed. 'Why not?'

I offered my hand. I wasn't sure what the gesture meant. He took it. His palm was moist. Then we went our separate ways.

I wondered whether both Natasha and I were already compromised beyond rescue. In which case, we had nothing to lose. And perhaps Podbirski *did* have a very Russian soul.

'About Poland,' Churchill says, almost as soon as he and Eden are seated facing Stalin and Molotov. 'You have, my dear Marshal, given us your assurance that free elections will be held.'

Stalin nods curtly, as if to say, Yes, of course, I have given my assurance, so what more need we say about this matter?

He is irritated by the way Churchill addresses him, so patronising – 'My dear Marshal' – as though Churchill is the one with 20 million troops under his command. This fat old man thinks he is superior to me, and superior also to Roosevelt. He is head of a country which has spent itself. That doesn't make him less dangerous, and he is a cunning one all right, and a snake in the grass. He is a thief who would knock you over the head for a *kopek*. Not like Roosevelt, who would need a bigger prize before he'd do it. But I've got both of them by the balls, and they know it. They call me Uncle Joe. The small children of Russia also call me Uncle Stalin. To the children, yes, I am an uncle, a good uncle. But if these old men imagine I am some kind of benevolent nincompoop of an uncle, they will soon get a big shock. They are a pair of gangsters. Still, I can't help liking these devils. Roosevelt knows what's what. If he were a Russian, and if he were not about to die, I could appoint him my successor. He would know how to run things. He would trust no one too much. He would divide and rule, which is the best way. He knew all along how important was friendship with me. I'm sorry Roosevelt is so sick. If he was strong enough to go on, then we could sort things out between us. And Churchill? Well, I have some liking even for that old scoundrel. He can drink like a Russian. He was our biggest enemy at the birth of our system. And why not? I would have done the same in his place. And, by God, he stood up to Hitler when he had nothing – a handful of weapons, a beaten army – to stand up with.

That took guts. He wrote to me in 1940, when we were, so to speak, on opposite sides of the fence as regards Hitler. He wanted to keep the door open between us. Yes, he was desperate, but it took guts to write to me in that way, and it showed the man had vision. He knew I only needed that pact with Hitler because I had to have breathing space. He loathed the Revolution and he loathed me. But he knew that hating – or liking, for that matter – is not a factor in big politics.

'Naturally,' says Churchill, 'between allies, such an assurance is received in the same sacred sense in which it is given. But my government, at some remove from events in that unhappy country, feels we are at a disadvantage in not having representatives in Poland who can keep us informed of what exactly is, um, going on.'

Stalin holds his palms together. His nicotine-stained fingers are surprisingly delicate for a man of such stolid, stocky build. A pianist's fingers, sensitive, intuitive, creative.

'Of course, it is necessary,' he nods, statesmanlike. 'Every country must have its eyes and ears. So, once the new Polish government is recognised, it will be open to Great Britain to send an ambassador, of course.'

Putting on a smile of great friendliness, Churchill asks: 'And can it be assumed that the ambassador will have freedom of movement within Poland?'

Stalin consults Molotov, not out of courtesy to his subordinate, but because he knows Molotov is crafty and loyal when it comes to foreign affairs. Molotov is the best of the bunch, though that shrew of a wife tries to poison his mind. Thinks she knows better than me about the Soviet State! I should have got rid of her before, but, by God, I will soon shovel her off to Siberia. Let those superior Jewish eyes look out on all that nothingness and dream about the Promised Land! Molotov won't object. He's the best of the bad bunch.

Stalin listens to his faithful minion and looks up at Churchill.

'The Soviet army at present is operating in liberated Poland, and as far as the army is concerned I can assure the Prime Minister there will be no interference with the movements of the ambassador.'

Churchill sits back, apparently satisfied.

'Of course, the government of Great Britain will have to make its own arrangements for the freedom of movement of its ambassador with the Polish government,' Stalin adds.

Eden's eyes flit to Churchill. There's the rub, his eyes say, we'll be dependent on the rulings of that Moscow-dominated gaggle. Stalin's guarantees are worthless. At the end of it all, he can throw up his hands and say: Yes, I know I promised there would be no problems, but it is the sovereign government of Poland that has the last say on matters like this.

Stalin enjoys the moment and knows he has this old aristocrat Churchill where he wants him. As a rule, such people know nothing about struggles and suffering and sacrifices, but Churchill *does* know. He was born with a silver spoon in his mouth, but he had to make his own way in life. He was a soldier and a writer, like me. He knows how to deal with his generals. If they're not helping the cause, get rid of them. I got rid of hundreds of the bastards because they were polluting the army. The real way to deal with these dogs of generals is to let them go hungry and fight each other for the prize. That's how to get the best out of them. Anyway, we'll soon see who knows how to handle his generals best. We'll see who gets his dogs to savage Hitler to death. Roosevelt has his Eisenhower, who has never commanded in battle and lives in fear of Montgomery and is too cautious to go for the German throat. I have Zhukov and Koniev straining at the leash. When the time comes – very soon – I'll offer the prize to the one with the fiercest temper and the sharpest tooth. The prize of taking Berlin. The prize of History. That is how one handles these generals.

Churchill moves on to the repatriation of allied prisoners of war. There are British and American POWs in areas coming under Soviet control. There are Russians who fought for Germany surrendering in droves to British and US forces.

He and Eden have debated the problem at length. The first difficulty is whether Stalin will be prepared even to discuss it. Soviet wartime publicity has never admitted that soldiers in the glorious Red Army have at any time been captured or surrendered, let alone joined the fascist side. To admit this is to admit that Soviet soldiers might not be eager to fight to the death in defence of the motherland.

Churchill knows that while some of these Russians in German uniforms deliberately chose to take up arms against the Soviet

Union, many of them fought in the Nazi ranks because they had no alternative – 'fight for the Reich, or die of starvation'.

'This large number of Russian prisoners is a matter of some embarrassment to us,' Churchill says. 'There are about one hundred thousand in all.'

They are treacherous pigs, Stalin thinks. Better you should machine-gun the lot, and save me from wasting bullets on them. They are traitors. Just by surrendering, they have displayed their treasonous tendencies.

Nevertheless, he consults Molotov, and they agree it's better to get these vermin back on Soviet soil and deal with them than allow them to fester in foreign lands.

'I hope they will be repatriated as quickly as possible,' he tells Churchill. 'And please, I request they should not be ill-treated.'

'We do not mistreat our prisoners,' Churchill responds.

That man is patronising me again, Stalin thinks. He wants to provoke me. What is better about the way they do things? They pretend to treat prisoners of war with kid gloves, but I know this is for show.

'The Soviet government looks on all of these prisoners as Soviet citizens,' he says. 'Never mind what they may say. And, please, there should be no attempt to induce any of them to refuse repatriation.'

Churchill glances at Eden who has a look of contempt on his face, which says: How dare this man intimate that we would seek to influence these POWs!

When I heard of the outcome of the repatriation issue, I shuddered at the fate of the 100,000 Soviet prisoners of war – whether they had fought for the Germans or fought in the Red Army. Regardless of assurances by Stalin, I felt that his paranoia concerning anyone who had been, in his eyes, 'contaminated' by contact with outside influences meant that most of them could expect a bullet in the back of the head or, if lucky, decades in a labour camp. I doubted whether the NKVD would spend too much time on individual cases, and certainly no more than a handful of prisoners – perhaps only the top military leaders – could expect a public trial, even a show trial.

Thinking about this, and the promises about Poland, and imagining the mask of false concern on Stalin's face made me realise once again that this man and his regime could not be trusted to give one the correct time of day, let alone stick to an agreement. I would have to do something drastic to get Natasha out of Russia as soon as possible, before the post-war winter of retribution really set in.

It also made me convinced that there was no point in telling Winston that an atomic bomb test might be so close at hand that he would have the means to deter Stalin. Winston, I was sure, knew in his heart Stalin could not be trusted, but he was an ally, and Winston would not countenance holding a gun to the head of an ally.

At the Livadia in the afternoon, before the final plenary session, I bumped into Ed. As we strolled in the gardens, discussing the conference, I was hoping he might say some more about the atomic weapon.

'Talk about days of infamy!' he exclaimed. 'Roosevelt will be remembered as the father of post-war appeasement, and Churchill as his poodle. What a pair!'

By this time, the broad outcome was no longer in doubt. I was as upset as Ed about the concessions we'd made, but felt I had a greater grasp of our lack of negotiating strength.

'How could we have squeezed anything else out of them?' I asked.

He raised his eyebrows.

'You really don't get it, do you? This is the big sell-out. Munich all over again.'

'That was different. We might have stopped Germany in 1938 if we'd shown Hitler we meant business.'

'And now? Are we showing Stalin we mean business?'

'I don't know. If we keep our military strength, we can still contain any Soviet threat.'

'Tell that to the Poles, the Hungarians, the Czechs! Tell it to...'

'For God's sake, Ed, you're starting to sound like Cassandra.'

'And she was right, wasn't she?'

We walked in silence for a few minutes.

'Well, I guess we're just going to have to live with the consequences,' he remarked. 'Peace in our time, eh, buddy?'

I asked, casually: 'D'you think that thing you mentioned yesterday could change the situation? I'd be interested in some details.'

He shrugged.

'Yeah, so would I, but it's better not to ask. Don't start digging. This is quicksand. Any information you get or use, you won't know if it's any good, and it will just drag you under – along with your sources.'

'Wild horses wouldn't drag the name of any sources from me,' I said.

'They don't use wild horses any more. They got more refined methods. You got to feed horses. Electrodes don't need food.'

'Still, out of interest, I'd appreciate a detail or two.'

'Jesus, Jim, I don't know what you're up to, and I sure as hell don't want to know, but sounds like you're already out of your depth. You don't want to get involved. Believe me, this isn't for amateurs. You want some advice?'

I wondered if he'd guessed something of my intentions. It wouldn't have taken a nuclear physicist to deduce that if I was desperate enough to try to rescue Natasha then I might use whatever resources were available. Maybe this was behind his original leakage of information – or misinformation – to me.

'Go ahead,' I responded.

'No one's going to bail you out if you land in the deep shit. This isn't some kind of public school game. So, think about it carefully, buddy. It's your ass. It's your goddam neck.'

He turned and strode away, quickly.

I stayed where I was for a few moments. I couldn't decide what he was up to. Offering me a morsel, then warning me against using it. Was he backtracking or trying to make me more credulous?

So where was I? I didn't have a solitary thing of substance to give Podbirski in exchange for Natasha, not a titbit of real technical information, not the name of a scientific expert who might give my gossip a shred of credibility. All I could offer them was Ed's morsel and the unlikely prospect of something bigger to follow. And the danger was that anything I said, any course of action I took, might put Natasha in more peril than she was already in.

As I walked back to the gleaming white palace under innocent blue skies, I felt discouragement drizzling down on me.

27

Yalta, February 10, 1945

Poland is finally done and dusted in the afternoon. Russia promises free elections and an agreement to redraw the map. Poland will lose territory in the east to the Soviet Union and, in compensation, chunks of Germany will be added to Poland's western borders.

Molotov says in his stolid, expressionless way that Poland must get back from Germany its 'ancient frontiers' in East Prussia and on the Oder River.

Roosevelt asks, appearing innocent, for how long these lands have belonged to Poland.

'Since a very long time ago,' says Molotov.

'If we take that as a precedent,' says Roosevelt, with half a glance at Churchill, 'it might lead the Prime Minister to ask for the return of the United States to Great Britain.'

'The Atlantic Ocean would prevent this,' chuckles Stalin.

Churchill is not amused. He glowers.

A haggle begins about the reparations to be seized from Germany.

Churchill says his government has instructed him to avoid figures.

'Instructed!' Stalin says, thumping the table in anger. 'Perhaps your government would prefer that Russia should get no reparations at all. If so, you had better say so.'

'I deny that categorically,' says Churchill, rising to his feet.

'Do you accept the principle of reparations?' Stalin demands.

'Naturally, we accept the principle.'

Round and round they go for a while. Roosevelt keeps out of it. Eventually, it's agreed that a joint commission will decide on figures.

'We bring our figures before the commission, and you bring yours,' Stalin snarls at Churchill.

Churchill smiles benignly. He's rather pleased he's managed to expose something of the real animal's primal behaviour.

'We seem to have established that whatever his other qualities, he is no gentleman,' he whispers to Eden.

'Now you can appreciate my difficulties in dealing with these people.'

'Ah, yes, Anthony, but perhaps you are a little too diplomatic. When you get my job, you will have to let your anger shine through at times – for effect.'

Eden, to his delight, is at last anointed as heir apparent.

'I have been learning at the feet of a master,' he murmurs with a smile.

Now, Stalin, again businesslike, tells his allies: 'The Soviet Union will enter the war against Japan within two to three months of the defeat of Germany.'

He does not mention the inducements Roosevelt has made to him in exchange for this firm commitment.

Finally, casually, as things wind down, Roosevelt says:

'Well, all that remains is the communiqué. We'd better get it finished and agreed by lunchtime tomorrow. I intend to leave at three in the afternoon.'

Churchill and Stalin protest that there is still much to be done and so little time if the President really means to stick to this departure time. Roosevelt says amiably that he does intend to stick to it.

Hopkins smiles to himself. The old boy's done it again; thrown the perfect curve ball to let them know that the United States is not going to run to anyone else's timetable. He's got what he wants in regard to the United Nations and the Soviet entry into the Pacific War. The other issues? Well, on paper, they're okay. Military agreement to smash Germany pronto, elections promised in Poland, reparations to be settled in due course. I guess we've gone about as far as we can. Now we can go home and recuperate.

When I saw Winston, on his return to the Vorontsov, he was enveloped in gloom and complaining bitterly about Roosevelt's attitude.

'He won't take any interest in what we're trying to do. Poland!

It hangs around my neck like an albatross. We must still try to get something more definite, something in stone, or Parliament will crucify me. Isn't a firm commitment on Poland more important to the President than going to talk to Arab potentates?'

'I don't think it's more important to the American people, Papa,' said Sarah soothingly.

'Bugger the people!' said Winston.

'Isn't democracy supposed to be about the people?'

'Sometimes I think democracy might be a better system if it were not always so dependent upon the people.'

'I used to think much the same about my audiences,' Sarah smiled.

'Yes,' Winston said, the irritation fleeing from his face. 'We are both performers, Mule. We strut and fret our hour upon the stage, hoping the cheap seats will bring their hands together in applause or votes. Well, I dare say, it will not be the issue of Poland that will bring me electoral defeat.'

'You will not lose, Papa.'

'Perhaps, perhaps. I see that Mr Bexley stays silent. It is likely that he knows something we do not.'

I chose my words carefully.

'The whole country admires you more than any other single human being,' I said.

He narrowed his eyes as they pierced into my skull.

'Indeed? Our people are also said to admire Marshal Stalin in great measure, but I do not for a moment think they would vote him into office.'

'If that brute is admired it's only because some ghastly newspapers have built him into a hero,' said Sarah. 'The people of England love you in their hearts for all you've done for them, Papa. Isn't that so, Jimmy?'

'And the people of Scotland, Wales and Northern Ireland,' I said.

She put her tongue out at me.

'Ah, the Welsh,' Winston sighed. 'We shall get a drubbing there.'

We all pondered the probable truth of his prediction. Then he brightened.

'But in Wales, at least, they will not badger me about Poland,' he chuckled. 'I fancy they would rather like Uncle Joe to take them over as well. Even now, in the Valleys, it may be there are songsters at work practising the Russian lyrics to 'Land of our Fathers'. Perhaps they hope he will help them to extend their eastern frontier.'

And off he waddled for a nap, restored to a modicum of good humour.

Among the rest of our delegation, there was a feeling of relief that the conference was almost over, a view that the meeting had made progress on the road to peace. Nothing to get euphoric about, but what more could we have expected?

The Americans were in general a lot more buoyant – apart from Ed and a few who shared his views. There was talk about how everything was going to be just fine in the world after the war.

'Poland?' one of the President's men told me. 'Who gives a fuck about Poland? It's a European affair. We're going to get out of Europe for keeps once this show is over – time you sorted out your own problems. Anyway, how is Churchill's meddling in Greece different from Stalin's meddling in Poland? They both want to install governments of their choice in another country.'

I pointed out that there were differences – the Greek government wanted help to ensure democracy, the Polish stooge government wanted to ensure there was *no* democracy – but my views cut no ice with the aide.

'Tell that one to the marines,' he laughed.

No one I spoke to even hinted about progress on the atomic bomb.

Later in the afternoon, as the Vorontsov staff were bustling about preparing for a banquet that Winston was going to host, I went for a walk in the grounds to clear my mind.

I was thinking of ways to get Natasha across the border – one fantasy being to smuggle her on to a plane in a borrowed dress and hat from one of Winston's typists – when I found Gerald Cross walking towards me.

'Penny for them, old boy,' he said, offering me a cigarette.

'My thoughts aren't worth that, Gerald. Day-dreams.'

'The best kind of dreams. One can shape those.'

We smoked in silence for a few moments, then he said: 'Been hoping I might bump into you. I've got my orders. Right after this talk-shop I'm Burma-bound.'

'Lucky you!'

I was genuinely envious.

'You could say that,' he smiled.

'How did you swing it, Gerald? I thought they didn't want able-bodied chaps like us to do anything useful, like fighting.'

'There is a way, James, but it probably wouldn't work for you. You have to do something disgraceful. Then they can't wait to be rid of you.'

I couldn't believe he was capable of anything disgraceful, and said so.

'Ah, depends on your definition of the term. My superiors said my behaviour was morally reprehensible, or words to that effect.'

'The shits!'

'Oh, I don't know. They were bound to react like that. They'd known beforehand about my inclinations, and weren't much bothered – especially those from public schools. But once I got caught at it, they had to wash their hands. I was given a choice, and going to the jungle is far preferable to a court martial.'

Ever since our schooldays, I'd been aware that Gerald was a homosexual. At first, I deduced his preferences from nuances, inflexions of tone and the absence of any expressed interest in females. Later, at Cambridge, he shared his secret with me. I wasn't surprised or bothered. Gerald's sexuality was his own business. What *did* disgust me now was that the military should want to punish him for being what he was.

'My mistake was to get caught, and I suppose to get caught with a fellow they deemed to be my social inferior,' he said.

'It's absurd, Gerald!'

'I should have been more careful, but how was I to know our comrade allies would capture it all on photographs and seek to blackmail me into working for them?'

'Christ!'

'So I had to come clean to our chaps. At least I wasn't forced to reveal the fellow's name, and I just hope no one takes it any further. In the end, I think everyone – except the Russians, I suppose – was relieved that it could all be dealt with quickly and quietly.'

'And this happened here, at Yalta?'

'And where better?' he smiled. 'Beautiful setting for a night-time moment of rapture.'

I shook my head.

'Don't I know it?' I said.

I could see from his face that he'd heard something of my reunion with Natasha. But he wasn't the sort to press me for personal information.

'Well, I wanted to let you know of my folly, James,' he said. 'A cautionary tale. Something comforting in being able to confide in a friend.'

'Yes.'

We shook hands in farewell.

'Think of me venting my feelings on the Japs,' he smiled.

'Shoot a couple for me, Gerald. See you in London when this is all over.'

'Will you stay on with Winston afterwards?'

'I have no idea. If he's still PM, and still wants me, I might have no option.'

'He won't be PM,' asserted Gerald.

'You sound pretty sure of that.'

'I've spoken to a lot of chaps in the other ranks. They'll cheer him to the rafters, but they won't vote for him.'

Still feeling angry about the way Gerald was being treated, I went into the Orangery. Anthony was sitting in an armchair, engrossed in a volume.

He glanced up.

'Know the play, Bexley?'

He showed me the copy of *Troilus and Cressida* he was reading.

'I've seen it performed, Foreign Secretary.'

'Really? Never seen a satisfactory performance myself. I don't doubt that the Elizabethan players would have put across Shakespeare's mood. They understood the themes: war, disintegrating world, ambition, love. The poetry bears reading and rereading, Bexley. Listen to this: Achilles, the greatest warrior in the world, asks if all his brave deeds in the service of his country have been forgotten. Ulysses – always the philosopher in this play – says, wonderful speech:

"Time hath, my lord, a wallet at his back,
Wherein he puts alms for oblivion,
A great-sized monster of ingratitude."'

He read with a melancholic smile on his lips.

'Does that not convey perfectly the way time treats us all, rich or poor, democrat or tyrant?' he asked. 'Impermanence, shifting sands, decay, oblivion. It puts the petty moment of triumph into perspective.'

'You read the lines very well, Foreign Secretary.'

'You're much too kind, Bexley. One day, when all this is over and forgotten, I'd like to get involved in the world of Shakespearean studies and productions. What matters are enduring values, and one of those is the beauty of poetic truth.'

He closed the book with reluctance.

'This is how I refresh my soul from time to time. The Prime Minister recites from memory; I drink from the written word. Enough of that. Our own mundane times call. We cannot dwell too much on the remote future.'

He stood up.

'A pleasant evening. Stroll with me before I dress for dinner.'

Outside, away from the interior microphones, he professed himself interested in the mood of the delegations.

'My conversations are always on the official level – or on a plain in which concealment is the common currency. One never knows what one's colleagues really think. One can only deduce – never easy when one is dealing with masters of duplicity. This is not a criticism of my colleagues from friendly nations; they perform as they are trained to perform.'

I told him what I sensed from some conversations I'd had, mentioning the talk of the 'Yalta Spirit'.

He smiled thinly at that.

'Our American friends do sometimes get carried away by the moment. But I venture to believe that the President is under no illusions about Stalin's intentions and that they will stay the course.'

'A few of the Americans I've talked to are worried that the President has been weak,' I said.

'Are they really? How very odd. And what do they advocate that he should do?'

'They believe he could deter our ally.'

'With what superior weapons, Bexley? A wooden horse?'

In response to his mocking tone, I said recklessly: 'If there were an awesome weapon, nearly ready for delivery, wouldn't it make them think twice about imposing their will on eastern Europe?'

His lips pursed beneath the perfect thin moustache.

'Threats? Against an ally? Super weapons? That sounds like Hitler talk, young man. *We* proceed on the basis of negotiated agreements. We need to have these agreements – we must be seen to be allies working together for victory, after all – and we have worked hard to get the consensus we have, whatever its shortcomings. It is true that we will have to see how the agreements are executed. But I find incomprehensible any suggestion that we could possibly use threats. I assume you have a grasp of the military realities.'

Clearly, he didn't think I had. His manner, and my despondency over the problems facing Natasha and me, pricked me into further indiscretion.

'An atomic bomb would surely change the realities,' I ventured.

He asked scathingly: 'Is nuclear physics a field in which you have some expertise, Bexley?'

'I have read about the possibility for years, in newspapers and the like. I had friends at the Cavendish.'

I surprised myself by the ease with which I was able to lie.

'I see,' he said slowly. 'And do your prognostications rely upon newspaper reports or upon the insights of your university friends?'

'They are pure supposition on my own part, Foreign Secretary.'

'That does not surprise me,' he said briskly. 'A word of caution, Bexley. Avoid guesswork. Don't deal in gossip. Do I make myself clear?'

I nodded.

He gave me a penetrating gaze.

'Very well. Be aware that you hold a position of trust, and there may be those – I am not saying there *are* such people, but there may be – who would try to exploit you. Be aware of that.'

Before I could think of whether to reply, he went on, more sad than angry: 'These are trying times. There is so much at stake. Two wars – one futile, the other made necessary by our stupidity. But it must not happen again. This is why we must go on talking to each other, not threatening. Hoping that reason will prevail. Not making threats, not fomenting rumours – that is a dangerous game, Bexley.'

I nodded again. It was better, I felt, not to utter a word, and especially not to utter a lie.

'Finally, let me say this. Even if a weapon of the sort you conjure up were feasible – and it is not at the moment – it would have little effect if brandished as a threat. When a country has had the entire German might thrust at its heart, and has withstood and repelled the aggression, I doubt very much whether it would take seriously any threat from us. They know that neither we nor the United States want to continue fighting in Europe after victory is achieved.'

Then he said, almost warmly: 'You know, as do many others, from personal loss and sacrifice, how two world wars have bled the whole continent white, reduced vast areas of it to rubble, killed millions. The Prime Minister and I have been through it all, two great wars, and we would not want our country to endure something similar again. Of course, if we had to face aggression, we should do so, but neither of us would want to do so until every other avenue was exhausted. This is not appeasement, Bexley, it is practicality.'

He hesitated, then turned his charming smile upon me and asked:

'Knowing me, as you do, do you believe I would ever – in whatever position I might be serving the country – stoop to appeasement when faced with a direct threat to our islands?'

I said I most definitely did not.

'Thank you, Bexley,' he said, almost humbly.

Russian soldiers sweep through the villa checking on security half an hour before Stalin arrives for Churchill's banquet.

The Prime Minister has lined up a regimental guard of welcome along the stone steps to the entrance. The guests are shown into a reception room, where Churchill presides benevolently over cocktails and chatter.

'How is Mr Hopkins today?' Stalin asks Roosevelt.

'Not too good,' admits the President. 'He's in bed. But he's a game guy. He'll be back. He always comes back. Presidents may come and go, but Harry will just roll on and on.'

'Like the Mississippi,' says Churchill. 'He may know something, but says nothing unless it is pertinent. Let us drink to him.'

Roosevelt sips his cocktail, but does not savour it. He knows how to mix them properly, and he knows a good deal more about Harry Hopkins than does Winston Churchill. He knows the man speaks his mind, and is invaluable on occasions, but sometimes, damn it, he imagines he is right about every darn thing.

'And he is not even an elected member of the government?' Stalin asks with a tone of innocent inquiry.

'He's not a member of the government at the moment, but he sure as hell could have got elected to Congress if he'd been willing to stand. I thought of him as my successor at one time, you know. The only problem was his health, and then he thought he could be more useful as my eyes and ears.'

'To Harry!' says Churchill, raising his glass.

'Amen,' says Roosevelt.

'A useful man, obviously,' says Stalin, joining the toast. 'I would like to have such a man at my side. Someone who would tell me the truth, not lies because he thinks I do not want the truth.'

Molotov stares expressionlessly ahead.

Then Stalin adds, as if the thought has just occurred to him: 'I am sorry that Mr Truman, also, did not accompany you to the Crimea. It would have been useful to meet him.'

'Why?' asks FDR with a smile. 'Because I might expire tomorrow?'

'Of course, I did not mean that!' says Stalin, in a voice full of shock. 'May God spare you to live for many more years, Mr President.'

'God?' murmurs Eden, glancing at Molotov.

'A figure of speech,' says Molotov in English.

'What did you say, Molotov?' Stalin asks in his Georgian-accented Russian.

'Only that you would be desolate if Mr Roosevelt were to be taken from us, Joseph Vissarionovich.'

'Not desolate. Do not translate this, Pavlov. But he is an easy man to deal with, once you get to know that he twists and turns like a mountain path. And I like him, Molotov. I like his deviousness. Perhaps he is a great man. Who can tell that a man is great while he is still alive. Only the future can crown us with greatness.'

'What the hell are they saying?' Roosevelt asks.

'Marshal Stalin was saying how much he admires you, Mr President,' says Pavlov.

'Ah,' says Churchill loudly, receiving a signal from an aide. 'Shall we go into dinner, gentlemen?'

At the table there are hints of underlying tensions, but little overt acrimony.

Proposing Stalin's health, Churchill says with a child-like grin: 'There was a time when the Marshal was not so kindly disposed towards me, and I remember I said a few rude things about him, but our common dangers and common loyalties have wiped all that out. May I add that I foresee a Russia, which has already been glorious in war, as a happy and smiling nation in time of peace?'

Stalin looks at him suspiciously. Is this old fool suggesting that the Soviet Union is anything but a happy and smiling country at the present time?

Molotov whispers that he should ignore the jibe, if it is that, because probably it is only meant as a joke.

Stalin stands up and pronounces: 'I would like us to drink to the health of King George of England.'

Churchill looks up misty-eyed. Perhaps there is really good in the heart of this Bolshevik blackguard after all.

'Naturally, I am opposed to the whole idea of kings,' Stalin adds. 'But I make an exception here because he is the boss of the Prime Minister.'

Roosevelt laughs. Churchill doesn't see the joke. He scowls and interjects: 'We are a constitutional monarchy. I am answerable to Parliament, and Parliament is answerable to the people.'

After this toast, Roosevelt goes into a rambling anecdote about a Catholic, a Jew and a member of the Ku Klux Klan. The moral is that the three of them manage to get on pretty well together in the local Chamber of Commerce.

'It's a good illustration of how difficult it is to have prejudices – racial, religious or otherwise – if you really know the other guy,' the President concludes.

'Yes, this is very true,' says Stalin in all seriousness.

'He did not mention the Negro,' Molotov whispers to his boss.

'The Negro was serving them drinks,' Stalin replies. 'That is how his great democracy works.'

Winston mentions the forthcoming British general election.

'Perhaps I will not be present when the three leaders of our countries meet again, after we have finished off the enemy. Perhaps you will have to deal with the estimable Mr Atlee.'

'I am sure you will win the election, Mr Prime Minister,' says Stalin. 'Who could be a better leader than he who has just won the victory in war?'

'We have more than one party, you know,' Winston says.

'Ah,' says Stalin, showing all his rotten teeth in a grin. 'Just to have one party is much better. Much easier to predict the result of elections.'

Molotov smiles cheerfully, but no one at the table laughs.

'In the election campaign, I will have to say some harsh things about the Communists who will oppose me,' muses Churchill.

'No?' says Stalin in feigned disbelief. 'The Communists are good boys. They will not support the Labour Party against someone who is such a friend of mine.'

'Perhaps you have some influence with the Labour supporters too,' Churchill beams.

'In my view, any leader must take care of his people's primary needs,' Roosevelt says. 'I remember that when I became President in 1933 the United States was close to a revolution because the people lacked food, clothing and shelter, but I told them: If you elect me, I will give you these things. Since then, there has been little danger of any social disorder in the country.'

Churchill applauds with a few discreet, unenthusiastic thumps of his hand on the dinner table.

'And now, I would like to propose a toast to my friend, the Prime Minister,' says FDR, who does not – cannot do so unaided – rise from his seat.

'I was twenty-eight years old when I entered politics, and even at that time Winston had long experience in the service of his country. Since those days, he has been in and out of the government for many, many years. It's hard to say whether he has been of more service to his country within the government or without.'

'Better outside when Chamberlain was the leader,' says Stalin.

'I did not agree with Neville, but he was a decent man at heart,' says Churchill firmly.

'Well, whatever the rights and wrongs,' says Roosevelt, 'and we all know there are rights and wrongs in every political situation – I have great respect for some of my deadliest political enemies – I would like to say that I personally believe Mr Churchill has been of immense service to his country even when he was not in government; for in those times, he forced the people to think.'

After the dinner, when Winston is showing FDR and Stalin round his map room – where staff dispense Napoleon brandy, whisky and a variety of liqueurs, as well as cigars and cigarettes – the mood is mellow until Stalin, studying the map of Europe with flagged pins showing military positions, implies Britain might be tempted to make an early armistice with Germany.

Winston begins to growl an angry response, but decides against descending to the level of this ruffian. He plunges his hands into his pockets and begins to sing: 'Let's keep right on to the end of the road'.

Stalin looks bemused.

Roosevelt tells Pavlov: 'Inform your Chief that the Prime Minister's singing is Britain's secret weapon.'

Stalin nods. He likes music, but this does not sound like music. He could sing better himself, but he prefers others to make fools of themselves. He loves ordering them to sing and dance after they've had too much to drink – Kaganovich, Beria, Molotov, Malenkov and the rest. He enjoys making them perform for him, the dolts.

Then he turns serious and says to Churchill and Roosevelt: 'More time is needed, I think, to consider and finish the business of this conference.'

Churchill fully agrees: 'Yes, yes. We must keep on to the end of the road.'

Roosevelt lights a cigarette and says firmly, as if to a child: 'Winston, I've made commitments. I must leave tomorrow.'

'But, Mr President, you cannot go,' Churchill cries. 'You must change your plans. We have within reach a very great prize. The future...'

Roosevelt smiles and says: 'I'm sorry, gentlemen, but I have three kings waiting for me in the Near East.'

It will be a pleasure, and a relaxation, to sort out the problems of that area after the difficulties of Poland and trying to cope with Winston's moods, he thinks. Yes, he'll bring everlasting peace between Arab and Jew in Palestine. Knock their heads together; get agreement on joint Moslem–Jewish–Christian control of the Holy Land. It should be child's play compared to the Polish impasse.

'Why the devil is he going there?' Churchill mutters to Eden.

Eden shrugs, as if to say: What does it matter? The Americans will never understand the nuances of Middle Eastern politics.

The President, eager to pre-empt further criticism of his early departure, puts the spotlight on Stalin.

'I'm a Zionist, Marshal,' he says. 'So is Mr Churchill. Are you one?'

Molotov coughs to catch his leader's attention, to suggest a diplomatic reply. Stalin ignores him but doesn't plunge in. He thinks and answers carefully. One thing you learn in long years as an underground agitator is to hide your true feelings. He is not going to show how much he dislikes the Yids.

'Yes, in principle,' he says warily. 'But I recognise the difficulties in solving the Jewish problem. We tried to establish a Jewish home at Birobidzhan, in our Far East, near China. A good area. It failed because the Jews soon scattered to other areas.'

He asks if Roosevelt will make concessions to the Saudi monarch, Ibn Saud. He means about the Zionist campaign for a homeland in Palestine. FDR, like Churchill, has a record of backing Zionist aspirations, but the issue of oil supplies from Saudi Arabia looms large.

'I'd like to review the whole Palestine question with him.'

Stalin finds it hard to believe that this American patrician can have any real love for Jews, however much they support him politically.

'The solution to the Jewish problem is difficult,' he says, as if imparting great truths to the Politburo. 'The Jews, I regret to say, are middlemen, profiteers and parasites.'

He smiles to show he is about to tell an amusing anecdote.

'You have heard of Yaroslavl? No? It is a town famous for the sharpness of its merchants, who are pure Russians, not Jews. We have a saying: No Jew could live in Yaroslavl. You understand the meaning? Because there even *they* could not make a profit better than the local merchants.'

Churchill and Eden study the contents of their brandy goblets.

Roosevelt says it is past his bedtime.

28

Yalta, February 11, 1945

Winston's irritation about FDR's imminent departure dragged on into the morning.

'The President appears to have lost his sense of proportion,' he said to Anthony as he puffed a cigar in bed, not inhaling. 'He wants to dally with these, these desert chieftains at a time when we are engaged in trying to settle the future of the civilised world for a generation or longer.'

'Possibly he is too ill to care about the next generation,' said Anthony.

'In that case, he is badly advised. Poor Harry is himself too ill to counsel him. But why does not Stettinius say something to him?'

Anthony shrugged. I wondered whether the American Secretary of State, who'd given up a successful business career to join Roosevelt's administration, would try to change the President's mind on a schedule he was so determined to pursue.

Leaving Winston's bedroom with a pile of paperwork, I came across Sarah. She'd dined with Anna Roosevelt Boettiger who said her father simply *had* to keep his appointments in the Middle East.

'As if the conference isn't so much more important than anything else!' Sarah said to me.

'Did you say that to Mrs Boettiger?' I asked.

'Don't be silly, darling. I'm much too diplomatic. I merely suggested that we drink to the next Big Three meeting. Mind you, I've gathered that the President's old mistress has come back into his life. Did you know that?'

I shook my head.

'Lucy something-or-other. It might be one of the more pressing reasons why he's so eager to get away from here and back to the States,' Sarah added with a giggle.

She asked me if I'd had any interesting encounters. I searched her eyes but could detect no mischievous curiosity in them. I told her I'd discussed *Troilus and Cressida* with Anthony.

'Beastly play to act in,' she said. 'It's one of those where the lovers end up badly because someone splits them up, isn't it?'

'That happens sometimes.'

'Oh, darling, don't despair,' she urged.

'I wasn't talking about myself, Sarah.'

'Of course not,' she said brightly. 'Anyway, I'd love to do Shakespeare again, but I'm more a dancer than a classical actor. No one would take me seriously as Juliet or Ophelia, would they?'

'You dance divinely, Sarah.'

'Thank you, ducky,' she smiled. 'I have a modest talent. After the war, d'you know what my dream would be? To dance with Astaire. Of course, my height would count against me. I'm much too tall for him.'

At the Livadia at noon, the leaders peruse a draft joint communiqué prepared by the Americans.

Churchill, spectacles halfway down his nose, skims through it.

Prosaic, he thinks. It lacks grandeur and the broad sweep of history. I should have written it. Ah, well, I shall deliver its essence in suitable phrases – for the benefit of posterity – when I have the time to write my history of these times.

He growls his disapproval at the use of the word 'joint' throughout the document.

'It conveys to me the Sunday family roast of mutton.'

'In my language, it means a place where you can get hooch and girls,' cracks Roosevelt.

Pavlov does his best to interpret this Anglo-American linguistic skirmish for Stalin and Molotov, who, almost for the first time in this conference, seem at an involuntary loss for words.

The word 'joint' is removed.

There is one final clash over Poland. The Americans have withdrawn insistence on Allied supervision of the elections, pulling the rug from under Churchill's feet. When Stalin asks Churchill if he accepts the decisions made on Poland, the Prime Minister, knowing there is nothing he can do about it, says:

'Very well. I am content with them, though I will be strongly criticised at home for yielding completely to the Soviet view.'

Stalin repeats his question, blandly, with an expression that conceals all trace of triumph: 'Does the Prime Minister agree with this section?'

'Yes, yes,' says Winston wearily, 'But I will be roasted at home for doing so.'

'Like the Sunday joint,' Roosevelt whispers gleefully to Hopkins, who stares at the document and does not laugh.

Thereafter, the communiqué is quickly approved.

It says that a defeated Nazi Germany will be divided into zones of occupation, that the United Nations will burst forth on to the world, the liberated countries of Europe will have the right to solve their problems by democratic means, the provisional government of Poland will have a broader democratic basis and will hold free elections, and an unspecified amount of war reparations will be extracted from Germany.

It does not mention things too sensitive for the public eye, including the conditions under which Russia will wage war against Japan. These secret clauses will be licked into shape and put into a protocol by the foreign ministers.

With this, the Big Three sign the statement, and the Crimean Conference is over, bar a final farewell lunch at the Livadia Palace. By this time, the major participants all have their minds on the future. Stalin is scheming on how to exploit his gains. Churchill is glum, but resigned to the fact that he has done all that could be done. Roosevelt is focusing on the speech he must deliver to Congress about the achievements of Yalta.

'It will be a tricky one, Harry,' he says to Hopkins at the lunch. 'I'm going to need all your skill to help me say what needs to be said.'

He seems to have forgotten an earlier conversation in which Hopkins indicated he would not be able to help on this – or perhaps he did not take it in.

'I'm afraid not,' says Hopkins sadly.

'What?'

'I mean, I'm too worn out, too damn sick to be of much use to you, Mr President. I feel like death warmed up. I'm going to have to take a rest and then go in for a spell in the Mayo.'

Roosevelt mutters: 'Of course.'

Hopkins knows the signs. FDR is angry and feels badly let down. He's not going to forgive me this time. He has a cruel and selfish streak at times, like kicking Winston when he's down and being more concerned about a speech than about my health. Well, fuck it, I have to get away from all this, and maybe I'll recover a bit, have a few more months to enjoy the small pleasures of still being alive, and having the delight of a lovely young wife. I've been damn loyal to Franklin and he's been good to me, but maybe this is the last chapter. It's been quite a life – battling the Depression, being at Winston's side during the Blitz, running Lend-Lease, winning presidential campaigns, winning the war, and now forging some kind of peace. And I'd be at peace too if it wasn't for the lack of a stomach and for the loss of Stephen.

Then he thinks of the meal awaiting him and feels nauseous.

During the lunch, I walked the grounds in search of Natasha.

Great issues had been debated, agreed, conceded, pushed into the arena of political and historical debate and dispute at this conference. Who would remember the travails of James Bexley and Natasha Khazan in 50 years time?

Ed saw and hailed me. I asked why FDR was in such a hurry to escape.

'Says he's going to try and get some agreement with the Arabs to allow lots more Jews into Palestine,' said Ed. 'Fat chance! The Arabs are about as keen on it as your government.'

I didn't rise to the bait. Britain's policy of restricting the numbers of Jews permitted to get refuge in their ancient homeland at a time when the whole race was under threat of extermination in Europe was something I was deeply ashamed about, but there wasn't time for a long debate on this with Ed.

'I suppose he's happy about the business here?' I asked.

'He may be,' Ed shrugged. 'Lots of people back home won't be. Stalin gave away zero. Roosevelt will boast he got a promise from him to open a second front against Japan and over the United Nations, but those cost Stalin not a bean. He gets territory and prestige. We got nothing out of it at all. We've sold the Poles out, and probably the rest of Europe as well.'

'What more *could* we have got?' I asked.

'What more? Jesus, the United States is the most powerful country in the world. That should count for something, shouldn't it?'

He spread his arms wide, palms outward, to indicate there was nothing more to discuss. He certainly wasn't going to talk about atomic weapons.

'I just wanted to say goodbye, buddy.'

We shook hands. Our friendship had withstood a lot. He'd been the one to come between Dorothy and me, but that relationship had died anyway. I'd used him as a scapegoat for my own feelings of humiliation. Now, I no longer felt deeply hurt. Perhaps I was learning wisdom, and the difficult truth that one had to try and shape one's destiny with one's own hands – even if the effort was doomed.

'Good luck,' I said.

'You too, Jim. Watch your back.'

I couldn't see Natasha near the palace. She must have known I was certain to be there today. Then I had a thought. I ran as quickly as I could – not bothering to conceal my urgency from the guards on the route – down the winding steps, along sandy paths to the stone bench where we'd met for the first time at Yalta. She was waiting. I sat down breathless, and we kissed.

'Natasha?' I said.

'Yes,' she replied firmly before I could ask the question.

'I will try everything. I will speak to people. I have ideas.'

My hopes tumbled out. She smiled, but without hope in her eyes.

'Yes, I would be willing to come with you. But there is no chance.'

'There may be a way.'

She searched my face for clues that I might not be offering a false promise.

'Tell me,' she said.

I shook my head and handed her a small envelope.

'Give this to Podbirski, Natasha. Please.'

She put it into a pocket in her tunic.

'This is the way?' she asked.

'We're not going to talk about it.'

'Jimmy, you want to do something dangerous for my sake. I can tell.'

I held her.

'There's no risk,' I said with a confidence I didn't feel. 'This is just a goodbye note. He might be able to help us.'

She pulled away.

'Then why do you not give it to him yourself?'

'That would be too risky. It's possible that every meeting I have with him is watched. Neither his people, nor mine, would believe it was only a friendly message if I handed him a letter.'

'Your people too?' She sounded shocked. 'Jimmy, they will shoot you. You must take this back.'

She removed the envelope from her pocket and tried to thrust it into my hand. I took her hand and kissed her fingers.

'Just do it,' I said. 'No one is going to shoot me.'

'Do you have to write to him? Why can't you say to him?'

'Because I may not manage to talk to him again. The conference is over. We're all going our separate ways.'

'I know,' she said sadly.

'Just take the letter.'

Her fingers closed over the envelope, and she returned it to her pocket.

'You promise me that there is no danger to you?' she asked.

'Believe me, it's okay.'

She sighed and I embraced her.

'We'll laugh about this when you're out of here,' I said.

I was trying to offer reassurance, but she detected only recklessness.

'This is not a joke matter,' she said sharply.

'No, it's not.'

'You cannot fool with Beria. They will hunt you down, even if takes years. They never forget. Like they never stopped hunting Trotsky.'

'I don't think so,' I said, trying to make light of it. 'Those things don't happen in England. If there's even the slightest risk, we'll go far away. New Zealand. South Africa.'

'Why do you say "we"? You know it is not possible I can ever go with you.'

'Let me work on the possibilities.'

We kissed intensely.

She looked at me with eyes wider than ever.

'You think?' she asked.

'With luck, I'll meet you in Berlin, just as soon as it's captured. And then I'll carry you off to England.'

She smiled as if she could imagine this. She touched my hand.

'How can you do this?'

I couldn't tell her. Podbirski had said knowledge was currency. Perhaps, but in their country it was also far more dangerous than ignorance.

'It's complicated,' I said. 'I hope it can work.'

'You are in the wrong country for hope, Jimmy.'

'If anyone asks you about the letter, tell them the truth. Tell them I spoke to you about nothing except love.'

'They never believe the truth, so it's better that I tell them nothing, nothing!' she said fiercely. 'Nothing about us. That is something in me they cannot reach. I will eat the letter, I will choke on it before I tell anything about us.'

Her angry desperation gave me black second thoughts about the whole venture. Now I wanted to take back the letter because possessing it was too great a danger to her. The hatred she felt might provoke her into some risky gesture of defiance.

My hand reached for her pocket. She knew why, and pulled away to prevent me from snatching the envelope.

She looked into my eyes, saw that my concern was for her, and shrugged.

'They can arrest me anyway, just for breathing,' she said, suddenly much calmer. 'Certainly for talking to you, even if just about love. So what is this extra risk? I will give this to Anatoly Mikhailovich and maybe it will work.'

She had her hand firmly over her pocket, to guard the letter.

'How many children you think we will have, Jimmy?' she asked.

She had tears in her eyes.

'Ten – at least,' I said.

We clung to each other.

'We must get back to the palace,' she said eventually. 'I will give the letter to him.'

The final session in the palace would soon be ending and the delegates dispersing for the last time.

I held her tight for as long as I could. Then we walked

hand in hand, and in silence, back up towards the palace and the sober reality it represented of an end to the present armed conflict but without trust between the victors. As soon as we saw the white granite walls, we walked apart from each other, like strangers, until we reached the gravel of the entrance grounds, and there we parted. A crowd of officials came through the doors and into the grounds, mingling, shaking hands in farewell. Yalta was over. I watched Natasha's small figure walk briskly towards a small group of Russian diplomats, including Molotov's arch henchmen, Vyshinski and Gromyko.

Both were smiling broadly. A good week's work.

I strolled over to a group of cheerful British officials, all looking relieved that it was finally over, as though it were the end of term. Then the black limousines rumbled into the courtyard to collect us and take us away.

Back at our villa, Winston abruptly announced we'd be off within the hour. We'd been preparing for a much more leisurely departure. He'd clearly decided there was no point in brooding over the diplomatic defeat. He must get away as quickly as he could from the scene and move on to fresh battles. The war wasn't over yet. He needed to sort out the situation in Greece, oversee the invasion of Germany, save the Empire, win an election. No time to lick wounds!

He was in a frenzy, like one who has survived the initial hopelessness of deep grief and flaps around in search of a purpose to life. Frantic activity was pushing guilt and regret into the shadows, as it ever had with Winston. Every five minutes, it seemed, he changed his mind about our departure time. Sawyers, poor man, was almost weeping with frustration as he was told to pack, and then to unpack.

Roosevelt and Stalin were already gone – departure operations mounted with preplanned, slick efficiency. Only we were left, fumbling with boxes and suitcases, not knowing when we were leaving or where exactly we were heading. Somehow, it all seemed like a metaphor for our position in the world.

Eventually, Winston made his final decision and we headed off by car to Sebastopol, from where we could visit battle sites of the old Crimean War, which had been still ripe in people's memories when he was a child.

Amid the gloomy rubble of Sebastopol, Sarah asked me solicitously: 'Did you manage to say goodbye to your sweetie?'
I nodded.
'The war's almost over. You'll see her again, Jimmy.'
I smiled at her. 'Let's hope so,' I said.
But I knew it rested on a gamble.
'I'd bet on it,' said Sarah as though she had read my thoughts.
'Like father like daughter,' I said lightly. 'Baccarat or lost causes, it's all the same to you Churchills.'
'Oh, Jimmy,' she said sadly, and kissed me on the cheek.

Podbirski was in the party escorting us to Balaclava, the site of that misguided, gallant Charge of the Light Brigade, doomed to be cut down by waiting Russian guns.
We managed a brief, whispered talk on the battlefield.
'Your letter, Jimmy, is interesting but gives nothing of real information to help. Is vague.'
His hands were plunged into the deep pockets of his overcoat. He had the look of a down-and-out merchant who has known better days and does not expect them to return.
'How could I tell you everything?' I said out of the corner of my mouth. 'When you deliver her to me, I'll give you the rest. It's better not to speak here.'
'You say you have information. How you know these things? You are not scientist, Jimmy.'
'I know the scientists,' I said.
My scribbled note, I felt, gave away no secrets. I knew none to give away. It was a falsehood from start to finish. It merely said that an unspecified research programme may have run into snags that would take years to resolve. I could elaborate if necessary. I did not mention a bomb or the word atomic. Podbirski, and his masters, would know what I meant. The danger – one of the many – was that Soviet spies might be telling their masters a different tale to mine.
I rationalised that far from giving secrets, I was feeding

misinformation. I would never have divulged to Soviet intelligence the few scraps that Ed had fed me about the Tube Alloys project. Instead, this was commendable, if unauthorised, black propaganda, I told myself with black humour: I might end up with a medal.

But no effort at internal frivolity could override the deep foreboding that British military intelligence would see my actions in a very different light – at the very least, as an overture to espionage. The fact that Russia was our current ally would carry no weight with them.

Nor could I rid myself of the overriding fear that I might be putting Natasha in terrible danger. It was impossible to push this dreadful apprehension away.

'How you know programme has run into such problems?' Podbirski asked. 'This is very big secret, my friend.'

'Come on, Anatoly,' I said with a bravado I didn't feel. 'Your informants must have fastened on to something similar.'

He didn't reply immediately, pacing away from me before coming back. Out of the corner of my eye, I thought I could see people watching me, former colleagues of Gerald. My disdain for them as they coolly observed my encounter with Podbirski allowed me to appear calm and unperturbed despite my mental turmoil. How could I stand in dread of such petty people?

Anthony and Alan Brooke were chatting to Winston, probably about the follies of the Charge – 'magnificent, but not war', a French general had remarked at the time. Everyone else seemed to be watching me. I told myself to stop being paranoid. They all knew it was only a discussion about a girl!

'If such big problems happen, why should it be such valuable information for my government?' Podbirski asked.

'For goodness sake, we can't discuss it now.'

'You worry about people over there. They think we talk about old days in Moscow. Jimmy, you are honest man, I think. Why you want to give secrets to Soviet Union? You are not Communist.'

'I want Natasha. You know that. This was your suggestion.'

'Jimmy, is okay. Always I like you, Jimmy. These questions, you understand, I have to ask. Not everyone trust you like I do.'

'Make them trust me, Anatoly.'

'I try,' he said, and walked off slowly in the late afternoon mist beginning to waft in from the sea.

365

The military men, who I felt had been watching me, now stood with their eyes turned towards the sea and talked among themselves. Normality seemed to be restored to the sinister setting of a few moments before.

But even the normality seemed menacing. I felt as though I were in a Hitchcock film.

29

Saki, February 14, 1945

We returned to Saki airport for our departure. All but the runway was still covered in snow, but slushy now, changing to a mud colour. The three flags of the allies fluttered limply. Winston walked down the long line of a guard of honour, staring hard at the men of the Red Army. I could see he respected them as soldiers who would constitute a fearsome foe, psychologically as well as numerically.

He made a brief speech: 'We bid farewell to Crimea, cleansed by Russian valour from the foul taint of the Hun, to your great leader, to your armed forces and to the valiant people of your country.'

It sounded to me like the tired reprise of a song that had once stirred the blood of those who'd welcomed Stalin to our side at last for good or ill.

Podbirski was among the small band of officials who'd made their way to Saki to wave us off. I wasn't near enough to talk to him, but he moved his head, unsmiling, in an almost imperceptible nod. It sent chills down my spine, a reminder that I'd put myself in their hands, and put Natasha at their mercy.

I looked around to see if Gerald might be among the military aides on the airport. He was not. Was he already on the way to steamy Asia?

Then we climbed into the planes – Winston giving his V for Victory sign at the top of the gangway steps – and took off, through the clouds and into bright sunshine over the Black Sea on our way to Athens and thence to the Middle East.

Once we were airborne, Winston summoned Sarah and me to join him. He looked bleak and troubled.

'I have done all that I can, but it is not enough. The world is changing and I am too old to change with it.'

'Oh, no, Papa, you are one of those men who *make* the changes. You'll go on doing that.'

'Perhaps, Sarah, perhaps,' he said without conviction. 'Nevertheless, this failure may turn out to be the end of me.'

'No one will blame you for anything,' she said fiercely. 'You did your best and anyway most of the voters think Stalin is the bee's knees.'

'I fear they do, but they will soon understand his real designs, and they will blame me for failing to prevent him. This is not self-pity, Sarah. I dare say, I have been guilty of feeling self-pity at times in my life, but not now. I have tried to do my best here, but the President and Stalin have outwitted me, and I shall be held to account for that. Do you not agree, Mr Bexley?'

It was time for an answer I'd rehearsed in my mind.

'They have outgunned you, Prime Minister, but not outwitted you. I'm sure the electorate won't see this as a failure, and even those who *do* see it like that will not fault you. There may be other issues, but you are still the man they most admire.'

'Ah, the other issues, Mr Bexley,' he said, nodding pensively. 'The other issues. You do not care to name them, I note.'

Sarah glared at me.

'I did not mean that there *are* other issues, Prime Minister,' I said. 'Just that your political opponents will try to claim there are, and will seek to exploit them.'

'The British people will not stand for such ingratitude,' snapped Sarah.

'Well, I believe I still have *some* credit with the British people,' said Winston. 'I trust it will counter those other issues you mentioned in passing, James.'

'There is no living man that the people more admire than you, sir.'

It was an answer of sorts.

'Very well, let us all take some rest now,' was all he said.

Afterwards, Sarah sidled into a seat next to me. She was seething.

'You ruined his mood,' she said.

'I don't think so.'

'You did! You're so wrapped up in your own little sordid affair that you don't care whether you hurt him or not.'

'Thanks for that,' I retorted. 'Perhaps he needs someone to tell him about the way things are going. I believe that's part of my job. The ordinary people are grateful to him, but the country's crying out for change. Has it ever occurred to you that a lot of people feel he may have outlived his political usefulness?'

'That's a lot of rot!'

'It may be, but that's the feeling.'

'Bugger the feeling!' she said with passion.

We frowned at each other, then simultaneously burst into laughter.

'Oh, Jimmy, I know you didn't mean to be horrid to him.'

'Sarah, you know how much I love the old chap.'

'Yes. And I know you have to counsel him. But the poor dear's been badly wounded by those two beasts at Yalta, and he feels so threatened.'

'Winston Churchill threatened?' I laughed. 'That's surely a contradiction in terms.'

'You're right. He'll bounce back. Wait till we get to Athens. Oh, Jimmy, did I say something very unkind to you? I'm sorry.'

'You were being mulish in your defence of your father, and maybe I deserved it.'

'There's nothing sordid about your love for Natasha.'

'I hope not.'

'What do you mean, darling?' she asked, concerned. 'What do you not hope?'

'A slip of the tongue.'

'Hmm. And I don't suppose you'd tell me if there was something.'

'I can't act for toffee,' I said. 'If there was something, you'd know it straight away.'

'All right. Message received. Will you take me to see the Parthenon?'

'You bet!'

In the event, we didn't manage to walk around the Parthenon, although we did see it, atop the Acropolis, lit by night from afar, a magnificent reminder of the birth of democracy – and of the need to preserve it from ruin. Our stay lasted a little more than 24 hours. A truce in the fighting between forces backed by Britain and the Communist rebels was in effect. Winston got a hero's welcome from a huge crowd in Athens' Constitution Square, and was buoyant as he flew to the Middle East for a farewell meeting with FDR.

On the flight, he explained with a puckish grin why Greece had been off the agenda at Yalta.

'To show how much I still trust you, James, despite your ill-concealed pessimism about the general election, I will let you in on a little secret. Stalin and I sorted out the Balkans, quite informally and without fuss, in Moscow last October. We agreed Britain would have ninety per cent of the say over matters in Greece, and Russia should have ninety per cent in Romania and seventy-five per cent in Bulgaria. I scribbled the percentages on a piece of paper and Stalin ticked his agreement with a blue pencil. A neat trade-off under the circumstances, don't you think, my boy?'

He didn't expect a reply, and I didn't dare remind him of the last time a British Prime Minister had extracted a promise from a dictator on a scrap of paper.

Off Alexandria, in the clear Egyptian sunlight, a few days later, Churchill visits Roosevelt on the President's vessel, the *Quincy*. He is determined not to recriminate with his old friend over Yalta.

Roosevelt greets him affably and Churchill asks if the talks with the Arab kings have been fruitful.

'I've had a darned good time, Winston. It's been an eye-opener, and very worthwhile. Ibn Saud came along with practically his whole court, it seemed. The fellow doesn't drink or smoke, but he's a noble chap for all that; lot of steel in him. He doesn't have much time for your Jews.'

'*My* Jews?'

'In Palestine, Winston. You still do have a mandate over Palestine, I assume. Or have you sold that off to pay your war debts?'

Almost immediately, he regrets saying this. Darn it, sometimes he just feels so low and weak that he behaves in the most stupid and insulting way. Like his recent uncivil attitude to poor old Harry.

Churchill does not allow his anger to show. Normally, he might have done so, even to the President, his old friend and past saviour; but things have changed. This man has only a slender hold on life, he thinks.

'It is a grave problem,' he admits. 'The Jewish people have suffered grievously for thousands of years, and most appallingly under Hitlerite Europe, because of their lack of a homeland. Surely, it is time for us to make some restitution?'

'So half the Democrat party tells me – the other half doesn't care to have Jews in the country clubs – but these high sentiments aren't going to appease the Arabs.'

'You are right, Mr President, and it is up to us, in this new world, to find some justice for both sides.'

'I'll get Morgenthau on to it as soon as I get back to Washington,' FDR jests. 'He'll turn all the swords into ploughshares.'

Churchill summons a smile. The Treasury Secretary's plan for transforming post-war Germany into a mainly agricultural nation, without heavy industry, was a foolish idea, but he himself might have come up with some similar vengeful medicine if he'd been a Jew like Morgenthau.

They talk of other things, of war and its weapons, and peace and its promises.

Churchill proposes that atomic bomb research should be developed in Britain after the war.

'That sounds fine with me, Winston,' says FDR. 'We're hoping to do our first important trials in ... in September, if I remember correctly.'

'In about seven months,' says Winston, counting on his fingers. 'That is gratifying, Mr President. Let us hope that by then hostilities will be over – but if not, such a potentially powerful weapon should hasten the end.'

'It certainly will, but I share your hopes that the war – in Europe, at least, and in the Pacific if Uncle Joe keeps his promises – will be over long before we're ready to drop one of them. From what I hear of the potential, I hope we never have to use one, ever.'

'Possession alone will surely be a decisive weapon in the future.'

'Let us hope so, Winston.'

Roosevelt holds out his hand in limp farewell, and Churchill grasps it.

'We've been through a hell of a lot together, Winston. A great adventure.'

'Indeed,' says Churchill, his eyes moistening with emotion. 'We have done great things in a great endeavour. The world, and especially the British Empire, will never forget your selfless help to my country in its time of need.'

'So long, old friend,' says Roosevelt, sensing a speech and cutting him short.

'Goodbye, Mr President. Until we meet in London in the summer.'

'I look forward to that, and to renewing my acquaintance with the King and Queen. You'll pass on my very best regards to them, please?'

Churchill nods, while thinking: He cares more for my monarch than for me.

On the flight back to London, Winston said sadly: 'I believe I shall never see the President again. He was vague and almost not of this world. He tried to be jocular, as of old, and to be affectionate, but, alas, he was not. He is a great man, though like all men – great and small – he has human weaknesses. One failing is that he can brook no rivals. Me, he fends off with attempts at ridicule, which I am sure are not really meant; his political rivals he defeats with brilliant tactics and stratagems and with wit. Stalin too brooks no rivals, but he is somewhat more unpleasant in his manner of disposing of them.'

He dictated a summary of his last talk with Roosevelt, concluding: 'We discussed some issues regarding the development of an atomic weapon. The President informed me that there was little or no likelihood of producing an effectively workable version for us in this war.'

I prepared to gather up my papers and leave him, when he said, in a conversational manner: 'You have some knowledge, I understand, of this subject of the, um, ultimate weapon?'

Denial was out of the question. Either Anthony had spoken to him, or our intelligence people knew already about my dealings with Podbirski.

'No knowledge, Prime Minister. Just speculation. I felt, in a moment of optimism, that the boffins might be able to perfect something sooner rather than later to make the Russians more amenable.'

'A fertile imagination, indeed. And you have not, I trust, spread this optimism beyond your own thoughts?'

'I mentioned it to the Foreign Secretary.'

Winston nodded.

'That is acceptable, of course. No doubt he found it of trifling importance. And beyond that? To friends, to colleagues, to allies?'

'No, Prime Minister.'

I thought it unlikely that he would believe me, and expected to be hauled over the coals. But there was no anger in his eyes as he peered at me above his spectacles.

'You would do well to restrict yourself in future to cold facts and not to foolish fantasies. Now to the question of your lady friend in Yalta, this Russian Juliet of yours – did you resolve anything in relation to this problem?'

I decided there was no longer any need to deny what I had previously denied to him – that there *was* an attachment between myself and Natasha. He'd made up his own mind, anyway, that there was.

'We talked, she and I. Circumstances did not permit any resolution, Prime Minister.'

'You talked. And you made no suggestions as to how the matter might unfold after the war?'

'I could not, Prime Minister. She and I both know there is no question that she will be allowed to leave the Soviet Union at present. We accept that reality.'

'You are wise to do so, said Winston. 'However, let me assure you that after the general election I intend to discuss with Marshal Stalin the possibility of entering into an agreement on allowing nationals of our two countries to have free passage between us.'

I nodded, though I knew this was so improbable as to be nonsensical. I would dearly love to have riposted by accusing *him* of foolish fantasies, but I hadn't yet reached the point of career suicide.

'I do not have high hopes of the outcome,' he added. 'But

if such an agreement were reached, James, would you wish this lady to travel to London?'

'As quickly as possible.'

'And your feelings for her are of a romantic kind and not ideological?'

'Purely romantic, Prime Minister,' I smiled. 'The Soviet ideology has no attraction for me whatsoever.'

I wondered if someone had put him up to this interrogation. He seemed uncomfortable.

'I am certain of that, and you may well wonder why I raise these matters with you,' he said, lighting a fresh cigar. 'Naturally, I am always interested in my personal staff and considerate of their needs. In this case, too, my daughter has mentioned your difficulties to me. She very correctly reminded me that I should be more considerate to my staff. I confess that my dear wife had occasion to give me similar advice in the earliest days of my premiership. I was somewhat brusque and impolite even to my Cabinet and senior civil servants then; I trust I have successfully modified my behaviour in the years since.'

It was a statement, not requiring confirmation, so I was silent.

'Brusque' was an understatement of his behaviour in those early days when nothing mattered to him but Britain's survival. If he believed himself to have mellowed now, I wondered, how difficult must it have been for his staff in 1940?

Back in London in late February, gloomy London as cold as I could ever recall, memories of the warmth and luxuries of Yalta and Alexandria taunted me.

The German V2 rockets were still flying in, eerily silent until they exploded with the sort of random devastation we hadn't seen since the worst days of the Luftwaffe Blitz five years earlier. In one way, this was worse because there was no warning, no escape if your name was on one of them. In another way, it was better: there was nothing one could do – no hasty, undignified scramble to a shelter, because no air raid signals sounded – but sleep in one's own bed and be thankful if one woke up in the morning.

During this period – it was almost the Phoney War in reverse, as we waited for the end of fighting in Europe and yet continued to suffer the same privations and fears of the war years – I phoned Gwen and suggested we meet.

I wasn't trying to rekindle anything. All I wanted was to talk to her as an understanding friend. I felt alone and cut off from the rebirth of love and closeness anticipated by so many parted couples. I had no emotional connection to my mother despite our wartime *rapprochement*. Ed and Dorothy were far away in every sense. Dr Bergsen was in a remote and alien land. Douglas was up to his eyes in work, and anyway I wanted to avoid a confrontation with him over my doings at Yalta. I didn't feel I could talk to Sarah; our recent level of mutual confidentiality had been due to the artificial hothouse atmosphere of the Crimean experience.

Gwen and I hugged each other with real friendship, but almost before we'd disentangled, she was telling me that she expected Binky back at any time as soon as his POW camp was liberated. Friends of his who'd managed to escape and make their way back to England had told her that he was as hearty, brave and encouraging to others as ever. He'd managed one escape himself, and been captured.

'But, thank God, they didn't shoot him or anything,' she said with feeling. 'I hope he doesn't try anything stupid again. I want him back, safe and sound. I need someone to take care of me again. Don't be hurt, Jimmy, I mean permanently.'

I told her how pleased I was for her. We discussed Natasha.

'Oh, gosh, Jimmy,' Gwen said. 'Mr Churchill will make sure she can join you once the war's over. Then we'll all be happy.'

'You're one of my few good friends, dear Gwen.'

'Thank you, darling. We had some good times, didn't we? And I'll always love you a lot; like a sister, though.'

She smiled impishly.

'You were damn sceptical when I told you that Dorothy wanted just that with me,' I laughed.

'Ah, but *I'm* not going to end up in bed with you again, Bexley.'

'Not even once more? For the road?' I teased.

She kissed me very fondly.

'Take that for the road, my dearest.'

We went to dinner and talked easily of the good and bad

times of our lives. Afterwards I walked her back to her front door and we embraced and said good-night and goodbye in the manner of old comrades in arms who cherish their friendship but know that past passions will never be reborn.

And just as well, I thought, as I strolled briskly back to my place. Much as I found Gwen as desirable as ever, it was Natasha who was central to my life and hopes.

The weeks that followed passed in a routine of work as Winston and his office dealt with the inexorable closing movements of the war in Europe, clearing the decks before the election campaign got underway.

For Winston himself, there was a joyous interlude. He insisted on travelling to the Rhine and wandered inquisitively about despite German snipers and shells, happy as a schoolboy on the first day of holidays until ordered back by an American general worried about losing a British Prime Minister on his watch.

No word came to me from Natasha or Podbirski. I forced myself to stay optimistic despite deep fears. On the plus side, to my relief, I got no indication that the security services were interested in me.

Then, one night as I returned home to Pimlico, I noticed a man sauntering along on the opposite pavement. I was suspicious and nervous, but then berated myself for being paranoid. Inside the flat, I peered through a window in a darkened room. He was still there, standing on a street corner, looking towards the flat. His attitude, which seemed insolent, angered me. I decided to go outside and confront him. After all this wasn't a police state yet!

I went back into the dark, dank night. I walked towards him. He looked up, unsurprised as I approached him.

'If you're keeping tabs on me, you need some basic training, chum,' I said aggressively.

'You are Jimmy?' he asked.

He wasn't British, for sure, from the accent.

'And you?' I asked.

I guessed he was Russian and probably from the embassy. He shrugged my question away.

'I go to bus-stop next down road. If no one follow me, if no one follow you, you come there in ten minutes.'

I checked that there was no obvious tail on either of us and joined him. Just two people waiting for a bus to appear from out of the darkness.

'So?' I said.

'In Crimea, you promise more information.'

'Why should I talk to you? I haven't the foggiest idea who you are.'

'You are worried about your friend, no?'

I wanted to grab him and shake the truth from him, but restrained myself.

'Is she okay?'

'Yes.'

'You have proof?' I asked.

'We hear tests going to happen soon with that thing.'

My mind was racing. I had to keep the conversation going.

'There are major problems,' I said.

'What problems?'

Here goes, I thought. In for a penny...

'I can't go into them here in detail, not standing here like this. Look, they have to make sure it doesn't go off prematurely – early, understand? – and that the radiation won't kill anyone who handles it. They have to develop a proper mechanism to make sure it works.'

'Okay, you give details. On paper.'

'Can you give me concrete assurances that she's safe and will be allowed out of your country?'

'I will try find out. You give me details on paper, same time tomorrow, I wait here.'

'No, my friend,' I said. '*You* give me proof first. Then I'll supply the details.'

A bus appeared out of the gloom and stopped.

'I catch this one,' he said, and jumped on board, without looking back towards me. The bus pulled off, and I was left feeling that I was being slowly pushed into a corner, without achieving anything.

I still hadn't thought of a way out by the following evening, but I went to the bus-stop and waited. He didn't appear. Not that night, nor the next, nor for the next fortnight during which

I kept the appointment each evening. Finally, I stopped going. Probably, his masters had decided I had nothing of value to offer or that any information I gave would be bogus. Or perhaps it had been an attempt by *our* intelligence people to entrap me into offering sensitive information to an outsider. I knew I might never find out for sure.

German resistance to the invasion of the Fatherland was crumbling perceptibly. It was only a matter of time before the end.

Like everyone else, I'd longed for the peace to come, and yet it seemed to me that nothing was changing or likely to change in a world without war.

In the Foreign Office for a meeting, I overheard one young man say to a colleague: 'All this concentration camp stuff bores me silly. I expect it's all propaganda by the Jews. Did we fight this war just to save them?'

'They'll end up top of the heap, anyway,' his colleague replied. 'They always do.'

I couldn't help thinking of the heaps of corpses discovered when Belsen and other concentration camps were liberated.

The Russians were showing every sign of going back on the Yalta agreement as regards Poland. They were also applying pressure to turn Romania into a pro-Moscow satellite – which was probably regarded as justified under Winston's secret percentages agreement with Stalin. I felt deep in my bones that most of eastern Europe would go the same way, and Germany too. I couldn't feel any real sympathy for Germany – though the stories of Red Army brutality and rape there were horrifying – but I feared that a Stalin-held German state would be a dagger at our heart.

I heard Winston muttering that the Russians were trying to cheat him over Poland and other promises.

'I won't stand for it,' he growled. 'The Bear advances. I am prepared to go to the verge of war.'

But what did that mean? Only, perhaps, that we were incapable now of doing anything but issue empty threats to the new looming enemy in Europe. FDR wasn't going to do anything to upset his rapport with Stalin, especially as the Pacific War was boiling towards the invasion of Japan proper.

I heard nothing more from the Russians – no news of Natasha, no further request for details. It was a hopeless game, I felt. Surely they already knew far more than I could ever tell them?

One evening in late March, Gwen phoned and asked if I'd come around and see her. She sounded distraught.

The butler showed me into her drawing-room. I glanced at the paintings hanging on the walls: a Renoir of two teenage girls looking out at life to come; a Canaletto above the large mantelpiece showing a panorama of the Thames glowing quietly in the sunset. Civilised, privileged life!

Gwen floated in, eyes red. I hugged her.

'There's a story doing the rounds that Hitler's going to retreat to Bavaria and hold out to the end, with all the British and American POWs as hostages,' she said. 'If we attack him, he'll kill them all. Have you heard that report, Jimmy?'

'I've heard rumours,' I said cautiously. 'No more than that. Guesses and speculation.'

'But he'd do it, wouldn't he?' she asked desperately.

'It's just a wild story, Gwen. I'm sure Binky's not in any danger. I'll check it out for you, though.'

'Thank you,' she whispered.

I left her, realising there was only one person who might be able to help – and not relishing the prospect of a conversation with him. However, there was nothing for it. Gwen was dear to me. I had to try to get some information for her.

I managed to see Douglas in his office the next day. To my relief, he was amused when I told him the reason: a friend of mine was worried about her husband who was a POW in Germany.

'Always happy to help one of your mistresses, James, even if it means delaying the final attack on Germany for a few hours.'

'Thanks, Douglas, but the lady isn't my mistress, she's an old Cambridge friend.'

'Good Lord, not the Communist one?'

'Actually, no, Douglas, it's Lady Harding. Binky Harding's wife.'

'I see. Yes, well, obviously there are all sorts of theories circulating about how things will end. The possibility your friend has heard is one of them, but I think unlikely. Our people are pretty sure Adolf and his henchmen will stay in Berlin to the bitter end. Anyway, it's improbable they could move any significant numbers of POWs even if they did make a break for Bavaria. For one thing, I doubt if the German army would help with the transport; everyone's desperate to ingratiate themselves with us – to avoid war crimes accusations and to stay out of the clutches of the Russians. I think you can assure her that Lord Harding should be safe. His Stalag may already be in Allied hands.'

He put his hands together and studied his fingertips. Apart from a couple of brief encounters during his visits to Number 10, this was the first time since Yalta that we'd had a chance to talk.

'I gather you were a trifle indiscreet in the Crimea, James,' he said.

'I suppose I was, Douglas.'

'Care to explain why?'

'Do I have a choice?'

'I'm your friend, not your interrogator,' he smiled. 'It might help you if you're frank with me.'

'Are you the one who's kept them off my back so far?'

'I imagine the Prime Minister has more influence than me in that regard. But it has been in my in-tray for a while. Sooner or later, I'm going to have to make a recommendation – which may or may not be accepted.'

'I suppose I was indiscreet,' I repeated. 'What else could I have done? I've told you how much Natasha means to me. Meeting her again at Yalta confirmed all that. You've loved, haven't you, Douglas?'

I'd never dared ask him this before.

'You're a passionate man, James,' he said. 'It's not surprising; both your parents were too. Not that either of them showed it very much to the outside world. You know, it was a great passion that brought them together.'

After all these years, it was the first time he'd told me about the love between my father and mother. My mother had never let a word of her marital feelings slip out to me.

'They were totally unsuited, but Clive was besotted with her. She was a great beauty – of course, you knew that,' Douglas continued. 'A great beauty, and with a great deal of passionate intensity. They couldn't escape marriage. An affair might have been more suitable, but in those times, before that war, it would have been difficult. The families were middle class, dedicated to respectability.'

I listened, scarcely breathing. For almost the first time in my life, I thought I could understand the marriage. For the first time, the idea of my parents as a couple became a reality rather than a disturbing puzzle.

'I argued against it,' Douglas continued, staring at his fingernails. 'I urged Clive to reconsider. She was not his match in intellect or moral fortitude. I was wrong to intervene, but I did. Your father ignored me. To his credit. The marriage, of course, was by and large a wretched one. After the passion died down, they discovered there was little in common; except you, James. That, at least, was a common bond. In the end, I was pleased that my advice was ignored and that they had married. What they had, even for a fleeting time, was more than many people have in a lifetime.'

I nodded. I couldn't speak.

After a few minutes, Douglas said: 'So, I understand the feelings that impelled you to indiscretion. I sympathise with you.'

'Thank you,' I muttered.

'On the other hand,' he said with a smile. 'I had rather hoped that my little efforts to guide you along moral ways might have deterred you from doing anything so reckless.'

'It was a bad situation, Douglas. If the price of helping her was to put myself in the wrong, then I believed I had no alternative. I still feel that way. But it *was* indiscretion, as you said yourself, and likely to harm only myself.'

'To place yourself in the wrong may in the abstract appear an admirable choice. However, it was more than just yourself, was it not?'

I didn't hold this bleak appraisal against him. It was typically Douglas: never let sentiment cloud the cold truth.

'Yes,' I responded, 'and if anything happens to Natasha, I'll hate myself for life.'

'And aside from that, James? Did you consider that you might be doing something to the detriment of your country?'

'I don't believe I did anything that could harm my country, Douglas.'

'You don't *believe*? What exactly did you do?'

'You'll have to take my word that I did nothing that could possibly damage national security – now or in the future. I'm sure of that.'

'How can you be sure of that?'

'Because the thought did occur to me, Douglas. I might have been prepared to betray my country if I was absolutely certain it would lead to Natasha's safety and exit. I suppose I might even have been very tempted to take a chance on this if I'd had the means. Luckily, I didn't.'

'But you purported to have the means, didn't you?'

'I lied to them, yes, Douglas. I was asked a question and I lied. Anyone might have done that.'

'Anyone else might not have put himself in such a position,' he said sharply.

I made no reply. I knew that I had erred in almost every way.

Douglas took a few minutes to tame his temper.

'All right, James, you've been foolish, and perhaps worse than foolish. But I'm not going to judge you beyond that. I don't know all the facts, and I'm not the right person to press you on this.'

'I suppose I'll still have to face the music,' I said, feeling relieved that at least my meeting with what I believed to be a Soviet Embassy man had apparently not been observed.

'I doubt whether it's a great priority at the moment, but, yes, you will probably have to give an account to the people who are interested in these things.'

'And I suppose my father would have understood my weaknesses?' I ventured. 'Or not?'

'I imagine he might have,' Douglas said with just the hint of a smile. 'Unless he'd forgotten his own.'

'Do you have any weaknesses, Douglas? I've always imagined that you were immune from temptations.'

'Let us not venture down those avenues,' he said, shuffling some papers on his desk to indicate our conversation was at an end.

As I left the War Office and wandered down Whitehall, my thoughts were on a love affair long before my own. I reflected on how fortunate I was to be born into a more open society than the previous generation. The inter-war period had given Europe a rough ride, but it had also permitted a freeing of experience and emotions for those too young to have fought in the last war. I also thought with a kind of happiness in my heart of the passion, however brief, that my parents had felt for each other in the dim Edwardian past. The sun was shining weakly and some buds on the trees, and something in the air, suggested that spring would soon replace our bitter winter. However, it was not the sun that made my eyes water as I dwelt on the past.

A week later, I got the news that Gerald had been killed in Burma. The officer who came to see me said Gerald had left a letter saying that two people who needed to be informed if he died were his father and myself.

'How did it happen?' I asked.

'Bad business. Our chaps were pushing towards Mandalay. One of *our* shells got him, poor devil.'

I thought of darkly beautiful young Gerald, passionate, confident rebel and loyal friend. I undertook to inform his father.

'When you see him,' the officer said, 'tell him Captain Cross was killed in action – that's all!'

I went on the sad mission to bring the news of Gerald's death to the family home in Wiltshire. The general looked old and defeated by sorrow. He'd been a widower for years. He vaguely acknowledged that he'd once met me at a parents' visiting day at school, though I doubted if he really recalled the occasion.

'You were a friend?' he asked.

'At school, university, during the war. A close friend.'

'Strange boy, Gerald. Had some odd views as a boy, but grew out of them.'

'Yes,' I said.

'Never married. Was there a girl, d'you know?'

'I think there were several,' I lied.

'Dark horse. But I loved him. Love my daughters too, of course, but Gerald was the only son.'

* * *

Another death, the following month, came as little surprise to anyone who'd seen Franklin Roosevelt at Yalta.

'I have a terrific headache,' the President suddenly said while on holiday at Warm Springs in the southeastern US state of Georgia. Then he fell into a coma and suffered a cerebral haemorrhage.

Among those with him was Lucy Mercer Rutherford. She left Warm Springs soon after he was pronounced dead – before his wife Eleanor and the rest of the family arrived.

I felt as though I'd suffered another personal loss, but nothing like the grief that struck Winston when he heard the news. He eventually decided not to attend the funeral in Washington; international developments made it impossible for him to leave Britain, he said.

Sarah thought the reason was different.

'I'm sure it's because he doesn't think he could cope with the emotion,' she told me. 'They were a couple of old cronies who'd been through the mill together, good times and bad, laughter and arguments – and then one of them ups and dies. All that's left is the black hole of memories and regrets. And that's too much for Papa.'

There was a memorial service at St Paul's, which had stood like a domed beacon of Britain's defiance throughout the bombings and bad wartime news. The sound of the 'Battle Hymn of the Republic' sung in the great interior of the cathedral proclaimed the friendship of two nations and two great men.

After the service, I saw Winston standing on the steps of the cathedral, tears in his eyes. I felt I was viewing a scene in an historic tableau: a great old man, to whom we all owed so much, mourning a fellow giant of the times.

Someone touched me on the shoulder to break the spell; it was Leo Roth. He told me he'd been in the United States for several years, but had returned to Britain a few weeks before and had been waiting for an opportunity to talk to me.

'I didn't want to risk a phone call, so I came here today, knowing you'd be at the service. Can we have a cup of tea together? Somewhere private.'

We found a café on Cheapside, close to the cathedral. I wondered if he was going to tell me about his family in Germany. I knew from his uncle that some cousins had managed to emigrate, but the fate of the others, including Leo's mother and sisters, and an aunt, could only be imagined with horror. Probably this was all too painful to discuss; in any event, there were other issues he wanted to put to me.

'In America, I was working on the project,' he whispered to me after a waitress set tea and toast on our table. 'You know the one?'

I nodded.

'I resigned when it was certain the Nazis could not build such a thing. I could no longer see the need for such a terrible thing.'

'If you've quit, then why such secrecy, Leo?'

'Because there are things I know. I am under surveillance, Jimmy. They don't like people resigning. They don't like people having information when they are no longer part of the team.'

He risked a surreptitious look around. No one in the café showed the slightest interest in us.

'I'd heard vaguely a test might be imminent,' I said. 'Is that the case?'

'I don't know how imminent. Not for months perhaps, not for years perhaps, but it will take place and they will proceed. This project is irreversible. They have spent so much money already, and they want to see something from that.'

He stirred his tea slowly, and again looked around the café. No new customers had entered.

'What will happen is this. They will test the apparatus on the ground, and if it works they will find a way to explode it in the form of a bomb or a shell. That is probably quite some way ahead, but we believe the development should never get to that stage. There has to be a political decision to shut the lid on the secret.'

'We?'

'Scientists, on both sides of the Atlantic, who have some idea of what energy might be unleashed. Jimmy, we don't even know for sure that we can prevent a chain reaction from destroying the world. Some fear the atmosphere will be ignited. That may be unlikely, but this apparatus will be able to cause such devastation that a future war will threaten the world.'

'And you, and your colleagues, believe a political decision to stop the development will not be made?' I asked.

'The spear was designed, and it was used. Explosives were invented, and they were put into shells. The aeroplane was invented, and they used it to drop bombs. That's the human mentality. This thing, though, is so dangerous to all of mankind that we must use every effort to persuade these people to see reason. Mr Churchill is a visionary. Would he be able to see the dangers?'

'I don't know, Leo. I imagine he'd weigh up military necessity against morality.'

'Precisely! That's what we all do. But what is the military necessity now? The Nazis were the only other people working on such a project, but no longer – and they are being defeated with ordinary weapons. The Japanese too are certain to be defeated. Is there any other enemy?'

I shrugged. The answer was obvious, and Leo himself supplied it.

'Possibly, probably, in the future, the Russians,' he said. 'Our information, though, is that they are not seriously interested in a project like ours. They believe it is caught up in too many difficult problems and will not be a reality for a very long time. They're wrong.'

I pondered this.

'What's the rationale in America?' I asked.

'The logic is: you spend millions to develop something, then you have to use it. Also, the planners say it's the only way to avoid an invasion of Japan and all the loss of life that would entail. We disagree. We think there is a way to get them to surrender without an invasion or using the apparatus. Offer them reasonable terms.'

'Unconditional surrender is the policy,' I murmured.

'You can get around that by offering some sensible concessions – assurances that the entire nation will not be destroyed or enslaved, that the institution of the monarchy won't be thrown away.'

I said nothing. I wasn't convinced the US was in the mood to give the Japanese any concession, and I doubted whether Japan was likely to surrender without a desperate and bitter fight on its home soil. Also I wondered how the young men facing death in the Pacific War might feel about dragging the war on because of moral scruples about a new weapon. I wondered if Gerald – a pacifist sucked into a just war – would have traded his life for a ban on the bomb.

'I've taken too much of your time,' Leo muttered. 'I wanted to see you because of your position. Will you mention our opinions to your boss?'

'I'll think about all you've said, but even if I dared broach the subject my arguments wouldn't carry any clout. Why don't you write to him?'

Leo gave a hollow laugh.

'The letter would not get to his desk, and they would lock me up and throw away the key. However, if a trusted aide like you were to drop some hints his way, then perhaps he may want to hear our views.'

'It's tricky. I can't promise anything.'

'Thank you, Jimmy. This is not some mad scientific nonsense. If we develop this, then the Russians will have no option but to follow us. None of us can say where it will all end, even though we all have an idea of *how* it will end. In a holocaust.'

Afterwards, I thought about the implications of Leo's remarks, but while I felt he and his colleagues might have a case for curbing further development of atomic weapons research, I didn't seriously consider that any good would come of my bringing this up with Winston. I *did* mention it to Douglas. He called me a misguided young idiot, adding that I clearly hadn't absorbed much about the workings of the world despite all the opportunities I'd had.

I reckoned I was lucky to get off as lightly as that.

30

London and New York

The war came to an end, first in Europe as the Red Army captured Berlin and Hitler killed himself, and then in the Pacific after the United States exploded two atom bombs on Japan. My thankfulness that the conflict was finally over was tempered by a lack of any communication from, or news about, Natasha. Since the bus-stop conversation in Pimlico, there had been an ominous vacuum of information.

News reports said that on VE Day westerners living in Russia were hailed as heroic and glorious allies, but when I applied at the embassy for a permit to visit the Soviet Union, my request was turned down coldly and without any reasons.

I asked colleagues who accompanied Winston to his meeting with Stalin and Truman at Potsdam near Berlin in July, 1945, to try to contact Podbirski, if he turned up there, or to try discreetly to find out anything they could about Natasha.

However, Podbirski was absent from the conference and Soviet officials were apparently even more uninformative on just about every subject than before. The Spirit of Yalta, such as it was, was disappearing into the unforgivably freezing air of the incipient Cold War.

I felt sure that the Russians were straining every muscle to construct an atomic weapon. Despite Leo's assessment of their intentions, I believed that they had seen through all the misinformation – including my pitiful efforts – about the lack of progress in America's nuclear bomb project. In that case, Natasha would be doomed.

I resigned from the Prime Minister's office when Winston was evicted from Number 10 after a resounding defeat in the general election of 1945. I was invited to stay on, but declined. This was not because I disliked the new incumbent, Clement Atlee – indeed, I considered myself a socialist, and admired the aims of his reforming Labour government – but merely because working for any prime minister after Churchill would have been like drinking flat Champagne.

Winston asked me to visit him not long after the election. He was sad and depressed, though he occasionally bubbled into his old form.

'It was a humiliation, James,' he said. 'My darling wife tells me it is a blessing in disguise. If that is so, it is very well disguised.'

I said something about the strange ways of democracy.

'Ah, but I detect that these vagaries meet with your approval,' he said with a smile. 'And there is some merit in so believing. God forbid that I should ever have been tempted into seizing dictatorial powers.'

'You would never have done so, sir.'

'And yet, and yet, such a course might have saved the nation from pernicious state socialism.'

His eyes twinkled with amusement at his own jest. Then he added with a solemn shake of his head: 'No, as a deep-dyed democrat I could not have contemplated that for an instant. We fought the war for the cause of democracy after all, did we not?'

He brightened as he regaled me with anecdotes from the last of the Big Three wartime conferences. He disclosed that when Truman received news at Potsdam of the successful test of an atomic bomb, there had been some discussion about whether or not to tell Stalin.

'I recommended that he should do so. Despite all, Stalin remains our ally, does he not? And it was his army that had taken Berlin. The President casually mentioned to him that we had acquired a weapon of immense power, a passing remark. Stalin appeared totally uninterested – but he is a master of disguise. I suspect that beneath his attitude of unconcern, he was considerably apprehensive.'

'And you think he was taken by surprise?' I asked, wondering if faulty intelligence, perhaps even misinformation, might have helped delay Russian research.

'I am sure of it,' said Winston. 'There was no evidence, but I had the feeling he was uncomfortably surprised.'

So Leo *had* been right, I thought. But far eclipsing any glimmer of satisfaction that I might in a very small way have contributed to the set-back to Soviet nuclear weapons development was a sickening emotion of dread over Natasha's fate.

'I have been in this business of negotiating with powerful men for many years, and I have an instinct about their real thoughts,' Winston plodded on. 'I was not in the least taken in by Stalin's attitude at Yalta – by what some saw as his reasonableness and willingness to compromise. No. I saw what he was and what he wanted and, indeed, how it would all pan out. But what could I do, with my limited resources, my weary armies, my flagging influence? Could I have done any more, eh?'

I was still sunk in my own despondent world of self-recrimination, when Winston glared at me and repeated: 'I am sorry to intrude on your deep thoughts. Could I have done more to deter Stalin?'

'No, Prime Minister. You did all that you could have done.'

'You speak an untruth, sir!' he thundered.

I was struck dumb. How had I offended him?

He saw the puzzled concern in my face, and said gloomily: 'Pray, do not be alarmed. My meaning was merely that you uttered a solecism in addressing me as Prime Minister, when I am nothing more than a down-at-heel leader of the opposition – and *that*, perhaps, for not very long if Anthony has his way.'

My first idea after leaving Winston's employ was to get to Moscow as a foreign correspondent. No luck! Every newspaper I tried, including the *Review*, turned me down. I wasn't told the exact reason, but inferred it was because the Foreign Office had put a veto on me.

'If it was in my power, I'd send you there,' said Tom Rathbone, still the *Review*'s editor. 'Alas, it can't happen, and I'm not at liberty to tell you why it can't happen.'

I decided not to burden Douglas yet again with my problems, so went to see Eden, who was already heavily engaged in rebuilding the Tory party into a machine he hoped he would soon be leading. He was friendly and courteous and said he had no knowledge of any Foreign Office order concerning me – there had certainly been no such decree during his tenure, he assured me – but he would look into it. I took his subsequent silence to be a confirmation that in some official circles I was not to be trusted.

This left me in a state of limbo. I was unhappy, trapped in apathy, not drawn passionately to any line of work that would be permitted me. Salvation of a sort came with an offer to write a weekly political column for the *Review*. I accepted. It gave me a modest income and the illusion of a purpose.

I received, around this time, two sad letters from Germany. The first came out of the blue, sent to me at the *Review*, from Bertha Wolf, husband of my friend in the German Embassy in Moscow in 1939. She wrote to say that Guenter had been killed on the eastern front in 1944.

'He hated the whole regime,' she wrote. 'But he joined the army like a good German to fight for his country. I thought you would like to know that some of us in this country also paid a terrible price for putting up with Hitler. Our children cannot understand why we did so, and it is not easy to explain.'

The second letter was in response to one I'd sent to Frau Siegendorff's address, enquiring if she was all right and whether she needed any assistance from me. Her reply, in a shaky hand, said she was in good health and that mercifully her house was not as badly damaged as others in the road.

'I manage to survive, but it is not always so easy these days. Gregor, my son, is dead. He was in Latvia where they said he was a war criminal and executed him. But everyone here has troubles, some more than me.'

I sent Frau S regular food and clothing parcels from then on. Financial regulations prevented me sending her money.

Winston continued to take his defeat badly. It wasn't so much that he blamed the electorate but that he hated losing, and believed he had lost his last battle. He felt there was nothing left in life for him but to await death. What restored him to a large degree was a holiday on Lake Como in Italy.

Sarah wrote me a chatty letter from their villa:

Papa is amazing. Having shown his ability to conquer the world (well, nearly!) he's now setting out to conquer painting. It's an idyllic place, which has soothed his soul. Yesterday, he completed a delightful scene of the banks of the lake, all greens, blues and yellows, very positive. He talks with affection about you, Jimmy, but tinged with sadness about your Natasha. The other day he said, tears in his eyes, that he would have gone down on his knees to Stalin if it would have helped.

This last was typical Churchillian hokum.

It did, however, tend to confirm that Winston, despite all he may have heard from intelligence sources about my attempts to barter Natasha's freedom, had quashed any suggestion that I be hauled in for interrogation. He was probably both amused and impressed at this romantic streak in me!

Douglas must also have argued vigorously against treating me as a security risk.

Obviously, though, neither of these two powerful friends had persuaded the shadowy investigating authorities that I could be trusted enough to be permitted to go to the Soviet Union as a journalist.

I was left to hope that the Labour government would not want to re-open an inquiry into my dealings with Podbirski. However, that wasn't the reason I wrote sympathetically about Atlee and his team in my column: I believed they were doing their best to bring Britain up to date in social justice as well as in its weakened post-war international role, which needed to include dismantling the Empire.

My mother deplored the Conservative election defeat. Her experiences during the Blitz had made her think a little bit like a socialist in those days; she'd been all for general solidarity, sharing and ending distinctions. Gradually, though, as the danger of losing the war receded, she returned to her old ideas of the need for privileged classes to preserve civilised society.

'Don't be a bore, James,' she said when I berated her. 'Yes, it was wonderful when we all stood together against Hitler, the lower classes together with us. But now it's no longer a case of equality. *They* want to be the ruling class. Can you imagine what would happen? It will be exactly like Russia unless we stand firm.'

'Hardly. Even Winston doesn't think that.'

'He said there'd be a socialist Gestapo running the country if Labour won. I heard the speech.'

'And it probably cost him millions of votes, but he knows now what a mistake it was. Actually, he has a fairly high opinion of the new government.'

'Really?'

'Well, yes, though he can be quite wicked about them.'

To amuse her, I retailed a couple of his waspish comments about the Labour leadership. It was nice to share a joke. Ever since Douglas had revealed to me the passionate, albeit short-lived, love she and my father had had for each other, I'd begun to view her with much greater sympathy, rather than merely as the cold and autocratic woman who'd ruled my early life. We still thought differently on just about every topic under the sun, but I found I could argue against her without the fury that I'd felt in my adolescence and young manhood.

In late 1945, Tom Rathbone offered me the post of the *Review*'s American correspondent, based in New York.

'I'd rather go back to Moscow,' I said ungraciously.

'Not a chance, old boy. Hands tied, and all that. Apparently, the Russians wouldn't accept you anyhow, and even if they did the *Review* wouldn't risk it. As it is, we're only hanging on in there by a thread: Stalin distrusts western reporters more than ever. America's a fascinating place these days, capital of the world, for good or ill. I really think you should go.'

I took the job. It was a chance to escape from depressing London and its ration books, and to see at first hand how the United States was faring without Roosevelt.

I went to say goodbye to my mother and she told me that she'd been diagnosed with cancer. She tried to be cheerful, but I could see she was in pain. Robert told me the prognosis was bad; she'd be dead within months. I was sadder than I could have imagined.

Almost the last thing she said to me was: 'Your father and I didn't really get on after the first few years. We were just very different people, but he was a decent man, and I wanted him to come back to me from France. I was cross with him because he didn't. "Damn him!" I used to say. Not "Damn the Boche" or "Damn the politicians", but "Damn him".'

I'd almost never seen eye to eye with her. She'd been remote and unloving when I was a child and discouraging when I was a young man. We disagreed fundamentally on almost all the great issues of life. The war had brought some reconciliation; at last, we were both on the same side. Now, the fact that she was dying forced me to look into myself and made me realise that I had so little to rely on, and that she was, in her own way, a cornerstone of my rickety, personal architecture. How dare she just fade out of my life like that?

A few days before I left for New York, I met Dr Bergsen for a drink in a shabby club in Soho where German refugees and graduates of the internment camps tended to gather.

We'd had a few brief meetings since his return from Palestine. In one of them he'd told me that Leo had finally received confirmation that his mother, sisters and aunt – Sam's sister Naomi – had died in Nazi extermination camps. 'Even so important a scientist like Leo could do nothing for them,' he'd said, a tremor in his voice.

This time, he talked about his disillusionment with Zionism after his brief flirtation with it in Palestine.

'And Dinah?' I asked.

'Ach, what can I say? I was on a kibbutz with her, but it was not good. She was too much with building Israel – like she called it – and with hating the Arabs. I could perhaps give her a good life in England, a comfortable life. But to her, England, where she was born, is the foreign land. Palestine, she has chosen.'

He was happier now to discuss the essence of Jewishness than he had ever been in Germany, when he had trusted in the traditions of the Fatherland.

'Ach, Jimmy, why should the Jews need a homeland, even if such a thing was possible? That is not our genius. Being a Jew is a state of mind. We can be Jews wherever we are and still be full citizens wherever we are.'

I didn't agree with him. I'd seen too much of anti-Semitism to doubt that it would easily be removed from the recesses of the average person's mind, whether in England, Germany or the Soviet Union.

'Why *shouldn't* the Jews have a homeland, Sam?' I countered. 'Most other peoples do.'

'Because it corrupts us. We were not meant to be nationalists of that sort. You should see the sort of Jews you find in Palestine. They are blond, they are arrogant, they are blind to the ideas of others.'

'You mean they're like every other race?'

'Exactly,' he said glumly. 'It pains me to see that. Then I ask myself: Would Hitler have done what he did to the Jews if Zion had already existed? And I am troubled because I don't think he would have been able; the Irgun fighters would have sent some people to kill him. So, back to the square one, eh, Jimmy? A conundrum. Without a country, we shine, but we are murdered. With a country, we will be as ordinary as everyone else, but at least there is a chance we will survive.'

'Is there an answer to your conundrum, Sam?'

'For me, it doesn't matter, but for your children, I hope.'

He meant my children with Natasha. They would be Jewish, according to Hebraic law.

'If I ever have them, it will be their battle,' I smiled. 'It's not one of my major dilemmas at present, Sam.'

'You will have them for sure. Don't despair, my good friend. People escaped from Hitler, also they can escape from Stalin.'

I mentioned my reaction to my mother's illness.

'More than anything, it surprised me that I should weep for her,' I said.

'This was disturbing also, my friend?'

'I suppose so. I mean, is it unnatural to dislike a parent and then to cry because they turn out to be so damn mortal?'

'Neither is unnatural. Even the Bible – a book, which neither of us believes is anything more than a great work of literature, but which wants to teach people how they should live their lives – even the Bible commands one to honour your parents, but does not say you have to love them. And to cry because your mother is dying, Jimmy, that is the same as crying over a Greek tragedy. Your tears are for humanity, and for yourself as well as for your mother, and for your Natasha and for your unborn children.'

I was forced into flippancy to conceal my emotion.

'I always knew you were a good lawyer, Sam, though I never expected so much psychology. But thanks for telling me.'

We were both silent, then he asked: 'Tell me, my friend, have you ever sat down and cried because of Natasha? I think not, Jimmy, because always you English need to hide your feelings. But perhaps in the train, coming from your mother's house, perhaps you for the first time were weeping for this woman you love and believe you have abandoned.'

'Perhaps,' I said. 'It's a thought, Sam.'

'A thought, yes.'

One of my first assignments in the United States was to interview Harry Hopkins. He was in hospital, but his wife Louise said he'd agreed to see me.

'He still has so much to say to the world,' she told me over the phone.

He was even more gaunt, even more sallow than he'd been less than a year before at Yalta, but he was courteous, remarked that he had great respect for the *Review*, and would be happy to talk as long as we kept it short. He didn't appear to recognise me at first.

We were about five minutes into the interview when he suddenly said: 'Bexley, huh? Yep, I remember you. Tried to kidnap me at Yalta. I remember your face. Why didn't you tell me that before you started asking me questions?'

'I didn't want to be presumptuous, Mr Hopkins. I was only a cipher at Yalta, fetching and carrying for the Prime Minister.'

'Fetching *me*, I seem to recall,' he laughed. 'Fetching and carrying, huh – sounds exactly what I did for the President most of my life. Call me Harry. You must be okay. Winston's got a great capacity for picking people. Roosevelt had that too, but he liked getting his advisors to fight with each other over issues, then he'd step in like a god and make whatever ruling he'd already decided upon.'

He chuckled.

'No flies on Franklin. But he could be damn ruthless if he thought you were anything less than loyal. He'd drop you like an old mistress who's lost all her charms. Did it to me a couple of times. He was one of the two greatest men I knew – Winston was the other – and also the most devious, apart from Stalin. He'd go to most any lengths to get his way. Don't want any of this negative stuff on the record, mind!'

He talked about a mission to talk to Stalin he'd undertaken for President Truman just before the end of the war.

'On the record, I felt it was better to talk to the Russians than not to. Things were beginning to fall apart between us, and I felt it was important to let them know that we understood some of their concerns, but that they could only push us so far. Poland was still the big stumbling block. They weren't going to budge on how it should be governed. My meetings kept the door open for dialogue, I guess.'

'Do you still feel that dialogue with Stalin is worthwhile?' I asked. 'Do you think his word can be trusted on anything?'

He grimaced, whether from pain or from the questions I did not know.

'I didn't think then, when I met him in Moscow, and I don't think now, that we should break off with the Soviets.'

Then he smiled: 'That's all you'll get from me on the record. Off the record, I don't think things will get any better until after Stalin dies. It's a hell of a different world from what we had at Yalta. Two of the giants of that world are gone from the stage and the remaining one can't see how much things have changed. The atomic bomb means there's no goddam alternative to us all living together in peace.'

'Can I quote you on that last bit?'

'Not until I'm dead and buried, son.'

When we'd finished the interview, he said: 'Weren't you a friend of Brewster?'

'We were at Cambridge together.'

'You talk to him at Yalta?'

'Once or twice.'

'You know he was peddling a line that we ought to threaten Stalin with the A-bomb?'

'I gathered something like that.'

'Did you tell Winston?'

'I didn't dare,' I admitted.

He laughed.

'He'd have balled you out for that! We were *all* courting Stalin at Yalta. We knew the son of a bitch couldn't be trusted in the way you'd trust a friend, but Winston didn't want him to ease up on the Germans and Roosevelt had his eyes on licking the Japanese and on how the post-war world could function.

'I don't know who put Brewster up to all that stuff about the bomb being ready in time to scare the pants off Stalin. Someone was behind it, for sure. There were plenty of people who believed Roosevelt would sell out. This was a ploy to make Stalin more tractable. These were the same guys who later on – like now – would be willing to drop the A-bomb on Moscow.

'Anyway it was a pretty dumb idea. As if Stalin didn't know exactly where we'd got to at Los Alamos! He had an army of spies and informants and sympathisers over here. And even if he didn't know, d'you think it would have deterred him if we'd already got the bomb? If anything, trying to threaten him would have had just the opposite effect: he'd have gotten even more pig-headed. That's his nature. He'd probably have welcomed an atomic attack on Russia – it would've made him the people's sweetheart once again, like after Hitler invaded. Hey, I'm rambling. Do your worst in the article. Build me up or knock me down any which way you want. I'm used to both. Now I'd better rest, and then I'm going to write to Winston, kind of thank you letter – for everything.'

He sank back into his pillows, exhausted.

A little over a week later, he was dead.

On the first of many trips to Washington, I looked up Ed and Dorothy. I had learned that you couldn't bury the past without decent consideration.

We behaved as civilised people, declining to discuss the acrimony of our former love triangle and talking about everything else under the sun.

I decided not to disclose to either of them that I'd begun an effort at Yalta to bargain for Natasha's release. All I told them was that I'd had no word from her since leaving the Crimea. But it turned out that they knew I'd made some kind of overture to the Russians.

One night after an evening spent drinking heavily at their comfortable Georgetown house, Ed became maudlin. He blamed himself for giving me information about the bomb that I subsequently passed on, implicating both of us in a conspiracy of treachery.

'It was insane. It was hubris. I believed I could save the world, and all I did was put a noose around a woman's neck.'

'It didn't happen that way,' said Dorothy sharply. 'You weren't giving away secrets. It was a silly game. You wanted to impress Jimmy.'

'Ed, I never mentioned your information to a soul,' I said.

'That's not what I heard. I just hope it wasn't because of that that she's gone, maybe executed.'

'Stop it!' said Dorothy. 'We have no idea of what happened to the poor woman. We certainly don't know if Jimmy actually gave away anything to them.'

'What exactly *did* you hear about me?' I asked Ed.

He had put his head in his hands, staring down at the floor as though contemplating all the woes of this world. Dorothy did the talking.

'You were seen in deep conversation with an awful secret policeman,' she said. 'That was all he heard. Why were you so friendly with someone like that?'

'Podbirski? He was a contact. Friendship didn't come into it.'

She gave a sneering little laugh.

I looked at her face, which had once filled me with unendurable longings. Age had robbed it of the fullness that had made her wide mouth and eyes so attractive. What I saw now was a thin, mean face with an almost hunted look. Her straggly greying hair – once so vibrantly, electrically auburn – was the last thing on earth I would have liked to run my fingers through. I wondered how I could ever have loved her, and then remembered the excitement of her smiles and her audacity, and thought that I'd probably aged badly myself.

'You can stop worrying about it, anyway, Ed,' I said. 'You're in no danger of being an accomplice to my treason, because I didn't engage in any. I told the contact a pack of lies that I invented; and if anything got her into trouble, it was *that*. It was a desperate, bloody foolish thing to do.'

Ed lifted his head and smiled a little. I couldn't tell whether it was relief at being let off the hook, or because of my stupidity.

Dorothy said: 'I doubt that she was punished because of you, Jimmy. She was working for them, anyway. If they've disposed of her it's because she'd outlived her usefulness. Those people live by devouring their own.'

I couldn't resist saying: 'It was always thus, Dorothy.'

She glared at me and retorted: 'The best of our generation were taken in by their lies. At least, we had ideals for a better world.'

I didn't argue with her. It seemed so futile to trade insults over past mistakes. The conversation veered towards foreign policy in general.

I said everyone was disturbed at the way the Russians were behaving, but what could be done about it?

'We've got the atomic bomb – perhaps we should show them we mean business,' Dorothy burst out.

Ed looked fondly at her.

Again, I thought about the sadness of change. When I'd first known her, she'd been gloriously, carelessly idealistic, albeit in a flawed cause. Her enthusiasm had been pure, even if her logic was twisted. Now, she'd lost the humanitarian fire. All that was left was a bitter vengefulness, stemming, I supposed, as much from self-hatred as from genuine political vision. She knew she'd been duped, and she was going to make sure that a price was paid for that by everyone, alive or dead, who had hoodwinked her.

She and Ed welcomed signs of a hardening US stance in the world, although they feared the impact on their own lives of the unforgiving line growing inside the country towards anyone with a past tainted by Communist association.

They spoke of Truman with admiration.

'He's some tough cookie,' said Ed, now fully recovered from his earlier self-pity. 'He gave Molotov hell at the White House after Roosevelt's funeral, said he should tell Stalin to deliver on those so-called promises about democracy in Poland – or else! Then he told the bastard to get out of his sight.'

Ed and Dorothy both smiled grimly as he recounted this.

I recalled Harry Hopkins on his deathbed saying there was no alternative to peaceful co-existence in a world of nuclear weapons.

'What does the "or else" mean?' I asked.

'We licked Hitler and Tojo, we can do the same to anyone,' Ed said.

'You had a little help,' I said mildly.

'Yeah, sure. Mostly verbal.'

I let it drop and said my goodbyes.

Like much that had touched my life in the 1930s – good and bad – my friendship with Ed and Dorothy appeared to be dwindling into sadness and disillusionment; but we stayed in contact.

America, in 1946, was a fascinating, if bewildering, place for a foreigner to live and work. After down-at-heel Britain, still licking its wounds, the abundance of good food and shiny gadgets in New York was almost too much for the stomach and the senses to digest. On the surface, the mood was raucously optimistic.

And yet, the country seemed to be strangely confused about itself and its international role. The United States had won the war – and, unlike all the other belligerents, avoided the physical devastation of its home soil. It had emerged as one of the world's two great powers, with huge armed forces and advanced weaponry. And yet Americans seemed to have a foreboding about the future.

This was due in part to unexpected post-war problems, mainly economic. Armed forces veterans, who'd expected the world would be at their feet when they returned from fighting abroad, found it difficult to adjust to a lack of job opportunities and to the self-discipline of family life after years of separation. People feared a new Depression might be just around the corner, and worried about losing the high standard of living that had spread into many homes during the war.

I liked the freshness and immense openness of the American hinterland, and the stark skyscape grandeur of the great cities, though I sensed that behind the doors of thousands of freshly painted homes in the suburbs or in smaller towns a growing conformity and materialistic lust was dulling the sensitivity of a free-spirited people.

I stayed for three years, during which a basic wartime American desire to get on with the Russians quickly gave way to acute anxiety as the Cold War began. It was not so much the challenge of a rival global power, as a fear of internal destabilisation.

People who thought of themselves as patriots saw spies and saboteurs behind every tree. The congressional House Un-American Activities Committee probed every nook and cranny for subversives. Intellectuals and artists and the film industry came under particular scrutiny, and, of course, anyone with even vaguely leftish political connections. People ran scared and were prepared to betray their friends and colleagues.

It was not an American, though, who fired the first resounding oratorical shot of the new international era. This was done by Winston – out of office in his own country but still honoured elsewhere as a prophet. In a speech at Fulton, Missouri, he said an Iron Curtain had descended across Europe. This was an admission of the central failures of Yalta – namely that Stalin's promises about eastern Europe were worthless, and that the Soviets would contribute to the United Nations only by using their veto to block any censure of their actions and methods.

As the unease grew in the United States, Dorothy's anti-Communist stance became more and more strident in media interviews and rallies, and she became something of a celebrated spokeswoman for this new crusade.

Neither she nor Ed publicly admitted their old Party connections. They feared that if their past came into the open, they would be reviled and their careers and lives shattered. This didn't stop them seeking to destroy others with similar pasts.

When I voiced concern at the witch-hunt being conducted against suspected Party members and sympathisers by Senator Joe McCarthy, Dorothy turned on me with vehemence.

'There is no alternative but to root out this thing completely. I support the hearings with all my heart and soul.'

'Will you tell all?' I asked.

'Ed wouldn't allow that. And neither would the FBI. The Bureau knows all about me, of course, and is happy to have someone of my eloquence and status – I had a reputation for my humanitarian work during the war, you know – speaking out against the evils of Stalinism. But they'd rather I didn't come clean to the whole world. If I did, they'd be forced to throw me out of the country.'

There wasn't much I could say.

'I know what you're thinking,' she added. 'It's a bit like the way the comrades work, isn't it? Dirty, dishonest. But this is a battle between good and evil – and we're on the right side.'

Later, I heard that Ed was going to testify against some of his State Department colleagues at McCarthy's congressional hearings. I read his exculpatory evidence with distaste, and wondered if he'd tried to curry favour by blabbing to the FBI about my dealings with the Russians. One thing in his testimony, though, reflected well on him in my eyes. He stated categorically that his wife was in total ignorance of his own earlier 'un-American' contacts, and she had never, he swore, been a member of the Communist Party.

Unluckily for Ed, some reporters probed into Dorothy's background. She did a deal that allowed her to give a brief and unchallenged testimony about her involvements in the 1930s, and permitted her to remain in the US.

Ed was jailed for perjury, but under the deal negotiated by Dorothy it was a token sentence and he was released after a couple of months.

I wrote to Dorothy expressing my sympathy for their problems. She and Ed had once been a central part of my life and, however much we'd drifted apart, I found myself saddened by their plight.

I couldn't taunt Dorothy with changing her spots, or for her original blind faith in Marxism as the cure for the world's ills. I knew that, except for a difference in temperament, I might have joined her in embracing the Party when nothing else was standing up against the beast of Nazism. And why had I not joined her? Not because I was wiser, more far-sighted, or stronger of will. It was due to a congenital inability to commit myself body and soul to any course of action that might lead me down a blind alley. It was only later, during the war, that I came to understand you can't always avoid blind alleys; that sometimes one simply has to take action to protect what one loves – one's way of life, perhaps, or a person as dear as one's life.

After America, I returned to England and wrote a book about the United States and the Cold War. One of the points I made was that isolating countries from their ideological enemies was more dangerous than engaging in debate and exchanges with them. In a chapter on the Soviet Union and its satellites, which had deliberately sealed themselves off from 'foreign contamination', I argued that it would be beneficial for them to allow their citizens freedom of travel. What they would gain in technological and practical knowledge would greatly outweigh the perceived danger that they would return as spies or foreign agents.

I sent a prepublication copy to Douglas. He didn't think much of the way in which I'd tried, clumsily, to further my own mission to get Natasha out of Russia, though he saw some merit in the book.

'It contains a measure of original thought, but the idea of conceding to our enemies the right to pick and choose the benefits of cohabitation with the West is flawed,' he wrote. 'Whatever you personally, or other individuals, might gain from such an arrangement, would not be mirrored by any benefits to us or our allies. As to whether the book will aid or hinder your efforts re Natasha, I cannot say. Nor would I condemn you for trying. In the longer term, James, keep working for your goal. The climate may change.'

I wrote back thanking him for his views and chiding him for putting the needs of the state above those of the individual.

'Sounds like a totalitarian idea, Douglas,' I wrote.

His scrawled response was: 'Sometimes you have to fight like with like.'

It saddened me that he had descended into the bedrock of pragmatism on which the whole world seemed to have settled. What hope was there for anyone when all that mattered was for a country to have irresistible weapons and impenetrable defensive walls – and never mind human happiness? Perhaps that was why the whole damn planet was becoming so grey and miserable and selfish.

In October 1951, Winston became Prime Minister again. He'd survived the five years out of office by writing a panoramic, if self-serving, history of the war, and by painting. At the age of 76, he was back in Number 10. My first thought was that I might have a powerful ally again in my quest to rescue Natasha. My second was that it was a pity the socialists hadn't had a longer period to complete the reforms that Britain desperately needed. My third was that Winston was too old for another term. I knew it would take wild horses to make him relinquish his last grip on political power, and I sympathised with Anthony who must have begun to despair of ever taking over.

Sarah, on a visit to London, met me for lunch. She was divorced from Vic, had married again, to a successful photographer, and had achieved her ambition of dancing with Fred Astaire, in a film called *Royal Wedding*.

I'd seen it and been unimpressed by her performance. Her dancing was technically good, but she lacked sparkle and the sort of glamour the big screen audiences demanded. I didn't tell her that.

I recalled how, on arrival at Saki in 1945, amid the greyness of the weather and the assembled bureaucrats, she'd struck me as having film star quality.

'And now you're the new Ginger Rogers,' I said.

'Don't be such a blatant liar, darling. I did what I'd always dreamed of doing. Dancing with Fred is one thing Papa never managed; a foxtrot with Stalin was the best he could do. But I've never been one to fool myself.'

She seemed happy both in her private life and her new niche as the star of a successful American TV drama series.

We talked about Natasha.

'Do go to see Papa,' she urged.

'I wouldn't presume to at this stage,' I said. 'I can hardly ask for his help in something so – at least in this climate – insignificant.'

'I very much doubt if he looks at it in such a way.'

The next day I was invited to Number 10 to meet Winston, no doubt because Sarah had suggested it.

He had aged considerably. The newspaper and newsreel images of him did not adequately reveal the ravages of time on his features and his movements. He shuffled now, rather than strode. His eyes, which had once flashed and glared witheringly at enemies, colleagues and subordinates, were now rheumy and almost opaque. But his mind was sharp. He seemed pleased to see me and accepted with satisfaction my congratulations on his election victory and on his wartime histories.

'Well, we are both successful writers now, James, though I do not aspire to be as prophetically profligate as you,' he chuckled. 'I rewrite the past to a certain degree, you seek to modify the future.'

I was immensely chuffed by his praise and warmth.

'Your concisely written volume had specific, indeed personal, designs,' he said.

'I'm afraid it did, Prime Minister.'

'Never be afraid to acknowledge a legitimate aim, young man,' he boomed with something of the leonine manner of old. 'But let me come quickly to the point. We will return later to your profoundly difficult, but not, I hope, insoluble, personal problems. I would like you to rejoin my staff in the capacity in which you served me so efficiently and with such dedication during the recent conflict.'

I tried to think of a polite form of refusal. I was surprised to be asked, especially as he must have known that the presence in his office of someone still under suspicion as a security risk could become a political embarrassment. I decided it was likely that his romantic nature, his nostalgia and loyalty, had pushed him into inviting me back. I was touched that he had done so.

My hesitation irked him.

'Pray, what is your answer?' he asked a little petulantly.

'To be asked, Prime Minister, is a great honour. Under different circumstances...'

'You refer to your career as an author. As one scribe to another, I understand very well your ambitions, but the experience of being so close to the centre of power at a time of such international gravity will be of immense benefit to your future works. I could envisage that when the time comes and I am called to meet my Maker – who will, I feel sure, be as apprehensive as I myself at the prospect of such an encounter – then, together with Randolph, you would embark on a biography of me. Of course, it might be some decades before I would be, um, sufficiently extinguished to allow such a project to begin.'

His eyes were twinkling now. As so often, his eloquence had lifted his mood. I seized the moment to decline his offer of a post. The reason, I told him, was that I was determined to work for Natasha's right to leave Russia and I felt this could lead to a conflict of interests if I was one of his private secretaries.

In reality this *was* one reason, but not the only one. I did not relish the prospect of watching from close quarters as this giant of a man went into decline, which I knew must happen. I wanted to go on writing, but not as a biographer. And I did not in the least fancy collaborating in anything with the unpredictable Randolph Churchill, already legendary for his rudeness and alcoholic over-indulgence.

Winston accepted my decision without rancour. He passed

quickly to the next subject. He feared another world war was looming and that the use of nuclear weapons would end in global catastrophe.

'I am going to do my damndest to prevent such a holocaust,' he said. 'I will go – I will not crawl, but I will go – to any lengths to educate Stalin and Truman on this issue. And if, by some chance, I do not succeed, then I will hand over the reins to Anthony, who will carry on the struggle. This is about the very existence of civilised life on our planet, and no government should be too proud to seek for some way out of a military confrontation, which none can win and all must lose.'

I muttered my agreement.

'And you, my dear James, you are young and you must search for happiness. If not in one quarter, then in another. I do not mean to be unkind or insensitive but one should not invest too much of oneself in lost causes.'

I opened my mouth to speak, but he waved me to silence.

'Loyalty in love is admirable, it is the stuff of poetry and great drama. It is not, however, always the path to that contentment which alone can sustain a true spirit in the long, long road of personal endeavour. Where are the snows of yesteryear? The answer to the poet's question is that they are gone. Wipe the slush off your boots, and trudge forward. I too have had my disappointments, in love as in life. But I have kept right on to the end of the road and I have had my rewards. A loving wife and family. I have been fortunate. I have been blessed.'

I could see he meant these words kindly, but I resented them – though I didn't dare show my feelings. My love for Natasha, my guilt about her and about so much else – my father's death, my inadequacy as my mother's child, my ineffectiveness as an opponent of injustice and as a faithful lover – made me abhor the idea of trudging forward, as Winston put it, without a backward glance. Still, I couldn't remonstrate with Winston, or feel great anger towards him. He had done too much for us all, and for me, to permit any discourtesy towards him.

Having given me this fatherly advice, he changed tack a little. He seemed to understand my deepest feelings.

'However, you are not a man who will stray from the path of fidelity,' he said, looking out of his window to the cobbled expanse of Horse Guards Parade. 'You will not heed my weasel words of advice. I applaud you for that even as I fear for the loneliness of your road. All I will say is that if you sincerely believe I can be of any assistance in your endeavours, pray do not hesitate to ask. There need be no pleading. Do you have such a belief?'

I shook my head sadly.

'Alas, I am in agreement,' he said. 'I would myself go to Moscow to track down your young lady, if you so desired it and if my advisers believed there were the slightest chance of success. I have enquired and been told there is none at this moment. Despite this, I could still try, but I could not guarantee, of course, that Stalin will, as the Americans are wont to say, "play ball".'

I did not take offence at his realism and the slight hint of playfulness over something that burned my soul. That was Winston, I thought. Fight to the death, of course, and never surrender. Brace yourself, and never despair. Even when up against an intransigent Russia, and trying to rein in a bristling America, he would go on scrapping to the end. But there was no point wasting your tears over hopeless endeavours.

His eyes were moist as we shook hands and said goodbye. To this day, I don't know whether it was the emotion of finally saying goodbye to a trusted member of staff, or a friend, or out of compassion for my burden and my lost love. The latter, I suspect. He was always a sentimental fool in his way, and this – among so many other qualities – was what made him a great man.

His old confrères of Yalta never possessed that ability to indulge in the softer side of human existence, and perhaps this was one reason why neither of them reached his level of humanity. FDR was brilliant and witty and sophisticated and wise, but it always struck me as unlikely that he would have wept at a friend's distress (though he *did* cry when his close friend and adviser of many years, Pa Watson, died on the way back from Yalta). And Stalin had such a stunted emotional interior that it is doubtful whether he could even vaguely empathise with the pain of others.

31

London

'I feel like I am really home now,' Dr Bergsen said to me as we watched the Coronation on a small, rented television set in my flat in Westminster.

On the screen, tiny black and white flickering figures performed the ritual of anointing a new monarch, a symbolic regeneration of the nation.

'But *you* do not, Jimmy, feel at home,' he said sadly.

'I've come to terms with it.' I smiled.

'I like what it means "at home". Comfortable, yes, complete, and also "*in der heimat*", which means the homeland of one's choosing, I think, not simply the place where one has had no choice except to be born.'

'Very philosophical, Sam. It must be the occasion.'

I had taken to calling him by the diminutive of his first name – at his earnest request – some time after he'd returned, disillusioned, at the end of the war, from Palestine, which had turned out not to be *his heimat*.

'One day she will be here too, your Natasha, and it will be complete,' he said.

I nodded, though I didn't believe in happy endings.

The sun on Coronation day should have been smiling brightly on the streets and on the people of London instead of being obscured by a spoilsport layer of cloud. The mood of the day was joyful optimism. It was an uplifting ceremony, even for someone as vaguely opposed to the hereditary monarchy as myself. The young Queen, delicate and fragile as a dove, symbolised the mystique of patriotism (or call it what you will) that had brought most of us to arms when we were threatened with foreign domination. Among the guests in Westminster Abbey on that June day in 1953 was the man who, far above all others, had embodied our will to resist. Winston, enveloped in the ceremonial robes of the Order of the Garter, looked like an old man, misty-eyed and made up of distant memories; yet he was Prime Minister again, presiding over the start of a new Elizabethan age.

No one I knew was touched more by the Coronation than Sam. It was for his sake that I hired the television set for the occasion. I was well rewarded. He glowed with loving loyalty towards his Queen and his adopted country and had to wipe away tears on several occasions.

He'd been pleased, seven years earlier, to leave Palestine, which was racked with Arab–Jewish unrest. He had been uncomfortable with the acute nationalism of many of the Jewish settlers, but was pessimistic about whether the Jews as a people could survive the eternal hostility of the world without a country of their own, and dubious as to whether the world would allow them to claim Palestine as that home.

In the event, Palestine – or the partitioned part granted to the Jews – *had* become Israel. Despite this, Dr Bergsen still had doubts about its future.

'What's the answer, Sam?' I'd asked when we discussed the topic a few weeks before the Coronation.

'Like always for the Jews, maybe no answer,' he said gloomily. 'Either they make a strong Jewish State or they go back to being outsiders wherever they live. Either way, there will be troubles on the road.'

'I hope *you* don't feel an outsider here.'

'What I feel is not important, Jimmy. Important is what the English feel about me. I feel at home, yes, for certain, I love this country. Like once I love Germany. But with a country – and sometimes also with a woman – love may be just a picture in the mind unless it is ... it is ... help me, Jimmy.'

'Reciprocated?'

'Yes. Otherwise it is just illusion. That is same word in German and English?'

'Yes, Sam, illusion.'

After the ceremony, we went into the street to watch the Queen's procession pass through London in all its pomp and sparkle. As we caught a glimpse of her golden carriage, Sam cheered as loudly and hoarsely as the millions of other Londoners and visitors thronging the city.

The Coronation was a fulfilment of peace, of what we'd fought for. Our post-war austerity was beginning to ease and, as if to confirm that our situation in the world was beginning to pick up, the news came through on Coronation eve that a British-led expedition had made the first ever conquest of Mount Everest.

I heard the news about Everest at the Hardings' house in London where Gwen and Binky were throwing a small party. I watched with pleasure as Gwen clucked happily around her two golden-haired children, a boy of seven and a girl of five. Binky was a benevolent host. The staff dispensed food and drink with quiet efficiency. Gwen and I caught each other's eye a few times, and exchanged smiles. I delighted in her domestic happiness; she still had hope that I would find mine.

By this time, eight years after Yalta, I'd reached a comfortable plateau in my career, and a plain of grudging acceptance in my personal life. I had schooled myself to believe that even if Natasha were still alive, she would never be able to join me in England.

Nothing had come of my efforts, made to Podbirski in the Crimea, to put myself forward as an informant to the Soviet Union. Apart from the one brief, vague encounter with the man I presumed was a Russian near my home in 1945, it was as though I'd never made the offer.

All my efforts to contact Natasha, or get information about whether she was alive or dead, through diplomatic channels, Russian officials, the Red Cross, and Russian émigrés, led to a blank wall. I believed she might, at worst, have been executed for complicity in my plot, or exiled to remote wastelands of snow, dying there or in transit along the Vladimirka Road. I forced myself to accept that she was gone from my life. I was to blame. I had lit up paths of false hope for her and given false information to her superiors. When I'd heard in the summer of 1945 that the Americans had dropped atomic bombs on Hiroshima and Nagasaki, I felt, with sickening certainty, that my lies about the snags in developing such weapons could have been the final nail in her coffin – that she had been murdered in angry revenge for my attempt to fool Stalin. This dread feeling stayed with me through the years.

Gwen tried to persuade me otherwise.

'From what you've told me, her parents and her contacts with you – just falling in love with you – were the things that may have hurt her. Not anything you did. You oughtn't to feel guilty, darling. It's a futile emotion.'

'I know that, Gwen.'

'Natasha would want you to channel your emotions into something useful. Why don't you write about it?'

'Inflict my guilt on the world?'

'Not your guilt. Your anger. Towards them, towards yourself. That's what's eating you up.'

'And to think there was a time when I believed *you* needed educating,' I said.

'Is there a compliment somewhere in that?'

'You're the one with the psychological insights, my love; work it out for yourself.'

'You beast, Bexley!' she said, and then, in a different tone: 'Now go and put it all down on paper – everything you feel about everything.'

But I couldn't write about it, except, occasionally, and very late at night, in attempts at self-destructive poetry.

I tried to lay my ghosts in other ways. I had several affairs, but they all ended badly, and I blamed myself; always, a part of me held back from full commitment to the relationship. I could not fault the women; only myself.

When I spoke of this to Gwen, she reminded me that the same failure to commit had run through my life, both in love and in politics – 'with the exception of Dorothy, and that was only because you fell in love with a kind of idea of the heroic female, as unlike your mother as possible.'

'You've forgotten to list Natasha as an exception,' I smiled.

'I'm sure you love her deeply, but is that partly because the circumstances make her so unattainable? The trouble with you, Bexley, is that you're an idealist by nature and a bloody foot-dragger by breeding.'

She spoke with kindness, but with the same direct honesty she'd always shown, and I sensed she might be uncomfortably close to the mark. Was I in love with Natasha herself, or merely with the idea of rescuing her from the Soviet dragon? I knew that she was gone from my life – but still I tried to find her, pursuing every avenue I could, enlisting Douglas's help. He made great efforts, but, as with my own, they had no results.

For eight years after the war, we tried. Nothing happened. Stalin died, and still nothing happened.

In the meantime, I was kept busy and for that reason found my life fulfilling to some extent. Perhaps thanks to Douglas, I had enough offers of employment to be almost spoiled for choice. I could have chosen diplomacy, journalism, business or lucrative authorship – there'd been several proposals for a candid biography of life with Churchill, all of which I turned down.

In the end, I applied for a post as head of a charity to help refugees from post-war eastern Europe. I got the job at a salary that was adequate for my needs. Some of my acquaintances thought it was the start of a bid for a parliamentary career, but I was not tempted.

Nor was I tempted to associate with the anti-Communist movements that had sprung up all over the free world, as it was called. Arthur Koestler, a leading repudiator of the Soviet ideology and system, tried to entice me on board one of those organisations. I declined. Even if I hadn't still been hoping for a miraculous Soviet about-face over Natasha, I couldn't see myself as a propagandist of this sort.

'Don't you think Stalin is a worse man than Hitler?' a Polish friend asked me.

My answer was that no greater menace than Nazism had threatened the modern world; it promised only bigotry, systemic hatred, murder on an industrial scale and the obliteration of rational thought. If Hitler had triumphed, we would all have been plunged into a new Dark Age, as Winston had put it in 1940.

'And do you think my country is not in the Dark Ages now?' my friend asked, scathingly. 'If you were Polish or Romanian or Czech or Hungarian wouldn't you feel differently?'

'One always fights for what one loves,' I said.

It was the only answer I could think of giving.

'You think Stalin is any better than Hitler?' he persisted.

'I'm pleased I didn't have to choose between them. In the war we chose Stalin as an ally – an uncomfortable choice. But I know I could *never* have been an ally of Hitler. I think the civilised world will survive Stalinism. It's inconceivable that it will last forever.'

'That will be a great comfort to my countrymen,' my friend retorted with heavy sarcasm and disdain.

The conversation took place early in 1953.

In March that year Stalin died. Like many others, I searched for signs of a real change in Russian attitudes to the world and its own citizens. There was none. Within months, the Korean War had ended, but a hoped-for thaw in East–West relations failed to materialise. Pro-Soviet regimes proliferated around the world. The United Nations, Roosevelt's great hope for the future, was already showing its limitations as an institution to prevent war. The Americans were building an arsenal of hydrogen bombs, which made the atomic weapons that had blasted Japan into surrender seem almost puny by comparison. The Soviet Union responded in kind. The nuclear arms race had entered an alarming new phase, which threatened to bring about global destruction.

Not even the national euphoria in Britain over the Coronation could offset my growing depression over a world solidifying into two vast implacably opposed armed camps – with myself cemented in one, and the woman I loved trapped in another.

My depression was heightened when Ethel and Julius Rosenberg were executed in the United States after being found guilty of conspiring to give atomic secrets to the Soviet Union. The whole grisly episode seemed to me the height of hysteria. I was sick to the stomach and close to despair. In times like this, what hope was there for the world, for Natasha, for myself?

One Friday morning in late summer, a letter arrived at my flat, addressed to 'Mr Bexley J'. Inside was a brief note – 'Meet for talks at St Paul's on Monday at noon'. It was unsigned and written in a spidery hand I did not know.

I was puzzled, but these were times when any straw was worth clutching. On the Monday, I went to the majestic cathedral, climbed the steps and stood between the great pillars looking towards Ludgate Circus and Fleet Street. In the streets, I could see no one I knew or who seemed the least interested in me. I went inside. It took a moment for my eyes to get accustomed to the darkness, and then I heard some footsteps, and out of the shadows stepped a figure I recognised instantly.

Podbirski.

'Anatoly, my God, what are you doing in London?' were my first words. 'Is this about Natasha? Is she all right?'

'Jimmy!' he said, taking my hand in a pudgy grip.

He looked nervously about, then steered me to a pew. We sat next to each other, like two casual worshippers.

'You have some news for me?' I hissed.

'I know nothing for definite,' he said in a low voice. 'I was told she was sent to work in Ukraine. Nothing more I know so far. Not good news, not bad news.'

She's alive, I thought. Then I wondered how much he was to be trusted. Was he going to try to blackmail me into espionage? It was ridiculous to be thinking this, but my mind was racing.

'Who told you this?' I demanded. 'When was she sent?'

'Jimmy, I have heard this. I don't know when it was they send her. I wish something more I can tell you than this.'

'What are you doing in London? Are you in the embassy?'

'In embassy, yes,' he said nervously. 'Jimmy, my friend.'

'What is it, Anatoly?'

'Jimmy, I take big risk to be here. I think you like to know is no bad news.'

'I'm grateful for that.'

We sat in silence. I couldn't help seeing a funny side to the situation. First, a bus-stop in Pimlico; now, a pew in St Paul's. This was progress of a kind.

'Listen, Jimmy. Always I help you, and Natasha. I like you both. I like when you love each other. Sometimes I did things which bring me trouble. But you are right. Is not about this only that I want to talk. Is about now. Jimmy, I need your help.'

Alarm bells rang in my mind. If the enemy wanted favours, it was time to raise the barriers.

'Why?' I asked curtly.

'You are so cold to me, Jimmy.'

'What do you want?'

'I want to leave Soviet Union for ever. I want to come to England. I want to defect.'

'Well?'

'Is not so easy, Jimmy. If England not want me, then Russians find out and they shoot me. I need guarantees. I need agreement. You can help me.'

'I have no influence whatsoever, but I might steer you in the right direction.'

'You will speak to Mr Churchill?' he asked hopefully.

'I don't work for him any longer, Anatoly, and, anyway, this sort of decision is taken at a lower level. I'll get you some names and addresses.'

He nodded sadly. Perhaps he had expected more.

'Look, you help me and I will risk everything then to find out where is Natasha,' he said desperately. 'Everything, I risk. Okay?'

I was pretty sure that he *did* know something but was holding this back as a leverage for my assistance.

'I don't like this method of dealing, Anatoly,' I said. 'If you have information about her, tell me now. I'm going to do what I can to help you, but this isn't a bartering session. This isn't Yalta, for God's sake.'

'Jimmy, always you joking,' he said, making an attempt to be the old humorous, in-charge-of-the-situation Podbirski. 'This is not barter. I will find something out. But is dangerous. Questions are dangerous, Jimmy.'

'Stalin's dead,' I said.

He looked around, horrified that someone might be watching and listening. Then he whispered: 'Now is maybe worse than before. Big battles in Kremlin. Everyone is thinking: What happens next?'

I could see this unpredictability scared him as much as anything did, had probably tipped his decision to defect. His former boss Beria had just been removed and arrested – and no doubt the business of liquidating Beria's men was already on the go. It was probably only a matter of time before they got to Podbirski.

Perhaps, after all, he was being truthful in saying he knew nothing more about Natasha's fate, but would try his damndest to find out. What had I to lose? And he *had* brought Natasha and I together.

'Okay,' I said. 'I'll do what I can.'

416

32

London

My first stop was Douglas's office in Whitehall.

'I've been approached by a Soviet diplomat, so-called, who wants to defect.'

'To this dreary country?' Douglas smiled.

'His name is Anatoly Podbirski. He was the NKVD man who helped arrange my meetings with Natasha at Yalta.'

'Ah, a friend of yours.'

'Douglas, this is a serious request. I believe it's worth pursuing.'

'Is he worth helping?' Douglas asked.

I said I was sure Podbirski had a good knowledge of the workings of the Soviet security and intelligence forces. At the very least, he would have information about the reasons for the fall of Beria and what it might mean for the organisation and the Soviet leadership. I suspected he was of moderately high rank and the possessor of secrets that could be of interest to British intelligence.

Douglas stared hard at his pristine, paperless, walnut desk on which the only personal item was a framed sepia photograph of my father in army uniform.

I was sure he knew everything available about Podbirski, perhaps even his desire and motives for defection.

'And you've come to me as his emissary because of your friendship?' he asked eventually.

'He asked me for help to get him asylum. He's not a friend and, obviously, I do not trust him. He claims to have been a friend of Natasha's father. I thought it my duty to pass on his request to you. Should I have kept it to myself?'

Douglas made no answer. His eyes bored into mine.

'All right,' I admitted. 'He said that if he got what he's after, he might be able to dig out something about what's happened to Natasha. He claims he has no idea where she is now, or even if she's alive.'

'Ah,' said Douglas, with just the slightest suspicion of a smile.
'Not that that is my motive,' I added hurriedly.
'No one would dream of assuming it was,' said Douglas drily.
'I know he might be lying. He might be a Soviet plant. He might have executed Natasha himself. I know all these things, Douglas.'
'As long as you do,' he said.
I nodded.
'I'll make some enquiries,' he said.

Within a day, I had news from him, which he said I could pass on to Podbirski at our next meeting, which Podbirski had requested should take place in the National Gallery. We met in the hall where I had listened to lunchtime concerts during the war. The frames on the walls were empty no longer. The great oil paintings were back from storage and on display, and Myra Hess's recitals belonged to what seemed like a distant, historic era.

I knew that our conversation was being watched and probably listened to by our intelligence people, and perhaps by his too.
'You'll be contacted, Anatoly,' I told him.
'Already, I have been,' he smiled.
He was more confident than the last time we'd met.
'So, Jimmy, I thank you. We have been great friends, no? Perhaps again some day we will meet when everyone is free. Now goodbye, maybe for long time. I will not be back to Russia, but I will do best to find out what I can for you about Natasha Khazan. I must tell you, Jimmy, that I never heard that she has told anyone anything about you. Never once. I would know if she did. I would know if she talked about you when they threaten her.'
'You know that she was threatened?'
'I make guess, Jimmy. Many people get threatened. Is good guess.'
'And do you guess that she is still alive?' I asked.
'I think yes. I think maybe in Ukraine, maybe in Siberia. Is only what I think.'

I could get no more out of him for now. I knew very well that he might be lying, but I preferred not to believe that. Instead I took comfort from the thought that she was still alive somewhere, and perhaps still had hope.

Podbirski and I shook hands briefly and he walked off, out of the gallery into the sunshine. I was convinced now that MI6, or whatever outfit was handling him, had allowed this meeting – had arranged the time and venue – in case he blurted something incriminating to me before they began his interrogation. Perhaps they were just as interested in me as in him.

I was not informed what happened after that, but I surmised that at some stage he would be granted asylum. I didn't ask Douglas, and he never raised the matter.

Nothing was reported or even vaguely alluded to either in the Western or, naturally, in the East Bloc press.

When news came of the execution of Beria and other NKVD henchmen, I imagined Podbirski's relief at being spared the fate of his superiors. I felt neither regret nor pleasure at my part in helping him.

I waited for months without any word about Natasha. Hope turned to a dull realisation that Podbirski's promises of gleaning information had probably been empty words or incapable of fulfilment, and that I would never see her again.

One evening I had an unexpected phone call.

'Name's Harris,' the caller said casually, in the flat accent of a man devoid of class or regional roots. 'Don't ask questions. Meet me in Regent's Park at noon. Bandstand near the lake.'

Another unsolicited meeting, unlikely to be of any real assistance to me! Nevertheless, I decided to go.

I was there by ten to twelve and, despite my protective scepticism, checked my watch every few minutes. As it turned twelve, a nondescript little man touched me on the elbow. He was carrying a neatly-folded copy of *The Times* and looked like a clerk on his lunch break.

'I'm Harris, your girl in Russia is alive,' he said matter-of-factly. 'That's all we know.'

'Where is she?'

'Afraid that's all we know.'

'Can I talk to Podbirski?' I asked.

'Can't say I know anyone of that name, so can't help you on that one. If anything else surfaces, you'll be told.'

He hesitated, then asked: 'Are you planning a visit?'

'To Russia? No. Should I be?'

'Let us know if you decide to,' he said. 'Doubt if they'd let you in unless you were sent by some newspaper. Any chance of that?'

'I'm no longer a journalist.'

'Pity,' he said. 'Well, let us know if you decide to get back into that line of work. Good money, I'm told.'

He looked at his watch and said apologetically: 'Have to be off, I'm afraid.'

He walked away, leaving me on a bench, but after going only a few yards, he turned and came back to me.

'A word to the wise, old chap. Don't probe without letting us know. Just a bit of friendly advice.'

'Who, exactly, is *us*?' I asked. 'Just for the record, old chap.'

He smiled sadly without replying, nodded goodbye and sauntered off.

I was left wondering whether I ought, perhaps, to seek a return to the *Review* and plead for a job as its Moscow correspondent. Despite previous forebodings, the paper was still accredited there. However, I didn't believe editorial management would consider sending me – they'd sense they were being used – and even if they did agree to post me there, I knew from the way Harris had talked that I'd be pressured into working for British intelligence, or suspected of doing so by the Russians. This would only endanger Natasha even more. She'd cease to be a prisoner with some possibility of release, and become a hostage.

In early 1954, about five months after my meeting with Harris, Douglas wrote asking me to come and see him at Trinity. It was no surprise to me that he'd returned in his late years to the place he loved most.

'I'm happy to say that I'm no longer needed as a full-time civil servant, and have been restored to my natural habitat,' he wrote. 'I am back in my old rooms and have resumed a small amount of tutoring, which, taken together with reading, walking and good conversation, affords me a very contented way of life.'

I drove down to Cambridge and walked through the Great Gate of Trinity into the court with its immaculately manicured lawns. I felt as though I was strolling back into my own past. Memories flooded back. Ed striding along in animated, enthusiastic conversation; Guy Burgess (who'd defected to Moscow in 1951) proclaiming the moral and political superiority of the Party; myself hurrying off to meet Gwen or Dorothy. The courtyard seemed to echo with old talk and emotions.

Douglas looked older and more tired than when I'd last seen him. I was stricken with fear. Was his summons to tell me that he was dying? He had been like a father to me for almost my whole life. I was closer to him than I'd been to my mother and, of course, to my natural father whom I'd barely known. I couldn't imagine life without Douglas in the background.

But it wasn't his health he wanted to discuss.

'I know you won't ask how I've come by all this information, James,' he said after greeting me affectionately. 'It's become increasingly clear that your friend is a very valuable commodity.'

'Friend?' I asked.

I wondered if he meant Natasha or Leo or Ed, or even Dr Bergsen.

'Podbirski,' he said. 'High-ranking. Higher than you guessed. Not the top echelon, of course, but a man who was able to impart some pretty solid information – assuming it turns out to be true, of course. There's a slight caveat that he may have been planted on us. There always is such a probability in cases like this. In any event, if he's of value to us, he is of equal value to them.'

'Why?' I asked.

Douglas shrugged.

'Who can tell?' he said. 'They're rather keen to get their hands on him.'

'To kill him,' I said.

'Perhaps to reward him,' Douglas smiled. 'Medal for valorous service and all that. Order of Lenin. We just don't know.'

'Douglas, you know as well as I do that if they get him back they'll execute him. That's their way. Even if he's a genuine double agent.'

'They want him,' said Douglas. 'And they're prepared to exchange him for one of ours.'

I supposed Douglas was telling me all this because I had been the go-between and because Podbirski had been a big part of my history with Natasha.

'I doubt if anyone wants my opinion, Douglas,' I said. 'But for what it's worth, I'd be horrified if he was swapped. You'd be sending him to certain death.'

'I would not be involved at all,' Douglas protested. 'I'm just the messenger.'

'That's what Anatoly said to me in Yalta.'

'Yes, well, I am passing this on to you because my informants are considering exchanging this man for what are regarded as two political hostages, a British businessman imprisoned on trumped up charges – and a Soviet citizen currently serving a lengthy sentence in Siberia.'

'Natasha!'

'Yes,' Douglas said, looking past me into the Trinity Great Court.

I was stunned, but not so much that I asked Douglas how he had managed to achieve this. I knew he must have had a hand in this, even if he was supposed to be in leisurely retirement from the intelligence business. I knew too, that he would not want to acknowledge it.

'Natasha for Podbirski?' I said.

'My informants feel they've gone as far as they can with him. Milked him dry, as the saying goes. For whatever reason, he's a prize the other side wants. And they've got people we want. Two for one. A good deal, don't you think?'

'But why?' I asked. 'Natasha is of no use to ... your informants.'

'No use whatever,' he said, permitting himself a smile. 'But I gather the Prime Minister has an interest in her case, and of course in the businessman whose name I am not at liberty to disclose. Naturally, Winston would be very careful about seeming to interfere in a security issue of this sort, but he has made his interest known. I gather some people are rather unhappy, feel it could be a dangerous precedent to bargain for the release of political hostages. I gather their view is unlikely to prevail.'

'When you tell me this,' I said, choosing my words carefully, 'are you asking how I feel about it? Or is this a *fait accompli*?'

'It's a work in progress, or so I'm told. We don't know how those on the other side might react.'

'I wish you hadn't told me,' I said.

'My dear James, I was rather hoping you'd be pleased to hear of this.'

'How could I condone sending a man – someone I've known for years – to a certain death?' I asked bitterly.

'You're not being asked to condone it. On the other hand, could you condone allowing this woman, whose liberty is of such importance to you, to remain where she is?'

He was not being unkind. I understood that. He wanted to make me see the pointlessness of feeling guilt about this whole business.

'It's not as clear-cut as you suggest,' I said. 'I'll get her out somehow. I couldn't be a party to a deal that involved murder.'

'Murder is a strong word. Much too strong. In any event, it isn't your choice, James.'

'Can't it be stopped, Douglas? Natasha wouldn't want it either.'

'The wheels are in motion,' he said. 'And it is not being done for Miss Khazan alone – or, as you appear to believe, for the sake of *your* considerations.'

Despite his words, I was convinced that this whole deal had been arranged – at the urging of Douglas or Winston, or both – for my sake. The British businessman was probably window-dressing in case the news ever leaked to the public.

'I'll go and see the Prime Minister,' I said.

Douglas looked at me as though I was eight years old and had suggested I might throw all my toy soldiers into the pond.

'I wouldn't do that, James. I really wouldn't. It takes him an age to make decisions these days, and he would not take kindly to being asked to unmake one of them. Especially this one. It would do neither you nor the lady any good at all. He wouldn't change his mind on the swap, but he might decide it would be more valuable to get one of our agents out of the Lubyanka than to get your girl out of Siberia.'

I knew he might be right. Winston, when piqued – especially by perceived ingratitude – could be extremely vindictive.

'Why did you tell me all this, Douglas?'

'Not to torment you, as you seem to believe. I thought I'd be giving you some hope. I hadn't realised your attachment to Podbirski.'

'He's a man, a person,' I said angrily. 'Or don't you see people like him as human beings any more?'

'Perhaps I don't,' said Douglas sadly. 'The wretched price of my insignificant contribution to victory.'

'I'm sorry, Douglas,' I said, immediately contrite. 'You've always been so good to me. You've always...'

'Please,' said Douglas, smiling now and holding up a hand to silence me. 'Would you care for tea?'

I spent sleepless nights after this.

The prospect of being reunited with Natasha was something I'd longed for, ever since we'd parted in 1939. But the cost of the proposed method, as outlined by Douglas, was so grave, so enormous, that it made me go cold. And yet if I'd had to kill someone in the Crimea in 1945 in order to snatch her from imprisonment, I believed I'd have pulled the trigger or thrust the knife without any compunction. So why was I fretting now?

What was wrong in exchanging her for someone who had probably been responsible himself for God knows how many deaths and disappearances? Would I hesitate if someone proposed exchanging her for, say, a Nazi concentration camp commandant already sentenced to death *in absentia*?

How impossible were all these questions? If killing is wrong – and I'd always held that it was, except in time of war or in self-defence – then it is wrong *per se*. I opposed capital punishment. On the other hand, if Natasha had been sentenced to death and I'd been given the chance of substituting another victim for her on the gallows, would I have done so? The answer to that one was: I'd have substituted *myself* for her in those circumstances. It was easy enough to give glib answers to hypothetical questions. In the here and now, though, it was a torment to struggle with the awful ethical equation. Natasha would walk free and into my arms, but the price would be Podbirski's days of icy fear, the pitiless torture he would suffer, the bullet (at best, the bullet) that would finally end his existence. It was all so grotesque, like a question posed by a taunting Devil's assistant in the deepest depths of hell.

Eventually, the person who gave me help in trying to live through my moral dilemmas – as he almost always had – was Douglas, though not in the way I would have hoped.

A month after our last conversation – a long month in which

I'd had no word on whether the projected exchange of Podbirski for Natasha was going ahead or not – I received an early morning phone call from the Master of Trinity. Douglas had died in his sleep. Had I known how ill he was? No, I admitted. I'd been too wrapped up in my own concerns.

'Don't blame yourself for not knowing,' the Master said. 'Douglas wasn't the sort to discuss his declining health with anyone. He wouldn't have wanted to place that type of burdensome knowledge even on those closest to him. His doctor told us that he – Douglas – had known for some time that his heart would give in before too long.'

'I always put my burdens on him,' I said.

'He named you as his next-of-kin.'

This surprised me a little. I knew he considered me a blood relative, but I had always assumed that while he had no living immediate family there must be cousins, nieces and nephews, perhaps lovers, in the shadows of his secretive world. Apparently, though, there weren't. I arranged for the funeral to be held in the unostentatious and irreligious way I knew Douglas would have wanted, and put a death notice in several newspapers.

I sent a telegram to Ed, advising him of the death, but received no answering communication.

The funeral was attended by many of Cambridge's best and brightest, as well as several anonymous distinguished elderly men. One, rather diffident and almost embarrassed, shook my hand and muttered: 'Old friend of his, old colleague.'

I asked the Master who this was and was told, in a whisper at the graveside: 'Alan Spenser – knighted for unspecified wartime services. You can probably guess what they were. Douglas merited a gong too, I'm told, but turned it down. Didn't like the fuss, I dare say.'

At the brief ceremony, a young Trinity pianist played some of the music Douglas had most loved. One of the items was a bitter-sweet Gershwin melody that Ed might well have introduced him to in the thirties, 'A Foggy Day'. As it was played, I sang to myself a line from the lyric: 'How long I wondered could this thing last?'

The Master spoke of Douglas's academic accomplishments and 'important sensitive research in the course of the last global conflict'. I said a few sentences to express my gratitude for the friendship he'd had for my father, for the way he'd watched over me and for the wisdom he'd imparted to many students over the years.

Sam Bergsen and his nephew Leo Roth were there, too. We didn't talk much, but Sam's eyes were moist as he clasped my hand and murmured his condolences. He, and possibly Leo too, owed a great deal to Douglas. Sam's tears, however, were for my loss rather than his own gratitude – and it was for that, as well as for our long friendship, that I hugged him in the graveyard on that dull, chill morning.

After the funeral, I had a meeting with Douglas's solicitor who informed me that I was Douglas's sole heir and, thus, the recipient of a small legacy. Douglas had never gone in for riches.

He had also left a letter for me, written a few weeks before his death. It was characteristically devoid of sentimentality.

My dear James,
I have greatly valued your friendship over the years. After Clive died, I decided to keep an eye on you, and I hope I've discharged that duty successfully. If I've tried to teach you anything, it is that life is mainly about making difficult choices within the parameters of a constant morality. In many cases, this isn't easy. One thing you will have learned, though, from your own experience as well as from your years with Winston, is never to brood over a decision taken. Life doesn't offer enough time for irremediable regrets and wrong turnings. It offers only a short span for enjoyment. Seize the day. I always have, thank goodness, learning from mistakes, though still managing to repeat them, and having fun in between. Follow me in that, if in nothing else.
Yours affectionately, Douglas

How, I wondered, would I manage without him? The truth was that he had shown me, over the years, exactly how I could do so. I couldn't emulate Douglas, and I knew he wouldn't have wanted me to. Nor, given my character, would I ever be able to walk away from a decision without having second thoughts. This applied even to choices that I had no say in making, like the one about Podbirski and Natasha. Douglas, I thought, was the one who had probably taken that decision – and then invited

Winston to endorse it – to spare me having even the remotest chance of a say in its outcome. Now he was telling me that it was pointless and destructive to be overwhelmed by guilt about it.

Once I'd digested his message – and his injunction to seize the precious day – I slept a little easier on some nights.

33

Berlin and London

In Berlin I waited at the Friedrichstrasse border post in the divided city. I checked my watch. The exchange was scheduled for 10 p.m. Five minutes to go.

A car pulled up nearby and three figures wearing overcoats got out. The one in the middle was Podbirski. I dreaded having to speak to him, but felt I had to. I began moving towards the group, but my companion, a British army captain, put his hand on my shoulder and shook his head firmly.

One of the two people with Podbirski offered him a cigarette and lit it for him.

He puffed eagerly as though it was his last taste of something good. He hadn't noticed me, standing in the dark. Then it was a minute to ten, and his group began walking to the Allied checkpoint. As they passed, Podbirski finally saw me. He looked surprised, then smiled and shook his head in what appeared to be resignation.

'Is okay, maybe, Jimmy,' he called out, before they marched him into the stretch between the American and the Soviet posts. I wondered if it had suddenly dawned on him what this exchange was about – not one spy for another, not a professional payback, simply a tawdry transaction in which he was the dispensable pawn.

In the dark, I could not see anything of what happened in this no-man's area, but within the space of a minute or so, the two men who'd taken Podbirski to his doom were returning with two people between them. One was a small figure who walked with hesitation, as though she feared some dreadful end to her journey. Then she saw me in the shadows. She blinked as though she could not believe her eyes.

When they had crossed into the American sector, I was allowed a few minutes with her, under supervision in a guardroom. We held hands. She was trembling. Neither of us was capable of expressing our feelings.

'I saw Podbirski walking to the plane,' she said. 'He arranged this?'

'In a way,' I said.

Then she was taken away for medical examinations and, someone told me, 'routine debriefing – just a day or two'.

Two days later she joined me at my hotel in Berlin. We embraced. She seemed exhausted and spent most of the time in her room; sleeping, she told me. We ate together in the hotel, but talked little. When I risked a question about her time in the Gulag, all she said was: 'Not so bad as I expected.'

Her English had become rusty in the camps. I told her about the externals of my life. I told her about my new job with an organisation set up to produce independent research into human rights abuses around the world. I told her about Sam Bergsen, now running his own successful wine importing business, and Leo Roth, doing research – presumably of a non-military nature – at the Cavendish, much to his uncle's delight. I told her about Douglas, and about Ed and Dorothy.

One evening, while Natasha slept in her room, I got a message to say Herr Klaus Friedrich was waiting to see me at the reception desk. I went down, and saw a slight, light-haired man smiling at me. It was indeed my old Social Democrat friend, the chap who fought Nazis and led illicit excursions to the Berlin Zoo. Meeting him again was a surprise, though not a shock. On the day before Natasha's arrival, I'd bumped into an old Sozi friend in Berlin who told me that Klaus was living in Bonn and that he'd get a message to him.

Still, I hadn't expected Klaus to fly to Berlin. The last I'd heard, in 1933, was that he was in a concentration camp. He'd been released after a few years, he told me, and managed to flee to Scandinavia, living out the war in neutral Sweden.

'Then I came back and now I am a big businessman. Can you believe that, Jimmy?'

I gave him a quizzical look.

'In my spare time,' he laughed. 'Never mind, I've made some money – West Germany needs rebuilding. It's good for the economy.'

'Are you still a Sozi, Klaus?'

'But, yes. My money and connections with the Americans will be of help to the party in the future – once we stop being slaves to socialism and start trying to win votes in this new capitalist society.'

Klaus had never been an ideologue. Perhaps it was because of that – and because of his bravery – that I'd liked him so much.

I told him about my meeting in 1933 with Dieter, Dorothy's old Communist boyfriend, turned Gestapo informer, and wondered what had become of him.

'The poor bastard went to the East,' said Klaus. 'He must have been mad to think the commies would want him. I heard he was murdered. Probably by someone with a score to settle.'

We reminisced a bit more over a few drinks and agreed to stay in contact in the future.

A day or two later I went on my own to Wilmersdorf and gazed from the outside at Frau Siegendorff's house, still standing, where I had first met Dr Bergsen and Dorothy – and first had my eyes opened to the cruel realities of the twentieth century. It was also the house in which I'd mooned over my first real experience of love. Frau S. had died in 1949, finally broken in spirit. She'd lost her husband in an unnecessary war and her son to necessary justice.

When I judged Natasha fit enough, we flew to London. I'd redecorated a room in my flat for her. I'd known even before the exchange that she would need lots of privacy. From the start, it was difficult between us. She barely spoke, and then only in generalities but not about her experiences. I had decided against pushing the issue. She seldom smiled. When she did, it was at a memory, it seemed, of something good from the past, rather than from being with me. These smiles only flickered briefly and then disappeared, like falling stars, into nothingness. I took her shopping, which she enjoyed more than anything else. She allowed me to buy her some calf-length dresses. Once, I went shopping without her and bought her a sleek Dior creation. She did smile at that, then said sternly: 'You shouldn't do these things. I am not your wife.'

I didn't want to put her under pressure of any sort, so I merely nodded benignly and squeezed her hand.

A few days later, she brought up the subject again.

'Sometimes, in the camps in Siberia, I think about being married to you. Then I know it all was a dream. Did you ask me to be wife to you, Jimmy?'

I said it was no dream, and that I *had* asked her.

'Maybe better if just a dream,' she murmured.

'Is that what you really feel, Natasha?' I asked gently.

'I don't know, Jimmy,' she said sadly. 'How can I know a thing like that? I am here, and so many friends are still in Siberia. There is place of ghosts and being hungry. How can I let myself be happy? So, I don't know, Jimmy.'

I discussed the situation, awkwardly, with Sam Bergsen, who said firmly: 'Give her time, my dear Jimmy. Sometimes, they are strange creatures.'

'Russians?' I asked.

'Women also,' he smiled.

So, I gave her time, which was what I'd intended to do anyhow.

She had taken to watching television for long spells, but apparently simply staring at the screen, without taking it in. I took her to the cinema several times, and she sat silently staring at the bigger screen.

One evening, the television news mentioned that the Americans had tested another hydrogen bomb in the Bikini Atoll. The Soviet Union would no doubt respond in kind shortly. She wiped her eyes, then said, accusingly: 'Why did you give me the letter for Podbirski?'

'I shouldn't have. I should have left you out of it.'

Then she began to weep a little. I put my arm around her, but she broke free. She dried her eyes.

'You could not leave me out of things. I know you did things so they would let me go. I know you wanted to bargain with them. You cannot bargain with people like these. You cannot come to terms with them.'

'Yes,' I said. 'It was a terrible mistake.'

Then she began to talk, a torrent of words.

'But it did not matter, Jimmy. Even without letter, they would have arrested me. They thought I must know something of

431

value. Those stupid people! They thought all we would have talked about was politics, not about love. I knew nothing, so I could tell them nothing. They questioned me – days and nights without sleeping, but otherwise no torture. Such stupid people! Even if I had read your letter, I would have told them nothing.'

She said Podbirski had been one of her interrogators.

'He was not so harsh as the others, but still he did the job they wanted him to do. I think he was worried they would blame him if I said nothing, because he was the one I always was supposed to report to. They all hoped I would confess something, anything.'

'Did you know Podbirski had been close to your father?'

'Close?' She allowed herself a smile.

'So he told me.'

'I learned some things in Siberia. Not very nice things. You don't expect to hear nice things. He told me also once, Podbirski, that he was a protégé of my father. I believed this. But in the Gulag, I heard the true stories. It was he – this same Anatoly Mihailovich Podbirski, who told you he was a friend of my father – it was he who gave information about my parents to the secret police, so they could make charges against them. False evidence, you understand?'

I nodded and let her talk on, asking no questions, not asking who had told her about Podbirski's alleged betrayal of her parents, not asking her if this embittered story was the true one. Who could you believe in this world?

She began to tell me about life in the Gulag, about the unbearable cold, the hard labour, the desperate hunger. She told me about beatings she had witnessed and of people dropping dead from exhaustion or starvation.

Several times, she broke down and wept copiously.

'But there was one good thing. There, from people who knew lots of things, I learned how my parents died. My father was executed with a bullet in back of the head while he was still in jail. Why Stalin decided he must suddenly die, I do not know. Perhaps they needed more space in the prisons. I met someone who was with my mother when she died in the labour camp. She was just too weak to go on. She had gone a little mad and imagined she was a little girl again with her family. So now I know.'

She let me hold her for a long time as she cried and trembled.

Then she went back to talking about people in the various places she'd been. Sometimes she did so in an almost chatty way as though she were giving me news about old friends of mine. At other times, I could feel her pain at having been witness to all this.

She told me about the friends she had made in the camps – the Ninas, the Olgas, the Tanyas, young women and *babushkas* – all with their lives and families shattered because of connections, trumped-up charges.

'Before, I never knew them, but they became my family in the camps. We lay close together when we needed warmth, we helped and protected when one was sick. We gave some little bits of food we could save to those who were starving. And then, of course, when we were family, they moved us again, one away from the others. Another heartbreak, another separation. The worst word in the camps, Jimmy, you know what it was? "*Etap*". You know what it means? Transport from one camp to another. Away from friends. Away from Lena, away from Katya. "*Etap, etap, etap!*" the guards shout. Away, away, away. For no reason, sometimes. Just so any small human comfort is denied.'

'Were you sick?' I asked hesitantly. 'Can you talk about what happened to you in the camps?'

'Oh, I was all right,' she said brusquely. 'I was young. I had still hope.'

She looked at me, but without smiling.

Day by day, after that, she talked for hours on end sometimes about what she had seen, and even a little about the deprivations she'd suffered herself, but always playing down her own experiences.

'It was not so bad for me, Jimmy. I always believed that one day I would be released. But for the others, there was never such hope. There was no good thing, no noble thing, about their suffering. They were not sacrificing for the greater good, even though some of them, old Bolsheviks, still tried to convince themselves that they were. And when the war ended, in those camps the problems got worse, not better.

'Then one day we hear – a miracle, he is dead. Stalin is dead. We cannot believe is possible. But, oh yes, everyone says it is so. Myself and Tanya, we cry – for joy. Then we laugh and think of freedom. Being free. It's no more maybe than just a dream. I see some other women crying and I go to comfort them. "It's all right, Vera, my dear, it's true. He's dead. Now perhaps is all over, your parting from your children and your grandchildren. Soon you see them, eh?" Still she weeps. And she says: "Comrade, I am crying because our beloved leader, our father is dead. What will become now of our Russia?" Yes, Jimmy, she cries because the bastard is dead, because she knows no other leader, and she even thinks he *is* Russia, that Georgian crook. And not only her. Others cry also. Those who that man sent to camps because of no reason except he needs to fill camps with people, so he accuses their husbands, their sons, their daughters, and some he shoots and others he sends to camps. And, Jimmy, they *weep* for him!'

And she wept. I put my arms around her and she wept into my chest, heaving and crying for the lost people and the lost souls of the Gulags.

Gradually, over months, she was able to talk about what she had witnessed in the camps with a little more detachment. I did not know if this was a good or a bad thing. Had she been bruised beyond repair? Or was she healing?

'Yalta was no good for any of us,' she said out of the blue one day. 'Not for you and me, not for the British or the Americans, not for the Soviet people. Only for that man, Joseph Vissarionovich Stalin, was it good. He got everything he wanted. You know what he was saying? "All my rivals are finished now. Hitler and Roosevelt will be dead soon. Churchill is finished. And now I can finish off any who challenge me here. If any general gets too big for his boots, any Politburo member, any Jew, any writer, any person, I can finish them off without any problems. I am the most powerful man in the world now."'

I found it hard to say anything in response, but finally ventured: 'I suppose it – Yalta – was another step towards ending Nazism.'

'For you, perhaps. For us, we still had Nazism, even if they called it another name. We still had secret police, torture, deportations, killings. It still went on.'

I was silent.

'I notice since I come here that people do not talk about what the Nazis did to the Jews. Is that true all over Europe?'

'There's a conspiracy of silence. No one wants to rake up the past. No one wants to remember very much.'

'Because they have things to hide?' she asked.

'In some cases.'

'Or because it is too painful?' she asked hopefully.

'I think because it is convenient not to remember. People, countries, want to rebuild. The Nazis – Hitler – were the originators, but they had willing helpers in a lot of places. Some of those people, even some former Nazis, are in high places now.'

'No!' she exclaimed.

'They just serve new masters now.'

'My God,' she whispered. 'But it does not surprise me so much.'

'Sometime, though, people, and governments, are going to have to confront this awful history,' I said. 'That's the only way we'll learn.'

'Oh, Jimmy,' she smiled, almost fondly. 'I love that you are still so optimistic, that you think the best of people. It's lovely, but it's wrong. Mankind is awful. You should understand that. They won't learn. They will say it never happened, or if it did it was the fault of the Jews. Some new Nazis will crawl from the gutter. New names, maybe, but same Nazi ideas. And always, especially, the Jews will be attacked.'

'That's not the way it will be,' I said. 'The world won't let it happen again. Besides, the Jews have their own state now. Even Sam Bergsen, who is no Zionist, admits that the existence of Israel means a guarantee of Jewish survival.'

'Maybe for now, Jimmy. But one day the Jew-haters will attack this Jewish state. They will find reasons for liquidating it. They will not say: "Let us try to understand the Jewish position." They will say: "Let us kill all Jews."'

Her moods swung wildly in these days.

One day she expressed support for Israel, the next she said it was Hitler's final triumph to herd all Jews into one vulnerable territory – 'like Stalin also wanted to do'.

She taxed me for not telling her at Yalta that the Americans were close to testing an atomic weapon, saying such information would have helped Stalin's opponents to overthrow him. She accused me of aiding a vast conspiracy to cement Stalin's power.

'You and your Mister Churchill and that old fool Roosevelt blundered at Yalta. They turned Stalin from one of the Big Three into the Big One of Europe. They crowned him. They believed his promises. The democracies gave away everything they could to this dictator, and for what? Did it end the war more quickly? Did it guarantee the peace?'

She said all this with eyes blazing, and then lots more. And eventually when she attacked my motives – 'You were interested only in what would win you medals' – I responded with equal anger. For the first time since our reunion, I let my feelings loose. From both of us, everything poured forth, all her anger and resentments and bitterness, all my anguish, guilts and delusions. Eventually, it ebbed and we sat back exhausted. I suggested a walk, but she shook her head and stood up. Her eyes were red. She came and kissed me on the forehead. I held her hands and did not let go. I stood up and we embraced.

Then she asked, softly: 'It was for **Podbirski** that they exchanged me, wasn't it?'

I nodded.

'Yes,' she murmured. 'First, I thought it was him who arranged it. Then I understand it was not him who arranged for me to be released. So, you got me, and they sent Anatoly Mikhailovich to be murdered.'

'I had no idea that was what was going to happen, Natasha. Not until they told me it was all decided. It was another bit of betrayal.'

'And if you had known?' she asked.

'I would have let it go ahead.'

'Because of me?' she asked.

'And because of me.'

The outpourings from both of us had been a marvellous release of tensions. We began slowly to feel quite easy with each other, but it was not all smooth going. She got depressed, I felt helpless in response. We got angry at times, with each other, with the world. Gradually, however, the wounds were healing.

One evening, after dinner, after listening to the 'Moonlight Sonata' on the gramophone, we'd said good-night and kissed lightly on the lips, as we'd been doing for some weeks. She went to her room and I put on the record again, and finally thought: 'Perhaps I'm seeing too many minefields.'

So I knocked on her door. She said I should come in. She was in bed, tucked up. She smiled at me. Neither of us said anything for a few minutes, then she said: 'Jimmy, you want to come to bed?'

'I wanted to say good-night again.'

She nodded and moved the sheet to allow me to lie beside her.

After that, the slow process of returning to normality continued. Her moods became more consistent, my responses easier. We could talk, we could make love. We could be angry at each other without triggering a major crisis. I had often – almost from the time of our reunion – suggested a holiday, but she had always rejected the idea as absurd.

'You think I am not on holiday from Siberia?'

She said she was quite happy where she was, didn't want to go away, wasn't interested in anywhere else.

Then, one morning, over breakfast, feeling jaded, I said: 'We simply have to have a break. Will you come with me? We'd go somewhere quiet, sort ourselves out finally, come back to life.'

She looked thoughtful, creased her forehead, spoke at last.

'What about the Crimea?' she asked. 'What about wonderful Yalta?'

She giggled.

'All right, Jimmy, to make you happy I go on holiday.'

Discussing the possible destination was exciting to both of us, and a glow began to come into Natasha's eyes.

Finally, it was Gwen who decided the issue.

I'd invited her round to meet Natasha.

The two eyed each other and made very polite conversation for a while before mutually deciding they liked what they saw.

'Binky and I have a cottage on the Norfolk coast,' Gwen ventured. 'You could laze in the garden, go for walks, sail on the Broads.'

'Sail!' Natasha's eyes lit up. 'Oh, yes, please, Jimmy, let us go. Always I want to go in boat. Away from the land.'

'Good,' said Gwen as though that settled the matter – which it did. She kissed my forehead and Natasha's cheek.

After she'd left, Natasha asked: 'You were lover with her?'

'It was a long time ago.'

'Not so long, I think. All right, I forgive. I will not hate her. I can see she is happy for you, so I forgive.'

'Thank you, Natasha. She's happy for both of us.'

'All right. And you will teach me to sail boat?'

'I will.'

'And we will be like a man and wife there all the time?'

'Yes, we will.'

'Like family,' she smiled, and then sank into gloom as she added sadly: 'Ah, Jimmy. Our families all are dead.'

'This will be another family.'

'With children, you mean?'

'If you want that, Natasha. Otherwise, just us two.'

'Us two is okay,' she said. 'But children, no. How can we bring children into such a world?'

'At Yalta you said you wanted children, lots of them,' I teased.

'At Yalta! Everything at Yalta was hope and empty promises. You and me never will have children, Jimmy. Never!'

But she was wrong.